DATE DUE

OCT 07 2013

PRINTED IN U.S.A.

TELL ME

Center Point
Large Print

Also by Lisa Jackson and available from Center Point Large Print:

Wicked Game
Malice
Without Mercy
Running Scared
Devious
Born to Die
Afraid to Die
You Don't Want to Know

TELL ME

LISA JACKSON

CENTER POINT LARGE PRINT
THORNDIKE, MAINE

This Center Point Large Print edition is published
in the year 2013 by arrangement with
Kensington Publishing Corp.

The text of this Large Print edition is unabridged.
In other aspects, this book
may vary from the original edition.
Printed in the United States of America
on permanent paper.
Set in 16-point Times New Roman type.

9/13
CENTER PT
$36.95

ISBN: 978-1-61173-784-4

Library of Congress Cataloging-in-Publication Data

Jackson, Lisa.
Tell Me / Lisa Jackson. — Center Point Large Print edition.
pages cm
ISBN 978-1-61173-784-4 (Library binding : alk. paper)
1. Family secrets—Fiction. 2. Abused children—Fiction.
3. Investigative reporting—Fiction.
4. Women journalists—Georgia—Savannah—Fiction.
5. Georgia—Fiction. 6. Large type books. I. Title.
PS3560.A223T45 2013
813'.54—dc23
                                                        2013020269

Dedicated to the people of Savannah.
I love your fair city,
even if I do take liberties with it.

Prologue

His hand was cool as it slid up her leg, smoothly brushing her calf, tickling and teasing, causing her spine to tingle and a warmth to start in the deepest part of her. Ever upward it traveled, slipping effortlessly against her, nearly undulating.

"Don't," she wanted to say but couldn't, because her voice wouldn't work, and really, she didn't want him to stop. His touch was magical. Divine. And downright dangerous. She knew all this even though she hadn't yet woken.

Hovering somewhere between consciousness and sleep, she thought she was on the edge of a dream, a warm sensation that lulled her into wanting to snuggle deeper inside the covers.

Still, his touch was sensual. Arousing. And because of it, she was in trouble. Big trouble. But she couldn't stop. Even now, when she knew it was the worst time ever for him to be sliding his hand along her bare skin.

The smell of wood smoke filled her nostrils, and the bed was warm and cozy, even though she heard the sigh of the wind as it rattled the windows.

Amity vaguely remembered that she wasn't at

home, that her mother, ogre that she was, had forced her and her two younger siblings out here in the middle of no-damned-where for the night.

That's right. Amity wasn't in her room at the house her mother rented. There was no lock on the door, no way to ensure privacy.

But Mother was out or asleep, and now Amity was with him.

Right?

Did that make sense?

On the edge of dreamland, she decided he'd taken a risk to come to her . . . of course he had. Despite the danger. But she'd dozed and now was still in that blissful state between being fully awake and dreamland. Somehow avoiding Blondell's watchful eye, he must've sneaked into the cabin and slid beneath the covers. God, he was good. Experienced. Made her feel like a woman, not a girl.

Of course, not everything was perfect, and now . . . now there was big trouble. Amity had needed to talk to someone about it, so she'd called her friend. She'd begged Nikki to sneak out and come to the house by the lake, and her friend had promised she would, but like everyone else in Amity's pathetic life, Nikki had abandoned her. Well, good. Then she wouldn't have to share her secret.

For now.

And *he* had slipped in unnoticed, come to her,

loved her. For the first time in her life, she felt secure.

Yet something wasn't right. Even in her semi-dreamlike state, she knew they had to be careful.

Quiet.

Nearly silent.

Hoping the darkness was enough of a cover, though soon, of course, they would let the world know of their love. That thought warmed her as much as his touch.

Her lips were dry, her mind still fuzzy with sleep. She thought she heard a dog barking in the distance but wasn't sure, and it didn't matter, of course. Nothing did but him. Realizing that since he'd started touching her, he hadn't uttered a word, she said softly, "Come closer." Anticipating his weight, anxious to feel his body against hers, she was disappointed. All she knew was his arm, long and fluid, sliding across her bare skin.

Was he just being careful?

Or was it something more?

It was strange that he wasn't pressing himself urgently against her, wasn't nuzzling her neck, or reaching around her to touch her breast. He should be tangling his hands in her hair, his lips hot and anxious as they found her own.

But tonight he was aloof. Playing his game. Toying with her.

And Mother was so close. Wasn't she? Or had Blondell left, assuming yet again that Amity would babysit the younger ones? These days, who knew?

However, him being here was dangerous. They couldn't be caught together. Not yet. She writhed a little, anxious for more of his touch, but he kept stroking her, sliding his arm against her.

With his silky smooth touch, he trailed his hand along her thighs, along the outside of her hips, and ever upward, across her rib cage, trailing the length of her.

Oh, Lord, this was magical. And playing with fire. Which, of course, she already had. That's why she was in so much trouble already.

His arm slid between her breasts and ever upward, yet somehow managed to move against the skin all along her thigh and abdomen and . . . ? Wait! That wasn't right.

She was waking now, dreamland fading . . .

Letting out her breath in a sigh, she opened a bleary eye. The room was dark, aside from the merest light from the fire and the lowest setting of the kerosene lantern on a nearby table. Lying on the hide-a-bed tucked beneath the loft of the cabin, she heard rain beating against the roof. A hard, steady tattoo. But . . . she was alone. There was no one with her. He wasn't stretched out on the mattress beside her. No. It was all a dream.

The only others in the old shack were her brother and sister.

Just Blythe and Niall, upstairs in the loft,

sleeping. And Mom was probably still on the porch. That's where she said she was going when you started dropping off, when she grabbed her opened bottle of wine and a glass and walked through the connecting door.

Still, something seemed off. The dream was so real. But if *he* wasn't here, beside her, then what the devil . . . ?

Alarm bells clanged through her mind.

Someone, no, make that some*thing* had been touching her and even now . . . Oh, Mother Mary! . . . it was rubbing up against her, only to stop suddenly, the length of it trailing over her.

Oh, *no!*

Hissss!

The sibilant sound echoed through her brain.

For the love of Jesus! No!

Screaming in sheer terror, she frantically threw back the covers and scrambled backward on the bed in a single motion. The snake, its reptilian eyes reflecting the red of the dying embers, hoisted back its sharp, triangular head.

Shrieking, trying to fly off the bed, her legs tangling in the covers. "Mom!"

Too late!

Quick as lightning, the snake struck, its coppery head still visible. Fangs sunk into her leg, hot pain searing.

"Mom!" Amity screamed, reaching for the side table, her fingers touching the base of the

11

kerosene lamp, turned so low as to barely glow as the snake slithered quickly off the bed. "Oh, God, oh, God, oh, God! Mom!" In a full-blown panic, Amity grabbed the lamp and threw it hard against the wall, glass shattering, kerosene bursting in a blinding flash that quickly died.

The snake.

Where the hell was the snake?

I'm going to die . . . Oh dear God. "Mom! Where the hell are you?

"Mom! Help! Snake!" she yelled. Afraid to get off the damned bed, she turned toward the door to the porch, only to see a dark figure hiding in the shadows. "Help! Oh, God, I've been . . ." Her heart was pounding, sweat collecting on her body. "Mom?" she whispered, scared out of her mind. "The snake just bit me! It's still in the house, oh, holy crap! Did you hear me?" Tears began running down her face, her heart pounding wildly. "We have to get to the hospital!"

Movement.

Was the figure one person? Or two?

In the dark, without her contacts, Amity couldn't tell. Didn't care. Were they kissing? For the love of God! No, maybe wrestling?

"Mom!" No, wait. That wasn't Mom, was it? It was only one person, kind of wobbly on their feet. Or not? Chaotic footsteps pounded in the loft above her. Her siblings!

"Niall! Blythe! Stay upstairs!" she cried when

she saw, in the faint light, silhouetted in the figure's hand, the image of a pistol.

Was Mom going to shoot the snake? In here? In the dark? Why the hell didn't she turn on the lights and—

She realized the gun's muzzle was aimed at her.

"No!" Cowering in the corner of the sofa bed, she pointed toward the corner where the snake had slithered. "It's over there. A damned copperhead, I think. Mom—"

Blam!

A deafening blast roared through the cabin.

A flash of light.

The muzzle of a gun as it kicked back a little.

Amity's body slammed against the musty pillows of the couch, pain searing through her abdomen.

Disbelief tore through her mind. She'd been shot? Someone had shot her? No way . . . but the blood running through her fingers told a different story, confirmed to her unwilling mind that someone wanted her dead.

She was still screaming as the world went black.

December 2nd
First Interview

"Just tell me what you know about that night. Let me tell your side of the story to the rest of the world. If you didn't try to kill the children, if you didn't mean to hurt them, then tell me the truth. Let me be your mouthpiece. Trust me, I can help!"

The eyes beyond the glass don't so much as blink. I'm not sure she's even heard my question. Then again, did someone who'd tried to murder children in cold blood ever hear anyone else? Ever really try to explain?

As I sit in my tiny stall, an open booth with an uncomfortable stool, a heavy telephone receiver and thick prison glass separating the free from the incarcerated, I try my best to be convincing and earnest, hoping to wring the truth from the person on the other side of the clear barrier.

But it seems impossible.

The prisoner suspects I'm up to something. That I'm using the information I might get from this interview for my own purposes, which, of course, isn't far from the truth.

As I stare through the smudged glass at the woman who's agreed to be contacted, a woman whom the public has reviled, someone with whom I've been through so much, I wonder if I'll ever get through, if the truth will ever be told. Suspicion smolders in her eyes, and something more too, something almost hidden. Hopelessness? Fear? Or is it accusation?

As if she knows.

But then, why wouldn't she?

It isn't as if we're strangers.

My heart trips a bit, and I want to bolt, to hide. But I force myself to sit on the worn-down stool where thousands have sat before me.

"I can help," I plead, and cringe at the tone of desperation in my own voice.

Her expression falters a bit, and even dressed in drab prison garb, without makeup, her once-shiny hair streaked with gray, a few pesky wrinkles appearing on what was once flawless skin, she's a beauty, with high cheekbones, large eyes, and full lips. The years since the horrific crime of which she's accused have been surprisingly kind.

There is noise in the hallway, on my side of the thick window, whispered voices from other booths filtering my way. There is no privacy here, not with the cameras mounted on the ceiling and the guards watching over the line of free people attempting to speak to inmates.

I hear sobbing from the elderly woman to my right as she tries to speak in low tones. She shuffled in before me and wears a bandanna on her head, dabbing at her eyes with a hanky. Her wedding ring is loose on her finger, her sadness palpable.

The stool to my left is vacant. A man in his thirties with tattoos climbing up his arms and a neatly trimmed soul patch, the only hair on his head, storms out angrily, his footsteps pounding away, echoing the loneliness of the worn souls who reside within.

But I can't be distracted by the hum of conversation, nor the shuffle of footsteps, nor the occasional burst of bitter laughter. There is little time, and I want only one small thing: the truth and all of it.

"Come on, I can help. Really," I insist, but in my little nook, where I can sense the prison cameras filming this interview, there is only silence as she stares through the glass at me, quiet as death.

Chapter 1

"I know, I know. I'm working on it. Really! I just need a little more time to come up with the right story!" Nikki Gillette glanced up at the skylight as rain drizzled down the pane. Above the glass, the sky was a gloomy shade of gray, the clouds thick with a coming twilight hurrying across the city. Beneath the window, inside her loft and curled into a ball on the top of the daybed, lay her cat, Jennings, his eyes closed, his golden tail twitching slightly as he slept. Seeing him, Nikki reminded herself yet again that she needed to pick up Mikado at the groomer's tomorrow. Her head was so full of her own problems, she'd forgotten him today. Luckily, Ruby had assured her she could pick up the dog tomorrow at no extra fee, a kindness she wasn't generally known for.

Hunched over her desk, Nikki held the phone to her ear with one hand and fiddled with a pen in the other. The conversation was tense. Nearly heated. And for once, she knew she was at fault. Well, at least partially.

As her agent described why her latest book submission had been rejected by her publisher,

Nikki glanced at her computer monitor, news stories streaming across the screen—an alert that yet another storm was rolling its way inland, the latest breaking news.

"What was wrong with the Bay Bridge Strangler idea?" Nikki asked, but deep down, she knew the answer.

Ina sighed audibly. "For one thing he's in San Francisco."

Nikki could imagine her agent rolling her expressive brown eyes over the tops of the bifocals that were always perched on the tip of her nose. She'd be sitting in her tiny office, cup of coffee nearby, a second, forgotten one, maybe from the day before, propped on a pile of papers that had been pushed to one corner of her massive desk.

"And you've never met him," she added in a raspy voice. "And since good old Bay Bridge is big news on the West Coast, I'll bet a dozen stories are already being written about him by authors in that enclave of mystery writers they've got out there. You know, I probably already have a submission somewhere here on my desk, if I'd take the time to dig a little deeper through my slush pile."

Another good point. Irritating, yes, but probably spot on. "Okay, okay, but I also sent you an idea about a story surrounding Father John in New Orleans."

"Who knows what happened to that freak? A killer dressed up as a priest. Gives me chills. Yeah, I know. He's a better match, closer geographically and infinitely more interesting than Bay Bridge, but really, do you have a connection with him? An inside look?" There was a pause, a muffled "Tell him I'll call him right back" on the other end of the line, then Ina was back, never missing a beat. "As near as I remember, Father John disappeared. Either moved on or, more likely, is lying dead in some Louisiana swamp. Crocodile bait or something. No one knows, and right now, not a lot of people care. He's old news."

"No one really knows what happened to Zodiac, and he hasn't killed in decades, but there're still books being written about him. Movies."

"Meh. From authors and producers without any new ideas. The reason your first two books did so well was because they were fresh, and you were close to the investigation."

"Too close," Nikki said, shuddering inwardly when she remembered her up-close-and-personal experience with the Grave Robber. That horrifying episode still invaded her sleep, bringing nightmares that caused her to wake screaming, her body in a cold, damp sweat.

"I'm not advocating you ever become a victim again, trust me. But you know you have to write something that you're emotionally connected to."

"So you keep saying," Nikki admitted as she looked around her little garret, with its built-in bookshelves, easy chair, and reading lamp. Cozy. Smelling of the spice candles she lit every morning. A perfect writing studio, as long as she had a story to put to paper.

"Here's the deal," Ina said. "The reason your first book worked so well, or at least in the publisher's eyes, is your connection to the story, your involvement. That's what you need."

"That might have been a once-in-a-lifetime thing," Nikki said as she twisted her pen between her fingers and rolled her desk chair back.

"Let's hope," Ina said. "Look, no one wants you to be a victim again. God, no. But you had a connection with the second book too."

Therein lay the problem. She'd sold *Coffin for Two*, her first book, a true-crime account of the killer she'd dubbed the Grave Robber, a psycho who had rained terror on Savannah before targeting Nikki herself. She had no intention of coming that close to a psycho again—book deal or no book deal. *Coffin for Two*, into which she'd infused a little dark humor along with her own personal account of dealing with the madman, had sold thousands of copies and caught the eye of a producer for a cable network that was looking for particularly bizarre true-crime stories. The book was optioned, though not yet produced.

Her second book, *Myth in Blood*, also had a

personal hook; she had been close to that true-crime story as it had unfolded. Working for the *Savannah Sentinel,* Nikki had pushed her way into the investigation, stepping on more than a few toes in the process and pissing off just about everyone in the crime department at the newspaper. That case, involving the rich and ill-fated Montgomery family, had had enough grotesque elements to appeal to the public, so another best-seller had been born. While trying to get close to that investigation, she'd met Detective Pierce Reed, and their relationship had developed to something deeper. Now they were engaged, and she was supposed to be writing book three of her publishing contract, but so far, no go. She just didn't have a story.

Ina said, "You know, dozens of true-crime books come out every month, but the reason yours stood out was because of your personal involvement. Take a tip from Ann Rule; she knows what she's doing. You've read *The Stranger Beside Me.* The reason that book is so damned chilling is because she knew Ted Bundy. She was there."

"She seems to have done well with other books, where she didn't know the killer."

"I'm just sayin' that we could use another *Coffin for Two* or *Myth in Blood.*"

"Or *The Stranger Beside Me.*"

"Yeah, I'd take that too." Nikki heard the smile in her agent's voice.

"I bet."

"You can come up with something. I know it."

"Easy for you to say." Stretching her back, Nikki stood. She'd been sitting for hours, working on a story for the paper, and now her spine gave off a few little pops. She needed to get out. To run. To start her blood pumping hard. For as much as she was arguing with Ina, Nikki knew her agent was right. She was itching to get to work on another project, couldn't wait to sink her teeth into a new book about some grisly, high-profile murder.

Cell phone pressed to her ear, she walked to the window, where she was lucky enough to have a view of Forsyth Park, with its gorgeous fountain and display of live oak trees. From her vantage point above the third floor, she could watch people in the park and look beyond the trees over the rooftops of Savannah. She loved the view. It was one of the selling features that had convinced her to buy this old, converted mansion with her advance from the book deal. She'd leased the two lower floors to renters and had kept the third, with this nicely designed loft office space, for herself. She was in debt to her eyeballs.

"Look, Nikki, it's getting to be crunch time. Maybe you should talk to Reed, see if he'll let you help with an investigation."

Glancing at the diamond sparkling on the ring finger of her left hand, she said, "Yeah, right. You know I won't use Reed."

"I know just the opposite."

Ina wasn't one to mince words.

"Thanks so much." Inwardly, Nikki winced as she glanced at a picture propped on her desk. In the photo, she and Reed were huddled close together, beach grass and dunes visible in the background, their faces ruddy from running on the sand. The wind was up, her red-blond hair blowing across Reed's face. They both were smiling, their eyes bright. The photo was taken on the day he'd proposed on that same beach.

So now she was considering compromising their relationship?

"Okay, maybe not *use* him, of course, but maybe he could, you know, let you get involved in some way with a current case?"

"That's not Reed's style."

"Seems you managed to squeeze into an investigation or two before," her agent reminded her, and she squirmed a little in her chair. There was a time when she would have done just about anything for a story, but that was before she'd agreed to become Mrs. Pierce Reed.

"Forget it, Ina, okay? Look, even if I could get him to agree, and let me tell you that's a gigantic *if,* it's not like knife-wielding psychopaths run rampant through the streets of Savannah every day, you know."

"Every city, or area around a city, has bizarre crimes. You just have to turn over the right rock and poke around. It's amazing what you might find. People are sick, Nikki."

"And I should be the one to capitalize on that." Nikki didn't bother to keep the sarcasm from her voice.

"It's what you do best. So dig a little," Ina suggested. "Turn over those rocks. Squeeze Reed for some info on a new case, even an old one. There's got to be something. What are the police working on now?"

"Reed doesn't confide in me. Or anyone. It's just not his deal."

Ina wasn't persuaded. "Not even pillow talk? You know, men really open up in bed."

"Let's not even go there."

Ina sighed loudly. "Don't play the blushing virgin card. I know you, Nikki. If you want something, you go after it and, hell or high water be damned, you get it."

"Come on, Ina. Think about it. If there were another serial killer running loose in Savannah, don't you think I would know about it?"

She could almost hear the gears turning in her agent's mind. In her mid-forties and shrewd as hell, Ina was barely five feet tall and the only agent in New York who had wanted to take a chance on Nikki when she'd submitted her first manuscript. Ina had seen what others couldn't, and now, damn her, she was trying to wring out of Nikki that same essence and perspective for a

24

brand-new *sales-worthy* story. "So get creative," she suggested, and Nikki heard bracelets jangling as she shifted her phone. "Maybe this time not a serial killer per se."

"Just a really sick monster with some kind of a blood fetish?"

"Or foot, or hand or breast. Or whatever twisted obsession turns him on." Ina gave a laugh that was deep and throaty from years of cigarettes. "Yeah, that would probably work." Clearing her throat, she added more earnestly, "You know the book is due in six months. It has to be published next year if we don't want to piss off the publisher and if we want to keep the Nikki Gillette brand out there."

Oh, Nikki knew all right. The date was circled in red on two calendars and highlighted in the virtual office on her computer as well. She wasn't about to forget, and she really couldn't. The struggling *Sentinel* was a slim remnant of its former self. Layoffs had been massive and painful. Nikki was working part-time for the paper and lucky to have a job. More and more, she relied on the advances and royalties from her books. Between the economy, the new technology, and her own ambition, she'd backed herself into a financial corner. She would be an idiot if she didn't make this work. "Okay, okay. I'll come up with something," Nikki heard herself say. As she hung up, she wondered what the hell that something would be.

She didn't take the time to think about it now. Instead, she flew down the circular stairs to her bedroom below, peeled off her jeans and sweater, and stepped into her running gear; old jogging pants and bra, a stained T-shirt, and favorite, tattered sweatshirt with a hood. She'd never been one for glamour when she was working out. Her running shoes were ready, near the back door, and after lacing them up and tossing the chain with her house key dangling from it over her head, she took off down the interior stairs and out the back, then sprinted around to the front of her home, ignoring the coming darkness. Her mind was a jumble, not just from the pressures of coming up with a blockbuster idea for a new book, but also from the fact that she was about to marry Reed. In her family, happily-ever-afters rarely occurred, and now she was planning to marry a cop—one with a tarnished reputation who'd left a string of broken hearts from San Francisco's Golden Gate to Tybee Island here on the Eastern Seaboard.

"You're a masochist," she muttered under her breath as she jogged in place, waiting for a light so she could run through Forsyth Park. *And deep inside a hopeless romantic.* The light changed, just as one last car, an Audi exceeding the speed limit, scooted through on the red, and Nikki took off again.

Starting to get into her rhythm, her heartbeat

and footsteps working together, she ran beneath the canopy of live oaks, their graceful branches dripping with Spanish moss. Usually the park had a calming effect on her, brought her a sense of peace, but not today. She was jazzed and irritated; Ina's call had only added to her stress level.

Get over it. You can handle this. You know you can.

The air was heavy with the scent of rain. Deep, dusky clouds moved lazily overhead, and the temperature was warmer than usual for this part of November. She sent a worried glance toward the sky. If she were lucky and kept up her brisk pace, she might just be able to make it home before the storm broke and night completely descended.

With that thought, she increased her speed.

A few pedestrians were walking on the wide paths, and the street lamps were just beginning to illuminate. A woman pushing a stroller and a couple walking a pug made her feel a little calmer, because the truth was that Nikki wasn't as confident as she seemed, wasn't the pushy cub reporter who'd been irrepressible and fearless in her youth. She'd had more than her share of anxiety attacks since her up-close-and-personal meeting with the Grave Robber. To this day, small, tight spaces, especially in the dark, totally freaked her out. So she ran. In the heat. In the rain. In the dark. Even in the snow during the rare times it fell in this part of the country. She didn't need a shrink to tell her she was trying to run from her own demons or that her claustrophobia was because of her past. She was well aware that she was walking on the razor's edge of some kind of minor madness.

Hence, she flew down the cement sidewalks and cobblestone streets, along asphalt county roads or muddy paths, speeding along the beach or cutting through woodlands. Mile after mile passed beneath her feet, and as they did, the nightmares that came with restless sleep and the fears of closed-in spaces seemed to shrivel away and recede, if only for a little while. Exercise seemed safer than a psychiatrist's couch or a hypnotist's chair or even confiding in the man she loved.

You're a basket case. You know that, don't you?

"Oh, shut up," she said aloud.

By the time the first raindrops fell, she'd logged three laps around the perimeter of the park and was beginning to breathe a little harder. Her blood was definitely pumping, and she slowed to a fast walk to alleviate a calf cramp that threatened, veering into the interior of the park again, only to stop at the tiered fountain. Sweat was running down her back, and she felt the heat in her face, the drizzles of perspiration in her hair. Leaning over, hands on her knees, she took several deep breaths, clearing her head and her lungs.

Straightening, she found herself alone. Gone

were the dog walkers and stroller pushers and other joggers.

No surprise, considering the weather.

And yet . . .

She squinted and found she was mistaken.

On the far side of the fountain, beneath a large live oak, stood a solitary dark figure.

In the coming rain, she and the man in black were alone in a shadowy park.

Her heart clutched, and a sense of panic bloomed for a second as the stranger, an Ichabod Crane figure, stared at her from beneath the wide brim of his black hat, his eyes hidden.

Every muscle in her body tensed. Adrenaline fired her blood.

It was so dark now that even the streetlights cast an eerie hue.

It's nothing, she told herself, cutting her rest period short. With one final glance at the man over her shoulder, she took off again, feet splashing through new puddles, her lungs burning as she cut through parked cars, ignored traffic lights, and sprinted home.

He's just a guy in the park, Nikki. Sure, he's alone. Big deal. So are you.

Nonetheless, she raced as if her life depended upon it, and as the rain began in earnest, fat drops falling hard enough to splash and run on the pavement, she came around the huge, old mansion she now owned and, taking the key from the chain on her neck, unlocked the back door, then ran up the stairs two at a time.

Once inside her own space, she threw the dead bolt and leaned against the door, gasping for breath, trying to force the frantic images of confinement and darkness from her brain.

You're okay. You're okay. You are o—

Something brushed her leg.

She jumped, letting out a short scream before recognizing her cat, who was attempting to mosey through a series of figure eights around her legs. "For the love of God, Jennings, you scared the crap out of me!" She slid onto the floor.

When had she become such a wimp?

But she knew . . . trapped in the coffin, listening to dirt being tossed over her, feeling the horror of a dead body beneath her, the smell of rotting flesh surrounding her . . . in that moment her confidence and take-the-world-by-the-throat attitude had crumbled into dust.

She'd been fighting hard to reclaim it ever since.

She was safe now, she told herself, as she reached up and checked the door to see that it was locked a second time, then a third, and after pushing herself to her feet, she made a perimeter check of the house. All windows and doors were locked tight, and no boogeyman hurled himself at her when she opened closets and checked inside.

Unconcerned about Nikki's paranoia, Jennings hopped onto the counter while Nikki, still edgy, downed a glass of water at the kitchen sink and stared through her window to her private garden three stories below. Rinsing her glass, she sneaked a glance at the gate. Still latched. Good. She took another look around the garden area, with its small table and chairs and huge magnolia tree, now devoid of leaves, but saw no malicious figure slinking through the shadows, nor, when she stepped out onto the small balcony, was anyone hiding on the fire escape that zigzagged its way to the ground. Double-checking that dead bolt as well, she decided her home was secure.

Finally, she let out the breath she hadn't realized she'd been holding.

For the love of God, pull yourself together, Nikki. Do it, now!

Kicking off her wet shoes, she walked through her bedroom, where she saw her wedding dress, wrapped in its plastic bag, hanging from a hook on the closet door. Her heart tightened a bit, and she ignored the thought that perhaps she was marrying Reed for security's sake.

That wasn't true, she knew, peeling off her soaked sweatshirt and stripping out of the rest of her clothes. She loved Reed. Wildly. Madly. And yet . . .

"Oh, get over yourself." In the shower she relaxed a bit, and once the hot spray had cleaned her body and cleared her mind, she felt better. There was no dark, sinister madman after her any longer. She loved Reed, and they were going to get married. Her bank account was low, but she could sustain herself for a few more months . . . so all she had to do was come up with a dynamite story for her publisher.

"Piece of cake," she said as she twisted off the taps and wrapped her hair in a towel. "Piece of damned cake."

Within twenty minutes she was back at her desk, a power bar half eaten, a diet Coke at her side, her hair air-drying in wild ringlets. Scanning the newsfeed on her computer, she noticed a breaking-news report running beneath the screen:

Blondell O'Henry to be released from prison.

She stared at the words in disbelief. "No!" Quickly, she googled for more information.

Blondell Rochette O'Henry, a beautiful enigma of a woman, had already spent years behind bars, charged with and convicted of the heinous crime of killing her own daughter, Amity, and wounding her two other children in a vicious, unthinkable attack.

Nikki's heart pounded as she remembered all too clearly the blood-chilling crime. Her mouth turned to dust, because Amity O'Henry had been her best friend back then, and Nikki knew, deep in her heart, that in her own way, she too was responsible for the girl's untimely and horrifying death.

"Oh, Jesus," she whispered, wondering if the report was true as she worked the keys on her computer, searching for verification of the story. In her mind's eye, she saw the image of Amity, who at sixteen was whip-smart and as beautiful as her mother, with thick, auburn hair framing a perfect, heart-shaped face, wide, intelligent eyes, lips that were sexy and innocent at the same time, and legs that wouldn't quit. And Amity O'Henry had the same naughty streak and sexual allure as her mother.

Nikki skimmed story after story, but they were all the same, nothing of substance, no details as to why Blondell was being released.

Nikki worried her lip with her teeth. She'd never really told the truth about the night Amity had been killed at the cabin in the woods—never admitted that Amity had asked her to come—and she'd buried that guilt deep. But maybe now she'd have her chance. Maybe now she could make right a very deeply felt and festering wrong.

Her search earned her an article about Blondell, written years before. The picture accompanying the article didn't do the most hated woman in Savannah justice, but even so, dressed in a prim navy-blue suit for her court date, her blouse buttoned to her throat, her makeup toned down to make her appear innocent, almost as if she were about to attend church in the 1960s, she was beautiful and still innately sensual. Her hair was pinned to the back of her head, and even though her lawyer was hoping she would appear demure, it was impossible to hide her innate sexuality.

Staring at the photo, Nikki knew one thing for certain: Finally, she had the idea for her next book.

As for a personal connection to the story?

She'd been Amity's friend. If that wasn't personal enough, she didn't know what was.

Chapter 2

Nikki drove like a madwoman to the new, downsized offices of the *Sentinel*. The newspaper had been a Savannah standard for generations, a bastion of the Southern press, but it was slowly dying, doorstep delivery and print pages giving way to electronic data zapped to computers and handheld devices, detailed stories cut into sound bites or tweets.

Many of the writers she'd worked with had moved on or were contributing to the electronic blogs, posts, tweets, and whatever was the latest technological blip in the ever-changing face of communications.

Located on the third floor of an old warehouse that had been converted to offices, the new headquarters were tucked into a weathered brick building that had stood on the banks of the Savannah River for centuries. Inside, the sleek interior, steeped in electronics, was about a third the size of the old offices where she'd spent so many years at a desk.

Nosing her Honda CR-V into a spot in the near-vacant parking lot, she grabbed her bag and braved the weather again. Dashing across the lot, through the rain, she skirted puddles as she locked her car remotely. A familiar beep told her all was secure as she reached the front doors beneath a wide awning. Into the building she ran and, with a quick wave to the security guard, took the stairs, water dripping from the edges of her coat as she used her personal code to open the door at the third floor.

With a click, the lock released and she hurried into the newsroom, where a few reporters were still at desks near the windows, separated by partitions, and the interior walls were dominated by a bank of computers for the digital feed. The employee lounge was cut into one corner, the restrooms another. Slick. Efficient. No unnecessary frills.

Few reporters were still at their desks, the day crew already having left and only a handful working the night shift.

"Hey!" she yelled to Bob Swan, the sports editor, as he appeared from the direction of the lunch room with a folded newspaper under his arm. "Is Metzger still here?"

"Home sick." Shaking his bald head, Bob added, "Picked up the bug from his mother at the retirement center where she lives. Whole place is shut down by the health department. Quarantined. But not before Metzger got hit." Bob chuckled as he turned into his cubicle, and Nikki followed to stand at the opening near his desk. "Hear he's sicker than a dog. Maybe now he'll finally lose some of that weight he's been complaining about." He dropped the paper he'd been carrying onto his desk.

"Too bad," she said, without much sympathy as Norm Metzger, the paper's crime reporter, had been a thorn in her side for as long as she had worked for the *Sentinel*. "I saw something about the lockdown at Sea View on the stream at home," she admitted. "And I caught something else."

Above the lenses of his half glasses, Bob's dark eyes glinted. "Let me guess. About Blondell O'Henry? Helluva thing, that. But with Metzger down with the stomach bug, looks like you're up." Then, realizing he'd overstepped his bounds of authority, he added, "But you'd better check with Fink."

"I will." Since the Grave Robber story, Tom Fink had grudgingly allowed her to report some of the local crime, albeit they were usually the stories that Norm Metzger didn't want. Nikki had never understood why Fink relied so heavily upon Metzger, apart from the fact that the heavyset reporter was more of a veteran with the paper. And maybe, just maybe, Fink was a bit of a misogynist, compliments of divorce settlements by his ex-wives. Whatever the reason, he'd never really given Nikki the chance to prove herself. Hence her high-handed refusal to take over the crime beat after the Grave Robber case had wrapped up.

She'd thought she'd move on to a bigger, more prestigious newspaper in the Midwest or Atlanta, maybe even New York, but then she'd fallen in love with Reed and eaten a bit of humble pie, mixed with crow, and decided to work part-time here in Savannah, the place she'd always thought of as home.

However, since Metzger was home sick, this was her chance at a story that could go nationwide, be picked up all across the country, and gain her legitimate access to Blondell O'Henry.

"I assume Levitt is on deck," she said, mentioning the newspaper's photographer.

"You know what they say about assuming anything," Swan said from his desk chair. "If this *is* yours, getting Levitt is on you. And you might have to fight Savoy for him." Inwardly, Nikki groaned. Effie Savoy was a recent hire, a woman whose blogs on the *Sentinel*'s web site were gaining popularity, a pushy reporter who was always around and dead set on being Nikki's new best friend. She was a real pain in the rear.

"Again?"

"She's a go-getter," Swan said. "Kinda reminds me of someone else a few years back."

"Yeah, right." She wasn't about to argue the merits of one of the newspaper's reporters, but it seemed odd, in this era of downsizing that, out of the blue, Effie Savoy had been hired to write a blog about all things domestic, and more. Her articles—or musings or whatever you wanted to call them—were all over the place, as was Effie. Nikki was forever running into the newbie, but somehow Effie had connected with the younger crowd. The worst part of it was that she reminded Nikki of someone; she just couldn't remember who.

Now she said, "I just thought I'd check the news feed."

"You'd probably get more info from Reed," Swan advised, raising his thick eyebrows.

"Not likely." That was the problem with this place. Everyone assumed she had a quick link to more information because she was engaged to a detective, but as she'd already told Ina, Reed was decidedly close-lipped about all his cases or anything to do with the department. She couldn't count the times she'd tried to gain a little info from him. Only three days ago, at the breakfast table in his apartment, she'd asked what she'd thought was an innocent question about a current case, and he'd just kept right on reading his paper, taking a sip of his coffee, even a bite of his toast, before saying, "Talk to Abbey Marlow," without so much as making eye contact with her. "She's the department spokesperson."

"I know who she is," Nikki had grumbled, tossing down the rest of her orange juice and biting back her frustration. "I just want the—"

"Inside scoop."

"Nothing like that."

He'd actually folded his paper onto the table and cocked his head, as if sincerely interested. Brown eyes, light enough to show gold glints, assessed her. "Exactly like that."

"It's just that you're the lead detective on the Langton Pratt case."

"And you're fishing again."

"I just want an angle."

"Seems to me you've got plenty." His razor-thin lips had twisted into a bit of a smile, that same self-mocking grin she'd found so intriguing when she'd first met him.

Infuriating, that's what it was, she thought now, as she knew she'd get no further with him than any other reporter on the street. "Reed's on lockdown, too," she said and headed for the cubicle she shared with Trina Boudine, who worked with human-interest stories and was her best friend at the office.

The two desks inside the cubicle faced each other and were separated by a thin panel with a few shelves. Trina's was neat as a pin, the desk clean, even her trash can empty.

Nikki's area was more cluttered and, as she called it, "lived-in," even though she worked only part-time. Pictures of her and Reed were pushed into a corner, along with a framed photograph of her niece Ophelia, known as "Phee," who Nikki could barely believe had started kindergarten two months earlier.

Plopping down, she unbuttoned her raincoat and let it drape behind her on the back of the chair as she logged onto her desktop computer and checked her e-mail. Sure enough, there was a quick memo from Tom Fink asking her to handle the Blondell O'Henry case as Metzger wasn't available.

"Yes," she said under her breath, happy that her name would finally appear in a crime-story byline again. It still bugged the living hell out of her that she was the second go-to for the crime beat, even after nearly being killed by the Grave Robber. It just went to show that, as far as editor in chief Tom Fink and the owners of the newspaper were concerned, it was still a "good ol' boys" network. *Such a load of garbage,* she thought, but she intended, once again, to prove herself and get paid while researching her next blockbuster. Smiling to herself, she started perusing the feeds.

The trouble was, she thought, as she scanned the bits of news that came through, Bob Swan was right. No doubt Reed had a lot more information on Blondell's release. "Bother and blood," she muttered under her breath, repeating a phrase she'd often heard from her late father, Judge Ronald, "Big Daddy" or "Big Ron," Gillette. Known for his sometimes salty phrases of exasperation in the courtroom, he'd been held in high esteem by both prosecution and defense teams. Big Daddy had been a fair judge who put up with little nonsense in his courtroom.

So maybe there was a way to get information out of her fiancé, she thought, as she searched through the press releases. She was certainly going to try. All he could say was no, which he was pretty good at, but for now she was stuck with the wire services.

And then she saw it. The reason for Blondell's immediate release: the recanting of key prosecution testimony from none other than one of the victims himself. Niall O'Henry, Blondell's son, now a grown man, was changing his story and saying that he was mistaken when he pointed a finger at his mother in the courtroom and, with tears streaming from his eyes and his tiny chin wobbling, had sobbed and whispered, "Mommy had a gun." Across the screen of her memory, Nikki saw him as he'd been: a scared boy, blinking in surprise, as if he couldn't believe what he'd just said. Then as the courtroom grew silent, every ear straining, he'd forced himself to say more, his little lips moving awkwardly as he struggled with the horrid words. He'd looked at the prosecutor and caught the slight nod; closing his eyes, he'd added, "Mommy shot Amity."

"I can't believe it!" Sylvie Morrisette raged as she took a corner a little too fast and the police cruiser's tires chirped. They were heading back to the station, and she was doing a good ten miles over the limit on Victory Drive. "That bitch should be locked up for the rest of her life!" She slid a glance at Reed and eased up on the accelerator. "Even that would be too good for her. I say, fire up old Sparky again and let her fry."

"Nice," Reed commented as they sped along the tree-lined street. Giant palms rose in the median of the boulevard, and large antebellum homes and live oaks draped with Spanish moss graced the sides of the street. "Were you on the force when she was convicted?"

"Hell no! That was twenty years ago." She buzzed around a green pickup that was loaded with landscaping tools and lumbering slowly. "How old do you think I am? I was still in Texas, probably mooning over Bart or some damned thing," she said, mentioning her ex-husband, with whom she had a contentious relationship. "But I remember it—boy, oh, boy, do I." Her West Texas drawl was becoming more pronounced, just as it always did when she was agitated. "She's an abomination to women, that one. Beautiful. Smart. And deadly as a cottonmouth, I'm tellin' ya." Reluctantly Morrisette slowed for a light, but her fingers held the wheel in a death grip.

She was a little bit of a thing, tough as nails, not an ounce of fat on her, mother of two and always, it seemed, pissed off at the male population as a whole. With spiky platinum hair, little makeup, and a quick temper, she was a definite force to be reckoned with. She'd given up her eyebrow studs and toned down her bad language as her two kids had gotten older, but she was still, as Kathy Okano, the assistant district attorney, had said often enough, "a pistol" in her ever-present snake-skin boots and bad attitude.

"You have to remember the case," she said, sliding him another glance. "You're a Georgia boy."

"I was in San Francisco at the time."

"It was freakin' national! All over the news, for Christ sakes. What were you, hiding under a damned rock?"

He didn't honor the question with an answer. "So refresh my memory."

She stepped on the gas and made short work of a Volkswagen Beetle that wasn't as quick on the draw. Whipping around the smaller car, she said, "The long and the short of it is that Blondell took her three kids up to a cabin for the weekend or something. Two younger kids up in a loft, Amity, the teenager downstairs, I think. Blondell claimed that an intruder with a gun came in, a struggle ensued as she confronted him, and everyone, including Blondell, ended up wounded. Of course, there was no phone in the cabin, and it was twenty years ago, before everyone and their toddler had a cell, so she tried to get the kids to a hospital, almost wrecked the car, and the girl died on the way."

"And the others?"

"Not good." Sylvie had turned grim. "The son, Niall, wounded in the throat, I think, and the little girl . . . what was her name?" Her eyebrows drew together as she checked over her shoulder and switched lanes. "Bella, I think; no, no . . . Blythe!" Snapping a finger, she said, "That's right. There was all kind of mention of Blythe's bravery because she took a bullet in the spine, ended up in a wheelchair."

"Sounds a lot like the Diane Downs case in Oregon years ago."

"That's the hell of it. People think Blondell purposely copied Downs. Saw a way to get rid of her kids and used it. Who knows? Reach into the glove box and see if there's any more gum, will ya?" She slowed and cranked the wheel, guiding the car into the parking lot near the station house on Habersham, a brick edifice that had originally

44

been built nearly a century and a half before, as Reed found the pack of Nicorette and handed it to her. With the agility of a twenty-year smoker, she retrieved a piece and tossed it into her mouth. "I hate this crap," she muttered, and he didn't know if she was talking about the gum or Blondell O'Henry's impending release from jail. Probably both.

Morrisette pulled into a narrow spot and slammed the cruiser into park. "Here's the hell of it. Blondell had just recently miscarried when she shot her own pregnant daughter. How about that? It all came out in her hospital exam."

Now that she brought it up, Reed remembered something about it.

"She never said who the father was," Morrisette went on. "Was it her ex, Calvin? That might've proved messy as he was already involved with wife number two, who also was probably pregnant about that time. He would have been a busy boy. Holy crap, there must've been something in the water that year. Blondell, her daughter, and Calvin's religious nut of a wife, June, all knocked up, well, at least until Blondell lost hers."

"You're saying Calvin was the father of his wife's baby and Blondell's, before she mis-carried?"

"That's exactly what I'm saying."

"You're not suggesting he was with his own daughter too."

"*That* never came up, thank God. Even though Amity was his *adopted* daughter. But no, I don't think so. I'm sure they would've been able to tell from the blood work. But he could've fathered his own daughter with June, wife number *dos,* and maybe the baby Blondell lost. Stranger things have happened." Morrisette shot him a look. "Then again, Roland Camp could have been the father. He was Blondell's most recent boyfriend. He's another winner, let me tell you. Not that it matters, as the kid was never born." She glanced out the window as a couple of uniformed officers walked past her car and into the building. "Or there's a good chance that Blondell's baby's daddy was some other lucky stiff entirely. Enough men around this town stared at her with their damned tongues dragging to the ground. She was smokin' hot. But who knows? I'm not sure the guy who knocked her up ever found out he was a papa, and since the kid was never born, the point's moot. It only matters because Blondell said in her testimony that she was drinking and confused because she was depressed about losing the baby. But that could all be bull."

Reed glanced at the station house, a beautiful building built for a much earlier time. Yet even with recent renovations, the offices of the Savannah-Chatham Police Department were showing their years.

"We're gonna have riots in the streets, let me

tell you. Blondell O'Henry is one of the city's most reviled criminals." She cut the engine and opened the driver's door. "Look up the case," she advised. "It's got more curves and twists than a nest of sidewinders with stomach cramps. Flint Beauregard, he was the lead detective."

"Deacon's father?"

"One and the same." She closed her door as Reed climbed out of the car, and together they walked toward the main door of the station. The rain had temporarily ceased and the clouds were beginning to shift to let in shafts of a few receding rays of sunlight, yet Reed felt no warmth. He'd never seen eye to eye with Deacon Beauregard, who had recently been hired as another ADA, a lawyer who was just a little too smooth for Reed's taste and a man who, it seemed, rode to a certain extent on the coattails of his deceased father, a decorated cop whose reputation was nearly legendary in the halls of the station.

"The whole case was circumstantial, as I remember," she said as they walked inside, her snakeskin boots ringing on the old floor as they headed to the stairs. "The critical testimony was from the boy. And now he's recanting. Ain't that just the cat's goddamned pajamas?"

Chapter 3

Nikki read through old testimony, especially Blondell O'Henry's, about the night in question. As she did, she saw in her mind's eye the scenario that had unfolded in the old cabin. It was a small building, one Nikki had known well, as it sat on the edge of property belonging to her uncle. Blondell was contemplating the loss of her unborn child and her recent divorce from her husband, Calvin, whom she swore was abusive. That's why she'd taken her three children to the cabin; to think things over and get her priorities straight. Her relationship with Roland Camp had been unraveling, and she had been faced with a future as a single mother.

Blondell maintained that her two younger children had been asleep, tucked into the loft above the main living area; her older daughter, Amity, was on the pull-out couch downstairs. Blondell had been out back on the screened-in porch, wrapped in a sleeping bag on an old chaise longue, drinking wine and watching the rain pour from the heavens to dimple the dark waters of the lake and listening to it pound noisily on the roof. She'd said it was nearly impossible for her to hear much of anything else, but she didn't mind. Caught in her own troubles, she'd been lulled by the wind and rain and wine while her kids slept inside the tiny cabin—basically one large room with a loft and a small alcove for a kitchen, along with a closet-sized bath.

She'd intended to bed down for the night on an old recliner near the fire that she'd lit in the old rock fireplace but had taken a few minutes to herself.

And that had been her mistake.

Somehow she'd closed her eyes and nodded off to the steady rhythm of the rain. She didn't know how long she'd dozed, only remembered that she'd awoken sharply at the sound of a car back-firing in the distance and just before a dog began barking wildly. The rain was still steady, but not as strong. She had a sudden premonition that something was wrong. Very wrong. And then her daughter had started screaming about a snake, a copperhead in the cabin.

Tossing off the sleeping bag, Blondell rushed in and saw, in the half-light from the fire, a horror that made her blood run cold.

A stranger was inside!

The fire had died down to red embers, so the cabin was nearly dark, but she could see a man's silhouette as he stood over Amity. He had dark hair and a muscular build, but his face was masked.

As he spun, Blondell saw the pistol clenched in

his hand, above which, on his wrist, was some kind of tattoo.

The rest was a blur, Blondell claimed. She'd screamed and they'd struggled. She'd hit her head and the world went black for an instant, the darkened rooms swimming in her vision. She thought she'd heard a dog barking again. For a fleeting second she felt hope that someone was near, but hope vanished as her vision cleared. Amity was screaming that she'd been bitten by a snake, and the stranger, in the shadows, was leveling his gun at the girl. Blondell had wrestled with him but hadn't been able to stop the horror as he'd fired point-blank at Amity.

Blondell swore she'd screamed and fought for the gun as Amity, lying on the couch, moaned in pain and footsteps erupted in the loft upstairs. Frantic, she'd launched herself at the stranger just as he turned to face her, his gun pointed straight at her heart. She'd flinched, still struggling for the gun, managing to grip the barrel and twist it upward, and then she heard Niall cry out.

"Mommy! No!"

"Get back!" she'd yelled, struggling to gain control of the gun, but the stranger was stronger and twisted the weapon, pulling the trigger.

Blam! Pain jolted down her arm, and she lost her grip, stumbling backward and falling to the floor.

Dazed, reeling in pain, she remembered the rest only in flashes: blast after blast echoing through the cabin; Niall running down the stairs, then jerking violently as first one bullet, then another, struck and his body tumbled down the remaining stairs. Little Blythe chasing after her brother, only to be hit as well, slipping through the railing to fall to the floor of the first floor with a last scream and heart-wrenching thud.

Blondell had cried, "No! No! No!" as Amity, unconscious, was bleeding out, blood pouring from the wound in her abdomen. Her son and youngest daughter mowed down by the monster as well.

Barely conscious, she heard the dog again. Closer, she'd thought, but the stranger, rather than finishing her off, had suddenly fled, running out the door and into the rain.

Blondell's story was a chilling account, but it was at odds with some of the police evidence. No gun had been found. Amity had died on the way to the hospital as the result of the gunshot wound, though she did have puncture wounds in her leg and venom from the copperhead in her bloodstream. The snake's bite would probably not have killed her, but the bullet that cut through her abdomen and hit an artery had.

Blondell's two other children had been rushed into emergency surgery. Blondell herself had been treated for a bullet wound to the right arm and a slight concussion as well as a contusion to the back of her head. She'd obviously fallen or been struck, and there were scratches on her arms, all of which could have been self-inflicted. Her fingernails had been clipped, their residue, presumably, still in the evidence file at the police station.

Hospital workers claimed her emotions were "all wrong" for someone who had been through the type of trauma she described, that her interest was more in her own injuries than those of her kids. She'd seemed stunned when told that Amity was dead, but hadn't shed a tear. Nor had any motherly concern been evident while her other children spent hours in the operating rooms. When advised that Amity had been pregnant, her fetus dying with her, Blondell hadn't uttered a word.

Had she been catatonic?

Had her injuries so confused her and stifled her emotions that her reactions were out of sync?

Or was she a cold-blooded murderess who'd been sent to prison because it was determined she'd staged the whole horrific scene?

Nikki didn't know.

Had there even been an intruder at the cabin?

That too was murky, but it was possible.

The flattened body of a copperhead had been found in the muddy driveway. Even that was odd, for in the middle of winter snakes were commonly in a state of reptile hibernation, sluggish and dull. And then there was the cigarette butt discovered near the porch. Blondell didn't smoke that brand; in fact, she rarely smoked at all.

Nikki wondered. DNA had just begun to be used at the time of the trials, but now . . . ?

She thought of Amity, and her heart twisted in guilt. Could she have saved her? Hadn't Amity begged her to come to the cabin that night?

If she had, would Amity be alive today?

"Please come," Amity had cajoled into the phone. "I need to talk to someone, and you're my best friend."

"I don't think I can get away."

"But it's really, really important," she'd insisted. "About . . . about my boyfriend. You have to find a way to come and please, please, please don't tell a soul. If you do we'll both be dead." She'd seemed about to divulge some great secret, then said, "I just can't tell you over the phone . . . *She* might be listening." By "she," Nikki had believed, Amity had meant her mom. "Come to the cabin, okay? I'll meet you at the lake. After midnight. Around one, okay? She'll be asleep by then."

"The cabin?" Nikki had repeated. "What cabin?"

"The one by the lake."

"My grandmother's cabin?" Nikki had asked, feeling a little jab of guilt for once showing Amity the family's nearly forgotten cottage on the shores of the lake when they'd been horseback riding. "How does your mother—?"

"Nikki! Just come! Nothing else matters," Amity had interrupted. "I'm not kidding. Please! It's a matter of life or death."

Nikki hadn't believed that plea. Amity had always been overly dramatic. Nonetheless, she'd reluctantly promised to show, to find a way to get to the lake, but she'd never made it. She'd set her alarm and even sneaked to the top of the stairs, but had heard her parents arguing in the den, just off the end of the staircase, so she'd waited in her room and eventually fallen asleep, only to wake hours later with the wintry Savannah sun climbing high into the sky, mist rising above the surrounding fields from the recent rain. Though she hadn't known it then, Amity O'Henry was already dead.

It's a matter of life or death!

She hadn't been kidding. Nikki had felt awful. Confused. Angry. Trying to convince herself that Amity's death was *not* her fault.

The news had rocked the community as it had ripped a dark hole of guilt through Nikki's soul. Could she have saved her friend? Somehow prevented the horrid tragedy? Sometimes she felt as if she should have been the brave heroine who somehow averted Amity's murder; at other times she knew with a bone-chilling certainty that if she'd made her rendezvous with Amity, she too would be dead.

As for Amity's whispered warning, "Don't tell a

soul," Nikki had taken that to heart, never once mentioning their conversation to anyone, not even her uncle, who became Blondell O'Henry's lawyer. Not even when she learned that Amity had been three months pregnant at the time of her death, knowing her pregnancy had probably been the big secret she'd planned to tell Nikki.

Lots of conflicting evidence had been brought to the trial, and most of the defense's case was called "smoke and mirrors" by the prosecution. The whole case had taken on a carnival atmosphere, possibly because of the media circus that had ensued.

The prosecution had insisted that Blondell, estranged from her ex-husband, Calvin O'Henry, was involved with Roland Camp, a shady individual at best, a man who had no interest in raising another man's children. Speculation had run high that Camp was breaking it off with Blondell because of her kids and that, after losing her unborn child, she'd snapped. In a fit of desperation she'd tried to kill her own daughters and son, then blamed it all on a mythical stranger.

Did that make sense? No. But nothing else did either, and Blondell's disconnect over her injured children hadn't played well with the jury. Still, if she were truly guilty, she'd taken great pains, gone to horrifying lengths, to rid herself of her children in order to what? Hang on to the boyfriend who had sworn on the stand that he'd moved on already?

It was a terrible story. Cruel. Insidiously evil. An echo of the Diane Downs case that had taken place in Oregon ten years earlier. A case that Nikki, like many others, believed Blondell had used as a blueprint for her own heinous act.

The defense stuck with the unknown intruder scenario, the proof of which was a single cigarette butt left at the scene and the squashed body of a copperhead in the driveway. These pieces of evidence, they claimed, meant that someone else had been on the property. As for the gun residue on Blondell's hands, it could be explained by the struggle for the stranger's weapon.

Their take was that Blondell's own injuries were evidence enough that she wasn't the killer. The man she'd wrestled with, whom she hadn't really seen, his face always in darkness, had been in his twenties or early thirties, around six feet tall, with thick, bushy hair. She'd also thought he had a tattoo on the inside of his right wrist, the markings of which were unclear in the darkness; but in one of the gun's blasts, Blondell had seen something that reminded her of a snake, or serpent, or the tail of some beast. Most of the inking was hidden by the long sleeves of his wet hoodie. She'd been allowed to search through book after book of photographs of known felons and to speak with police artists, but she'd identified no one on file, nor had she been clear enough in the details of the man's features—partially because they were hidden by a mask—for the artist to come up with a clear picture.

The defense had insisted that despite going through the motions, the detectives in charge of the case had targeted Blondell from the get-go and had never seriously searched for another suspect, the real killer.

The prosecution's case was circumstantial and rested on the tiny shoulders of Niall O'Henry, who, because he was old enough to know what was going on, was put on the stand. It was he who, at eight, had, in whispered horror, sent his mother to prison for what was supposed to be the rest of her life.

Now that could change.

According to the information Nikki had gathered, Niall O'Henry, along with his lawyer, was going to make a public statement, his own personal press conference, which was bizarre, but what wasn't about the Blondell O'Henry case?

Nikki had put in a call to the attorney's office, left a message, and was working on finding a phone number or address for Niall O'Henry. "In time," she told herself and kept digging. Since she'd arrived at the newsroom, the information had started streaming in, and yes, she'd broken down and texted Reed, but he hadn't responded to her bold question: "Any news on Blondell O'Henry case?"

No surprise there.

As for Blondell, it appeared she was keeping her silence. No one had any idea yet what she thought about her son's turnabout and recanting of his story. Nikki had already sent an e-mail to the warden at Fairfield Women's Prison near Statesboro, requesting an interview, though she didn't hold out much hope that it would be granted. Over the term of her incarceration, Blondell O'Henry had been moved from one women's facility to another and, since her one escape years before, had been kept under maximum security at Metro State Prison in Atlanta until it had closed. Afterward she'd landed in Fairfield, which was a little more than an hour's drive from Savannah. No matter what, Nikki determined, as she left the offices of the *Sentinel*, she was going to get a private interview with the state of Georgia's most notorious femme fatale and murderess, if it killed her. And, oh, yeah, she was going to get it *first*.

She was already out the door when her phone chirped, the sound of her preset reminder. She checked the screen after she settled behind the wheel. "Right," she said when she saw the quick text that told her Mikado was ready to be picked up from the groomer's.

Fortunately, Ruby's Ruff and Ready was on

the way to City Hall, where Niall's lawyer, after he'd filed the necessary papers at the courthouse, planned to hold an impromptu press conference. She wondered, as she backed out of the lot and eased into traffic, how the police department was handling all the unusual events in a case that had been decided nearly twenty years earlier.

Traffic was snarled in the historic district, but she knew the back roads and side streets over by the parkway. She took side streets to an alley where Ruby Daltry had her little shop. Hurrying, Nikki made her way through a short gate and along a brick walkway to the back porch. Over the screen door, hung a hand-painted sign, RUBY'S RUFF AND READY, in script, with colored paw prints of various sizes surrounding the letters.

She rang the bell and stepped onto the porch, where several dog crates and beds had been placed. A large, tile sink dominated one corner, and unmoving paddle fans hung from the elevated ceiling.

"Comin'," a voice called from inside, and Ruby, a fiftysomething woman with fading red hair pinned into a knot on her head, appeared in one of the three, small, descending windows in the door, walking awkwardly before reaching forward to unlatch the door. A child of about three, her hair in pigtails, was wrapped around one of her grandmother's legs and seemed fastened there. "I was wonderin' if you'd show up," Ruby said, offering a gap-toothed smile.

"Sorry about yesterday," Nikki apologized, stepping into a large open room to be greeted by a chorus of barks and yips. Three or four dogs, tucked into crates, peered through the mesh of their doors, and within his carrier, Mikado, ecstatic at the sight of her, was turning in tight, little circles.

"I'm glad to see you too," she said to him, leaning down and wiggling her fingers through the mesh. "Hang on for a sec."

Mikado yipped excitedly as Nikki straightened.

"You're not the only one who left a pup here. I don't know what people are thinking. Must be the rain . . . or maybe all that business about Blondell O'Henry. You've heard about that, haven't you?" Ruby was always one for juicy gossip.

"Only that she might be released, that testimony is being recanted."

"Unthinkable what that woman did," Ruby said. "Those poor kids. One dead, the other two growing up knowing their mother tried to kill them." She sighed heavily. "I just can't imagine."

"Blondell has always claimed that she was innocent, that some intruder came into the cabin."

Ruby's eyes met Nikki's in an "oh sure" stare. "What else was she going to say? That she did it? I don't think so. Nope, she's guilty as sin, and if you ask me it was all because of a man. She was involved with that . . . oh, what was his name?" She let out her breath in a low whistle.

"Roland Camp," Nikki supplied.

"Right!" Snapping her fingers, Ruby added, "A nasty one, him. Good-looking, I suppose, but a real lowlife. Don't know what she saw in the likes of him when, in her day, she could have had any man in Georgia, let me tell you. I'm a little older than she is, but I'm telling you all my brothers had their damned tongues hanging out at the thought of Blondell. Sickening the way men acted around her. Boys, men, she dated them all."

"You knew her?" This was news. Good news, actually. Another source of information. Even if it was, at the worst, suspect and, at the best, laced with gossip.

"I knew *of* her. She went to the school across town, but the boys, they knew all the hot girls in the area, and by that time, I was out of the house and set on marrying Seth. Blondell, she had her eyes set on someone to get her out of a crappy home life, I think, and I swear she was involved with some older guy who was rumored to be the baby-daddy of her first kid."

"Calvin O'Henry," Nikki said, distracted; she clipped Mikado's leash to his collar and held him back as he strained forward.

"Uh-uh. He wasn't the father of her first baby, as I understand it."

"Yes, you're right. Sorry. Amity was adopted," Nikki corrected herself. "Mikado, slow down!"

"Who knows who the real father was?" Ruby went on. "The truth is, I didn't really think much about Amity, you know, until she . . ." Ruby glanced down at the girl still wrapped around her big leg and decided to let that thought go, but Nikki made a mental note that Ruby and her brothers had known Blondell as a young girl. Before she'd married. Before she'd had children. Before she'd become involved with Roland Camp and the horrid tragedy had occurred. Background information.

Ruby said to her granddaughter, "Come on, Janie, give me a break here."

Janie was having none of it, her waifish face twisting as she wound up for what looked to be a colossal wail. "Noooo!"

In a hurry, Nikki asked, "How much do I owe you?"

"Seventeen fifty. I clipped his toenails too."

She fished in her wallet and came up with two fives and a ten. "Keep the change."

Ruby's broad face brightened. "Thank you." She tucked the bills into the pocket of jeans that were a couple of sizes too tight and peered over Nikki's shoulder to the exterior door. "I hope the others come. I close up at five. Got dinner to get on the table, y'know. Seth, he comes home from the garage and he's hungry as a bear. Growly as one too, if dinner ain't on the table. Y'know what I mean?"

Janie was winding up again. "Hungry!" she cried.

"In an hour," her grandmother admonished.

"I want a snack!"

"You eat now and I know what'll happen. You won't want any of your dinner."

"Hungrrrrry," the little one insisted, grabbing hold of Ruby's leg again, clutching her rather substantial thigh.

"Oh, for the love of Pete. Here!" Ruby opened a drawer and pulled out some kind of packaged fruit snacks that looked suspiciously like red jelly beans though the wrapper proclaimed the health benefits of zero fat and a high percentage of vitamin C "in each and every bite."

Snagging the packet, Janie finally released her grandmother's leg and skipped off, her tears miraculously disappearing, her pigtails bouncing as she took off through an archway, separated by a series of child gates, toward the living room, where a television was visible, the screen flickering with the bright colors of a cartoon show.

"I swear, that one has me wrapped around her little finger, and it's worse yet where her granddaddy is concerned. Man oh man, does she get her way around Seth." Ruby was shaking her head as the beams of headlights flashed, splashing against the back of the house. "Oh, good. Looks like Margaret is here to pick up Spike. I was wondering. She's not the most reliable tool in the shed, if you know what I mean."

Nikki didn't comment. Glancing at her watch, she knew she just had time to run Mikado home before driving to City Hall to hear firsthand why Niall O'Henry had decided to change a story he'd clung to for nearly twenty years.

Chapter 4

Unprecedented was the first word that came to Pierce Reed's mind as he stood, collar to the cold wind, watching the growing throng of people gathered around the steps of City Hall. *Grandstanding* was the second.

Standing behind a podium that was set up under one of the stone arches of the portico was David Blass, a senior partner in the firm of Blass, Petrovich, and Sterns. A tall man with broad shoulders and what appeared to be an expensive suit, he leaned into the microphone. "Let me be clear," he said in a voice that boomed into the crowd, where reporters with cameramen jockeyed for position. He held up one hand, as if for effect. "There will be no questions. Mr. O'Henry is here just to make a simple statement."

The less-robust man beside him had to be Niall O'Henry, son of Blondell. He appeared uneasy, as if uncomfortable in his own skin, and was a good three inches shorter than his attorney. While Blass's skin was tanned by hours on the golf course, Reed imagined, O'Henry was pale in comparison, a smaller, nervous man in a much cheaper suit. His features were sharp, his lips tight, his eyes staring across the milling crowd rather than into it. Had he looked healthier, Reed decided, Niall O'Henry, with his large eyes, aquiline nose, and high cheekbones, could have been a handsome man. As it was, he had the aura of a trapped animal, ready to bolt at any second.

"This is all such bullshit!" Morrisette muttered under her breath. "Such bullshit!" She was chewing her gum as if by pulverizing it she could wring out the very last drop of nicotine.

"Mr. O'Henry would like to change his testimony in the state's case against his mother. Though the conviction of Mrs. Blondell O'Henry was nearly two decades ago, Mr. O'Henry was only a child at the time and now feels compelled to tell the truth." Blass stepped aside, his shock of white hair catching in the wind as Niall stepped up to the microphone.

To Reed, this smelled of total crap.

And he wasn't any more convinced when Blass stepped to one side and Niall, pale and wan, took the microphone.

His voice was thin and reedy, perhaps because of the injury he'd endured as a young boy, as he read from a prepared statement that he'd placed on the podium in front of him.

"I, uh, I just want to say that my testimony in the trial of my mother was false. I was young, impressionable, and confused. The night of the tragedy, when my sister Amity was killed, is a blur in my mind, still nearly a total blackout, and I, as a boy, was coerced into giving a statement that would ultimately convict my mother. I apologize to the state of Georgia, to my mother, Blondell O'Henry, and to God. Thank you."

That was it.

Hands shot into the air, and reporters barked questions, even though they'd been specifically told not to. They were ignored by Blass and O'Henry and were left dissatisfied, as was Reed, though he hadn't expected any major revelation in the first place, no new piece of evidence. The public and the police wanted something more. As he glanced around the crowd, he saw his fiancée, who, with her photographer, had pushed her way as close to the podium as possible. He'd caught a text from her earlier and knew that he'd be in for it later, that she was going to push him hard on this one.

But with Nikki that was to be expected.

"I'll meet you back at the station," he said to Morrisette. They had walked the few blocks over to City Hall to avoid the traffic knots and parking issues the impromptu press conference had created.

"Okay. I've already requested all the old files on the case." Her eyes narrowed at the podium, now empty. "Looks like it's going to be a long night."

"The first of many."

"Hell's bells. Guess I'm going to have to play nice with my ex so he can ferry the kids around. It pisses me off."

What doesn't? Reed almost asked, then bit his tongue as he knew that comment would piss her off as well.

"I'll be there soon."

"Pick up dinner, would ya?" she asked, heading in the opposite direction. "Your turn. The Dollhouse is right on the way. Get me a fried shrimp po'boy, extra sauce. With fries. And a piece of pecan pie."

"You want—?"

"Don't even say it, okay? I know it's a heart attack ready to happen. So bring it on!"

"I was going to ask about something to drink," he said dryly.

"Oh. Make it a Dr Pepper." And she was off.

Nikki couldn't believe it. As she watched Niall O'Henry being ushered away by his lawyer, she tried to step forward, to ask one of a hundred questions that leaped to her mind. She was thwarted, of course. She and a dozen other reporters were contained by security as they yelled questions at the retreating figures of Niall O'Henry and his lawyer.

Thwarted, she turned to Jim Levitt. "Tell me you got some good shots."

"Nope."

"What?"

"More like great shots. You know, Pulitzer material," he said sarcastically while glancing down at her as if she were a moron. He was a beanpole of a man with sandy hair and freckles who'd played basketball in college and whose reach allowed him to hoist a camera over a lot of heads; hence, he was able to get shots a shorter person couldn't.

"Okay, okay, sorry," she said, sensing how touchy he was about his work. Levitt, whose wife was pregnant with twins due around Christmas, was feeling the bite of the economic downturn as well as the newfound difficulties of his profession. These days everyone had a camera, or at least a phone, that could take decent photographs. Not only was he used less at the paper, but his studio business had fallen off sharply. No one wanted to pay for professional shots when they could have Uncle Henry with a timer on his phone do a fairly decent job.

Working with his digital camera, he showed her more than a dozen shots of Niall O'Henry, his lawyer, and the group of people gathered at City Hall. "Don't worry about the pictures, okay? Just write a piece worthy of them," he said.

"Pulitzer material. I promise."

"I'll see you back at the paper," he said as he headed off, and Nikki experienced that same uncomfortable feeling that she was being watched. She glanced around. No one was paying any attention to her, not with the focus on Niall O'Henry. Though night had definitely fallen, she was far from alone, the crowd still slowly dispersing, a few knots of people still huddled together.

And yet she couldn't shake the sensation that unseen eyes were observing her, scrutinizing her every move.

Don't be nuts, she warned herself, glancing over her shoulder, her gaze scraping the shadows. Nothing.

"Hey!" she heard as she scrounged in the bottom of her bag for her keys. Glancing up, she spied Reed walking along the sidewalk toward her. As always, her heart did a quick little galumph at the sight of him. Yep, she thought again, *hopeless* romantic.

His gaze found hers, and his lips twisted into that irreverent grin she found so damned endearing. A five-o'clock shadow was in evidence but couldn't hide his strong jawline. Warmth spread through her—happiness—and she felt the corners of her own mouth lift. How could it be that she'd missed him when she'd been with him less than twenty-four hours earlier?

Make that ridiculous, hopeless romantic.

She ducked around a couple who were deep in conversation as they shared a cigarette and met Reed under a street lamp. "Where were you? I looked."

"To the side." He hitched his head toward an area that was now cleared of people. "How about dinner?"

"How about some exclusive comments on the Blondell O'Henry case?"

"Down, tiger. You know where I stand on that."

"Yeah, yeah, but this is breaking news on a very old case."

"Keep pushing, Reporter Gillette," he said dryly, then took the crook of her arm and walked her farther from City Hall. "Seriously, I've got to stop at The Dollhouse and grab a sandwich for Morrisette. I thought we could catch a quick bite together. That is, if you promise not to be obnoxious and keep bugging me for information you know I can't give you."

She was hungry, and she knew there was no way she would be granted an interview with Blondell O'Henry tonight. However, she planned to be at the prison the minute the doors opened tomorrow. She hadn't had an answer to her e-mail yet, but she knew other reporters were probably clamoring for access as well, so she wasn't going to wait for permission.

"There's a certain amount of bugging I feel compelled to do," she explained, and he groaned dramatically as they linked arms and walked the three blocks to the small restaurant, located in a historic Victorian-era home that had been remodeled and retrofitted with a commercial kitchen, elevator, and veranda used for outdoor dining. Painted a soft pink, trimmed in white, with bay windows and a long porch, the restaurant did appear to be a classic dollhouse, and the owners, Kenneth and Barbara Sutton, added to the theme by shortening their names.

The restaurant was fairly crowded, but they didn't have to wait too long for a table, where they ordered meals for themselves and takeout for Reed's partner.

"Metzger's sick, so I've got the Blondell O'Henry story," she said, adjusting her chair. She was seated across from Reed, their table tucked into a corner of what had once been the parlor.

"I already know you're not going to let up until I give you an inside police perspective."

He didn't sound overly perturbed, so she added, "And maybe get a look at the old case files."

"You're dreaming."

The waiter appeared and set two glasses of sweet tea on the table. As he left, she took a sip, feeling the cool liquid slide down her throat.

"Come on, Reed. You don't have to give me any information that's classified or whatever you want to call it, nothing that would compromise the case, but—"

"What case? Blondell's been tried and that's it. If she gets out of prison, no matter what she did, she's free. If she's innocent, she paid a high price. If she's guilty, the nearly twenty years she's already served will have to be enough for the state. Either way, there's not really a case against her. The department will argue, of course, but when it's all said and done, she may walk. Guilty or not."

"But the case will be reopened," she said. "If Blondell didn't do it, then someone else did. Remember her story of the intruder breaking in."

"An intruder she didn't recognize. Maybe it'll be reopened," he said dubiously. "I can't say. I wasn't there. But Flint Beauregard, the lead on the case, is dead, so there's no help there. All I can tell you, as a reporter, is that the department thinks they got their man, or woman, in this case."

The waiter showed up again, this time with their meals—a steaming platter of fried chicken with collard greens and black-eyed peas for Nikki, barbecued ribs, corn bread, and slaw for Reed.

"So when are you going to the prison to try to get that exclusive interview with Blondell?" he asked, raising a dark eyebrow just in case she might try to deny the obvious.

"Crack of dawn tomorrow."

"I figured."

"It's my job, and I need to do it."

"No argument from me. Have at it." He was already digging into his ribs. "You know I'm all for your career—supportive as hell, as a matter of fact. Just as long as you stay safe, don't put yourself into harm's way again, and don't push too hard when you try to get information out of me."

"That sounded like a lot of rules."

He heaved a long-suffering sigh. "Maybe we'll agree to disagree for now. And then later we could . . ."

"Talk about the case?" She fought a smile.

"That wasn't really where I was going."

"Are you coming over, then?"

"I wish. I think it's going to be a long night for me and an early morning for you. How about a rain check?"

"I can do that," she said, hiding a stab of disappointment. Though she wanted to find out more about Blondell O'Henry, she let it go. For now. Pushing Reed only put his back up—in fact, he became a brick wall—but if she was patient and didn't badger him, he'd open up a bit. The trouble was, patience wasn't her long suit. For now, though, she decided, biting into crispy, butter-flavored chicken, she'd put questioning Reed on the back burner and concentrate on the O'Henrys.

Not only was there Blondell to interview, but her children as well. What was the real reason Niall was intent on changing his testimony? What about his younger sister, Blythe, wheelchair-bound since the terrible attack? And what of Blondell's husband, Calvin, now remarried? She'd known the O'Henry family far more intimately than anyone, including Detective Pierce Reed, realized, and she knew she had to jump on the story. Quickly. Before anyone else did.

They ended the meal sharing a large slice of hummingbird cake. As light as it was, Nikki could take only two bites of the banana and pecan confection. "Take the rest to the station," she said when Reed too put down his fork. "I bet someone there will eat it."

"Trust me, it won't make it past Morrisette's desk."

He motioned for the check. Once it was paid, they walked together to her car. "Going back to the office?" he asked as she drove him to the station.

"Working from home, I think. I've got to write the O'Henry article for tomorrow and, in the morning, drive to the prison."

"She won't see you," he said as she slowed for a yellow light two blocks from the police station. "Her attorney won't allow it."

"We'll see." As the light changed, she turned onto Habersham and eased around Columbia

Square, where water cascaded over the ledges of a central fountain and stately live oaks stood guard over the pathways.

Slowing, she edged her Honda to the side of the road to let him out.

He said, "Be careful."

"Of what? I'm not going to compromise your case, I swear." She held up three fingers and mouthed, "Scout's Honor."

"I just don't like the idea of you at the prison."

"I won't be in any danger." She saw the doubt in his eyes and loved him even more. He wouldn't tell her what to do, but he'd worry a bit. "This isn't a case like the Grave Robber, nor is Atropos at large any longer," she said, citing the most recent incidents in which a deranged serial killer had stalked the streets of Savannah. "This is a cold case where a woman was charged and convicted of killing her kids. Family members. No one else was hurt." She paused. "That is, unless you don't think Blondell O'Henry is guilty?"

"I haven't studied the case, but since she was tried and convicted, yeah, I think she did it." He leaned over and brushed a kiss against her cheek. "I'll see you tomorrow."

Before he could reach for the door handle, she took his face in both her hands and pressed her lips to his. A warmth fired her blood as his tongue touched hers and her bones immediately began to melt.

"You're causing trouble," he whispered into her open mouth.

"I know."

He lifted his head again and winked at her. "Hold that thought, would you? Tomorrow."

"Sure, Detective."

This time he escaped, opening the door and sliding outside. As he jogged into the old brick building housing the police department, she nosed her way into the flow of cars and headed home. Traffic was thin, and she easily drove past the wrought-iron fence of Colonial Park Cemetery. In the darkness, she caught only a glimpse of the headstones, but even so her skin crawled, reminding her of her ordeal a few years earlier. Glancing into her rearview mirror, where the reflected headlights nearly blinded her, she made her way toward Forsyth Park and, across the street from its perimeter, the antebellum building she called home. The tiered fountain was illuminated, the tall trees with their canopy of branches ghostlike as Spanish moss swayed in the breeze.

"It's charming," she said aloud, "not scary." But she couldn't ignore the little drizzle of fear that slid down her spine as she parked, locked her car, and hurried up the interior staircase. On the third floor she was greeted by Mikado's sharp barks as she let herself into her apartment. The little dog spun circles and did a happy dance that always ended up near his food bowl, just in case she felt generous. "You're a little pig," she teased, picking him up and petting him, only to be rewarded with a tongue to her face and the not-so-pleasant odor of doggie breath. "First, outside with you, then I'll think about it."

Jennings had shown up as well and was pacing across the back of her couch. "Yeah, you too," she said to the yellow tabby before she found Mikado's leash and, as promised, walked him downstairs and into the backyard, where the porch light offered soft illumination and the patio furniture and shrubbery cast weird shadows. She stood on the old brick veranda, shifting from one foot to the other, a cool breeze cutting through her light jacket, her mind on the article that was forming in her mind.

All the while, as she waited for the little dog to sniff and take care of business, she thought of Niall O'Henry and how she would spin the story about him.

"Are you about done?" she asked and looked around for the dog, who had disappeared into the shadows. "Come on, Mikado! I'm freezing."

No answer.

"Buddy?" Her gaze scoured the magnolia and crepe myrtle lining the brickwork, but she couldn't see the dog, nor did he respond. All she heard was the hum of traffic in the city. "Mikado?" Whistling, she walked toward the fence line, hoping he hadn't found a space to crawl under.

"Come!" Her heart started to pound a little faster when she finally saw him, unmoving, staring toward a corner of the yard. "What is it?" He growled, and her nerves tightened, even though she knew he could be focused on a cat on the other side of the fence, or a squirrel or some other rodent.

Hearing the soft rustle of something moving through the undergrowth, the hairs on the back of her neck raised. Reed's warning, "Be careful," echoed through her mind. Shivering, she said, "Let's go, buddy," and quickly picked up the dog. His little body was tense, his ears cocked, his eyes trained on the encroaching darkness. "Give it up," she said, and scratched him behind the ears as she hurried into the house and up the stairs.

Once in her apartment, she snapped off the lights and moved into the kitchen to look down at the garden below. Nothing appeared to be out of the ordinary. When she squinted into the darkness beyond the fence, she thought she saw movement, someone hurrying through the shadows of the yard and alley behind her property, but she couldn't be certain and chalked the image up to her overactive imagination.

Mikado barked for a treat, and she broke a small doggie biscuit into two pieces before making a cup of hot tea. She then headed up the stairs to her writing alcove and computer.

The article came together easily, but there

wasn't a lot of meat to it, nothing special, and she frowned at her cell phone as Niall O'Henry's lawyer hadn't deigned to return her call. "Par for the course," she grumbled and made the best of the information she had.

Tomorrow. If she could just get in to see Blondell, then she'd have a real story. Somehow, she had to make it happen. For now, she logged onto her e-mail account at the paper, found the pictures Jim Levitt had turned in and picked two. One was a close-up of Niall as he stood solemnly at the podium. The second was a broader shot that showed the crowd that had convened around the steps of City Hall. It still wasn't enough, so she searched through the paper's archives and located several pictures of Blondell O'Henry at the time of her trial. Even in grainy black and white, she'd been a striking, petite woman with dark hair that framed a heart-shaped face. Her features were even, her cheekbones sculpted. Her large, smoky-gray eyes were rimmed in thick lashes, and her full lips were parted, showing perfect teeth and creating a slight enigmatic smile that could only be called sexy. Despite having three children, she'd been thin, with a few curves that were, as her father had said often enough, "in all the right places."

After attaching the digital photos she'd chosen for the piece, she sent everything to the *Sentinel*, then started work on a synopsis of the book she planned to write. It would take her a week or two to put the idea together and then to flesh it out enough so that Ina and her editor, Remmie Franklin, would approve.

After working for two hours straight, she decided to call it a night, but as she was starting down the stairs, she spied her high school yearbooks piled on the bottom shelf of her bookcase. Her copies of the Robert E. Lee High School *Traveller*, named after the Southern general's famous horse, had collected dust since she'd moved in. Now Nikki walked up the stairs again and sorted through the four volumes to find the school year she was looking for—the last year of Amity O'Henry's life. Almost gingerly, she pulled the volume from its resting place to carry it downstairs.

Once she'd changed into an oversized nightshirt, she plumped up the pillows on her bed and settled in. Mikado curled up beside her, and Jennings found a spot near the footboard. Carefully, she turned the pages, spying pictures of classmates as they'd been twenty years earlier, wearing eager, fresh faces, once-cool fashions, and hairstyles that were no longer in vogue. She found Amity O'Henry's junior-year picture, and Nikki's throat tightened as she studied it.

As beautiful as her mother, Amity looked into the camera. Her dark hair fell past her shoulders, her big eyes a cool blue and the smile that touched the corners of her lips sensual. Not yet seventeen, she appeared to be a grown woman with almost innocent eyes. There had been something about Amity that had caused heads to turn and boys to fantasize.

And one had done more than that, obviously.

Amity had dated a lot of boys, her relationships as volatile and short-lived as a firecracker on a rainy Fourth of July, sputtering out quickly.

So who had gotten her pregnant? Flipping through the pages of the yearbook, Nikki saw the faces of the boys who had openly dated Amity. Brad Holbrook, the baseball jock, and Steve Manning, a do-nothing stoner who was Hollywood handsome, were the two Nikki remembered, but that was because Amity tended to date older guys, in their twenties—"men," she'd called them, though the ones Nikki had met hardly seemed like adults. Nikki, a year and a half younger, had been given strict curfews, and boys who dared to take her out learned very quickly that Judge Ronald Gillette expected his daughter to be brought home and walked to the door. She remembered one particularly excruciating experience. Tate Wheeler had asked her out, and upon his arrival at the house, they'd both been summoned into her father's den.

"You will have her home by midnight," he'd said, eyeing Tate as if he might be a deadly rattler ready to strike.

Standing in front of the desk where the judge had been seated, both Tate and Nikki had squirmed. Leather-bound books filled several tall cases that flanked the windows, while family photos, law degrees, awards, and antique weapons vied for the remaining wall space. Half-glasses at rest on his nose, the judge had selected a cigar from his humidor but hadn't bothered to light it, just fingered the rolled tobacco, as he repeated, "Midnight."

"Yes. Of course, sir," Tate had responded, and Nikki had withered inside. Why did her father have to be so old-school?

"Good."

Tate, in an effort not to shrink before the man, had said, "Nice guns," and nodded toward a wall of pistols and rifles mounted above a mahogany credenza.

"Thank you. I've collected arms all my life, and they each have a unique history." Pointing with his cigar at a long-barreled pistol, he'd said, "I have it on authority that this pistol was used in the War of Northern Aggression. I believe it killed at least one Yankee soldier, though of course there could have been more." His smile was cold as ice, and the look he sent Tate was usually reserved for prosecutors and defense attorneys who irritated the hell out of him in the hallowed walls of his courtroom. Getting to his feet, he added, "You know, son, this pistol is worth a fortune, I suppose, but the most important thing about it is that it still works. I took it out just last week. Hit a target dead on from twenty paces. The way I see it, a collection of firearms isn't worth a damn if the guns don't work."

She'd shot her father a "don't do this" look, which, if he caught, he'd ignored. "You kids run along. Have a good time." His fleshy fingers moved in a quick "be off with you" motion as he sat in his creaky leather chair. "And remember: midnight. Not one o'clock, not twelve-twenty, not even twelve-oh-one. Midnight."

That had been that. Any hoped-for relationship with Tate Wheeler had died a quick death in the judge's den.

She'd been home by ten-thirty, and Tate hadn't called again.

"You're trying to ruin my life," she'd charged the next time she and her father had been alone. She'd found him at the fence line, watching his small herd of horses; two mares grazing in the lush grass, a foal frolicking on spindly legs.

"What do you mean?" He hadn't taken his eyes off the field, where sunlight had played upon the mares' backs, giving their bay coats a reddish sheen.

"All that crap about the Civil War pistol and getting me home by midnight! No one does that anymore!"

"I do."

"Old-school, Dad. You just like embarrassing me. You get off on it."

He'd chuckled, which had only infuriated her all the more.

"What I'm doing, Nicole, is separating the wheat from the chaff. Any boy worth his salt will be back again and not be intimidated."

"Don't you know how scary you are?"

"Not if you get to know me."

"For the love of God, Dad, no one gets a chance! You frighten them all away." She'd let out a world-weary sigh and watched one of the mare tails twitch at a horsefly. "None of my friends' dads pull this kind of crap."

"Watch yourself, Firecracker," he'd warned, using the pet name he'd given her. Then, less sternly, he'd added, "Have you ever thought that your friends' dads don't care as much as I do?"

"They just don't enjoy mortifying their daughters."

"Is that what I do?" He'd actually grinned.

"Yes!"

"Good." He'd slid her a knowing glance. "And if you think what I put them through is bad, just be thankful they don't have to deal with your mother." His eyebrows had lifted over the tops of his glasses, "Now, there's a woman who can be scary!"

Nikki sighed. No, Amity O'Henry hadn't had a father who acted like a medieval king who was dead set on protecting his daughter's chastity. Amity had been allowed to do what she wanted, with whom she wanted, when she wanted. All that freedom that Nikki had so envied had been a curse, and she missed her father more than she could ever have imagined as a teenager. To think about the last time she'd seen him . . . She closed her eyes at the memory, a frigid wind cutting through her soul.

"Don't go there," she whispered, chastising herself. To push the image aside, she found Amity's picture again and remembered her friend's last anguished plea:

"Please come. I need to talk to someone and you're my best friend."

And Nikki, daughter of privilege and harsh curfews, had failed her.

Chapter 5

As Nikki had expected, she wasn't the only reporter waiting to interview Blondell O'Henry. Though she'd arrived at Fairfield Women's Prison before eight the next morning, two television news vans were already parked in the lot near the front gates. One reporter, Lynnetta Ricci, a tiny blonde from WKAM, stood in position for an exterior shot of the guarded entrance, her cameraman already filming. Another team, DeAnthony Jones and his cameraman were finding a spot for the obligatory exterior shot of the prison.

There were others arriving as well, reporters she didn't recognize, but all sharing the same eager fever she'd felt upon hearing about the potential of Blondell O'Henry's release.

The gates opened electronically at eight, and they were ushered inside to a waiting area where they each showed their identification and turned off their electronic devices before surrendering them, along with their valuables, to a grim-faced African-American woman seated at a desk behind thick glass. Her hair was white and close-cropped, her eyes dark with suspicion. Her ID tag read Officer M. Ulander, and she didn't so much as crack a smile as she received the items passed through the two-sided drawer. Asking for their signatures, she returned visitors' passes with dexterity, if not pleasure.

Nikki hoped to be the first person allowed inside, but she was disappointed. She was third, behind Lynnetta Ricci and a man she didn't recognize, who had introduced himself as Ryan Nettles, a twentysomething, eager stringer for a newspaper in Atlanta. DeAnthony Jones had to settle for fourth.

She fidgeted on the padded bench in the anteroom, all the while cognizant of the cameras that were filming this sterile room along with all the other corridors and common areas of the new prison. The gates were electronic, the guards stern, the air inside the prison filtered and yet stale-feeling.

Her claustrophobia was trying to raise its ugly head. She hated the idea of being locked away, be it in a closet, a prison cell, or a damned casket.

The reporters before her filed in and out, and finally she was led by a guard through a series of electronic gates that hummed and clanged, her footsteps echoing on concrete floors as she was guided to an office on the first floor.

"Wait here," the guard instructed, pointing to another small, windowless office, where a receptionist/secretary was hard at work on the keyboard of a computer. A heavyset woman with streaked hair meant to conceal her gray, she wore a telephone headset and glasses balanced on her pert little nose. A nameplate announced that she was Mrs. Martha Watkins, and several plaques that had been proudly hung on the walls led Nikki to believe Mrs. Watkins had been an excellent employee in the service of the state of Georgia for thirty-plus years.

"Warden Billings will be with you shortly," the woman said, not missing a beat in her typing, though she did slide a quick glance as Nikki entered and the door closed behind her, clicking loudly, as if it too were locked.

Nikki fidgeted in her seat for almost ten minutes before the inner door opened. A tall, serious woman in a slim skirt and collared sweater introduced herself as Warden Jeanette Billings, then asked Nikki into the inner sanctum of her office. A large window allowed sunlight into the room, where a Thanksgiving cactus was starting to show orange buds, and Nikki breathed a sigh of relief.

The warden's desk took up most of the office, where shelves of books and framed black-and-white photographs lined the walls. A laptop computer was open on one side of the desk and a tablet on the other. As if to add some age to the room, an antique globe, circa 1920, was positioned on a stand in one corner.

"Please, have a seat," the warden offered, and Nikki dropped into one of the two visitors chairs. "I received your e-mail about an interview with Ms. O'Henry," she said before Nikki could ask about it. "I did write you back this morning to let you know that Ms. O'Henry is seeing no visitors." Her features were sharp, her demeanor that of someone who was used to being in charge. "Obviously you, and the others, didn't receive it or chose to ignore it."

"I was on the road."

One of the warden's slim eyebrows arched as if she doubted Nikki's word.

Nikki hadn't driven for over an hour to end up

empty-handed. "If you read my e-mail, then you know I'm not just here for a quick article or even a series of articles for the *Sentinel*. I'd like to write a book, tell Blondell's side of the story."

The warden's smile was tiredly patient. "Again, Ms. Gillette, you're not the first. Ms. O'Henry has been approached many times by different authors interested in her story."

"But that was before. Now it looks like she could be released, a free woman for the first time in nearly two decades. I'd think she'd want the world to know how she feels, what really happened that night." Nikki was on a roll now, but she could see the censure in Jeanette Billings's eyes.

"I'm sorry, Ms. Gillette. There's nothing more I can do. I've passed your request along, with all the others, and Ms. O'Henry, under her lawyer's advice, will decide if she would like to contact you." She started to rise, as if the short interview was over.

"But I really would like to speak with her," Nikki argued, not budging. "I was a good friend of her daughter's. Amity called me the night she was killed, and I feel like I'm connected to it all in a more personal way."

Little lines of disbelief puckered the warden's eyebrows. "As I said, Ms. Gillette, I'll relay the information. Now, if you'll excuse me, I have to get back to work."

"I've met Blondell O'Henry. Spent the night in her house. Amity stayed at mine. My uncle was her defense attorney."

"Was?" She picked up on the one word she apparently considered a weakness in Nikki's campaign.

"Yes. Alexander McBaine."

"But he is no longer representing her."

"My uncle was forced to retire due to health issues, but I'm sure Blondell—er, Ms. O'Henry—will remember him and me as well."

The warden walked around her desk. If Nikki had made the slightest inroad past the woman's steely resolve, she couldn't see it.

"Thank you," Billings finally said, just as the door opened and the guard who had escorted her into the office was ready to usher her out again.

Great.

Just flippin' great!

She walked back through the series of gates to find DeAnthony Jones glancing up expectantly as the doors opened and she stepped through. By this time there were two more people waiting, and Nikki would bet her next advance that they were reporters as well. "Good luck," she said to DeAnthony as he rushed past and she stopped to collect her things through the drawer of the glassed-in desk.

Officer Ulander, seated behind the thick glass, didn't seem any happier now than she had been when Nikki had arrived. "Sign please," she said in a raspy voice before she slipped another form through the drawer. Five minutes later, Nikki was out of the prison, walking through the cool morning sunshine to her car.

One of the news vans had vacated the lot, but Nikki knew there would be more. Blondell O'Henry was going to be at the forefront of news, not only in Georgia but throughout the South and perhaps across the nation, and Nikki planned to be front and center on the story.

She switched on the engine, opened the sunroof, and pulled out of the parking space. Since Fairfield was a new facility, the long lane winding to the main highway was smooth, the pavement unbroken. She glanced in the rearview mirror and saw the prison receding through the back window. Though modern and backdropped by rolling hills, the concrete-and-steel fortress wouldn't be mistaken for anything other than what it was. Watchtowers rose from the corners of thick walls topped with coiled razor wire.

Nikki thought of being locked inside and wondered how Blondell had survived all the years behind bars. She'd made it out once, during her only escape, from the first prison where she'd been incarcerated. For nearly three weeks, the news had been filled with images of officers and dogs searching for one of Savannah's most notorious convicted killers—on the run.

Nikki remembered that time because it was the summer after her senior year of high school. At the time, Nikki was more interested in her boyfriend, streaking her hair, wondering how she would deal with being so far apart from Jonathan after their inevitable and oh-so-tragic breakup, which would happen as she went off to college. But the state had been abuzz about Blondell's bold escape via a garbage truck.

"Can you imagine?" her mother had said at the table on the veranda where Nikki and her parents were eating breakfast. Fingering the diamond cross at her neck, Charlene Gillette had wrinkled her nose as if she, herself, were hidden in those bags of sweltering, rotting garbage.

Their conversation had taken place just after the Fourth of July, and the Georgia summer had arrived in full force, the heat sweltering. "It's amazing that she made it out alive," Charlene said, adding, "Then again, I've heard that cockroaches can survive a nuclear blast."

"She's a tough one, I think," her father observed, reading the paper, a cup of coffee near his ever-present glass of sweet tea on the glass-topped table. The sun had already heated the flagstones on the veranda, and bees were vying with hummingbirds, whose shiny green backs gleamed in the bright morning light.

"More like callous. And heinous! Dear Lord, what that woman did was unimaginable." She'd physically shuddered, then sent Nikki an "I told you Blondell O'Henry and her kind were filth" look.

Nikki had finished her orange juice and ignored the fritters soaking up syrup on her plate, excusing herself quickly to catch up on accounts of the escape in the solitude of her room. At eighteen, in the throes of teenaged angst and lost in her own problems, she'd been awakened to her interest in the news by Blondell's bold escape.

In the ensuing weeks, the police had sent out a plea for help in finding her, asking the public's help in locating the notorious femme fatale and her newest lover—oh, God, what was his name? Nikki had thought she'd never forget it.

Nikki flipped down the visor and concentrated. Barry something? No. Not quite right. Larry. That was it. Lawrence Thompson. Now she remembered. It had been Thompson who had been spied in a trucker's cap, oversized sunglasses, and newly grown goatee at a gas station in West Texas that happened to have a surveillance camera and caught the tattoo on his right arm as he'd paid for gas, beer, and chips. The inky head of a chameleon had peeked out of his sleeve. The cashier had seen it and recognized the tattoo as belonging to Thompson.

Within hours, the police descended on a fleabag of a motel southwest of San Antonio, where the pickup Larry had "borrowed" from his sister had been parked, dusty and baking in the pock-marked back parking lot.

He and Blondell, it was presumed, had been on their way to Mexico.

Upon her capture, Blondell was returned to prison, and her accomplice stood trial. Thompson had been incarcerated as well for his part in her escape.

Damn! Nikki *needed* to speak to Blondell.

She tapped her fingers on the steering wheel as she drove, then found her cell phone in the pocket of her purse and clicked it on. Sure enough, she'd missed several calls and texts while she'd been at the prison. After giving the screen a cursory glance, she dropped her phone into her cup holder as she considered her options.

Surely she'd get a little more insight from Reed, though she knew it wasn't going to be easy. Aside from him, she also had another source at the police department, a contact she hadn't tapped since the Grave Robber case, her brother Andrew's best friend, who had leaked information before. But if she contacted Cliff Siebert and Reed found out, there would be serious hell to pay.

That said, there was, as Big Daddy had often intoned, "more than one way to go at this," she thought, as she tore around an RV that was ambling along the road, filling most of the lane and making it impossible for her to see anything ahead. She did have an ace up her sleeve, as

Blondell's attorney had been her very own uncle and, as she saw it, another personal connection to the story.

"Put that in your pipe and smoke it, Ina," she said aloud as she retrieved her sunglasses from a hidden compartment in the dash, then slipped the shades onto the bridge of her nose. Her mood elevated a little as she considered her next course of action after the bust at the prison. Of course, she wasn't going to give up on getting an interview with Blondell. Somehow she would manage to talk to the woman. She had to. Speaking directly to Blondell O'Henry would be pivotal for her book and would certainly add reader interest to the series of articles she hoped to write for the *Sentinel.* If she could just talk to Amity's mother, Nikki felt she could convince Blondell to tell her side of the story. Maybe Blondell would want money, but that could probably be arranged. Or maybe she just would finally want to set the record straight.

If she's not guilty, what if the police find another way, another piece of evidence to ensure that Blondell spends the rest of her life in prison? But no, she couldn't be retried for the same crime. That would constitute double jeopardy. Still, Blondell was far from home-free yet. The state of Georgia and the police department would want to see her kept behind bars.

It was time to pay a visit to Uncle Alex,

Blondell O'Henry's onetime attorney and Nikki's favorite uncle.

Merging into the traffic on the interstate, she ignored the lush farmland and thickets of pine and oak as she drove toward the lowlands and Savannah.

The problem, of course, was that Alexander McBaine was suffering from dementia, most likely early-onset Alzheimer's, and so his recollections would be spotty and undependable at best. But surely he had notes from the trial . . . ? If she could just see both the prosecution's and the defense's sides of the trial—how perfect would that be?

"You're dreaming," she told herself, as she glanced over her shoulder, switching lanes to exit the freeway on the outskirts of the city. Still, nothing ventured, nothing gained. And just maybe it would be one of Uncle Alex's good days.

Chapter 6

"It's a mess, that's what it is," Morrisette said, eyeing all the boxes and chewing her nicotine gum as if her life depended on it. She and Reed had been summoned by Kathy Okano, who had asked that they meet in the training room that was to be converted for a special use: reconstructing the case against Blondell O'Henry.

The state of Georgia wasn't giving up on keeping one of its most infamous criminals right where she was.

"It's not just a mess," Okano announced as she joined them in the area that was being set up primarily for the review of Amity O'Henry's homicide. "It's *your* mess. I'm putting you in charge, Reed. And, Morrisette, you work with him."

"We have other cases," Morrisette said.

"Oh, I know." Okano, a tall woman with a blond bob, wire-rimmed glasses, and a sharp mind, frowned as she eyed box upon box of dusty documents and information that had been archived for nearly two decades and that were now spread over two tables. "And you can't ignore them, of course. But I'll spread the wealth, trust me. But for now, you need to lock this down. The press is already all over this case, and the department doesn't need any new black eyes.

"You two weren't here at the time of the trial, so you'll have fresh eyes. No prejudice. Unfortunately, some of the detectives who worked the case are long gone, and their expertise and knowledge would have helped. The DA at the time, Garland Brownell, died two years after prosecuting the case. Forty-nine and dropped dead of a massive heart attack after working out at the gym. Jasper Acencio moved to Phoenix five or six years ago. He's still there, as far as I know, working for the Phoenix Police Department, so contact him. Flint Beauregard, of course, was the lead. He died a couple of years back. Too bad, that," she said, shaking her head. Reed didn't say what flicked across his mind: the scuttlebutt that Flint Beauregard had died from complications of emphysema and congestive heart failure owing, at least in part, to too many years of cigarettes and rye whiskey.

"I don't know if Deacon can help," Okano went on, mentioning Flint's ADA son, "but maybe." Her gaze locked with Reed's. "God knows, he's chomping at the bit. Anything to ensure his father's reputation isn't tarnished."

Reed nodded. He also didn't say that in his estimation Deacon Beauregard was a class-A prick.

"DNA has come a long way in twenty years," the assistant district attorney continued. "If they can now prove that a handkerchief that was supposedly dipped in the spilled blood from Louis the XVI's beheading really is his, then we can certainly come up with DNA, if it's not corrupted, from that cigarette butt left at the scene, for starters. And find out about that damned snake. Why was a copperhead found flattened at the scene?

"Also, we've got a bit of a problem. Most of the

evidence is here, but the tapes are missing. Videos of the crime scene and all the video from the trial, though I imagine if you dig deep enough you can find it on YouTube, or wherever. Everything else is out there these days." Okano glanced from Reed to Morrisette. "So if you see something that seems a little off, I want to know about it immediately."

Her cell phone rang, and she said, "Anything you need, just call," before clicking the phone on and opening the door to the hallway. Noise of the department filtered in: ringing phones, shuffling feet, buzzing conversation punctuated often by the ripple of laughter. Then the door shut behind her, blocking everything but the steady hum of the furnace.

"Jesus!" Morrisette shoved her fingers through her spiked blond hair as she opened an evidence box and peered inside. "What won't we need?"

"Good question." Reed eyed the crates, walking from one to the next. Everything—from the physical evidence, to the medical examiner's reports to the testimony at the trial—was there. Pictures of the victims and the crime scene, ballistics reports, hospital information, theories and interviews that had been bundled and locked away had been retrieved.

"Hey, here's something!" Morrisette said and reached into one of the boxes.

"What?"

She pulled out an evidence bag that held the

well-preserved carcass of a freeze-dried snake. "What do you think?" she asked, holding up one booted foot. "If we crack this case and prove that good old Blondell really did off her kids, maybe I could end up with this bad boy as a souvenir. Get myself a new set of boots?"

"Yeah, that's what's gonna happen," Reed said as he pulled up a chair and scanned the list of evidence. It looked like it would be a long morning.

"You know your uncle is ill," Aunty-Pen said gently. The epitome of a genteel Southern woman, with polite manners, effusive charm, a dulcet-toned voice, and a backbone of steel, she added, "I don't see how he can possibly help you."

She led Nikki through the marble-tiled foyer and past a grand staircase that wound to the second-story gallery, with its coved ceiling and enormous chandelier, the one Nikki's mother had once referred to as gauche. The house had been built before the turn of the last century and remodeled at several points over its lifetime, so that it resembled a Southern mansion on the outside but was modern and efficient on the inside.

Ever the hostess, Penelope Hilton (no dear, not one of *those* Hiltons) poured them each a glass of sweet tea and offered Nikki a chair on the screened back porch with its view of her sweeping gardens of magnolia, jasmine, crepe myrtle, and gardenias. Paths wandered through the lush, fragrant foliage to fountains and birdbaths. She and Nikki had never been close, but that was just how Penelope handled all people—at arm's length. Though sisters-in-law, Charlene, Nikki's mother, and Aunty-Pen had never really gotten along. Their rift had widened considerably when Penelope lost both of her children in a tragic accident years earlier.

"Even if Alexander were well enough to help you," Aunty-Pen was saying, "he couldn't, you know. Client-lawyer privilege." She sat in one of the cushioned chairs near a round wrought-iron table where a vase of fresh flowers had been placed. Tall and athletic, Aunty-Pen had once ridden dressage for her college team, and as she'd been known to point out, had *almost* been selected for the Olympic team a quarter of a century earlier. Her hair was clipped short, a warm blond touched with gray, her eyes as blue as a Georgia summer sky. "And he's not here. I had to move him three, no, dear Lord, it's been nearly five months ago, though, of course, I do bring him home once in a while."

"I know," Nikki agreed. "But it would be good to see him anyway. The case is really just an excuse."

"You don't need one, dear," Aunty-Pen said with her cool, knowing smile. "He'd love a visit, though it may be that he won't remember you." A dark cloud passed behind her eyes. "His is a very insidious disease. Robbing the man of being who he once was." She sighed and sipped from her tea. "I'm going out to Pleasant Acres today, of course, and you're welcome to join me. I always plan my stays between his lunch and nap."

"Every day?"

"Mostly. Well, except Sunday, when I go directly after church and eat with him."

"I would like to see him."

"All this business with that O'Henry woman," she said, waving off the idea as if it were a bothersome insect. "I don't know what the fascination is, but then what counts for news these days . . . If it were up to me, they'd keep that woman locked up and throw away the key. My God, what she did." Aunty-Pen glanced out the window to a plaque she'd had installed in her garden, a stone etched with her children's names. "Burning at the stake would be too good for her."

"Innocent until proven guilty."

"Which she was. Proven guilty. That's why she's in Fairfield."

"But the prime witness recanted."

"Her *son*. A boy who now questions what he saw with his own two eyes. To think what he and his sister have lived through. It's impossible to imagine."

"Uncle Alex might be able to help me."

"I wouldn't count on it."

"Still, I need to visit him."

Her mouth twisted downward at the corners. "But you'd better brace yourself, Nicole. It won't be easy. You were, or, I mean, *are* his favorite niece, I know, but . . ." She shook her head sadly, then lifted her chin. Aunty-Pen wasn't one to wallow in grief. "We can go this afternoon."

"Good."

"Oh, and how's your mother?" She asked out of duty; they both knew it.

"Okay, I guess." Charlene Gillette, never a particularly healthy woman, had, in recent years, grown frail to the point that she hovered somewhere just above a hundred pounds, which wasn't much for even her petite frame.

"She's got to be ecstatic about the wedding, though. You're her great last hope."

"She's looking forward to it," Nikki agreed, but she bristled a bit, knowing what was coming next.

"You'd think Lily would settle down."

"She doesn't want to."

"But for Ophelia? What's Lily thinking, raising her without a husband?"

"It's the thing now, Aunty-Pen. Women don't need a husband to start a family."

"Don't be silly, Nicole. That's ridiculous! Any woman needs a husband, and certainly every child needs a father."

"That's antiquated thinking," Nikki said, and

her aunt sent her a look guaranteed to cut through steel.

"You can be as modern as you want to be, but let me tell you, marriage is more than a ritual and a piece of paper. It's not just a privilege, it's a sacred union, not to be taken lightly. You're sure you're ready?"

"I think so," Nikki said, fighting her irritation. She knew the well of Aunty-Pen's grief and how it came out in these picky little ways. She would never get to be mother of the bride, never have grandchildren, or great-grandchildren. Rather than argue, Nikki changed the topic. "How about I drive this afternoon?"

"Let's just not speed as if we're running from a fire. The world won't stop if we arrive at Pleasant Acres five minutes late."

Reed spent most of the morning sipping bad coffee and reading through Flint Beauregard's notes. The case file was thick and seemingly complete, at least at first glance, but he intended to study the notes in greater detail once they'd sorted through all the physical evidence, read the statements, and gone over the testimony at the trial. There were depositions to read, witnesses to find, and lab work to scrutinize and double-check with today's technology. Along with all the physical evidence found at the scene, there was a bundle of letters, yellowed with age, written in

Blondell's distinctive loopy handwriting, all addressed to "My Love." None, it seemed, had ever been sent. They had been preserved in plastic, and as Reed read them, he felt as if he were invading a couple's privacy. The notes were intimate and sexy and flirty and spoke of undying love and desperate need, but gave no indication the author intended to do anything malicious or harmful. If anything, they seemed more like a plea for the same adoration the writer was offering.

Bothered, he set them aside and concentrated on the scientific evidence rather than the romantic yearnings of a woman who eventually would be found guilty of murder.

Meanwhile, Morrisette worked on organizing the evidence and sorting through what, in her opinion, was relevant and what wasn't. A junior detective was given the job of searching all the Internet databases looking for the addresses and phone numbers of the witnesses for the prosecution, as well as those who had spoken for the defense. The idea was to see if anyone else was changing his or her testimony and, if so, what would it be. The state hoped someone would come forward with more damaging evidence, but Reed wasn't betting on it.

Skimming the files, Reed made notes to himself. A few anomalies jumped out at him, not the least of which were Blondell's injuries. Had she somehow fallen against something on purpose to make it look as if she'd been attacked, and had she really fired a gun point-blank into her own arm to add credence to her story? If so, it was a gutsy move, but her injuries, for the most part, weren't life-threatening. No serious concussion or blood clot on her brain, no nicked artery in her arm. In that respect she had been much luckier than her children. While the defense had insisted she'd been wounded in a struggle with an assailant for the gun—hence the gunshot residue on her hands—the prosecution had argued that Blondell, a woman who could murder her own child in cold blood and try to kill the others, could certainly shoot herself. Reed wasn't convinced. Not completely. If she'd been dead set to get rid of her kids, why even drive them to the hospital? Why not finish the job and say she'd been knocked out in the attack, that the assailant had thought he'd killed her.

Why leave witnesses?

No, despite the outcome of her trial, it didn't quite jibe that she was a cold-blooded killer, so he figured it wasn't so much his job to find the evidence to keep Blondell O'Henry in jail as it was to uncover the truth.

Meanwhile, the press was all over the case, and he'd declined to take any calls he didn't recognize. The public information officer could handle any and all questions. Of course, that didn't include Nikki, who was already hounding him.

She was like a terrier with a bone when she wanted a story. He'd learned that lesson long ago, and while she'd irritated the hell out of him, she'd intrigued him as well, and he, who had sworn off women after the debacle in San Francisco, had found himself falling in love with her. He'd fought his attraction, of course, but in the end she'd gotten under his skin like no other woman, and he, once a confirmed bachelor, found himself proposing to her.

Now, as he looked at the autopsy report on Amity O'Henry, he inwardly cringed. She'd been so young, a child really, yet three months pregnant. He wondered if Blondell had known about the baby, though she'd sworn she'd had no idea that her daughter was even sexually active, let alone pregnant. Nor had Blondell been able to come up with the name of the child's father. Again, DNA testing would help, as long as the father was in the database.

Unfortunately, there was no blood, amniotic fluid, or anything from the fetus, and twenty years ago paternity testing wasn't as precise as it was today.

So who was the guy? Nikki said she knew Amity. Maybe she could provide a list of boyfriends the girl had been dating. Beauregard did have two names listed, but according to the reports, each had submitted to a blood test and had been ruled out as the father of the unborn child, whose blood had been O-negative, which, since Amity was A-positive, indicated the father had negative blood, a rudimentary identification test by today's standards, but still accurate.

His mind wandered for just a second to another paternity test a few years back, when he'd learned that a victim of the Grave Robber, a woman he'd been involved with, had been pregnant with his child.

His heart still twisted at that thought, and now that he was again dealing with a case in which an unborn child was a secondary victim, it made him all the more angry and determined to ferret out the truth.

Unfortunately, Beauregard's notes weren't as thorough as Reed would have liked, and the biggest piece of evidence against Blondell O'Henry—the testimony of her young son—was now being recanted. Reed would have loved to see portions of the trial, so he'd taken a quick look online and found some just-posted clips on YouTube, generated from the renewed interest in the case. He'd seen the defendant, demure and quiet, hands folded in front of her as the trial progressed. Garland Brownell, a former football star, had handled the prosecution's case well, his style subtle when it was called for and more passionate when that was needed during the examination of his witnesses. Alexander McBaine had been as smooth as silk, a good ol' Georgia boy who oozed Southern charm. He too had dealt with each witness expertly. However, the cut-up pieces of the trial that Reed had found weren't cohesive. He longed for the missing tapes.

One thing he noticed: in every clip he saw Blondell was the same. Cool. Beautiful. Serious. Judging from her appearance, no one could have imagined her capable of the evil of which she was accused.

Now she'd served nearly twenty years of her life sentence in prison, which was nothing to dismiss, but there certainly wasn't enough other circumstantial evidence to back up that conviction, and, of course, she couldn't be tried twice for the same crime, should she be released. Was she guilty of the terrible, blood-chilling crime, or was she, as she had always maintained, truly innocent?

His job was to prove her guilt and allow the DA to pursue whatever path needed to be taken to see that Savannah's most notorious female criminal remained behind bars.

Surprisingly, his fiancée, Amity O'Henry's best friend, might hold the answers.

Rotating his head, he stretched the muscles in his neck. Nikki had been pushing him for information about the case. Now their roles were reversed, and he sensed she might be able to help him. If nothing else, he'd learn a lot more about the psychology of the victim.

Yes, he thought, kicking his chair away from the desk. The tables were about to be turned.

Chapter 7

Unfortunately, Aunty-Pen was right. Alexander McBaine wasn't the man Nikki remembered.

Nikki had driven the five miles out of town to the Pleasant Acres Assisted Living Center, a long, low building set on the marshy banks of a creek. From the windows of their units, the residents could watch waterfowl in the reeds, but the alligators were kept away from the rolling expanse of lawn by a sturdy wire fence that encircled the yard.

Inside the facility, she and Aunty-Pen had made their way along a carpeted hallway with handrails and evenly spaced pictures to a wing housing the patients with dementia, her uncle's new place of residence. Aunty-Pen had admitted that she did take him home on some weekends, just because it "broke her heart" to see him in the small apartment. She hoped being in his own surroundings would jog his memory, make him recall himself more clearly. So far that was a no-go.

Today, seated in a wheelchair in his studio apartment, Alexander McBaine was wearing a cardigan sweater over a white dress shirt that obviously had once fit and now was two sizes too large. Slacks that needed to be cleaned and slippers on the wrong feet completed his attire as he stared out a single window at a courtyard where feeders were attracting winter birds. Nikki's throat tightened as she thought of the strapping attorney he'd once been, a man who had commanded attention, whose sharp mind had been pitted against those of the prosecution. He'd had flair, brilliance, and a winning smile that had hovered somewhere between sexy and hard.

Now, though, his grin was that of a simpler man.

For a second, she thought he recognized her, but soon she realized she'd been sadly mistaken.

"Hollis!" he cried happily, and tears filled his eyes as he beamed up at her from his chair and pushed himself unsteadily to his feet. Standing next to her, Aunty-Pen stiffened and looked away. "But I thought . . . oh, thank God! Silly me! I must have had a nightmare. Yes, Pen?" He glanced at his wife, whom he obviously still recognized, then turned his attention to Nikki again. "I was afraid it was true, that you really had . . . died in an awful accident. But . . ." His voice drifted off with his confusion as reality and fantasy blended. Obviously, he'd thought Nikki was his long-dead daughter, her cousin

Hollis, gone now, along with her brother, Elton. "Oh . . . dear . . . please . . . never mind. It's just good to see you." He blinked back tears, and Nikki, catching a look from her aunt, didn't have the heart to tell him he'd been mistaken, that she was really his niece and not his precious Hollis. Instead, she hugged him close. He smelled of the same cologne she remembered from her childhood, but now it was no longer tinged with cigarette smoke as he'd obviously been forced to give up the habit here at Pleasant Acres.

"How are you?" she asked, and he offered up a little smile.

"All right, I guess." He frowned a little then, his once-dark eyebrows knitting, his hazel eyes cloudy behind thick glasses that Aunty-Pen slid from his face.

"Look at these! How can you see anything?" she clucked, striding into the adjoining bathroom. Seconds later the sound of rushing water could be heard.

He chuckled. "Nothing's ever clean enough for your mother."

"She's my aunt," Nikki said. "I'm Nicole. Nikki. Ron and Charlene's daughter."

His expression went blank for a second, then worried lines etched across his brow. "Ronnie's girl?"

"Yes. Nikki," she repeated, smiling at him, and some of the clouds seemed to disappear for a second. "I'm a reporter with the *Sentinel.* The newspaper. You remember." *Please remember.* When he didn't respond, she added quickly, "I'm doing a story on Blondell O'Henry. You know. She was your client twenty years ago."

"Blondell," he repeated.

"Yes, she was accused of a horrible crime, of shooting her children."

He shook his head.

"She swore she didn't do it, and you represented her. She claimed a stranger burst into the cabin where they were staying and shot them all."

"All?" he repeated.

"Blondell was injured too. Shot at close range in the arm. Gunshot residue was found on her blouse and skin, and the prosecution claimed she did it to herself."

"Yes . . . Blondell." Was there just the hint of a caress in his voice as he said her name? Then his eyes clouded.

"You remember her?"

He nodded slowly. "Oh, of course I do. Beautiful woman. Interesting." His fingers moved a little, one hand straightening the cuff of his sweater with the other. "Not what she seemed."

"That's right," Nikki said eagerly.

"Dangerous. A siren . . ."

"Blondell was kind of a siren," she encouraged when he faded out.

His eyes focused somewhere in the middle

distance, then he looked at her again. "Nikki!" he suddenly crowed. "About time you came to visit your favorite uncle!" Then he paused, his expression changing. "When did you get here?"

"Aunty-Pen just brought me." He was back. Even if he'd lost the thread of their conversation, she was pleased he knew her. "You're right. I should've come sooner. How've you been?"

He lifted a hand and tilted it back and forth. "I've been better, or so I've been told. Getting old is hell, you know. My mother told me that, but I didn't believe her." He nodded sagely. "Now I see she was right. It's good to see you."

"You too," she said with heartfelt enthusiasm. She hadn't realized until that moment how much she'd missed the uncle who had spent so many hours in debate with her father as they'd smoked cigars on the veranda, both of their wives disapproving, two women who had been forced into a reluctant, often competitive, and sometimes icy relationship by marrying half brothers.

But Nikki didn't have any time to consider family dynamics or loyalties, for she was certain her uncle's moments of lucidity were shortlived. "I'm writing a story on Blondell O'Henry," she said. "You remember her. She was your client, and she was convicted of murdering her daughter. She's about to be released from jail. Her son's recanting his testimony."

Her uncle's head snapped up. "No."

"No?"

"She's dangerous!" he insisted, nearly spitting as he grabbed her wrist in a death grip.

"But you tried so hard to see that she wasn't convicted."

"No. Nikki, no!"

"Why?" she asked desperately, hearing the water still running in the bathroom.

He glanced toward the door that Aunty-Pen had left ajar. "Leave this alone!"

"What do you know? Did Blondell really kill her kids? Uncle Alex?"

He was shaking his head. "Don't touch this! You don't know what you're getting into."

"Alexander?" Aunty-Pen called from the other room. "What's the name of your nurse? I want to talk to her." The water stopped running and Nikki held her breath, but then Aunty-Pen closed the door for some privacy.

Nikki seized the extra opportunity and said softly, "I want to know what happened."

"Attorney-client privilege, Nikki," he answered sternly.

"Can you tell me anything about the case? Something not privileged, but—"

"Yes!" he interrupted suddenly.

"Let me get my recorder and notepad," she said, throwing a quick glance at the bathroom door.

She heard the toilet flush as she dug around in

her purse, just as Uncle Alex said firmly, "She didn't do it!"

"You know that for sure? How? Didn't you just tell me she was dangerous?"

"Did I?" He grew thoughtful. "I don't remember."

"How can you be so certain she was innocent?" Nikki asked. "Was it something in particular?"

He looked at her blankly.

"Of course, that was your position as defense counsel," she hurriedly tried again, "but you must've had your doubts or at least some proof to think that she was innocent."

She saw the clarity start to fade and wanted to moan with frustration. His strong jaw drooped, his gaze falling to the floor, where he saw a string and stooped to pick it up.

"Uncle Alex, how do you know that Blondell didn't shoot her children?" she asked one last time.

He plucked the string from the carpet and held it out proudly as if he were a five-year-old boy searching for worms and had found a night crawler.

"I'm going to speak to the administration here," Aunty-Pen was saying as she returned to the room. "They're supposed to keep you and all your things pristine, and these," she held up his spectacles, "were far from it." Frowning, she set her husband's glasses onto his face, carefully making certain the bows fit over his ears. "Now, Alexander, isn't that better?" she asked.

He looked through the sparkling lenses and really smiled for the first time since his wife and niece had entered his room.

"Hollis!" he said, spying Nikki as if for the first time. Again tears threatened. "Baby girl!" His throat caught. "I thought you were . . . I mean, I dreamed this horrible nightmare that you were gone." He blinked back tears of relief and joy while Nikki withered inside.

"Oh, Alexander," Aunty-Pen whispered under her breath, turning away to hide her own emotions.

Embarrassed, Nikki said, "I'm not—" but stopped short when she caught another of her aunt's warning glances and quiet shake of her head. Instead she held her uncle's hands in her own and felt a cold desperation slide through her as she realized he had retreated again into the fog that was his mind.

Looking into his suddenly happy eyes, Nikki smiled at him and decided her aunt was right to not try to force him to recognize her. For a few seconds she could be Hollis. What would it hurt? He seemed so relieved to see his daughter that once again Nikki didn't try to dissuade him of a truth he so desperately wanted, even if it didn't exist.

A gentle rap on the open door caught her

attention, and a young woman in bright scrubs stepped inside. "Oh, I'm sorry. I didn't realize Alex had company. It's time for his meds."

"We were just leaving," Aunty-Pen insisted, indicating to Nikki that their short visit was over.

Before Nikki could start for the door, though, Uncle Alex reached out and grabbed her hand, squeezing her fingers with a surprisingly strong grip. "Please," he said, an undercurrent of desperation in his voice, "About Blondell." From the corner of her eye, she caught the sudden stiffening of her aunt's spine.

"Yes?" Nikki said.

"Don't tell a soul," he whispered, then winked at her.

Again Nikki remembered Amity's words that night: . . . *please, please, please don't tell a soul. If you do we'll both be dead . . .*

She stared at him, shaken, but whatever glimmer of awareness had been there was gone now, dissipating from his fixed gaze as he stared blankly ahead of himself.

Aunt Penelope suddenly looked very sad. "Let's go," she said, and Nikki released her uncle's hand.

"Bye," she whispered, but he didn't respond, didn't even act as if he knew she'd been in the room.

As the nurse moved in to give him his pills, Nikki and her aunt made their way down a long corridor where the walls were a creamy white and sturdy handrails ran between doorways. The carpet had a tight nap so that residents in wheelchairs could navigate the hallways, and the pictures hung between the rooms were copies of familiar pieces in soft hues. Aunty-Pen didn't stop at the front desk. She appeared to have forgotten that she was going to lodge a complaint about her husband's care.

"Such a shame," she said as they walked through the main doors.

Outside, clouds were gathering, and what had promised to be a warmer day was now turning colder. Once in the car, Nikki adjusted the heat as she drove her aunt home.

"It's difficult," Penelope admitted as she stared out the passenger-side window. Biting the corner of her lip, she managed to shear off a flake of rose-colored lipstick. "He was such a dashing man, you know. Brilliant. That's what really got to me way back when. He could have had any girl on campus, and he chose me." She slid a glance toward Nikki, her mouth turning down at the corners, but then she visibly straightened her spine, the seat belt tightening around her shoulders. "Well, a lot has changed since those idealistic days when I was an undergraduate and he was a law student with his future stretching before him." She looked through the windshield again, gazing into a distance only she could see.

Nikki, still mulling over her uncle's warning, didn't know what to say. She and Penelope hadn't ever been close, and they had grown more distant with the deaths of Hollis and Elton. While Uncle Alex had embraced Nikki and her siblings, Aunty-Pen had found it too painful, a reminder of what she, as a mother, had lost.

And Aunty-Pen had another cross to bear: the persistent rumor that Uncle Alex had been involved with his notorious, beautiful client Blondell O'Henry. The stink of that gossip had never left Alexander McBaine, and along with his courtroom defeat, his rising star had fizzled. Soon thereafter the first signs of early-stage Alzheimer's began to manifest themselves.

Before Blondell, Penelope Hilton McBaine had thought she would rise with her husband as he moved ever upward into the political arena. She'd even had her eye on the governor's mansion.

"Hogwash," Charlene had muttered upon hearing Aunty-Pen's ambitions. "What a pipe dream! That could never happen with his clientele!" She'd never liked Uncle Alex and detested the fact that he would "stoop so low" as to represent the likes of Blondell O'Henry. "This has nothing to do with the law," she'd confided to Nikki once after having come from a luncheon at the country club and, smelling slightly of gin and cigarettes, picked her daughter up after school. "It's all about fame and money, let me tell you!" With a sly glance at Nikki in the passenger seat, she'd confided, "He has a thing for her, you know." Then, as she'd concentrated on slowing for an amber light, she added more sourly, "All the men in this town do."

"Oh, come on, Mom."

"Trust me on this one. It's just that Alex has the balls to do something about it."

"You think he's involved with Amity's mom?"

"I'm just saying no good will come of his taking her case. Mark my words!" The light changed and the conversation ended, but Nikki had never forgotten her mother's comments that day.

Now, as she drove home twenty years later, Nikki sneaked a glance at her aunt, sitting ramrod straight, and noted the firm, unhappy set of her jaw, the fist balled in her lap. She couldn't help but wonder just how much truth there had been in her mother's bitter prediction. Certainly a lot of pain had ensued.

And, she knew, it wasn't over yet.

The city was rising before them, rolling acres of lowland giving way to a sprawling suburbia, houses with yards lining the streets. Around the periphery of the town she drove until she returned to the old manor on Canterbury Lane where Alexander had brought his wife thirty-odd years earlier. The lots here were large, the grounds well tended, shade trees and hedgerows protecting each owner's privacy.

121

Nikki remembered the times she'd spent here, sharing secrets with Hollis in her oh-so-pink bedroom, keeping mum about Elton's fascination with a variety of drugs, most notably weed and ecstasy, and driving out to the farm outside Savannah where Aunty-Pen had kept her horses; after college, she'd continued to ride and insisted Hollis do the same.

"I'm not really into it," Hollis, who was fair and looked very much like her mother, had admitted to Nikki.

It had been a warm summer day, and Nikki remembered it clearly because her cousin had said, "Why don't you drive?" even though Nikki wasn't old enough and didn't have her license.

"For real?"

"Sure. You drive all the time with your folks, don't you?"

"But I only have a permit."

Hollis's blue eyes had twinkled with a naughty devilment as she'd scooped her keys from her purse and whispered, "I won't tell, if you don't."

"But Dad would kill me if—"

"If he found out? Well, he won't," Hollis said. "We all have our secrets, don't we? Including my mother." With a smirk she added, "I just found out I might have a half sibling somewhere. How about that? Can you believe that Mother actually *did it* with some boy while in high school and got herself knocked up?"Hollis had giggled at the thought. "It's so rich!"

"You're sure about this?"

"Oh, yeah. I overheard my aunt on the phone the other day."

"What happened to the baby?"

"I don't know if she even had it. Just that she was preggers. And I always thought that if I had a half sibling somewhere it would be from my dad."

"What are you talking about?" Nikki had felt embarrassed and uncomfortable.

"He was hot when he was younger. Still is, I guess, but it's weird to say about your dad."

"Sick."

"Enough about my twisted family, with all our skeletons neatly tucked away in their closets," she said with a shrug. Then, eyes gleaming, she asked, "Aren't you friends with Amity O'Henry? You know her, right, she's in my class?" Hollis's lips had stretched into a smile that hovered between pleased and something else, something almost wicked.

"Yeah. I like her."

"She's trouble, Nikki."

"How would you know?" Hollis ran with the popular crowd, the cheerleaders and dance-team members and prom princesses. Amity didn't. Nor did Nikki, at least not at that time.

"I hear things." Hollis's already arched eyebrow had raised in that "I've got a secret" manner that had always gotten under Nikki's skin.

"What things?"

"Elton and his friends have all . . . you know."

"No, I don't." She didn't like the tone in Hollis's voice. So much like Aunty-Pen's.

"Well, if they need a blow job, they can just call Amity and she'll oblige."

"What!" Nikki couldn't believe it. "That's dumb! Stupid older boys bragging about something they only wish they could do! Sick, Hollis!"

"Oh, Nikki, grow up, would you?" Hollis had rolled her eyes. "It's not that big of a deal except that Amity isn't very selective, if you know what I mean. She's just like her mother."

"That's crap." Nikki had heard the rumors about Blondell, of course, but had chosen to ignore them.

"Do you want to drive or not?" Hollis asked, annoyed.

"Yes." Nikki snagged the keys before her cousin could change her mind. Within minutes she was behind the wheel of Hollis's cool Camaro, driving to the stables where Aunty-Pen kept her horses, on property owned by Nikki's father, thousands of acres of lush Georgia farm-land surrounding a large lake. There was the old family farmhouse that had stood for centuries, built long before the Civil War, and far away on the other side of the lake, a small cabin still stood, a cabin where an unthinkable act would occur and Amity O'Henry would lose her life, though no one knew it then.

That day with Hollis was warm for autumn, sunlight dappling the ground where it pierced the canopy of live oak branches that shaded the road.

Hollis's head was bent forward; she was busily French braiding her streaked hair. "Me riding horses makes *her* happy, and so I do it so she's not always on my case. I have to placate her so she doesn't *always* stick her nose into my business. The way she acts, you'd think I was five instead of sixteen."

"I love riding," Nikki had enthused, and she'd meant it. She'd been one of those "horsey girls" in grade school and still loved hanging out in the stables with the animals. Of course, lately her interest in boys had cut into the hours she'd spent riding, but she still adored the animals and rode whenever she got the chance. She'd never really understood her cousin's apathy toward the beautiful mares and geldings that Aunty-Pen loved so much. But then there were lots of things about Hollis she didn't get. Like allowing her to drive the car. No way would Nikki ever be so generous if, and when, she got her own set of wheels.

"I know. You've always been into anything to

do with horses. Not me." Shrugging, Hollis had added, "I've got better things to do." She'd glanced through the bug-spattered windshield. "Hey! Watch out! The turnoff's just around the next bend in the road." Her words had been a little muted as she was holding a rubber band between her teeth.

"What better things?" Braking as she rounded the long curve in the road, Nikki gave wide berth to a couple of boys riding bikes while balancing fishing poles. In baseball caps, they were laughing and talking, seemingly unaware they were sharing the road with anyone as they pedaled along the asphalt, smack dab in the middle of Nikki's lane.

"Idiots!" Nikki had muttered under her breath and saw in the rearview mirror the kid with the backward turned baseball cap flip her off. Great.

"What would I do besides riding?" Hollis mused, double-checking that her blond braid was perfect in the mirror on the visor. "*Anything*. Waterskiing, or tennis, or hiking, or dancing, or getting a pedicure, for God's sake." She'd laughed, that soft trill that still lingered in Nikki's mind. Hollis then glanced in the passenger's mirror to survey her work and, apparently satisfied, snapped the band into place. "Any-damned-thing."

That had been the end of their conversation as Nikki had seen the gravel lane leading to the farm where Aunty-Pen's horses were stabled. She turned onto twin ruts where dry grass and weeds scraped the undercarriage of Hollis's car.

"You know what?" Hollis said then, a funny little grin stretching her lips. "Why don't you ask your friend Amity to come out and ride sometime?"

"I thought you said she was trouble."

"I know, but maybe I like trouble." Hollis had leaned back in her seat to stare out the window at the lush grass of the fields that butted up to the lake. Almost under her breath she'd added, "Being with Amity could be a lot of fun."

Now, reliving her conversation with Hollis, Nikki saw it in a whole new light, without the naïveté of her youth. Still, she experienced a deep and oh-so-familiar pang of emptiness when she thought of the older cousin she'd adored and the friend she'd lost not long afterward.

They had gone riding with Amity, but only once, because less than three months after that warm autumn day, Hollis and Elton were in the horrid crash that took both their lives. A sudden winter storm had swept through the South, snow falling, ice sheeting the roads, temperatures low enough to endanger the peach trees.

As Nikki understood it, her uncle was supposed to pick up Hollis from a friend's home, but he'd been busy and had tossed the keys to his son with a warning of "Be careful" and, when his wife had worried about the weather, had cast off her concerns. "He could use some experience in the snow. For the love of God, Pen, you can't mother-hen them forever."

Aunty-Pen had never let him forget those chilling words because of the tragedy that had ensued. Elton had gone straight to Hollis's friend's home, making it to her house without much trouble. But the storm took a turn for the worse in the two hours he spent there, and on the return trip they hit a patch of ice that sent the car skidding out of control and into a telephone pole. Hollis, who was not wearing her seat belt, had been flung through the windshield, her neck had been broken, and she had been pronounced DOA at the hospital. Trapped in the car until the EMTs and the Jaws of Life could free him, Elton had sustained life-threatening injuries. In the Atlanta hospital, he'd lingered a few days, unresponsive, his injuries so acute that he couldn't survive without life support. Though Aunty-Pen had pleaded with the doctors and her husband to keep him alive, in the end, after a harrowing week during which she was told that Elton was "brain-dead," the hard decision had been made.

Her aunt and uncle had buried both their children two days before Christmas. Aunty-Pen, though she professed to love him with all her heart and had stayed with him all these years, couldn't truly forgive her grieving, guilt-riddled husband.

Nikki remembered standing at the grave sites, fresh earth turned, coffins gleaming as winter sunlight played wickedly upon the thawing ice and snow. From somewhere in the distance, the sound of a Christmas carol had whispered hollowly through the pines surrounding the cemetery.

"God rest ye merry gentlemen, let nothing you dismay . . ."

Too late, Nikki had thought at the time. Far too late.

December 5th
Second Interview

She's desperate.

A young reporter scrabbling for a story. And not just a newspaper account. Oh, no, Nikki Gillette wants more than a quick recap. She demands details, deep secrets, all the juicy details for a book, no less. As if that were possible.

From my side of the prison glass of the "private" booth where I sit on an uncomfortable stool, I hold the receiver to my ear and try not to think about the germs lurking thereon or the dozens of other inmates who have used this very phone while their loved ones came to make the guilt-riddled journey to talk for a few minutes.

The guard is close behind me, my ankles shackled, even my hands rendered somewhat immobile with handcuffs that clink as I shift the receiver against my ear.

Yes, I'm one of Georgia's most notorious criminals, or so they all think, but they don't have the facts. Only I know what really happened in that lonely cabin twenty years ago.

I smell dirt and dust, and the air is filled with the despair of those whose fate is sealed. Mine is not. Soon, I'm certain, I'll walk outside again, a free woman, soaking up the sun's warm rays, hearing the soft sigh of the wind as it rustles the leaves of live oak and peach trees, smelling the sweet scents of magnolia and jasmine. I'll drink mint juleps and laugh again . . . I'm sure I'll laugh again. Won't I?

No, no, I mustn't even question. I won't be here long. Because, of course, the truth will set me free—a quaint saying but one that's oh so true.

For now, in this disgusting sty of a prison, with the smell of disinfectant unable to cover the odors of body fluids and filth, I hold my head high and ignore the guard whose job it is to make certain I don't flee, or fly into a rage, or hurt myself or the others huddled in their little spaces and whispering on their phones.

As if!

Now, looking at Nikki Gillette, the reporter, watching her facial expressions, I can almost see the wheels turning in her overly imaginative mind. This—my story—would be the key to her fame and fortune.

All because she thinks she knows me.

Because she believes she has an insider's view of what makes me tick.

What a joke!

I don't so much as smile. I'm able to force myself not to respond, to play my part, as I have always done. It doesn't matter how deeply she probes or how outrageous her questions, I can keep up the facade. Haven't I held my secrets close and maintained this mask for twenty years? Why would I rip it off now and tell all that I know?

For her? For her story? Not a snowball's chance in Satan's hell.

She's speaking into the phone now, trying to get to me as I inwardly recoil at the smudged glass, the tight quarters, the others who are locked inside this hellhole, all of whom stare at me with a jaundiced eye. Women who have no hope, common criminals who have no reason to live. I'm not one of them, and they know it, sense that I'm different. I do nothing to change their minds. Let them think what they want.

I know the truth.

I know exactly what I did.

And what I didn't do.

"Look," Reporter Nikki is saying, trying not to sound annoyed or desperate or needy, "so you don't like the questions I've asked of you. I get it. Really. You know I do. You know me, know that I'll tell the truth, your side of the story."

She's almost pleading now, her eyes, through the thick pane, beseeching.

"You need to let the world know why you maintain that you're innocent of such heinous crimes. You've let the horror of that night define who you are."

I can't argue that simple fact, so I don't. Just retain my stoic manner, as I have since the tragedy. Conjuring up the sweet faces of my children twists my soul and darkens my heart, but I feign innocence, because that's what one is to do. It was my duty to protect them and I failed.

I feel crestfallen and know that I've allowed a bit of emotion to show in my eyes, so I force my chin up as I hold onto the phone's heavy receiver. I refuse to let this woman, and the world, see my pain, so I will not flinch, not even at her most probing and personal questions. Nor will I allow my eyebrows to knit in frustration or thought, and I will keep my mouth a beautiful half-smile that won't betray the coldness I feel in my soul. With some effort, I force my gaze to remain steady, so that she won't see as much as a shadow pass behind my eyes. She thinks of me as callous and doubts my motives. As they all do.

But I will not crack.

Never.

"So why won't you talk to me?" Nikki asks again. "Is it to protect yourself? To maintain your innocence?"

I just stare back at her.

"Come on!" She's frustrated now. "If you don't explain what happened, the world will think that you're a cold-blooded killer. Is that what you want? How you want to be remembered? You can talk to me! I was close to your daughter!"

She stares hard, and I fear my eyes might give me away, that a tiny dilation of my pupils will indicate that she's getting to me, that she will know that I hear her and understand her pleas.

I concentrate on my breathing, taking in air slowly and letting it out evenly, keeping my heart from racing and my skin from flushing. It's something I learned to do as a child. To escape the pain of the world, to keep *him* from gaining the satisfaction of the knowledge that he'd gotten to me, that he'd broken through the icy facade I'd developed.

My stepfather. The giant. A gentle soul, so many said, but they didn't know his truth, didn't have to smell the stink of him as he rutted. My jaw tightens as I think of the bastard. May his black soul rot in hell.

"Please," Nikki is saying, frustration evident in her voice, "you have to let me help you."

Oh, right, that's what you're doing, Nikki. Helping me by writing and selling my story. As if I would believe her stupid pleas for a second!

"Talk to me."

Without a word, I hang up my heavy telephone receiver. "Guard," I say as I clamber to my feet, my shackles rattling. I don't bother looking over my shoulder as the foiled reporter stares after me.

So you think you know me, Nikki?

Guess again.

Chapter 8

"I need a smoke."

Reed, who had been reading testimony from the trial, looked up and found his partner pushing back her chair from the table where she'd been working.

"Thought you quit."

"I didn't say I was going to have one, I just said I needed one," Morrisette clarified. It had been her turn at the case file after a morning of sorting and double-checking that all the evidence was still intact. The flattened snake, the cigarette butt, and the clothes of all the victims had been sent to the lab for updated analysis; a partial list of names and addresses of witnesses who were still alive had been compiled; the autopsy report on Amity O'Henry and the medical records of the other victims had been reviewed. Even the clippings from Blondell's fingernails, taken the night of the attack, were being searched for DNA, but the theory was that since they'd been clipped after Blondell had been seen at the hospital, and presumably had been cleaned before she had surgery on her right arm, they would come up with nothing worthwhile, no epithelial tissue of the unknown assailant, who, of course, most likely did not exist.

Morrisette dug through her purse, found a pack of Nicorette gum, and tossed a piece into her mouth. "Let's take a break, grab some coffee or something. Talk this out. There's only so much sitting I can do." She checked her watch. "We kinda missed lunch."

"Fine. Let's grab something." The room was getting to him too. They'd already logged in hours sitting with dusty files and twenty-year-old evidence. He'd made several calls and set up some interviews, the first of which was with Niall O'Henry, to find out why he was recanting his testimony and to get his new view of what had happened the night his sister was killed. Since he'd been a child when he'd taken the stand, there was no talk of perjury—at least none Reed had heard. Unfortunately, the first time that was convenient for David Blass, who insisted upon being present at the meeting, wasn't for a couple of days. Rather than argue the point, Reed had acquiesced. It might be best anyway, because by the time he interviewed Blondell's son, he would be up to speed on the case, through his first look at all the evidence. "Crab cakes? At Hoppers?"

Hoppers was a beach house converted to a restaurant on Tybee Island and was a good half an hour away. "Trust me, we need the break," she said when she noticed he was about to argue about the loss of time. "Sometimes getting away from it, talking it out, helps."

She was right, and Hoppers, with its view of the beach and the pier that stretched into the Atlantic, would be a good place to find a new perspective. The food was excellent, the prices were reasonable, and she was right, they both needed a break, a change of scenery to discuss the case.

"Sounds good."

"I just need to stop off at the ladies' room." She was already heading for the door, chewing her gum frantically and eyeing her cell phone.

Reed took a quick detour to his office, skimmed his recent e-mail, then grabbed his jacket and side-arm from the back of his chair, logged out, and caught up with Morrisette at the stairs. Together they made their way outside, only to run into Deacon Beauregard heading into the building.

"I was just about to check in with you," the ADA said as they stepped outside. A cold blast of wind raced down the street, kicking up a bit of trash and a few dry leaves. "How's the O'Henry investigation going?"

"All right," Reed said.

"Helluva thing." Morrisette squinted up at Beauregard.

Unlike his father, Deacon was strapping and fit. Flint had, from all accounts, smoked more than he drank, while his diet had been rumored to revolve around a deep fat fryer. With a fondness for pecan and peach pie, as well as cheeseburgers, po'boys, and any traditionally Southern food, Flint, in his later years had become jowly in the face and soft around the middle. Department pictures taken the last years of his life revealed as much.

Not so with his boys. Deacon didn't smoke, avoided booze, and spent two hours a day at a gym. At six foot two, he had towered over his father, but he was just as dedicated and focused as his old man had been—at least, that was the current consensus in the department. The younger son, Holt, was a different story altogether. He too was athletic and tall, like his older brother, but there's where the resemblance stopped. Briefly, he'd become a cop like his old man, but he had bombed out. Reed didn't know that whole story but decided he'd check it out.

Currently he was dealing with the older brother, and he watched as Beauregard's lips flattened. "I just can't believe that after all these years the little prick is changing his story! What's up with that?" Obviously disgusted, he added, "Dad worked damned hard on that conviction."

Reed said, "We're talking to Niall O'Henry and his attorney later in the week."

"Maybe you can convince him to stick with his original story," Beauregard suggested.

"A little late for that," Morrisette said dryly.

"This was Dad's biggest case, and it's a shame to see Blondell O'Henry walk when she killed her own daughter in cold blood. She tried to take out the other kids too. And now one of them is saying she didn't do it?" He let out a huff of air. With a glance at his watch, he said, "I've got to run, but if there's anything I can do, just let me know."

"Your dad have any private notes?" Morrisette asked.

Beauregard's eyes narrowed a fraction. "What do you mean?"

"Just that. Lots of times when a detective is caught up in a case—when it becomes his life's work, so to speak, like I've heard it did with Flint—he keeps his own notes, unofficial stuff, musings, ideas that are, for one reason or another, cast aside, don't make it into the case file."

For a second, it seemed that remark got Beauregard's back up, but if so, he disguised it quickly. "Don't think so, but I'll check with my mother. She still lives in the same house, and Dad used the second bedroom for an office once my brother moved out."

"Flora, right?" Morrisette said. "The place on Stevenson, a few blocks off Victory Drive?"

"Yeah." The skin over Beauregard's face tightened a bit. "How'd you know?"

Morrisette's gaze was icy. "Been around the block a couple of times."

He eased into his smooth-attorney attitude again. "I'll check with her, and please, keep me up to date. Anything I can do to help."

Morrisette said, "Find us the murder weapon."

"What?" Beauregard glared at her.

"It would help if we had the damned gun," Morrisette clarified. "The .45."

Beauregard looked at her as if she were nuts. "I don't have any idea where—"

"She's kidding," Reed cut in. "We'll keep you abreast of the investigation." He started for the parking lot.

"Do that." Obviously irritated, Beauregard stormed into the building, and Morrisette caught up with her partner.

"Just because he's a prick doesn't mean you have to make him show it to you every time you say something," Reed observed.

"A prick and then some. He's already shoving his nose in our business. I'll drive," she added, keys already in hand as she headed to her aging Chevy Impala, the upholstery on the back seat showing the impressions of her kids' car seats.

"Beauregard's still an ADA," Reed reminded her as she unlocked the car and slid behind the wheel.

Morrisette made a retching noise.

Reed half-smiled as he sat down in the passenger seat. Their doors shut in unison, and before he'd snapped his seat belt into place, she'd started the engine with a flick of her wrist.

She said, "Beauregard's like his old man, only a little more polished, the rough edges smoothed out, but still rough underneath." She adjusted the rearview mirror. "Deacon goes to great pains to look smooth and refined. All an act. He's a bully. Just like Flint." Backing out of the parking space, she added, "I don't trust him." Throwing the car into drive, she eased out of the lot, and as soon as there was a break in traffic she gunned it. "As I said, too damned slick. Too concerned with appearances. At least Flint didn't give a crap about that."

"But you didn't like him, either," Reed said as she changed lanes and headed west on Liberty Street.

"I'm definitely not a member of the Flint Beauregard fan club, which puts me in the minority at the station. The way you hear Red DeMarco or Bud Ellis tell it, Beauregard was second only to Jesus Christ in working miracles, at least when it came to solving cases for the PD." Still working her gum, she shot Reed a knowing look as she drove out of town and, once past the city limits, hit the gas. "Sometimes I wonder how the department keeps running now that Beauregard's gone. Again, a goddamned miracle!"

Alfred Necarney's trick knee was acting up again, his arthritis throbbing. The damned docs at the VA said there was nothing much they could do about it, and he figured they probably were right. He'd had the bum knee for forty-odd years, ever since he took some shrapnel from a land mine in Vietnam.

A pisser, that's what it was, but then again, most things were. Like the way Mandy-Sue hadn't waited for him back then. While he was on a tour of Southeast Asia for Uncle Sam, she'd taken off and married Bobby Fullman, just like that. Alfred had come home to a hero's welcome, a knee that never worked quite right, and no bride waiting for his return.

He'd driven up to this cottage in the north Georgia hills, outside of Dahlonga—the one his granddaddy had left him while he was out of the country—settled in, and never left. As for Mandy-Sue, good riddance to bad news. He'd heard from Nola-Mae, his flap-lipped sister, that Mandy was a grandma now four times over and that Bobby, that son of a bitch who'd been one of Alfred's best friends at Tyler High, had died two winters ago of pneumonia.

Couldn't of happened to a nicer guy, Alfred thought for the two hundredth time. What a cocksucker Bobby Fullman had turned out to be.

But that was all ancient history; Alfred had settled into this three-room cabin, made it his own, made a few "improvements" to the place, and had his own thriving, if not exactly legit, business on the side. That is, when he wasn't logging. Which, just three months ago, he'd given up completely, even sold what equipment he'd collected over the years.

But he was set, at least money-wise. Social Security had kicked in just this past April, so times were good. He still worked a little, but that was about over too, and he wasn't sorry to give up rising before dawn to clear-cut a hillside with a bunch of damned kids, none of 'em past thirty-five or so. Besides, the damned environmentalists were gettin' in the way of that too. Just like everything else.

This evening, the rain had quit just before darkness had descended, and the forests surrounding his old cabin smelled fresh and clean. Yep, he loved it up here and had quit thinking how his life would have been different with Mandy-Sue in the suburbs of Atlanta. Shitfire, he'd have hated that. Probably that prick Bobby Fullman had done him a favor.

He was about to turn on the news when headlights splashed against the windows of his house. At about the same time, old General, his hound of indeterminate mix, sent up a ruckus that set off the chickens, who'd just roosted for the night. Now they were squawking, making a helluva racket.

Checking to see that his shotgun was propped near the front door, Alfred climbed out of his recliner, his nightly nip of whiskey waiting on the nearby table. It was his ritual: not a single drop would pass his lips until the six o'clock news came on the tube.

So who the hell would be stopping by? Alfred was, and had been, a loner all his life. People considered him odd, and he did nothing to discourage that opinion. The way he figured, the fewer people who knew him, the better. Absently scratching his beard, he stared out the window.

Whoever was driving the pickup had left it idling near the old pine tree, where he'd set up a picnic table that he used for target practice. Each Sunday afternoon, he'd line up his empties from the week and take aim. Though it had been a long while since he was in the army, he could still shoot the hell out of a Budweiser can at a hundred yards.

It took him a second to recognize the man who was striding toward the front porch. Dressed head to toe in camouflage, he'd been to Alfred's home before. A customer. A good-paying customer at that.

General let out a low, warning growl.

"Hush!" Alfred said, and the dog instantly quieted, though his droopy-eyed gaze followed the visitor. Through the screen door, he greeted the taller man. "Howdy. You here on business?" It was a superfluous question; they both knew the answer.

"Yeah."

"How many this time?"

"Not sure. But a few. Let's see what ya got."

Alfred was nodding and wondering just how much he could charge. He didn't want to lose the guy as a customer, but he had expenses to cover, and now that his logging days were over, he was on a fixed income. "Okay. Let's go out back and take a look."

Without further ado, he grabbed his keys and walked outside, down the long front porch and around the side of the house, where Alfred had several old trucks parked, all in various states of repair, another side occupation.

He unlocked the shed in the back of the house, then once inside, rolled up the old rag rug and found the trapdoor. He climbed down the ladder first, flipped the switch, and illuminated the concrete bunker, which he'd built himself. It was rudimentary but had everything he needed down here. Heat, light, water, and cases of canned goods. The place was ventilated too, and there was a toilet of sorts, though he hated to think that if there was ever a nuclear blast he'd be stuck down here waiting who knew how long for the radiation to dispel. He knew that idea to be a fool's game, but the bunker was here, just in case, and in the meantime he used it for another purpose.

For his babies.

The walls were lined floor to ceiling with Plexiglas-and-wood cages he'd constructed himself. Some held sand or mulch with ladders or fake tree limbs, along with the water and lights on timers. Most important, each terrarium housed one of his snakes.

He felt a swell of pride as he watched them move slowly in their cages, their eyes bright, their tongues flicking in exploration, the beauty of their scales glistening as they moved. It was in Vietnam that he'd first become fascinated with the pit vipers, cobras, and kraits of Southeast Asia. Here, in the hills of Georgia, on his grandfather's old estate, he'd decided to catch his own domestics and sell them.

Rat snakes, milk snakes, black racers, and hognoses—you name it, he had most of the nonvenomous kind, but Alfred knew that this customer, like so many of his, was interested only in his babies who had fangs.

"What would you like?"

His client walked to the far wall, where he eyed the terrariums for rattlers, corals, copperheads, and water moccasins.

"Coral snakes this time," he said, eyeing several cages. "At least to start with."

My banded babies, Alfred thought as he eyed the colorful rings on the coral snakes. *Red on yellow, kill a fellow. Red on black, friend of Jack.* These were definitely red on yellow.

"And let's make it three. That should do. Now, how about the copperheads?"

"Got a fine lot," Alfred bragged, showing the client his three largest—beauties each one, and a little different in size and color.

"They are. I'll take all three."

"Really?" Alfred was already counting the dollars in his head. He was thinking that this week he could buy the more expensive whiskey that was displayed on a higher shelf at Marty's Liquor Store, a luxury he rarely afforded himself, as practical as he was. Things were definitely looking up.

"Yep. That'll do it, I think." The customer looked him squarely in the eye and reached for his wallet. "How much do I owe you?"

Alfred wanted to bargain, start high, then accept something a little lower so that the customer would return. He never wanted to lose a customer since his business wasn't exactly sanctioned by the state of Georgia, but this guy worried Alfred a little. He was just one of those dudes you knew instinctively not to push too far; he looked like he might have a hair-trigger temper.

None of his clients were mainstream, of course, but this one, there was something a little unnerving about him. Still, they dickered a little over the cost, settled on a price that warmed Alfred from the inside out. Once the cash was exchanged, Alfred found his hook and tongs and began fishing out three of the best corals he'd caught in the last year, feisty little things that curled over the tongs.

The client handed him a leather pouch, one with holes in it, and swore he'd take them directly back to wherever the hell it was he came from and put them in a terrarium he'd made himself.

"I've seen yours, decided to build my own."

"Well, that's good." Alfred dropped the snakes, one by one, carefully into the pouch, and felt a pang to see them go. He'd caught each one himself, in the wilds of Georgia, and it pained him a little to know that he'd never look into their faces again.

The same was true of the copperheads, which took a little more work and were put into separate pouches, again with tiny little air holes. At least this customer came prepared.

"Here ya go."

The guy pulled the drawstring tight on the last sack and cinched it, the bags moving as the snakes jostled inside. Easily, he clipped them to his belt.

"Good doin' business with you," Alfred said as the customer reached the ladder with his new purchases strapped to his belt.

"You too."

Alfred was already thinking about his whiskey on the side table, ice melting as the news had already started, when the customer stepped on the first rung of the metal ladder. Alfred took one last look around the bunker and didn't see the blow coming, a sharp, painful crack to his skull.

"What the fuck," he whispered before his bad knee buckled and he went down. He was already losing consciousness when the client jumped over him and quickly took off the lids of the terrariums, one after the other. Alfred tried to reach for his gun, but it was too late: blackness was coming over him, and the guy had already vaulted him and was climbing quickly up the ladder.

He saw the first rattler moving in its case, raising its head, flicking its tongue, and then, sensing freedom, slide upward over the Plexiglas wall and slide down the side, dropping to the floor less than three feet from where Alfred lay, unable to stay awake.

"Sleep tight," the customer said as he climbed the rungs and snapped off the light before slamming the trapdoor shut.

Chapter 9

"I'll take a small caramel Jazzachino," Nikki said, placing her order at the local coffee shop, All That Jazzed. She'd spent a couple of days at the computer, digging up addresses and phone numbers, hoping for a call from Jada Hill,

Blondell's defense attorney, that had never come through, and she was frustrated as hell.

But things were going to break, even if she had to force them, she decided as the coffee grinder whirred and shots of steaming water hissed into cups. The tiny shop was full, not a table to be found, customers lounging in overstuffed chairs, or working on laptops, or reading or doing cross-word puzzles, or playing games on phones or tablets or whatever electronic device they had with them. The buzz of conversation was low, but constant, the lights a soft amber.

"Hey," a voice behind her in line called, "Nikki!"

Turning, she spied Effie Savoy three people behind her. She tried to muster some enthusiasm when she answered, "Hi." Sliding her debit card through the card machine, she left a tip, then moved to the end of the counter to wait. In the time it took for her drink to appear, Effie had caught up with her at the "pickup" end of the counter.

Great.

There was nothing really wrong with Effie, at least nothing Nikki could put her finger on, but the woman, a few years older than she was, bothered her. She always stood just a little too close, as she did now, not giving Nikki her space, and it seemed to Nikki that she was nosy, too nosy, a quality that of course came with the job, to some extent. The long and the short of it was, Effie was pushy and she had instantly made Nikki want to avoid her.

"How're the wedding plans coming?" Effie asked as they stood in the cluster of customers awaiting their drinks. She was a couple of inches taller than Nikki and, though not heavy, a big-boned woman whose blue eyes stared a little too intensely when you spoke with her, as if she was trying to figure out all the hidden meanings to what you were saying. She was just too damned intense, and she rarely cracked a smile.

"I've got everything put together." A bit of a lie, but who cared? What business was it of Effie's?

"It's coming up now, isn't it? Next month?"

"Around Christmas."

Where was her damned drink?

"A busy time," Effie pointed out. "Especially now, huh? Since you're, like, the go-to person at the paper about Blondell O'Henry."

"I suppose."

"Kinda funny," she mused aloud. "You getting that assignment and your fiancé investigating the case, or reinvestigating it, I guess. Oh, here. That's mine!" she said as the server was about to shout out the order. "Regular coffee with room for soy milk? Right?"

The barista, a redhead, nodded without looking up, and Effie snagged the steaming cup.

"Perfect."

The waitress was already handing out the next drink.

"Tom told me that I'm supposed to work with you on the O'Henry pieces," she said.

"What? I didn't hear this. I thought you did more homey, domestic stuff."

"Well, my blog's gotten big, y'know. Got men readers, and this story about a mom who killed her kids and is getting out of jail is perfect."

"One kid," Nikki corrected. "And now that's in question, and she's in prison, not jail."

Effie nodded. "I'll get the details straight later. The important thing is that it's to dovetail into yours, right? We can compare notes. I read that you knew Amity, that she called you on the night she died, so I was thinking that I might even interview you for the blog, get an insider's view. You were a teenager at the time, right? And a lot of moms of teens read me. It could be good. And it would add interest to your stories, get young readers who don't really remember Blondell O'Henry reading your articles, either online or in the paper itself."

Nikki's stomach dropped. The thought of spending hours being interviewed by Effie wasn't her idea of a good time. "You know, I work best alone, but I'll talk to Tom." *And tell him there's no way in hell I'm working with you.*

"Do that," Effie said with such conviction that

Nikki realized this was already a done deal. A ghost of a superior smile touched the corners of Effie's mouth, but it quickly vanished.

"Medium mocha, extra whip. Sugar-free vanilla latte!" the barista called as Nikki backed up to let two teenagers grab their frothy concoctions. Seconds later the same redhead announced, "Caramel Jazzachino" as she placed Nikki's hot drink on the tall counter while Effie doctored her drink at a cupboard where creams, milks, sugars, and artificial sweeteners were surrounded by lids, stir-sticks, and napkins.

Wending her way through a line of customers and emerging outside, where the Georgia rain was threatening, the skies darkening, a chilly breeze blowing over the river, Nikki tried to get over the feeling that her chance meeting with Effie wasn't just a coincidence. Lately Effie had turned up in a lot of the same places Nikki did and seemed to know a lot about Nikki's life. She hadn't quite reached stalker status yet, but there was something more to Effie than met the eye— at least where Nikki was concerned.

She'd just stepped onto the street when her cell phone jangled, and she plucked it from its pocket in her purse. Ina's name and number appeared on the screen.

"Hey!" she said, answering and glad for an excuse to ignore Effie if she tried to catch up to her.

"I love it!" Ina exclaimed, her raspy voice filled with enthusiasm. "This proposal is exactly what I was talking about! Oh. My. God. Nikki. You *have* to write this!"

"I hope to."

"No. Not *hope*. *Plan to!*" She was emphatic. "Of course, you have to flesh this out, it's just a bare-bones idea now, but this is the kind of story with that personal twist, it's just what we need! Look, if you could put it together quickly, as there's all this buzz about Blondell O'Henry's release right now, all the better. But we'll have to jump all over this. You won't be the only one with this idea, you know."

Unfortunately, that was a fact, Nikki silently agreed. A lot of true-crime writers would be interested in the story, just as reporters for rival papers and television stations had been at the prison to try to secure an interview with Blondell.

However, those authors wouldn't be able to claim to be best friends with the murder victim. And Nikki had come up with a twist.

"I know," she admitted, walking toward the office and the parking lot where she'd left her Honda, "but I thought I'd tell my story with a twist."

"Such as?"

"This won't exactly be the Blondell O'Henry murder retrial book—that's what everyone else will be doing. I want to put a new spin on it. The story won't be centered on Blondell O'Henry, but on her daughter Amity, the real victim. That's where I have the connection, and that's the angle that will cut more deeply emotionally."

"Huh. I don't know." Some of Ina's enthusiasm trickled away. "People *know* Blondell O'Henry's name. That's what's going to grab them."

"Yeah, yeah, I know," Nikki said, turning the corner. Pedestrians were scattered along the sidewalks—some tourists, some shopping and strolling, others, like Nikki, keeping a brisk pace. She glanced into the windows of storefronts that she passed, half expecting to see Effie's reflection as she hurried to catch up to her. Dear God, was that her, in the long, black coat? Glancing over her shoulder, she saw, sure enough, that Effie was half a block behind her, texting as she hurried.

What was her deal?

"Nikki?" Ina said, bringing her back to the present.

"Oh. Right. Blondell's name will be there, front and center, of course, but so will Amity's."

"Hmm. Well . . . sure. That concept really didn't come across in the pages you sent."

"It's a work in progress," Nikki assured her. "You know, Amity was killed first. Before Blondell was injured. At least that's the way Blondell tells the story. So I want to explore that. It just didn't make sense to me."

"It doesn't make sense," Ina declared as Nikki managed to take a sip of her drink. "Can you spell psychopath? What happened is nuts, just plain psycho nuts. And remember, the police think she lied. So did a jury."

"But why? That's what I don't get. Why the attack? I don't buy that she would try to kill her kids just for a new man's affection."

"Again. Nuts."

"There's more to the story, more to tell. I was Amity's friend. I knew who she dated. I think it's important to find out who was the father of her child." She took another drink.

"Amity's?"

"Of course."

"And Blondell. What about her? I know she miscarried, but who was the father of that unborn child? Is he still in the picture?" The wheels were really turning in Ina's head now. "Okay, you run with your gut. I passed what you sent me to Remmie, who's promised to read it in the next couple of weeks, but I think she'll get to it earlier, what with all the press this story is going to generate. So the sooner we get this going, the better."

Remmie Franklin, Nikki's editor, worked for Knox Publishing, an independent publisher in New York.

"Hey, slow down. Look, I'm glad you're all over this, but it'll take time to write the book."

She jaywalked across the street and said, "I'm hoping to put it together as the story unfolds, of course, but it's going to be months."

"Don't know if you have months. I gotta be honest here; I hear the sound of computer keyboards clicking all over the country even as we speak. Authors frantically putting together the Blondell O'Henry story. Publishers willing to pay for ghostwriters so she can put her name on her story, an autobiography. There's bound to be some shirttail relative hoping to cash in on this. People are desperate to sell anything to a publisher, you know, and a story like this . . . guaranteed best-seller, if the timing is right. We *have* to work fast. If we come in late and the market is already flooded with Blondell O'Henry ideas or unauthorized biographies, then we're in trouble."

"I can only do what I can do."

"Well, at least you've got an inside scoop," Ina agreed. "Friendship with the victim, your uncle being the accused's attorney. The cabin where the crime took place on property owned by your family. Yeah, we've got the upper hand on this one. So far. As soon as I hear from Remmie, I'll let you know, but I'm assuming we've got the green light. See," she said, a lilt in her voice, "I knew if you dug deep, you'd come up with the right story!"

Nikki didn't argue, even though she hadn't

really "come up" with the story idea; it had fallen into her lap. She glanced over her shoulder. No Effie. Good. She must've veered off somewhere.

"And it doesn't hurt that you're engaged to a detective working on the case. The more personal connections you have to Blondell O'Henry, the better." Nikki didn't put up her usual argument. They'd been through it before. "So, you said in your e-mail that you were going to the prison to interview Ms. O'Henry. How'd that go?"

"It didn't."

"No?"

"So far I've been roadblocked."

"Too bad. You'll need to talk to her, see what she thinks now, after all these years. Has she altered her story? Had a change of heart? There's no reason for me to speculate, of course. It won't do any good. You know what you're doing, so just run with it, and I'll get back to you the minute, and I mean the minute, I hear from Remmie, but I think we've got a winner here!"

"Good!"

"And trust me, if I don't get a call soon, I'll nudge again. Meanwhile you keep working! Talk later!"

Nikki dropped her phone into the pocket of her jacket and kept walking, sipping her drink, her mind lost in the story she was going to write. Ina was right, she needed something more than what any author could offer, something deeper about Blondell's daughter.

The wind nearer the river seemed more brittle, the air a few degrees colder, and as she stared across the steel-colored water, she watched a container ship as it chugged up the narrow channel. For a second she got that same unnerving sense that someone was watching her, but as she took another swallow from her cup, she glanced over her shoulder and saw no one who looked out of place, no one who reminded her of the tall figure she'd seen in the park—and now, thankfully, no Effie Savoy anywhere near. Her nerves were still strung tight, that's all it was, and reading about the O'Henry case hadn't helped calm her. Thinking of Amity and the horror she'd suffered only added to Nikki's anxiety.

Her gaze followed a couple walking into a restaurant, and she told herself she was being silly. Again. And it was getting old. She'd never been one of those mousey women afraid of their own shadow, and she certainly wasn't going to start now.

Nikki's cell phone jangled again, and as she fished it out of her pocket, she saw her mother's number flash across the small screen. "Hey, Mom," she said as she waited for a pedestrian light to change. "What's up?" she asked, but she had a pretty good idea of what was to come.

"I got a call from Ariella this afternoon,"

Charlene said, confirming Nikki's guess. "There seems to be some problem with the photographer, something about double-booking. Anyway she wants you to call her and straighten it out. You might have to hire someone else."

The light changed, and Nikki, not the least bit interested in her wedding at the moment, said, "I thought we had a contract with Jacques."

"I know, but there was a mistake on the photographer's end, and something has to be done. The wedding is only six weeks away, you know."

Inwardly Nikki groaned. How often had Charlene reminded her that her nuptials were soon approaching? As if she didn't know the date.

"There also seems to be an issue with the chairs for the reception, or the slipcovers. I think they can't get enough of the off-white ones, and to have some white and some ivory would look odd, I think. Also, I know we need to talk about the seating. Ten at a table just won't work—"

"Mom!" Nikki said, hearing the little tremor in Charlene's voice over the sound of street traffic and the sigh of the wind. "Look, I'm working right now. Can't Ariella figure it out? Isn't that why we hired a wedding planner?"

"But she can't get hold of you, and these decisions have to be made. By you. Soon. You're the bride."

"I know." This is why she'd wanted a simple

wedding, just family, but that idea had been squelched, not intentionally, but just as the guest list had grown, so had the event, and her frail mother had actually seemed healthier and stronger now that she had a purpose, that of marrying off her daughter. "Look, I'll call her as soon as I'm off work," Nikki promised.

"I'll let her know. Five, then."

"Mom, you know I don't work regular office hours. I've got a major story I'm working on!"

"That Blondell O'Henry business, yes, I know." There it was, the underlying tone of disapproval in her mother's voice—if not of Nikki's chosen profession, then of the woman who had been convicted of murdering her own daughter. Charlene had never minced words when it came to Blondell O'Henry.

"Just let Ariella know that I'm busy and not purposely avoiding her. I'll call her the minute I get a second."

"Do that, honey," her mother reprimanded gently, her Georgian drawl a little more evident. "Remember, this is your wedding we're talking about, the most important day of your life." And with those words of wisdom, she'd managed to lay down the law, along with a good measure of guilt.

Great, Nikki thought as she stepped off the curb. A horn blasted. From the corner of her eye she saw motion. Quickly she jumped backward, twisting her ankle just as a black sports car sped through the intersection.

"What the hell?" she cried as the BMW sped off.

"Whoa!" a teenage boy on a skateboard said, his eyes rounding beneath the edge of his watch cap. "That dude almost hit you! Man, it was like he was trying to run you down!"

"He missed. This time," she said, flashing a smile as she looked after the car that was racing away, windows dark, license plate smudged. An accident? Probably. Just some anxious, lead-footed idiot who hadn't seen her or maybe even wanted to scare her as he sped through a red light. Nothing more. Nothing the least bit sinister.

Right?

But she couldn't stop the little frisson of fear from running down her spine.

"That light just wasn't kinda pink," the kid said. "It was really red. That douche bag is lucky someone didn't T-bone him!" Then he took off, throwing down his board and pedaling with one foot as he streaked across the street. Ankle throbbing, Nikki hobbled in front of the stopped traffic to the far sidewalk. The pain lessened as she made her way to her car, and she told herself it was nothing, just a case of an impatient idiot wanting to beat out the cross traffic.

Still, as she climbed into her Honda, she checked the rearview mirror and tried to ignore the skateboarder's assessment.

It was like he was trying to run you down.

Shivering inwardly, she slid behind the wheel, then locked all the doors before starting the car.

Don't do this, Nikki. Don't fall victim to fear again. Especially where there is no threat, none. It's all in your mind.

Gritting her teeth, she backed out of the parking spot, then rammed her Honda into gear. Throughout the day, she'd made notes to herself on her cell phone after locating several addresses of people she wanted to interview.

Of course, Niall O'Henry hadn't picked up his phone, nor had his attorney returned Nikki's calls, but she figured she may as well try to locate Blondell's son and find out exactly why he had decided to recant his testimony after twenty years. What had happened to him to make him change his mind? Then there was Blythe, Blondell's daughter, who had survived the attack but was paralyzed from a ricocheting bullet. She was a grown woman now and still living in an apartment that was just off Bull Street, near one of the buildings housing the Savannah College of Art and Design, and happened to be less than half a mile from Nikki's home, which would be perfect.

She desperately wanted to talk to both Niall and Blythe. Since she'd struck out with Blondell, Nikki figured she'd go to the kids.

Checking her rearview mirror again, she watched the traffic behind her, but no dark

163

sports car was visible, no other vehicle following.

"Just your imagination," she told herself and considered calling Reed, just to check in. It wasn't to ask him about the O'Henry case, or so she tried to convince herself, as she turned onto Victory and headed a few blocks east to a quiet neighborhood with shaded streets.

Niall's home, a cottage with a large picture window and a raised porch, appeared to have been built sometime in the 1940s. The shrubbery wasn't as neatly pruned as some of his neighbors', and dead leaves were scattered over the tufted grass and skittered across the sidewalk. The house was in sad need of a new coat of paint, and one of the gutters dangled precariously from its eave. Parking across the street, she made her way up a concrete walk that was badly chipped in places, with weeds poking through a few cracks.

Inside, the curtains were tightly drawn, and wedged into the screen door was a pamphlet, fat from rain, yellowing with the sun. Once she'd stepped onto the porch, she rang the bell and heard it chime; when there was no response from inside, she knocked on the screen door.

Nothing.

No sound of footsteps hurrying across seventy-year-old hardwood. No barking dog. No movement of the closed drapes.

"Ain't no one there!" a voice called, and Nikki jumped, turning to find a woman in a broad-brimmed hat, bib overalls, a flannel shirt, boots, and gardening gloves standing on the other side of an untrimmed row of boxwoods. "Hasn't been for, oh, nigh onto a month now, I reckon."

Nikki stepped off the porch and crossed the soft lawn. "You know Mr. O'Henry?" Maybe this woman could help her.

"Oh, hell, no. No one does. I've lived here sixteen years now, and I never spoke but half a dozen words to him. Same with his wife, though I saw her with the kids once in a while. She never waved, just hurried to the car. Well, to tell you the truth, I'm surprised he's even married. He's a loner, you know, and really, who could blame him? Everyone in the whole damned town knows what he went through."

She was staring at Nikki through glasses that darkened as the sun peeked through the clouds. Without removing her gloves, she found a pack of cigarettes and a lighter in the voluminous pockets of her overalls.

"You aren't the first one to come calling," she added and managed somehow to light a long cigarette, holding it in lime-green gloves. "Lots of people been knocking on his door. I've watched 'em." She shot a stream of smoke from the side of her mouth.

"He used to go to work at seven-twenty every morning, on the dot—I'd hear his pickup fire up —then return around six. Just like clockwork.

The missus, Darla, I think her name is, if she left the house at all, it was during the middle of the day in that old red Dodge—a Dart, I think it was." She took another drag. "It was weird, though. I never even heard the kids playing in the yard. Kinda odd, don't ya know. Well, good riddance. That's what I say."

"Why?"

"They moved out. Oh, must've been three weeks now, maybe four. Went back to work on his father's farm, that's what I heard. You know Calvin O'Henry?"

"I know of him," Nikki said. "Blondell's ex-husband and Niall and Blythe's father. A strange man, from all accounts."

She frowned. "I know the wife, June. Her son and my boy were in the same class at school. She's a strange one, though, let me tell you. I'm sure as heck glad she's not my stepmother. I think she makes Nurse Ratched . . . from that movie, what's it called?"

"One Flew Over the Cuckoo's Nest."

"Yeah, that one. I think maybe they made a book from it."

Or the other way around.

"Anyway, June makes that nurse look like an angel, I'm tellin' you. Religious too, and not in a good way, y'know. I'm a Christian woman, mind you, go to church and Bible study and believe in the Savior, Jesus Christ, but June O'Henry, she takes it too far. That church she attends? It's one of those snake-handlin', speakin'-in-tongues sects. Let me tell you, it gives me a case of the willies."

Nikki had heard, somewhere, that Calvin O'Henry's second wife was part of a religious sect far outside the mainstream, but snake handling? Why had she never heard this? "In Savannah?" she asked.

"Not in town, but outside. Yeah, I know everyone thinks they only exist in Appalachia, in the mountains, but that's just not correct." She was rambling on before she realized Nikki hadn't introduced herself. "So who're you? Reporter or something?"

Nikki was remembering Amity's wounds from a snake bite, and it took her a moment before she extended her hand. "Nikki Gillette, *Savannah Sentinel*."

"That rag?" she said, then hesitated, "Wait a minute. Gillette?" Her eyes narrowed behind her glasses, and her pleasant, gossip-sharing smile faded. "I know all about you. Big Ron or Big Daddy or whatever the hell it was they called him, he was your father. Right?"

"Yes, and—"

"You're the one who was nearly killed by that psycho a few years back? Wrote a book about it?" Her lips compressed and she clucked her tongue. "I should've recognized you."

Nikki was nodding, but before she could say another word, the woman backed up a step, away from the overgrown hedge. "I got no use for you, nor that father of yours. I know he's dead and I say that's a blessing. He sent my Clarence up the river for twenty years." Hooking a thumb at her chest, she added, "Twenty damned years! I know it was his third DUI, but hell, no one died in that wreck. For the love of Christ, I ain't talkin' to the likes of you. What happened to your daddy was too good for him." Jettisoning her cigarette into the moist grass, she turned and stormed toward the neat bungalow she called home.

"Wait a minute," Nikki said, jumping over the boxwoods and following the woman to her porch. "I'm just looking to talk to Mr. O'Henry."

"You and the rest of the world. You ain't hearin' any more from me. I don't give Big Ron Gillette's progeny the damned time of day!" She hurried up the cement steps and reached for the handle of the door. "You've got about three seconds to get off my property before I call the cops and have you arrested for trespassing!"

Chapter 10

Two days later, before the interview they were scheduled to have with Niall O'Henry, Reed and Morrisette took a drive to the cabin where Amity O'Henry had been killed.

"This place certainly wouldn't win any awards from *House Beautiful*," Morrisette muttered as they walked into the cabin. Remarkably, the key the station had on file still fit the lock, just as the key to the gate at the end of the lane had. As the door creaked open, Reed had to agree with his partner.

It was as if they'd stepped back in time. A thick layer of dust covered the floor, mantel, and windowsills, and the carcasses of dead insects were visible, along with a myriad of spider webs. The air inside was musty and smelled stale, as if no one had cracked open a window during the past twenty years.

A few pieces of furniture remained, but the hide-a-bed where Amity O'Henry had been shot was gone, and the desk and table seemed to be falling apart.

The room was large, with a high, pitched ceiling where, it appeared, wasps had nested in the rafters. Stairs ran up the far wall to the open loft area that was about half the size of the lower level, and in the center of the room, on the wall opposite the loft, a crumbling stone fireplace climbed two stories to dominate the room.

"It's like time stood still," Morrisette remarked as she clicked on her flashlight and ran its beam around the small living area. The fireplace was empty, devoid of ashes or a grate, and yet there was the faint odor of soot lingering in the air. "Kind of gives a person the creeps."

"It could," Reed agreed, as Morrisette pointed the beam of the flashlight to the wooden stairs running up the far wall to the loft. Reed glanced up and wondered about the children who had been put to bed upstairs. Niall, barely eight at the time and little Blythe, not quite five.

How terrifying for them to hear . . . what? An argument? A door bursting open? Cursing? Gunfire? A smashed lantern? Screams? Whatever it was, it had to have been loud enough to wake them up and cause them to come stumbling down the stairs without knowing they were attracting a killer's attention.

If they'd stayed in their beds, would the attacker have come up the stairs and killed them as they slept, or would the killer have let them live? Had their own mother fired on them, or was it truly a stranger, a maniac with a gun and an unknown motive?

Beauregard and the team had theorized that Blondell had shot her daughter as she'd awoken following the snakebite, but how the hell did the sibilant creature get into her bed in the first place? On its own? Was it planted?

Beauregard's theory was that while Amity lay bleeding out, conscious or not, the little ones had tumbled out of their beds, only to be mown down by their own mother, who had been callous enough to shoot herself in the arm and smash her head against the mantel or some other surface to add to her alibi. Then, once she was clearheaded enough, she'd hauled her injured kids into the car to make that slow, harrowing journey to the hospital and get rid of the murder weapon. True, the car showed signs of being wrecked, and a tire rubbing against the wheel well and the alcohol in her bloodstream could have contributed to her inability to drive fast. Blondell swore that she had trouble focusing because of her head injury, and that driving was difficult also because of her shattered arm. And the car, after she'd sideswiped an oak, was nearly impossible to drive. All of the above hampered her speed to the hospital, she claimed.

Cell phones weren't prevalent back then, and there weren't many phone booths scattered throughout the Georgia countryside, so she couldn't call for help.

Other evidence that had thrown the cops off—

the snake that had apparently bitten Amity before being run over on the drive and a cigarette butt—could have been planted before she started her rampage. What the hell was a copperhead doing in the cabin in January, and who had left the cigarette?

"Beauregard couldn't find evidence of another person in the cabin besides Blondell and her children," Reed said as they stepped through the gloomy rooms.

"Not at that time. Too many people had used it back then." She eyed the empty interior. "It lost a little of its luster and popularity, you know, after the murder."

"Who owned the property?"

"Same people that do today," Morrisette said, running her flashlight's beam toward the archway leading to a small kitchen at the back of the cabin. "The acres surrounding the cabin and the lake belong to the Eleanor Ryback Trust, which is essentially her descendants." When he didn't respond, she added, "One of those descendants is your fiancée."

His head jerked up. "Nikki?"

"Unless you've got another one tucked away somewhere. Eleanor Ryback was married twice, first to Frank McBaine and after he died, to Marshall Gillette. She had two sons, Alexander McBaine with husband number one and Ronald with number two." Morrisette swept the beam of her flashlight up the face of the fireplace to where the chimney disappeared into the ceiling. "She's long dead now, but was the mother of Big Ron or Big Daddy or whatever you want to call him, the Honorable Judge Ronald Gillette, as well as mother to Big Ron's half-brother, Alexander McBaine, who was Blondell's attorney at the time of the trial."

"I knew that much. Surprised it happened. I mean, weren't there cries of nepotism by the prosecution?"

"Probably, I don't know. But Flint Beauregard and the DA at the time played poker with Big Daddy. Either side could have cried foul. And it gets even more incestuous," she added. "Jesus, is that a bat up there?" Her light was positioned in a crack between the main beam supporting the ceiling and butting up to the chimney stack. Tiny eyes reflected. "I hate those things!"

"How does it get more incestuous?" he asked, but he wasn't sure he wanted to know the answer as they were discussing Nikki's family.

"Well, the rumor was that Alexander McBaine fell in love with his client."

He hadn't seen even a hint of a love affair in Beauregard's notes and said as much.

She lifted a shoulder as she turned to run the light over the stairs. "Speculation, for the most part, but where there's smoke, there's fire."

"A rumor."

"You know, it happens more often than you'd think, the lawyer-client love affair, probably from working so closely together. But I just don't get it."

Reed offered up. "She was a beautiful woman."

"Oh, bite me! There are thousands of beautiful women right here in this town. And there were just as many twenty years ago. Come on. Blondell O'Henry is accused of murdering her daughter, and then her lawyer—no, rewind: make that her *long-married* lawyer—falls for her? Sick, if you ask me."

"But Amity's murder happened before Alexander McBaine took Blondell's case, obviously," Reed thought aloud. "Did he know her before? Why use this cabin?"

"That's a good question, but I think it didn't come through the McBaine side. Your fiancée knew Amity O'Henry, I think"—Morrisette scowled a bit—"so she might have been the connection between them."

"Because she was friends with the dead girl?" Reed said, bothered, refusing to admit that the same thought had crossed his mind. "That's a big leap. She was what? Fifteen or sixteen at the time."

"Even so, Nikki Gillette's father owned an interest in this cabin, where the murder occurred." Morrisette cocked her head and stared at him. "I'm just sayin'. So maybe you should ask her."

"I will," he said, and he felt an unanticipated premonition of dread seep through his bones. The evil that had occurred within these crumbling walls still hadn't evaporated.

He eyed the loft from the ground floor. According to Beauregard's notes, some of the evidence found in the cabin had supported Blondell's story, and some didn't. The case would have probably been a stalemate except for Niall's whispery testimony. Spoken through a larynx that was shattered by a bullet fired from the assailant's gun, his words convinced the jury that he'd seen his mother take aim at him and fire.

Yes, it had been dark that night, and yes, he'd been a terrified, myopic eight-year-old at the time, but frail, reluctant Niall O'Henry had been a convincing witness.

The defense had countered by insisting it had been far too dark for anyone to see clearly, much less a child who wore glasses and hadn't put them on when he'd bolted out of bed that night.

Blondell had insisted her son had seen her wrestling for the gun, but in his blurred vision mistakenly thought she'd aimed the weapon at him and pulled the trigger.

To this day, she repeated the same story and vowed she was innocent. The "intruder" with bushy hair and a serpent tattoo, with whom she claimed she'd fought, was never located, though many men, mostly those who knew her, had been questioned. Of course, the murder weapon had never been located. According to the notes, the police had interviewed neighbors of the cabin, but no one had been awakened by the sound of a car backfiring or by a barking dog. Then again, they were located so far away from the cabin, they might not have heard the gunshots over the storm. Both of the neighbors who had been called to testify, those with property abutting the property surrounding the cabin, could recall only the sounds of the pouring rain and the wind racing across the marshland.

Nor had a second set of tire prints or footprints been discovered that night, though the rain could have washed them away.

Other than the snake and cigarette butt, and Niall's now-recanted testimony, the police didn't have much.

Blondell's side of the events had continued with her panicked trip to the hospital, the swollen creek, the treacherous bridge, and hitting the tree and mashing her fender. Amity had died on the way to the ER.

Blythe had been rushed into surgery, but her spinal cord had been damaged, leaving her in a wheelchair ever since.

Niall's injuries—broken ribs and a shattered right ulna—had healed for the most part, and even his nearly destroyed larynx functioned, but as with his sister, Blythe, his mental scars would never heal, or at least that was the conclusion of one of the many psychiatrists he'd seen, who had testified at Blondell's trial.

"So what have we got here?" Using the beam of her flashlight, Morrisette walked to the stairs, tested them, then started up the rough-hewn steps to the loft. "Oh, man, take a look at this." She was halfway up the flight when she stopped and stared at the wall and stairs: dark stains were splattered against the wall and risers.

Reed's stomach turned.

Morrisette's attitude changed. "When I think of my kids and realize what that little boy and girl saw." Shaking her head, she stared at the twenty-year-old blood, then made her way up the remaining steps to the loft. Reed, more somber than before, followed her to the wide-open area with its open railing and dusty plank floors. In one corner, a bureau was still standing and supported a cracked, fly-spotted mirror.

So the little ones were up here. The frame of an old bed still stood, mattress long gone, but Morrisette ran the beam of her light over the rusted rails. "Damned nightmare for those kids. The way Blondell told it, she was surprised by an intruder with a gun, they wrestled for it, she got shot, and then he hit Amity. The kids up here, hearing the commotion, started running down the stairs, despite her yelling at them to stay where they were. The killer spied Niall running down and hit him midway. Where we saw the blood."

"And the girl comes to the top of the stairs, sees her mother, and somehow falls over?" Reed said, stepping to the rail.

"Gets hit, slips through the spindles, I think . . . see, they're handmade, not up to code, if there even was one when this place was constructed. She slides through and falls the eight feet to the floor below, breaking her back." Morrisette's jaw tightened, her lips becoming a razor-thin line as she met Reed's gaze. "A damned shame all the way around."

"Even if Blondell didn't try to kill them."

"Oh, she did. Her story is just that, a massively sick and tall tale." Morrisette was convinced. "Why in the world would a stranger follow her to the cabin? No one was supposed to know she was here, spending time with the kids, sorting out her life or some such tripe. So let's just say that she's telling the truth. Someone comes in, to what? Rob her? Nothing was taken. Rape her? Didn't happen, no matter how wounded she was. Wipe out her whole family? Why? Because they saw his face? Nuh-uh. It was dark. The kids can't even remember if another person was here or not. And then there was that damned snake. Maybe it was nothing, just a weird anomaly. But I don't like it. And it bothers me that Calvin married a woman who's into a church where they handle poisonous snakes."

Reed had seen the notation in the file about the Pentecostal church June O'Henry belonged to and their strange practices. In the file, Flint Beauregard had simply written "snakes" in a notation beside June's name, but if he'd further connected it to Amity's death, the detective hadn't left a record of it.

"You think June Hatchett or Calvin O'Henry brought a snake to the cabin, then proceeded to shoot Amity?" Reed asked now, trying to keep his skepticism to a dull roar.

"I know it doesn't make any sense, but still it's weird, something to consider, and we're running out of time. Jada Hill is pushing for Blondell's release. Could be any day now." She glanced around the loft one last time and said in disgust, "Let's go."

At the base of the staircase, Reed peered into a small bathroom. Once a minuscule "three-piece," the room was now composed of a tiny shower without fixtures, a basin that was as dry as a bone and held rusted pieces of pipe and dead insects, and a toilet with no lid on the tank that no longer held water, just showed rings and dirt from a time when it had actually functioned.

"Lovely," Morrisette said. "Reminds me of Bart's place." At least her black humor had returned. Bart Yelkis was one of Morrisette's exes, the father of her children, and a deadbeat who was always late on his child support.

"Oh, come on," Reed countered, "his apartment couldn't be *this* nice."

She spit out a humorless laugh as they headed into the kitchen, which was small and rundown, like the rest of the place, the warped linoleum looking as if it was pre–World War II and the windows leaking.

Opening a drawer, Reed thought about that night so long ago.

"Hoping to find a murder weapon?" Morrisette asked.

"Would be nice."

Another snort. "That's part of the big mystery, what the hell happened to the .45? We found the slugs—in the wall, in Blondell's right arm, in Amity and Niall and Blythe—but no damned weapon. Blondell claimed the stranger who attacked her took off with it." She looked through the grimy kitchen window over the sink. "My guess is it's out there in the water somewhere."

"The whole area was searched." Reed walked out through a swollen back door to a rickety porch with rotten boards and a view of the lake that stretched for at least a quarter of a mile. Reeds, marsh grass, and a few cypress trees grew around the banks of the rippling water. "And not just searched once, but over and over again." He'd read Beauregard's notes and the reports in the case file. This cabin, property, and lake had been scoured.

"Yeah, well, I'm saying that Blondell could have ditched the gun anywhere around here, or stopped somewhere on her way to the hospital. It wasn't as if she sprinted there, y'know."

That much was true: though she'd claimed she'd managed to get her kids into her car, then drove "like a madwoman" to the hospital, it had taken nearly an hour for her to arrive at the emergency room. If she were truly racing the clock, the trip should have taken less than half that. Would the extra time have saved her daughter and granddaughter's life? Who knew? As far as Reed was concerned, even considering hitting the tree and her own injuries, the length of time for the journey was a serious flaw in Blondell's testimony that she'd done everything possible to get her kids to safety.

Staring across the lake, he wondered what really had gone down. A flock of wood ducks swooped onto the ruffled waters of the lake. They seemed to glide on the surface, then, one after the other, tails up, dipped their heads beneath the surface.

"I guess we've seen all there is," Reed said as he and Morrisette headed around the exterior of the cabin. In the office, he'd viewed diagrams and pictures of the place, of course. The drawings were made by the investigating officers, and the photographs were taken the night and day after Blondell reported the attack, but actually walking around the cabin gave him a new perspective, and he now felt more connected to the case.

He checked his watch as he climbed into Morrisette's car. "We'd better get a move on. Blass is bringing in Niall O'Henry in about an hour."

"Good. This I gotta see." She frowned as she slipped behind the wheel. "I won't lie about it, I'm pissed as hell that he's recanting. You know, now that he's a full-fledged adult and all, but" —she slid a final look at the dilapidated cabin— "he was just a scared kid back then, terrified out of his frickin' mind and not much older than my Toby. Niall witnessed something unimaginable, so it's hard to be pissed at him." Flicking on the ignition, she said, "So let's go see what he has to say."

Chapter 11

With her recent string of bad luck, Nikki wasn't expecting much as she parked at Blythe O'Henry's apartment building in one of the five spots marked GUEST. The phone calls she'd made to Blondell's "friends" and family members had, for the most part, been busts. Half of them she couldn't find; the others didn't want to talk to her and wished no one remembered that they'd been associated with a woman convicted of such heinous acts.

As for the people besides Blythe who'd actually been at the cabin on the night Amity O'Henry was murdered, she hadn't been able to speak with either Blondell or her son. Grabbing her purse and recorder, Nikki bolstered herself with the old adage "The third time's the charm," while ignoring the "Three strikes and you're out" rule.

"Think positively," she told herself as she slammed her car door shut.

Blythe lived in a modern, two-story apartment building with a brick facade and white trim. Each unit, including Blythe's ground-floor apartment, faced a central garden area with azaleas surrounded by snaking tendrils of ivy. She found her way to apartment 1-D and rang the bell.

For a second, she heard nothing. "Come on, come on," she said under her breath, crossing her fingers. Surely she would get lucky.

Still she heard nothing, but the blinds in the front window fluttered a bit.

Knocking loudly, she waited again, and this time the blinds definitely moved as a black cat with tuxedo markings wedged himself between the slats and the window, hopping onto the sill, where he stared at her with round, green eyes.

"Well, at least I know someone lives here," she said just as the blinds snapped open, the cat jumped down, and Nikki found herself staring into the elfin face of Blythe O'Henry, who was glaring up at her through the window. Her lips were pursed, her eyes nearly hidden by a fringe of bangs, but she looked mad as hell as she let the blinds drop. A few seconds later, loud clicks indicated that locks were being sprung. The door opened, and Blythe, now twenty-five and still ensconced in a wheelchair said, "You're Nikki Gillette and you're with the paper, I know. You wrote those books too. I've seen you on the news."

Such was the price of fame in a small town. "I came here because—"

"Because of Niall's testimony. Oh, I know," she said heatedly on the other side of the screen. She was a tiny woman, her frame as small as her mother's, and her blond hair, razor cut and straight, feathered across her forehead in side-swept bangs that partially hid large, hazel eyes. "My phone's been ringing off the hook ever since my brother decided to change his story. Reporters, like you. The police. All of a sudden I'm the most popular girl at the prom." To add credence to her words, her cell phone began to play some classical piece, and she plucked it from a bag snapped to the rail of her chair, checked the numbers on the screen, and raised an eyebrow as if to say, "See?" Then she dropped her phone into the bag again. "I don't want any part of it."

"I understand, really I do," Nikki said quickly

before she lost any chance of the interview. "I've been on both sides of this. Yes, I'm a reporter, and I would love to interview you, but I know what it's like to be the victim, to be mobbed by the press."

Blythe hesitated. "The Grave Robber, I know."

Nikki was nodding, trying to come up with a reason for Blythe to allow her an interview. "I was lucky, not only that I survived, but that I worked for the newspaper and knew what to do, whom I could trust."

"Fine. But I really don't have anything to say." She moved to shut the door.

"Your story's important," Nikki said.

"Oh, mine is?" Her lips thinned. "Don't try to con me or flatter me or tell me any lies. I've had enough of that all my life."

"I just meant—"

"What do you want from me?" she cut her off.

"Insight, I guess. For a series I'm doing. I also want to write a book about what happened that night."

"Whoa! *What?* You think I'd agree to that? I'm not interested in any part of it! My father already sold his side of the story to some tabloid, and it was a nightmare. I was just a kid, but I remember. All the questions. The poking into my family's life, looking for dirty, scandalous secrets they could exploit." She shook her head violently. "I'm out." She started to slam the door.

"But I was Amity's friend," Nikki persisted,

desperate to speak with Blondell's daughter. "We hung out together all the time. In fact, she called me that night. Wanted me to sneak out and see her."

"*That* night?" Blythe repeated suspiciously. But the door remained open. "And you never told anyone?"

"She asked me not to."

"But she was killed. We all nearly died, and you didn't come forward?" Revulsion twisted her small features.

"Nothing she told me would have made any difference."

"You don't know that. What did she say to you? What did she want?"

"She asked me to meet her at the cabin. Sneak out. But I couldn't get there. My parents were up and fighting, and I fell asleep." The old pain returned, and it must've registered on her face because Blythe hesitated, her hand still on the door.

"Why did she want you to meet her?"

"If you let me come in, I'll tell you all about our conversation."

"Oh, for the love of God." She rolled her eyes.

"Look, I've felt awful about it ever since."

"But not bad enough to go to the police."

"It wouldn't have helped, but, yeah, I probably should have done something. I am now."

"Twenty years later. Wow. How heroic," she

said as she eyed Nikki. "But it'll change every-thing, you know. Even if Niall's new testimony doesn't get my mother out of jail, when the press gets wind that the daughter of the judge and the niece of the defense counsel withheld evidence, this whole thing is gonna blow up in your face."

"Probably."

"So how are you going to do it? Come clean in one of your articles?"

Nikki's guilt was nearly palpable, but she set it aside for the moment. "I'm really sorry for what happened to you and your siblings. What you went through was unspeakable, and I won't even suggest that I know how you feel, because I don't. But I'd really like to tell your side of the story."

"Back to that." Her smile was a smirk.

"Well . . . yes."

She inhaled and then exhaled slowly, giving Nikki a long look. "I'm going to have to talk to someone eventually, I suppose, and I can't stand that reporter from WKAM. Lynnetta What's-her-face."

"Ricci."

"Yeah, that one." Blythe rolled away from the door, leaving it open, a tacit invitation. "So I guess it may as well be you. At least you knew Amity. My only thing is this: it's got to be exclusive. I'm not going to talk to anyone else. No one. It's just too hard."

• • •

"I'm just saying that I was wrong. I got the facts mixed up in my mind. I was just a kid!" Niall O'Henry's voice was clear if sibilant and raspy, sounding a little like a snake, Morrisette thought. She reminded herself that he had only been a boy of eight, a little kid who had witnessed something out of a horror movie on the night he'd been shot, but as he sat in the interrogation room, with his high-dollar lawyer at his side, she couldn't help but doubt his motives. She'd been born suspicious, and a string of loser men in her life, along with her job in law enforcement, hadn't added to her trust factor.

In fact, she thought she had a pretty good handle on knowing when she was being peddled a load of bull, and right now, staring at Niall O'Henry—watching him fidget in his suit, and cast his nervous gaze to his attorney, and lick his dry lips—made her think he wasn't exactly opening up with the whole story.

"Why the change of heart now?" Reed asked. He too was in the room, seated across the table from Niall while Morrisette preferred standing by the wall. Cameras were running, of course; everyone in the room knew about and had agreed to the recording. They were also being viewed by others in the department, their faces hidden by a two-way mirror.

Niall pulled at his shirt and tie, as if they were

suddenly too tight, while beside him, David Blass, imposing as ever, showed no emotion whatsoever. He was taciturn and stoic, not one strand of his thick, white hair so much as moving in the warm breeze created by the heating system.

Niall's skin was beginning to glisten with sweat. The guy was nervous as hell. "I just . . . I just feel it's time. I've found Jesus Christ, and I can't live the lie any longer."

"It's been twenty years," Reed said.

"I *know!* I've been struggling with what happened that night all my life." Niall stared at Reed and didn't blink, as if his contacts were holding up his eyelids. "I'm sorry, but I have to do this. It's the right thing. I've . . . I've . . ." Another furtive glance at his attorney, which warranted an almost imperceptible nod from Blass. "I've been seeing a psychologist, and she's been working with me. Repressed memory treatment. I've seen doctors and hypnotists, psychiatrists and acupuncturists—you name it—to deal with my injuries from that night, the physical and the mental." His voice had taken on a wheezing tone as he became more agitated, serving to remind everyone of the trauma he'd gone through. "Finally, I found Dr. Williams with the All Mental Health team, and she's been wonderful."

Morrisette said, "I thought you found religion."

"Yes, yes, I did. I mean, I have." He was nodding enthusiastically. "I've always been

189

surrounded by Christians. My stepmother has a very strong faith."

"That would be June O'Henry?"

"Yes. She married my father not long after . . ." His eyebrows pulled together as he thought. "Well, I think it was during Mother's trial." Nodding now, remembering, he added, "June always forced us, me and my sister, to go to church service, and Bible study and Sunday school and everything"—he waved a hand as if to indicate that *everything* was all-inclusive as far as religion went—"well, all the services associated with the church, but I was a kid and I thought it was all baloney." He looked down, ashamed, a bit of red creeping up the back of his neck and then crawling across his cheeks and flushing his skin. "I was acting out, didn't like my new mom. Her faith was strong, rock-steady, and she was strict, not afraid to use the hickory switch, if you know what I mean. Of course, I wasn't happy and . . . well, I was confused. Rebelling. I know that now."

"And now you're not?"

"Of course not. I'm a grown man."

"And you go along with a religion that uses venomous snakes in its rites?"

"Last I heard, Detective, there was freedom of religion in this country," Niall said.

"And your sister Amity was bitten by a snake the night she was killed. Correct?"

"You can't blame that on my stepmother's church." He glared at her. "Do you know how many snakes there are in Georgia or the southeastern United States? They're everywhere. In the wild and in homes as pets. Or used for research or whatever." His lips pursed angrily. "All I'm getting at is that now I see things more clearly. Much more clearly. I see them for what they are. When I testified, I was a kid and I was scared. I just did what I thought I should . . ."

Morrisette waited. *Here it comes.*

He swallowed hard. "I was kind of talked into saying what I did."

"That your mom shot you," Morrisette reminded.

"Maybe bullied is the right word. That detective, Mr. Beauregard, he was nice to me and . . . and I wanted to please him." A drip of sweat slid from his temple to his chin. Absently he swiped at it with the back of his hand.

"You're saying Detective Beauregard asked you to compromise your testimony?" Reed put in. "To lie?"

"No! Not directly . . ." Niall blinked and shook his head. "He just kind of steered me into what he deemed was the 'right' direction. I couldn't talk to my mom, and my dad was just angry all the time, furious at what had happened. Whenever her name came up, he went through the roof.

"But Detective Beauregard took time with me. Gave me soda and cookies out of the vending machines, that kind of thing. It meant a lot to me." After another glance at his lawyer, he folded his hands on the scarred table. "In response to his kindness and because I wanted to please him, I was influenced by him and what he wanted from me."

"Which was," Morrisette encouraged.

"To testify against my mother." He let out a long sigh. "So I did."

"Are you now saying you *didn't* see her shoot you or Amity?" Morrisette asked. She didn't much care for Flint Beauregard or his uppity son, but this total turnaround smelled of something rotten.

"A faithful witness will not lie: but a false witness will utter lies. Proverbs 14:5."

Morrisette caught Reed's eyes and sent him a "Can you believe this?" look. To O'Henry, she said, "You're quoting Bible verses now?"

"Yes!" Niall was emphatic, one hand slapping the table. "I've found the Lord, and I cannot shame Him. I'm a follower of Jesus Christ, our Savior, and I cannot bear false witness! That's the ninth commandment."

"I know it's a commandment." Morrisette let her annoyance slip into her voice.

David Blass held up a calming, diplomatic hand. "Mr. O'Henry is cooperating," he reminded them. "Trying to help you with your investigation of his own volition."

"You're not just trying to spring your mother?" she asked Niall.

"I just want to tell the truth!" Niall was glaring at Morrisette now, his eyes narrowing in a newfound hatred.

Well, fine. Morrisette knew he'd found God, had taken his father's and his stepmother's extreme religious views to heart. She also knew this weakling facade was just that—window dressing—because she'd checked. Niall O'Henry now worked on his father's farm, pitching in with the hard labor, so he was tougher than he looked. Also, he wasn't just a devout Christian, he was a card-carrying member of the NRA and had joined a vigilante group that was considered extremist, like his father. Married, with a wife and two sons, he seemed intent on policing his own property and keeping others away as if it were Fort Knox.

"You and your father," she said to him, "you're tight, right? Good buds."

"I like to think so," Niall said cautiously.

"You work for him, on the family farm?" She already knew this much, but wanted to see his reaction.

Blass was obviously irritated. "Where's this going, Detective?"

"Just checkin' my facts." Morrisette saw Niall's clenched fists, the vein beginning to throb near his temple. He might be all dressed up and putting on the soft-spoken act, but Morrisette wasn't buying it. She hadn't from scene one in front of

City Hall. The guy had been coached and prompted by David Blass as much as he had by Flint Beauregard twenty years ago. She couldn't help but wonder what really made him tick, deep down in the darkest parts of him. She suspected he was a bomb about to explode. "What's your father think of your change of heart?"

"What does Calvin O'Henry have to do with any of this?" Blass demanded.

"Calvin O'Henry's gone on record for years about how he feels about his ex-wife. Now his son wants to get her out of prison?"

"Be that as it may, it's Mr. *Niall* O'Henry's testimony that concerns us here. This has nothing to do with Calvin." Blass was riled now, two points of color showing on his face.

"Okay." Reed, who'd stayed back and let her run with the interview, now gazed over Niall's shoulder at her before turning on his "good cop" charm. "We're here to listen, Mr. O'Henry," he said equably. "Why don't you tell us what you remember of that night? In your own words. No pressure. Okay?"

"Maybe this is a mistake," Blythe said, second-guessing herself as she glanced at her watch. They were seated in her living room, she in her wheelchair, her back to the dining area, Nikki on a sleek modern couch in front of the window. Two other chairs, one black leather, the other a leopard

194

print, faced a flat-screen TV that was flanked by four guitar stands, each displaying a different type of electric guitar.

"Do you play?" Nikki asked as the black and white cat strolled across the living room.

"They're my boyfriend's," she said. "He moved in about four months ago." Then, as if she realized she'd gotten off track and said too much, Blythe turned serious again. "You said you knew Amity. Before you start asking questions, why don't you tell me about that?" Blythe acted as if she suddenly doubted Nikki's claim. "Amity was a year older than you, and you didn't come from the same neighborhood. Considering what I know about my sister, I doubt you were in the same Brownie troop together."

"Amity and I both went to Robert E. Lee. We had a couple of classes together," Nikki said. "P.E. was required for both freshmen and sophomores, a blended all-girls class. We saw each other there and in biology. We were lab partners.

"I tested high enough as an entering freshman to skip general science and was pushed into biology, which was a sophomore class," Nikki explained when Blythe looked suspicious. "Your sister ended up being stuck with me as a lab partner."

"Amity wasn't into school all that much." Blythe said it as if it were a documented fact.

"That was probably true."

"You carried her, didn't you?"

"Sometimes." Nikki remembered a time when she'd actually helped Amity cheat on a biology exam.

"You did her homework?"

"Once in a while. Yes."

"You weren't helping her, you know. That was part of Amity's problem, getting others to do her work for her, or so my father used to say. Then again, Dad and June were strict. Unbending. Even with Emma-Kate, and she was their darling, of course."

Nikki nodded, remembering Calvin and June's daughter, born just after Blondell's trial.

"Dad told me that Amity had nearly been flunking out and didn't seem to care."

"That was the next year."

"I guess you weren't there to bail her out."

"No."

"How about Hollis McBaine?"

"How do you know Hollis?" Nikki asked.

"I don't. But I've learned a lot in the past few years. I had a lot of questions about what happened and not many answers. I knew that Dad and June saw things one way, in black and white, as they do with everything, so when I could, I read all there was to read about my mother. I was, like, obsessed with what had happened. My shrink says I'm looking for answers I can't find, but I think that's crap. The answers are out there. Someone knows the truth."

"That's what I'm trying to find out. I'm hoping to talk to your mother."

"Good luck with that." Behind her shaggy bangs, Blythe rolled her eyes. "For a few years I visited her in prison, with a social worker. My dad and stepmother wouldn't be caught dead near the prison, and then, when I was older, I went by myself. I'm not completely bound to this chair, y'know. I can drive and walk with a walker, but it's hard. Anyway, like I said, obsessed."

"What about your mother? Was she anxious to see you?"

"Never," she said, then amended that statement. "That's not really true. I think she was glad for a break from the boredom and routine, but I don't kid myself into thinking it had anything to do with motherly love. To me, she's always been indifferent. Maybe even cold, and certainly narcissistic." She glanced at the recorder, its red ON light glowing. "Anyway, I just pieced as much information together as I could. I knew my mother's lawyer had a couple of kids who had died, so I googled them and read all the articles and realized that Hollis was the same age as Amity, and she had died just a couple of months before my sister. How weird is that?" Blythe lifted her shoulders in the tiniest of shrugs. "But, then, what isn't weird about all of this?"

"Nothing," Nikki admitted.

Chapter 12

Niall O'Henry squeezed his eyes shut for a second. "I heard something. Loud voices, I believe. My mother. Angry. No, no, furious was more like it," he said, looking from Reed to Morrisette in the interrogation room. "I've always thought she was yelling at Amity, but now . . . now I believe she was yelling at the intruder. Anyway, I shot out of the bed. I was in the top bunk, and I hurried to the stairs when I heard a shot. I couldn't see much. I've worn glasses since I was three or four and hadn't put them on, just ran to the stairs and started going down. The only light was from the fire, but I saw Amity on the bed and then a blast, a bright light, and I was hit. I thought my mother was the only person in the room, so I assumed she'd shot at me, but now, thinking back, I think there might have been someone else down-stairs. Someone threatening us. Attacking us."

He appeared earnest and sounded a little desperate, his wheezy breath more apparent as he became more agitated. "Look, I really don't know what I saw. I was just a kid, a myopic kid in the semidark with bullets flying. I heard screaming, yeah, and then Blythe was behind me. I remember that. As I fell down the rest of the stairs, I saw her near the top and there was another shot and she . . . somehow slipped through the rails." He closed his eyes tightly, almost cringing, his face seeming to fold in on itself. "And then . . . I kind of blacked out, I guess. I remember Mom carrying me to the car. Amity and Blythe were already inside, and Mom was bleeding."

"You didn't see anyone shoot her?" Reed asked.

Niall was shaking his head. "I don't know how it happened."

"You testified that she shot herself."

"I know!" He held up both his hands. "That's what Detective Beauregard wanted. He suggested it, I think. Because my mother was shot in her right arm and she was left-handed, but I'm telling you I didn't see it."

"Did you see anyone else in the cabin?" Morrisette said.

He looked weary, as if he'd been battling demons for years. "I just don't know. But the point is I cannot, in good conscience, allow my mother to spend one more night in jail because of what I said. All because I wanted to please a man who gave me Snickers bars."

"She won't get out today."

"I know, but I've done my part." His spine seemed to stiffen a bit as he slid a glance at his lawyer, then stared Reed straight in the eyes. "I'd like to make a signed statement. Immediately."

• • •

If Nikki had expected a big breakthrough from Blythe, so far she'd been disappointed. Blythe's information on her family wasn't much more in-depth than what Nikki had already read. Though pressed, she swore she had no idea who the father of Amity's baby was. She'd been too young to know.

"I only heard things after the fact," Blythe said, one hand resting on the arm of her chair, the other stroking her cat. "And usually it was something I just happened to overhear when June and my dad didn't think I was around. All I know is that they were death on some older guy she'd been seeing, but I don't know who, and there were a couple of boys from high school whose names came up." Her eyebrows drew together as she concentrated. "Steve Something-or-other, a baseball player, I think."

"Steve Manning, but he didn't play ball," Nikki said. "Brad Holbrook was an All-State pitcher. They both dated Amity for a little while."

"And Holt Beauregard," Blythe said.

"Flint's son?"

"I'm sure I heard his name."

"His father—"

"I know. Was the lead detective on the case."

"That never came out in court," Nikki said, certain she would have remembered if Beauregard's youngest son's name had been connected with Amity O'Henry.

"I only heard about it years later, when my dad and June thought they were alone. Dad and June were in the kitchen in the farmhouse; she was cooking breakfast and Dad was at the table, drinking coffee after the morning chores. I was just coming down the stairs and they were discussing Amity and the boys she'd dated. They didn't see me. The stove was on the far wall, and Dad was facing it, away from the hall and the stairs, so I ducked back into the hallway and listened. It was hard to hear over the frying bacon, and they were talking kind of low. But I know I heard four names. There could have been others. But the ones I definitely heard were Steve, Brad, Holt, and Elton."

"My cousin Elton?"

"You know another one?"

Nikki felt as if she'd been sucker-punched. In the past few days she'd read and reread articles about the trial and she'd known Amity. "She never mentioned Holt or Elton."

"Maybe it was the secret she was going to tell you if you'd shown up at the cabin that night."

"The lead detective's son and the defense attorney's son? Both linked with Amity?"

"And Steve and Brad."

Nikki had just shaken her head and moved on, asking her instead about the night Amity died, but Blythe could tell her little more than what she already knew. She'd heard screams and gunfire.

She didn't remember sliding through the railing, hitting the floor or anything about the ride to the hospital. The next thing she recalled was being released to her father's care.

"And that was a nightmare too," she admitted. "Believe me, living with Calvin and June and Leah and Cain was about all Niall and I could take. Leah, she's older, and she was like our nurse or something, or June, at least, gave her that responsibility. Really? A twelve-year-old? But Niall liked that. I think he kinda had a crush on her." She pulled a disgusted face. "He and Leah . . ." She shuddered. "I don't care if there's blood involved or not, a stepsister is a *sister,* a *relative* in my book."

"Niall and Leah were, what? Lovers?"

"I didn't mean *that, exactly,* but . . ." She gazed off into the distance, lifted a shoulder. "They were tight, and she got kind of silly around him. Not at first, of course, we were both just kids, but as time went on, when Niall was in high school, it was pretty obvious that they were interested in each other. June did *not* like that at all. As crazy as her religion is, and it's . . . nutty, the whole incest thing is frowned upon. I would have left if I could, but I didn't have a choice. Things didn't get any better when Emma-Kate was born. She was a crabby, colicky baby."

Before she could expound, the roar of a motorcycle's engine reverberated through the apartment, only to stop suddenly. Blythe looked up sharply. "That's A.J." Her shoulders sagged for the first time since Nikki had arrived. "He might not be thrilled about this."

"Is it his business?"

"He thinks so," she admitted at about the same time that her boyfriend swaggered inside.

"Hey, babe," he said, bending down to kiss her cheek before he noticed Nikki getting to her feet.

"Hi, babe," she replied. "This is Nikki Gillette. She was a friend of my sister's and is a reporter for the *Sentinel*. She, uh, wants to write a story about my mother."

"True crime," Nikki said, extending her hand.

"More like true cash, don't you mean?" He was a tall man, over six feet, with beard shadow covering his chin, his lean body draped in black leather, his hair pulled back into a scrawny black ponytail. He carried a helmet tucked under one hand and didn't bother to remove his gloves or boots. "You wrote a couple of other books, right?" One eye was squinting as he considered her for the briefest of seconds, and Nikki thought she recognized him from somewhere, maybe.

"That's right."

"You payin' her?" Hooking a finger at Blythe, he said to his girlfriend, "She payin' you? Or givin' you credits or royalties or whatever they're called?"

"I'm here as a reporter for the *Sentinel*," Nikki said, pocketing her recorder.

"I don't care if you're here for the fuckin' *New York Times*, we deserve a cut. Look at her! Still in a fuckin' wheelchair because of her fuckin' lowlife mother. She's got a disability, I mean, for the fuckin' rest of her life!"

"I can speak for myself," Blythe said, stiffening.

He dropped his helmet unceremoniously onto the couch. "Sorry, babe. That's the way I see it."

He didn't sound sorry in the least.

"I can handle this." Blythe's lips were taut.

"Hey." He cocked both wrists, palms out in gesture of surrender, as he took a step backward. "I'm just lookin' out for us." Then as if Nikki's name and face had finally made an impression on what was outwardly a Neanderthal brain, he said, "Wait a sec. You were with Sean Hawke for a while, right?"

Nikki didn't respond.

"He's one badass dude," A.J. added, nodding, as if agreeing with himself, a note of envy evident in his voice, "Can fuckin' play a guitar, I mean fuckin' play it."

"Yes, he can," Nikki agreed.

"He lives around here now."

Bully for him. "I heard."

"How's that for a fuckin' coincidence."

Not much of one. His cell phone must've vibrated because he turned his attention away from Nikki and Blythe, while reaching into the pocket of his jeans. Seconds later he was reading a text.

Good. She really didn't want to talk about the former boyfriend who had dumped her years ago. She'd dated him during her rebellious period, when his bad-boy good looks and irrepressible, irreverent attitude had fascinated her. He'd even taken on her father, not letting Judge Ronald Gillette intimidate him. But in the end, he'd found someone else. When his white-hot affair with Cindy had sputtered out, he'd attempted a reconciliation with Nikki, his rekindled interest concurrent with the Grave Robber's reign of terror. Thankfully, by then Nikki was over him and his dark side. These days she didn't want to even think about him.

If Sean hadn't left her, she might never have met Pierce Reed, fallen in love, and become his fiancée. Oh, crap! She was supposed to call Ariella, the wedding planner.

"It's really time for me to go anyway," she said to Blythe, grabbing her keys from her purse, sliding a business card from her wallet, handing it to her. "If you think of anything else, call."

"She won't," A.J. said, not bothering to look up from a text he was writing. "Not unless you think of some way to pay her for her trouble, and even then it's a big maybe." He managed to glance at his girlfriend as his fingers flew over the tiny keypad. "I say go with the highest bidder, babe."

Blythe's jaw hardened, but before she could say anything, A.J. headed into the kitchen, where he opened the door of the refrigerator and peered inside. "Babe, we got any beer?"

"I don't know." Blythe added under her breath, "He's really not like this when we're alone, you know."

"Get the hell outta here!!" he yelled sharply and stomped the floor. Like a bolt of greased lightning, the cat streaked from the kitchen.

"I'm sure," Nikki said dryly, as she witnessed A.J. hold the fridge door open with his shoulder, grab a carton of orange juice, then open it and start chugging. Yep, a lover if there ever was one. At the door, she said to Blythe, "If he can't treat you with a little respect in front of other people, then maybe he's not worth the trouble." God, she sounded like her own mother, and Blythe shrank back as the hapless cat again vaulted into her lap.

Geez, Nikki, when are you going to ever learn? Now you may have lost a valuable source! "Sorry," she apologized. "It's none of my business. I was out of line."

Blythe didn't respond.

"I'll be in touch. Thanks. Good-bye. See ya, J.A."

Blythe said, "It's—"

"I know." *But Jack Ass is more like it.*

December 10th
Third Interview

"Okay, so you don't like that line of questioning. I get it, but don't you want to let the world know you're innocent?"

I sit on my stool in the prison communication area, hoping beyond hope that I can break through the icy facade of the woman holding the receiver to her ear, but I know it's pointless.

The eyes behind the booth's thick glass reveal nothing, and I think of her as she once was: beautiful, smart, a woman who would make men's heads turn. A woman who instilled envy in other women, who wished their husbands wouldn't look in her direction.

She is still slightly imperious, despite the drab prison garb and the fact that her graying hair hasn't seen a touch-up or professional cut in months.

"I can help you. You know that. Your story needs to be told."

The face beyond the glass doesn't so much as flinch. No twitch in the corner of the mouth. No movement in the cold, cold eyes. Could anyone be so outwardly callous and still be innocent?

"Why not tell the world exactly what happened that night, not the same old story you've been repeating since you were incarcerated?" I ask, wanting so desperately to know the truth. "Are you trying to protect yourself? Your reputation?" I lean closer. "Well, it's too late for that. Now only the truth, and I mean the whole truth, not some whitewashed, lawyer-sanctioned story, will help you."

She won't respond. It's almost as if she's a statue as she sits on her stool, locked up for what could be the rest of her life. It's incomprehensible to me, but there has to be a way to get through to her, so I try a new tack.

"If you don't explain what happened, the world will go on thinking that you're a cold-blooded killer, that you have no heart, none whatsoever. Is that what you want? Is that what your final epitaph will be?"

Is there just the tiniest dilation of her pupils, a hint that some of what I'm saying is piercing her icy, unbending exterior? Can I reach her?

With an effort, I keep my own voice even, since I don't want her to have the slightest inkling of how much this bothers me, that I too am involved personally, that my own guilt is immense. Could I have seen this coming? Prevented it?

Two stools down, a middle-aged man coughs and next to me, partitioned off, a woman softly weeps, her voice tremulous as she whispers into her phone to the woman seated so close to her, but separated by glass.

I can't think of them now, I have to concentrate, to find a way to get to the truth. "What about Amity? Tell me again. Why was she a threat?"

Is there just the slightest tightening of those lips, a speck of cruelty in the set of her chin, the tiniest spark of evil within her eyes?

"Is that why Amity died? Because she was young and beautiful and somehow in your way?" I throw the questions out there, thinking about my innocent friend and how she died, how she became the central point in Blondell O'Henry's sordid tale, but, of course, once again I get no response. The once-beautiful face beyond the glass is for the most part impassive, as if nothing matters, the people who died, the innocent victims, were all just pawns in a master killer's cruel game.

"Come on," I whisper, and she hears the desperation in my voice, sees my frustration, and that must please her because she smiles. I can imagine that same cold, hard grin crossing her face as she pulled the trigger . . .

Chapter 13

"Well, that was a bust," Morrisette said, collapsing theatrically into the side chair near Reed's desk. "So Niall O'Henry found God, the one that tells him it's okay to play with rattlers and copperheads, then finally recants. Great. Just effin' great." She ran a hand through her already spiked hair and twisted her lips in an expression of disgust. "I see why he was confused, but why all the change now? He recently loaded up the whole damn family and moved back to Daddy's farm. What's that all about?"

"Maybe he just couldn't afford his house."

"He left his job to go back to farming. I'm checking to see if that was voluntary, or if he was let go."

"Could be the old man needed him."

She snorted. "Calvin and June O'Henry, they're like a Tim Burton version of *The Brady Bunch*. Yours, mine, and ours, and add in the creep factor. Calvin sues Blondell for the wrongful death of Amity and her unborn child." She shook her head in disbelief. "What he thought he could get out of Blondell is anyone's guess, though he did manage to sell his side of the story to one of the tabloids."

"We have a copy of that?" Reed asked.

"Might be in the archives. Anyway, I think he made some money off it, and he kinda basked in the quasi-fame of it all. Even did a round of talk shows. Paraded his kids on one of our local shows. Milked it for all it was worth until no one was interested anymore." She spit her gum into the trash. "A scumbag of the lowest order. Played the victim himself. It was all such crap. And now, hallelujah, we get to talk to him again." Her cell phone rang and she checked the screen. "Not important," she said. "Bart. Since he doesn't have the kids, I'm not taking it." She clicked off and slid the cell into her pocket.

Reed returned his attention to his computer monitor. On the screen were photographs of the original crime scene in the cabin.

"Our job is to build a case against Blondell, or rebuild it, this time without Niall's testimony," he said.

"There's always his sister, Blythe."

"Five years old at the time, twenty years later. Not credible."

"But she's in a wheelchair. A real victim. The judge will connect with her."

"Not solid enough," Reed said.

They both knew Morrisette was grasping at straws, that they'd lost the only credible witness at the scene. Other than Blondell, that is, but she was sticking to her story of the masked intruder.

Reed had learned that from her new attorney, Jada Hill. Nonetheless, he still wanted to interview Blondell face-to-face, get a little insight on what made her tick. Though he was as disappointed as everyone else in the department about Niall's change of testimony, he figured if Blondell was really guilty, as she probably was, then they'd figure out a way to keep her behind bars.

"You know there are already protests," Morrisette said. "I saw it on television. People with placards at the governor's office, demanding Blondell O'Henry stay in prison."

"Caught it on the noon news. But there are still some people who believe she's innocent. They're out there as well."

"A sucker born every minute," she muttered. "If that's true, what the hell happened to the masked stranger who came in, guns blazing? And why would she never name the father of the child she lost? Why act so distant and cold in the ER after a drive that took way too long, long enough for Amity to die? Blondell's guilty. That's all there is to it." When she saw he was about to argue and play devil's advocate, she waved him off. "If Flint Beauregard bribed the kid and somehow coerced him to testify against his mother, that's a problem. But it doesn't change the fact that she tried to kill all her kids in cold blood. All for the attention of a jerk-wad of a boyfriend."

"Who hasn't been located."

"Do you blame him?" she asked. "Roland Camp is no damned prize, sure, but he thought his nightmare was over."

"Guess he was wrong," Reed said.

She reached into her pocket, found a pack of antismoking gum, and popped in a fat, little stick. "So where are we?"

"The lab is working overtime on the blood samples and cigarette butt, anything they can find that might be able to help. They've got Blondell's clothes, which, presumably, still have GSR."

"Gunshot residue she claimed came in the struggle for the gun," Morrisette reminded. "Means nothing."

"We've still got the remains of the snake."

"I sure as hell hope Blondell O'Henry's incarceration doesn't hinge on what's left of a twenty-year-old copperhead."

"I've got Lyons searching for the new addresses of all the players from back then." A junior detective, Denisha Lyons was the latest addition to the unit, smart as a whip, twenty-six, and eager to make her mark. "I've also got a call in to Acencio in Phoenix. He was out of town, but I spoke with the secretary for the Phoenix Detective Unit, and she said he should be back tomorrow."

"Hopefully he can shed some light, since Beauregard's no longer with us," she said, chewing thoughtfully. "I'm thinkin' we're gonna need all the help we can get."

• • •

"I know, Mom. I'm late, I get it. I'm on my way! You and Ariella can figure out the problem with the chairs!" Nikki clicked off and tossed her cell into the passenger seat, then swore a blue streak, hitting the gas.

"Calm down," she told herself, easing off the accelerator a quarter mile later. There was no reason to drive like a madwoman through the city and hit a bicyclist or pedestrian like that ass who'd nearly hit her earlier—all because the color ivory wouldn't go with white.

She shook her head in frustration. She really didn't care about all the silly details that her mother found so important. All she wanted to do was get married in a simple ceremony, which she should have arranged to have done at the local courthouse. If she'd wanted something more romantic, she would have eloped to Fiji, Barbados, or Timbuktu. She could have gotten married anywhere other than her mother's church, and she certainly didn't have to have a reception at her father's stuffy old country club.

She'd pointed all that out for the last time in late August when she'd dropped by to talk about the wedding with her mother and found her sister and niece already at the house, Charlene in the kitchen squeezing the last of the tea out of bags she'd had steeping in the sun. Pressing hard against the bags with a wooden spoon, Charlene watched the dark tea swirl into the already-amber water inside a glass Pyrex pitcher as Nikki had breezed in, armed with all kinds of excuses as to why the wedding needed to be scaled back.

"Hi, Mom," Nikki had said, tossing her purse onto a bench in the entry hall and pressing a kiss into her mother's pale cheek, seeing Lily and Phee already at the table.

"Were your ears burning? We were just talking about you," Charlene said.

"That we were," Lily agreed, grinning that secretive smile Nikki found so irritating.

"Aunt Nikki!" Phee ran toward her aunt to be swung off her feet. Her dark hair was untamed by pink barrettes that were barely visible in her mop of wild curls. Ophelia was six years old, full of questions and irrepressible energy, and Nikki adored her. If she'd ever thought she might not have children of her own, Phee had changed her mind completely. The little girl was definitely the apple of her eye.

Lily had never named Phee's father, preferring to raise her daughter on her own. She loved being anti-establishment, loved butting up against her oh-so-traditional parents. Her hair was nearly long enough that she could sit on it, though she braided it and pinned it in an unruly coil on the nape of her neck.

Lily always looked so perfectly rumpled that Nikki bet she took pains to achieve that slightly unkempt style. In Nikki's biased opinion, it was as time-consuming and self-involved as primping for the prom.

Nikki had played with Phee for a little while, chasing her through the house while her mother poured the tea over sugar and ice in the large glass pitcher her own mother had once used.

"Okay, sweetheart, I've got to talk to Grandma for a while," she said to her niece.

"Why don't you draw something for Aunt Nikki?" Lily had asked, and Phee flew to the table, where crayons and art paper were already waiting.

"A horse!" Phee proclaimed, her dark eyes sparking. Her skin was olive in tone, her eyes a light brown, nearly gold in color, her hair thick and near-black, unlike anyone else in the Gillette family. Obviously the dominant genes in Phee's makeup came from her father, but on that topic Lily had remained mum since the day she'd broken the news to her parents that she was going to have a baby, and that the delivery would be without any husband or known boyfriend waiting in the wings.

Big Ron and Charlene had been scandalized, of course.

Lily, at least outwardly, hadn't given a damn.

When the precious little girl had been born, however, all perceived shame had disappeared into thin air. Of course, there had been questions about the baby's paternity, but Lily had blithely refused to name the baby's father and had kept the secret close to her vest.

After years of prodding, Charlene had finally quit asking questions or speculating or even being ashamed of the circumstances of Phee's conception, because she adored her slightly precocious granddaughter, as did Nikki. No child was more loved, even if there wasn't a strong father figure in Phee's young life.

That day in August when Nikki had driven to her mother's to explain about her feelings on the wedding, Phee had finally wound down and was coloring at the table, Lily standing at the island of their mother's kitchen and rearranging a vase of roses and gardenias while enjoying the argument brewing between Nikki and their mother.

Charlene Gillette's appearance was frail, as it had been for the past five years, but her hands were steady as she had carefully poured them each a glass of sweet tea. "Lemon?"

"None for me. Look, Mom, I just don't want it to be such a big show," Nikki had said. "I think a wedding should be personal, between two people."

"Why even bother?" Lily snagged her glass and stirred it with a long spoon she'd found in a drawer. "It's just a formality, you know. Nothing more than a piece of paper."

"It is not!" Mother had been highly offended, her cheeks coloring, her eyes snapping fire. "I don't know where you get your obscene ideas! Marriage is an institution, a sacrament!"

"If you live under Pope Pius the Fifth in the sixteenth century, maybe," Lily replied lazily. "But come on, Mother, we're not even Catholic, and the last I checked we're in the new millennium."

"Don't get so high and mighty with me." Despite all her health issues, Charlene Gillette still had a lot of spunk. "I'm just saying that a woman needs a man, legally, socially, and morally. Marriage is the answer."

"Not for me. Not legally. Nor socially, and especially not morally," Lily said.

"I've heard all about your marching to a different drum, Lily, but it's not for everyone, dear."

"Nor is marriage."

Their mother had carried her tea into the family area and sat in "her" chair, an apricot-hued, tufted wingback with a tiny ottoman that, separated by a small table, was dwarfed by her deceased husband's recliner. Though Big Ron had been dead for four years, his La-Z-Boy, complete with favorite throw and empty cigar humidor, stood at the ready, as if the judge were expected to burst through the door at any second.

Charlene had eyed Nikki as she'd joined her in the family room. "We've already reserved the country club and spoken with Pastor McNeal. It's too late to back out now," she'd said. "Besides it's expected. You're Judge Ronald Gillette's daughter."

"It's not his wedding," Nikki had pointed out.

"No, you're right," her sister said as she'd reached for her pack of super-long, black cigarettes. "Apparently it's Mother's."

"Oh, Lily, for the love of God, don't smoke in here."

"Dad did."

"He smoked on the veranda," Charlene said tightly.

"Whatever," Lily dismissed. "Watch Phee for a second, will you?" She slid her gaze from her sister to her mother. "I'm going out to the *veranda,*" she said, carrying her cigs and glass of tea.

The memory faded. Nikki had lost the battle over the country club, conceding to her mother's wishes more as a means to keep peace in the family than because it was anything she wanted.

Now she pulled into the long drive of her mother's home and parked behind a white van decorated with images of happy brides painted on its sides. The script over the sliding doors read A TO Z WEDDINGS, ARIELLA ZONDOLA, THE WEDDING PLANNER.

Nikki inwardly groaned. This was so not her. She should have probably tried harder that day in

August, but she hadn't had the heart to destroy Charlene's dream of watching at least one of her children walk down the aisle. Andrew was dead, Lily a lost cause, and who knew when, or if, Keith would even have a girlfriend. Nikki, in her mother's eyes, was her only chance.

Switching off the ignition, she picked up her phone and speed-dialed Reed. He answered on the second ring. "I was wondering if I would hear from you."

"Wondering or dreading?" she teased.

"What's wrong?"

"Care to drop everything and come over to Mom's to discuss chairs and the color of slipcovers with Ariella?"

He groaned audibly. "Is that where you are?"

She glanced at the house, where her mother was just turning on the lamps and gazing out the window. "Uh oh, the jig is up. Mom's seen me." Charlene was standing on the other side of the glass, impatiently waving her inside.

"I think I'll take a pass."

"Chicken."

"You can handle it."

"Why do I feel abandoned?"

"Because I'm bagging out on dinner tonight too."

"Again?" she asked, disappointed.

"But I'll be over later, if I'm still welcome."

"You're never going to be welcome at my place

again and you know it." As he laughed, she caught her reflection in the rearview mirror and saw the twinkle in her eyes.

"You're a tough woman, Nikki Gillette."

"That's why you love me."

"Just one of the many and various reasons."

"I'll expect a list tonight. *When* you come over."

She heard another voice, muffled in the background, as, no doubt, someone at the station needed his attention. "I'll see you later," he said.

"You'd better," she said, but he'd already clicked off.

Her mother was still in the window, hands on her hips, giving Nikki the evil eye, so she tucked her phone into the pocket of her purse and steeled herself for her entry into the lion's den of white linen, ivory lace, and furrowed brows.

Chapter 14

"So that's it?" Charlene eyed the chiffon bows with a dubious eye, and her lips turned down a bit. "No slipcovers? Just this fabric woven and tied through the wooden slats on the backs of the chairs?" Tapping a fingernail on the portfolio, open to a picture of a table set for eight, chairs visible, Nikki's mother obviously wasn't a fan of anything so untraditional as the sleek bows.

"I love the look," Nikki said, daring to speak up. She'd been at her mother's house for nearly two hours and was wired, her nerves jangled from the three cups of coffee she'd drunk as they'd discussed in excruciatingly minute detail every aspect of the reception decor. They'd settled on a beach theme, with shells and candles on off-white linens.

"But I thought you were doing a Christmas theme. Holly sprigs, mistletoe, and white and red roses," Charlene had whispered at one point.

"Reed and I like the beach. The ocean. You know, something fresh. Airy."

Charlene, poring over the array of idea books set upon the table, slid one across for Nikki's perusal. The book was open to a photo of an elegant lobby of white lights, with snowy-looking blossoms tucked into holly wreaths. A heart-shaped ice sculpture held center court in a room bedecked with cedar garlands and tables draped in white. "It's December."

"In Georgia. Mom, people won't be coming here in sleighs."

"I think you're becoming a bride-gorilla," Charlene said tartly.

"The term is bridezilla, Mom, and no, I'm not."

"I *know* the term, Nicole. I was just double-checking to see if you were even paying attention."

"What Nikki's chosen will be really beautiful,"

Ariella cut in, spreading oil on the emotional waters yet again. Slim, with olive skin, dark eyes, and ringlets of dark hair, she'd gone to school with Nikki years before and after college had somehow gravitated to wedding planning. Her business had taken off, and she now had three assistants on the payroll but, because she knew Nikki, was handling this wedding herself. "We can twist a little bit of metallic ribbon in the bows, the same aquamarine shade as the place settings, and the look will be stunning." She found a narrow strip of sea-blue ribbon that shone in the light. "The metal will reflect the light from the candles and the holiday pearl lights, which will not only touch on the ocean theme, but the season as well."

"You're certain?" Charlene said, unconvinced.

"Absolutely." Ariella's confidence was infectious.

"Done deal!" Nikki was already pushing back her chair. "Does that do it?"

Ariella started packing up her portfolios. "For tonight."

"If you say so." Charlene was still frowning as she picked up her now-cold cup of coffee. "I don't think you're taking this seriously, Nicole."

"Mom . . ." Nikki fought back a sigh as she bussed her mother on the cheek. She then grabbed up her coat and purse while Ariella picked up her display books and samples.

"I, uh, heard you saw your uncle the other day."

A shadow passed behind Charlene's eyes. "How is he?"

She thought about his lucid moments and the warning he'd sent her but kept it to herself. "Not so great. But . . . he didn't seem unhappy."

"Well, that's good, at least. Living with Penelope had to have been trying."

"You should visit him," Nikki said. "Either at the retirement center or when Aunty-Pen takes him home."

"Yes, I should," Charlene said without an ounce of conviction.

Nikki knew it would never happen. "I'll call you tomorrow."

"In the afternoon. I have bridge luncheon, you know."

Like clockwork. "Yeah, Mom, I remember."

To Ariella, Nikki said, "Let me help you with these," and she picked up two small baskets of samples, as Ariella's arms were overloaded, and helped her tote her portfolios to her van.

Once they were outside and the door was shut firmly behind them, Nikki said, "She's wrong, you know. Mom thinks I'm not into the wedding or the marriage, at least not enough to suit her standards, but I'm just dealing with it differently."

"I get it." They made their way along the lighted, curved path through the lawn to the drive. "Everyone's different." Ariella clicked the remote, and the lights of the van flashed.

"So you do this for a living, but you aren't married?"

"Haven't found the right guy."

"What do you mean? You're still with Jim, right?"

"Living together, but he's traditional in ways that I'm not. He wants me to take his last name."

"And you don't want to?"

"It's Smith. James Smith. Which is fine. Really. But I'm not giving up my business. A to Z, get it? Ariella Zondola. My initials. Not A to S."

"Can't you keep both?"

With another click of the keyless remote, she opened the van's sliding door, causing the happy brides painted on the side panel to appear to dance out of the way before she placed the baskets and her portfolios inside. "I don't know why, but Jim and I aren't in any hurry. I don't feel my biological clock ticking, at least not yet. Some people, like you, are sure, and thank God for you all or I wouldn't have a job!"

Nikki smiled, not admitting to her own doubts. It wasn't that she didn't love Reed, and she wasn't put off that he was a cop, which would make lots of women think twice. The truth was that marriage was a big step, and the unions in her family had never been all that solid. Not her parents' marriage, despite their facade, nor her aunt and uncle's, with its rumors of infidelity. And going backward, even her grandmother

Ryback had been married more than once. As for her biological clock, it was ticking so loudly it sounded like a time bomb in her head.

"You don't get any pressure from your family, or Jim's, you know, about having a kid or passing on the family name?"

Ariella shook her head. "None I can't handle. I tell them my life is my business and they back off."

Nikki glanced back at the house, where her mother was standing in the front window, the lights of the living room throwing off their warm illumination as Charlene squinted into the darkness at them. "I don't know what it would take to convince my mother to take a step or two back."

"Different strokes for different folks, right?" She hit the button again and the brides on the panel were restored to their normal position.

"Right."

"Looks like tomorrow we get to see her majesty, the queen of all things evil," Morrisette said as she walked into the training room now dedicated to the O'Henry case.

Reed said, "Innocent until proven guilty."

"We did that once. Proved the guilt." She strolled around the long table where Reed was working, her gaze scraping the pictures he'd placed on display on the long bulletin board

226

across one wall. The photos were gruesome, showing the extent of Blythe, Niall, and Blondell's injuries as well as full-body shots of Amity O'Henry lying on a slab in the morgue. Her color was already blue, the gunshot wound visible just under her sternum, tiny puncture wounds from the snake's bite showing just below her hip. "So young," Morrisette said, as if reading Reed's own thoughts. "So senseless."

"I know."

"Here's my problem," she said, "Why the kids? Really? The theory was the same as with that Diane Downs case in Oregon, that she wanted to get rid of them for her new lover, Roland Camp, because he didn't want them. But she had an ex-husband, and obviously Calvin O'Henry and June would have taken them if she really needed to get rid of them."

"Some people don't want something they have, but they don't want to give it to anyone else either, especially not an ex-spouse."

"I know, but attempting to kill your kids? Wounding yourself?" She shook her head. "That's just so unnatural for a mother."

"Maybe she didn't do it."

"You're buying the masked stranger with the serpent tattoo?"

"I'm just saying we're here to find the truth, not manipulate the facts to keep Blondell O'Henry in jail."

"Has the femme fatale of Savannah reached through the prison walls to ensnare you too?"

"Oh, so you found me out. Just don't tell Nikki, okay? It might make for an awkward wedding ceremony."

"Funny, Reed. You're a funny man." She plopped down in a chair. "Okay, convince me."

"I don't know if Blondell's guilty or not, but the motive's weak, as you said."

"Then let's look for another one."

"Yep," he said, and they turned their attention back to the board.

After hours at the computer, checking facts and finding names, addresses, and phone numbers of the people she wanted to interview, Nikki stood and stretched, clambered down the stairs from her loft, and took Mikado outside. The night was cool, but dry, thin clouds scudded across a half moon, which she viewed through the branches of her magnolia tree.

"Hurry up," she told the little dog, who sniffed at every bush and shrub before doing his business and racing her into the house again. The lights of the downstairs units were dim for the night. Charles and Gloria Arbuckle lived on the second floor. Happily childless in their midforties, they were fitness buffs who left early in the morning for their separate jobs, usually met for dinner, which they ate out, and were seldom around on the weekends, as somewhere there were mountains to climb, rivers to kayak, and marathons to run.

Tonight, on the first floor, which was occupied by Dorothy Donnigan and her thirtysomething son, Leon, a flickering bluish light was visible through the drawn shades of Leon's room. Perpetually unemployed despite the college degrees that gave his mother bragging rights, Leon was a loner. A true gamer and marijuana enthusiast, Leon, tall and scrawny-bearded, rarely stepped outside their apartment except to smoke a cigarette and talk softly on his cell phone. Nikki had said "hello" a few times when she'd returned from her run or a trip to the store and received a nod from deep in the hood of his sweatshirt. His apple-cheeked mother was middle-aged and fighting a losing battle with her weight; she was quick with a smile, but her son seemed just the opposite. Nikki supposed Leon took after his never-seen father, who, Dorothy had explained once as Nikki had helped her haul groceries inside her apartment, was "a bit of a do-nothing, if you know what I mean. Not that I would bad-mouth Leon's father, you know." She'd actually looked ashamed at admitting what she thought.

"Maybe you should," Nikki had suggested as she'd set her grocery bag on the counter and seen a pile of dirty dishes in the sink.

"Well, then I'd be just another bitchy ex-wife, wouldn't I?"

"I'm not sure I would worry about it, if I were you."

"Maybe you're right." At that moment Leon, unshaven and wearing his uniform of sweatpants and hooded shirt, had lumbered into the kitchen. Seeming as if in a fog, he'd dropped yet another dirty dish onto the pile, and without a word had walked outside onto the brick veranda, where he'd unceremoniously lit up.

"All he needs is a job," his mother said, her gaze following after him as he closed the door. She'd cranked on the hot water, squirted liquid cleaner into the filling sink, then started putting away her groceries, Nikki had said a quick good-bye and escaped. Outside, she'd skirted Leon who, puffing away while kicking at leaves, already had his phone clamped to his ear, and as she'd hurried up the exterior stairs, she'd felt his assessing gaze follow her every step of the way.

Like father, like son, Nikki had thought at the time, and her opinion hadn't changed in the nearly two years that Dorothy and Leon had been her tenants.

Now she wondered just how long Mrs. Donnigan would take her son's lack of ambition. Not that it was her business or her problem, but time, as they said, was marching on.

With Mikado yipping at her feet, she climbed

the outside stairs to her third-floor retreat and stepped inside. Tonight, the apartment seemed empty. Lonely. She wondered how it would be when she and Reed married. To date, he'd left a shaving kit, a pair of jeans, a couple of shirts, and one suit in her unit, but after the wedding he was planning to move in permanently, and they'd talked about having a child.

Life would be very different, and she figured eventually they might have to take over the rest of the house, or at least the second floor.

A baby. She smiled to herself as Mikado raced into the kitchen and danced at her feet while she, by rote, found him a tiny scrap of a biscuit. In her early twenties she hadn't thought much about children, but then Lily had brought Phee into the world and Nikki had done a quick one-eighty. For the first time, she'd envisioned herself having a child, a cousin for little Phee, and had imagined them playing together. Of course, she'd been with Sean then, and thankfully that relationship had disintegrated. The bad news was that the years since then had rolled quickly by, and now, even if she got pregnant on her wedding night, there would be nearly seven years between the cousins. Quite a gap. But certainly not one that couldn't be bridged.

The little dog barked again, demanding attention or food, probably the latter. "Enough," she said. "Dinner was over hours ago." While Mikado was a frenetic bundle of energy with an insatiable appetite, Jennings, always looking for a place to curl up, could barely be bothered with the mundane task of eating. Tonight's Tuna and Chicken Delight, guaranteed to make any housecat's mouth water, had been left, untouched as usual, and she'd been forced to put the bowl on the counter, out of marauding Mikado's quick eye and sharp nose. Unlike Jennings, Mikado always found the cat's food absolutely enticing.

Her cell phone rang and she pulled it from her pocket. Reed's name and picture appeared on the display and she felt her heart soar.

"Where are you?" she asked.

"Guess."

"Still at the station."

"Yeah, but on my way, in"—he paused, as if checking his watch—"less than an hour."

"Dinner's cold," she told him.

"You cooked?" Disbelief tinged his words.

"In my fashion. Thai takeout."

"Isn't that cheating?"

"Depends upon who's the judge."

"Doesn't matter. I can reheat. You have a microwave."

"My most-used kitchen appliance."

He chuckled. "And I have a confession to make: I had barbecue two hours ago."

"Of course you did." She smiled, leaning a hip against the kitchen counter and stared through her window. "So how's it going?"

"Slowly. Tomorrow I have to run up to States-boro."

"What?" she said, suddenly all ears. "You're interviewing Blondell at Fairfield Prison?"

"I figured that would get your interest."

"You have to take me with you! I've been trying to see her since this story broke."

"You know I can't do that," he said. "It would break all kinds of policies and rules. The reason I'm telling you now is for you to digest it, work it out, and deal with it."

"Because you knew it would be a fight."

"Well . . ." He trailed off. "I'll be home in half an hour, maybe forty-five minutes."

"Fine, I'll see you then."

"I can't be talked out of this, Nik. This is my job." He hung up, but she held onto her phone for a minute longer. This was going to be a problem, but she wasn't going to let it get the better of her. All problems had solutions; she just had to find hers.

Climbing the spiral staircase to her loft, she was working on the list of people she wanted to interview when she heard footsteps on the building's interior stairs and smiled when the familiar click of a lock announced Reed was home.

"I'm up here," she called down the stairs and saved the information on her computer before hurrying down to the living area. Reed had already tossed his keys onto a small table near the front door and hung his jacket on a curved arm of her hall tree. "Beat?" she asked and without invitation threw her arms around his neck.

"Beyond." The dark shadow of his beard, deepening crow's feet near the corners of his eyes, and wrinkled shirt attested to his state of mind. But he kissed her just the same, strong arms wrapping around her, hands flat and warm as they pressed against her back. When he lifted his head, he kept the tip of his nose within a hairbreadth of hers as he gazed down upon her. "What about you?"

"Rarin' to go."

"Must've been all that talk about bows and flowers and menus and seating arrangements."

"Don't remind me." Sliding a glance up at him, she added, "You were right. We should've eloped."

One dark eyebrow lifted. "There's still time, Gillette," he said and made a big show of glancing at his watch. "We could make the border by midnight."

"What border? Canada? Florida? We're not underage or running off to Mexico or Las Vegas or wherever."

"Not after your mother's deposit on the country club ballroom or whatever it is."

"Her idea, not mine," Nikki reminded him, still slightly bugged that Charlene had insisted on paying for the church, pastor, and reception. Nikki had picked up the tab for her dress, bought on sale, Lily's gown as maid of honor, and Phee's frothy frock, as she was slated to be the flower girl. Nikki had argued, but her mother knew her financial state and had waited years to put her stamp on a wedding, so behind her daughter's back, she'd high-handedly put down a substantial and only partially refundable deposit at the country club to secure the wedding date. "It's what your father would have wanted," she'd said after Nikki, horrified, had learned of the deed, a week after the fact.

"I thought we were just looking at the place," Nikki had protested.

"We had to move fast. Snap it up. The Christmas season, it's very popular, weekend dates don't last past June," was Charlene's excuse.

So now here she was, facing a large wedding that had never been her idea. At least, though, she was marrying the love of her life. Standing on her tiptoes, she kissed Reed a little more soundly and felt his hands slide down to cup her buttocks.

"This won't work," he said, around her open mouth.

"What won't?"

"Seducing me into letting you come with me to the prison tomorrow."

"That's not what I'm doing."

He squeezed one of her buttock cheeks. "Then,

by all means, seduce me to your heart's content."

"I will, Detective," she said, sliding a hand beneath his shirt to touch the taut muscles of his abdomen. "You can count on it."

"One," he whispered into the shell of her ear. "Two." Her fingers delved beneath the waistband of his slacks. "Three." She released his zipper and it slid with a slow hiss. "Okay, darlin'. That's it!" He swept her off her feet and carried her unceremoniously to the bedroom, where he fell with her onto the mattress. "One hundred."

Chapter 15

"If she asks, I'll put in a good word for you. That's the best I can do," Reed said, knotting his tie at the full-length mirror and seeing Nikki standing behind him in the reflection. She'd gotten up first, showered, dressed, spent time on her hair and makeup, and now, having gathered her coat and computer case, looked as if she intended to either jump in the car with him or follow him to Fairfield Prison.

"You have to let me come with you," she insisted for the sixth or seventh time.

His gaze found hers in the mirror. "Nikki, don't. Okay? We discussed this."

"But really, I'm sure I could help. She's more likely to open up to me."

"She won't even see you," he said, jerking on the tie and scowling.

"But I knew Amity, I was in their home a couple of times, even met Blondell before."

"Doesn't change anything."

"And I recently talked to Blythe."

He sent her an irritated glance. "I know, and I wish you'd back off. I'm the lead detective, and I can't have my soon-to-be-wife out messing with my witnesses. Don't you see how impossible that is?"

"I'm a reporter and a crime writer. This is what I do."

"Not on my cases," he said sharply. "Go report on the serial murderer who's terrorizing Chicago."

"You want to get rid of me?"

"You know what I mean. I'm not giving up my work, just because we're getting married. Nik, if our relationship is going to work—"

"If," she repeated.

"You can't undermine me—"

"I'm not."

"Or compromise my work in any way, shape, or form."

"Is that what I'm doing?"

"Just let me do my job," he said and stalked to the closet, where he found his sport coat hanging between two of her jackets.

"I need to do mine too, Reed." She looked so earnest and so damned beautiful, with those wild, red-blond curls and that dusting of freckles across her nose, and those green eyes, rounded with sincerity. "Just take me with you. I don't even need to see her."

"You're going to ride all the way up there just to sit in the car?"

Her gaze slid away.

"You want to overhear my conversation with Morrisette."

"No." Her eyebrows drew together. "I just need to be a part of it. I'll sit in the waiting area. Whatever."

"No dice." He slid his arms into his blazer. "Tell ya what. I'll meet you tonight for dinner, and I'll give you my impressions. No dialogue, nothing like that, just how I feel about the case. And I'll tell the warden that if Blondell is going to talk to anyone in the press, which I don't think her attorney will allow, you would be a good candidate."

She rolled her eyes. "Won't help. If Jada Hill knows I'm engaged to you, she won't allow it." She paused. "But I did do a nice piece on her about four, no maybe five years ago."

Jada Hill was a local, born and raised in Savannah. "That might work for you."

"Unlikely."

Reed didn't respond, though he silently agreed.

Jada was the oldest child in a middle-class African-American family. Through hard work and perseverance, she had put herself through school, graduating summa cum laude from Tulane University before attending law school. She'd married, had a child, divorced, and was back in the workforce.

Nikki touched him on the arm as he headed for the bedroom door. "Reed, I need this."

"I said I'd put in a good word with the warden and Blondell's attorney. Other than that, darlin', you're on your own."

"You're insufferable," she muttered.

"It's a curse." He kissed her on the cheek and ignored the storm of emotions gathering in her eyes, because that could be deadly for him. He found her the sexiest when she was on the edge of anger with him, and he didn't even want to think about what kind of psychological implications that might have, so before his thoughts wandered too far down that erotic path, he said, "Dinner tonight?"

"And now you're deflecting."

"Making plans with my bride," he countered, but the narrowing of her eyes told him she wasn't buying his story.

"Fine." She tossed her hair over one shoulder. "But only if you pay."

"Something tells me I will, over and over again."

"You got that right, buddy." She broke into a small smile despite herself.

Grabbing up his briefcase, he patted his pockets to make sure he had his keys and smartphone and headed out the door.

He was to meet Morrisette at the station, talk briefly with Kathy Okano and probably Deacon Beauregard, then drive out to the prison, where he'd finally meet the woman who had become the center of his work life, the topic of gossip around town, every reporter's wet dream, and his fiancée's ultimate fantasy.

He wondered if Blondell would live up to the hype.

All dressed up and nowhere to go, Nikki thought, as she caught her reflection in the mirror. She heard Reed's old Cadillac fire up and purr out of the parking lot and, looking out the window, caught sight of it lumbering down the alley. "Thanks for nothing," she said as she let the blinds fall back into position, then gave herself a quick mental shake.

Of course he wouldn't talk to her about the case, nor take her to a police interview. She'd known that, but she still had to try, didn't she? She wouldn't be the reporter she was if she didn't push the boundaries a bit. The truth of the matter was that she was a little nervous. After being a victim herself, she'd had to fight the urge to shy away from tough, life-threatening situations.

Before the Grave Robber, she'd been brash and bold, and would have done just about anything to get close to a story, no matter how dangerous it might be. Now that wasn't the case. Having been so near to death once before, she was more cautious.

Sometimes too much so.

She'd been working with a psychologist for the past four years, off and on, dealing with her anxiety.

Last night, after making love to Reed, she'd felt wired and energized, while he, exhausted, had fallen asleep. His briefcase had been in the living room, and all she would have had to do was sneak out of bed, pad silently into the living room, and close the door. With him snoring in the bedroom, she could have opened his case and pored over the documents therein or, even better, taken pictures of the most important ones with her smartphone.

But she hadn't.

Because she loved him.

Because he trusted her.

And because, deep down, she figured there would be a more forthright and honest way to get the information without potentially ruining his case, not to mention their relationship. She still had a source at the department, she thought, though in recent years Cliff Siebert, her brother Andrew's friend and coworker, had been reticent about giving her information.

Before that Cliff had often talked to Nikki and given her inside tips. She'd protected his anonymity all the while, pretending she didn't know that he'd been interested in her and maybe, just maybe, had somehow harbored survivor's guilt after Andrew's death. Now, however, her relationship with Cliff was thin and strained, but she knew that if she really pressured him, Cliff might give her the information she needed.

However, she would have to go behind Reed's back to do it, and so far she had resisted that temptation.

Instead of placing a call to Cliff just yet, she sat down and wrote her article on Blythe, then set it aside before she did a final edit. Afterward, she organized her notes, sent out e-mails, checked social media sites, and searched for the people she needed to interview. Of course, Blondell O'Henry was at the top of the list, and she could only hope Reed would grease those skids so she might have a chance to talk to the woman. In the meantime, she listed all the people who knew Blondell best, including the men who could have fathered the baby she'd miscarried. Aside from Blondell's ex-husband, Calvin, Nikki wanted to locate Roland Camp. The same went for Amity. Nikki knew the kids Amity had hung out with in high school, but she wanted to figure out who could have gotten her pregnant.

Then there was Larry Thompson, Blondell's lover, who had helped her escape from prison in the garbage truck. Nikki figured that if Blondell had wanted to admit to something different from the story about the stranger with the tattoo, she might have confided in the one person who had risked his life and freedom to spring her. Thompson was out of prison and had been for more than five years, but with his common name, he'd been able to disappear and was hard to track down, though Nikki figured maybe Reed could get to him. Surely the guy had a parole officer.

Yeah, she'd find him somehow. She was nothing if not dogged, and she'd thought she'd located the right L.C. Thompson in Charlotte, North Carolina, though that guy was no longer a journalist and worked as an auto mechanic. Her phone calls to "L.C." had remained unanswered, but she wasn't about to give up. She figured she could drive up there and track him down.

After spending a couple of hours at her desk, she stood and stretched, contemplated taking another run, and glanced at her watch. Was Reed already talking to Blondell? Would she change her story? Would Jada Hill even allow her infamous client to speak? Damn, but she wished she was there.

Sitting on the window seat of the bay window,

243

she tried not to think about the interview in progress and instead made more notes to herself. Though she'd interviewed Blythe, she still wanted to talk to the rest of Blondell's family, especially Niall and Calvin, her ex. Then there was June Hatchett O'Henry, an odd duck if there ever was one. How did she fit into this? Was it coincidental that her church practiced snake handling and Amity O'Henry had been bitten by a snake before she was shot?

She started writing down questions she'd ask the people most closely associated with Blondell and Amity, and within ten minutes she heard the sound of a car rumbling down the back alley. Nikki looked out over her garden and saw a navy-colored BMW swing into the small parking lot. Seconds later her tenant, Charles Arbuckle, climbed out. Leaving the engine running, he hurried up the outdoor stairs to the second floor.

Nikki circled the name Holt Beauregard on her legal pad and wondered how close Flint's younger son had been to Amity. Why had she never heard of any supposed relationship? At least it would be easy to talk to him, as he was a private investigator in town. It wouldn't be so easy to check out Amity's relationship with Elton, her own cousin, since he'd died a couple of months before Amity, and talking to Aunty-Pen about him would only be pouring salt into the wound. But if that was the way it was, so be it. According to

Blythe, like Holt, he'd been interested in Amity and possibly dated her.

Could either of them have been the father of her unborn child?

Elton had dated Mary-Beth Emmerson, a girl who had gone to school with Nikki. Elton and Mary-Beth had been a couple, on and off, for at least two years before his death.

"They're destined to get married, you know," Hollis had once confided to Nikki after Elton's car had roared out of the driveway of the McBaine home, the tires of his seventies Porsche squealing on the asphalt of the long drive. A yellow streak, the low-slung car's engine had whined loudly as the Porsche disappeared around the hedgerow.

"And why is that?" Nikki asked, staring at the empty lane. Even at fourteen she was just getting into boys and was curious about all aspects of the mysterious male-female relationship.

"Because Mother and Daddy approve, that's why." Hollis had arched a knowing eyebrow as she and Nikki had returned to the house. "The Emmersons belong to the club, and Mary-Beth's dad is a doctor. Pediatrician, I think."

"So what?"

Hollis rolled her eyes upward, as if thinking hard. "So it's a big deal. Mother said it was a good match."

"All because Mary-Beth's dad is a doctor?" Nikki had found that hard to believe.

Hollis lifted an "I'm just telling you" shoulder. "Compared to some of the other girls Elton's been hot for, Mary-Beth looks like royalty, and to Mother, that's important."

"Then Aunty-Pen must be a snob," Nikki had decided.

Hollis laughed, amusement filling her sky blue eyes. "Of course she is, Nikki! Come on, really, aren't we all?"

Maybe she was right, Nikki thought now, as she scribbled down Mary-Beth's name next to Elton's on her legal pad. Jennings trotted into the living area from the bedroom and hopped onto the window seat next to her. Staring out the window, he let out a pitiful cry as he saw birds fluttering through the yard.

"You're okay," she said, stroking his downy head just as a downstairs door slammed, thudding loudly.

The cat scrambled off the seat.

Half a second later, Nikki saw Charles Arbuckle appear again on the staircase. He ran down quickly, then jogged to his idling car; he threw his briefcase onto the passenger seat as he climbed in, then yanked the door shut. Backing out quickly, he barely missed the garbage cans lining the side of the alley before ramming his car into gear and taking off.

"Always in a hurry," she muttered, recalling Arbuckle's intense demeanor as he'd flown out of the house, then thought the same phrase applied to her. She wondered if marriage would exacerbate her compelling need to get things done yesterday or if she would slow down a bit, "enjoy life" and "smell the roses," as her mother always advised. "All those deadlines, Nicole, they're making you a crazy person."

Until now, she'd thought it was just a matter of age, that, in her early thirties, she was merely running at full steam, while her mother embraced the fact that she and all her friends were in the retirement set.

"Nah," she decided now. She'd been born revved up, always in third gear, and that was probably the way she'd die.

As she started to turn from the window, something glinted in the weak sun, something near the bins. She squinted. Probably nothing, she told herself. Maybe an errant piece of trash.

She glanced back at her notes, to Elton's name. His father had become Blondell's attorney. It was all so deeply entwined, she thought, scribbling Uncle Alex's name with an arrow pointing to Blondell and Elton. How well did Alex McBaine know Blondell O'Henry when he took her case? Had they met before? Possibly because of Elton? Was that the connection to the cabin? At the time of Amity's murder, the rumor mill had been churning out theories and speculation about Blondell. Some people had thought that the baby

Blondell had lost had been fathered by Roland Camp, the man who supposedly wanted nothing to do with her existing children. Others believed Calvin O'Henry, Blondell's mercurial ex, still the most likely candidate for the child's baby-daddy. Still others, the crueler bottom-feeders of the gossip chain, had sniggered that Blondell's attorney might be the man.

Nikki's own family, from Charlene to Aunty-Pen, had pooh-poohed that catty theory as the rubbish it was, but now Nikki couldn't help but wonder. She couldn't ask her aunt, because Penelope would either be furious with her for bringing up old, painful nonsense or go glacially silent on the subject.

Either way, Nikki wouldn't get an answer from Penelope McBaine. Nor would Nikki have any more luck with her uncle. With his advancing dementia, there was little chance of getting through to him.

And if she mentioned the rumor to her mother, Charlene might have a stroke, so for now she had to find a back-door way to get the information, something DNA could certainly confirm or deny.

There was a chance the paternity of Blondell's unborn child wouldn't matter in the least, just as naming the father of Amity's unborn child might not make a difference. However, those little facts made for interesting speculation and certainly good reading. She could almost see the ending of a chapter midway through the book where she named one or the other of the heretofore unknown fathers.

She had her work cut out for her, but there was something else, another way to discover further information, if she dared consider it. As Alexander McBaine's favorite niece, she knew where there was a key to his house—and the den that had become his home office before his mental health had started to decline. She might not be able to get info from Reed, but should the right opportunity arise, she could search through the defense team's notes.

Maybe.

If they still existed, and if Jada Hill hadn't gotten her hands on them yet.

Nikki would have to work fast.

Chapter 16

What the hell was Alfred up to this time?

Nola-Mae drove her old Ford Taurus up a final turn on the rocky, once-gravel road that led to their granddaddy's shack, a place her brother had called home ever since returning from that god-awful war where he'd gotten himself all torn up. He'd never been right since, she thought;

then again, maybe he never had been. The war might just be an excuse.

As she rounded the corner and the trees surrounding the lane opened up, she spied Alfred's old pickup where he always parked it. General was lying on his rug on the porch, and a light glowed from within. Or maybe it was just the television.

If that was the case, if Alfred was sitting in his chair watching the latest sporting event, she might just have to kill him. She'd driven twenty-five miles because she couldn't get him to answer his damned phone. To Alfred, the phone was a one-way device. He called when he wanted you, and if not, he didn't bother to answer. However, ever since caller ID had come to this backwoods area and he'd upgraded to be able to see who was phoning, he'd started picking up for her.

But not for the last three days—or was it four? Enough time for her to worry. Her cousin Vera had said she hadn't seen him in town at all. That might not mean much, loner that he was, but still Nola-Mae had decided to make the drive. Even brought him a batch of his favorite bar cookies: blondies that Great-grandma Simms always made for Christmas.

But if he was just holing up, pulling his head into his shell like a damned box turtle, she might just throw the blondies into his stupid flat-screen, the only modern convenience he'd allowed himself.

Climbing out of the car, she slammed the door shut and stalked toward the house as General, baying, bounded over to her and scattered the chickens that were searching for bugs or seeds near their coop. The fence that was supposed to keep them contained was down again, and three hens and a rooster had escaped into the yard.

"Hey, there, buddy," she said and gave the dog a scratch behind his long ears. General was having none of it, running and howling, as if he'd gotten himself into a tussle with a porcupine and come out on the losing end. "I'm comin', I'm comin'," she said and felt the first little premonition of dread. Usually by the time she pulled up, Alfred had climbed out of his chair and was standing at the screen door.

Sure enough, the heavy oak door was wide open, only the screen separating the house from the porch. "Alfred!" she called, carrying the paper plate covered with the cut brownies and wrapped in plastic. "Hey, I've been trying to get hold of you. Did you know the chickens are out again?" She pushed through the door, and General, still putting up a fuss, shot inside. "Alfred?"

The door slapped shut behind her, and she stood in the living area. Yes, the television was on, a game show playing. That was odd in and of itself, but the fact that there was a drink sitting untouched by the chair, watered-down, from the looks of it, as if ice cubes had melted, was damn unnerving. She'd never known her brother to take a nip before six or so, but she supposed that could have changed.

"Alfred, are you here?" She walked past the tiny kitchen and down a short hallway that led to the bath and a single bedroom. Opening both doors, she found no one.

"What the devil?" she said, then saw General at the door, whining, half-jumping to get outside again. "Where is he?" she said, as much to herself as the dog.

Letting General outside, she followed after, and the big dog tore around the corner of the house. "Oh, no," she whispered, and her skin crawled a little.

The dog was heading to the shed, where, beneath the floorboards, Alfred kept his snakes in some kind of bunker. She'd never seen his collection, and they'd never spoken of it, but she'd heard the rumors about Alfred, confirmed by that ever-gossiping Vera, that he bought and sold all kinds of vipers.

Vera had said he kept them belowground, out under his shed, and today it looked like Nola-Mae was going to see for herself. "Alfred," she called loudly as she opened the door to the out-building and stepped inside. "Look, come on up!"

General was barking and going out of his friggin' mind. "Shh! You stop!" she ordered as she couldn't hear a thing. "Alfred!"

The dog held his nose to the trapdoor, which was visible as an old rug had been thrown off it. Alfred had to be in the underground space. "Oh, great." Steeling herself, she yanked hard on the ring that served as a handle, and the door creaked open. As the light from the shed pierced downward into the cavern below, Nola-Mae spied a hand on the bottom rung.

And then the hand began to move, fingers twitching. She started to call her brother's name again when General began growling, and there, on the uppermost rung, so close she could have touched it, was a diamondback rattler, its tail vibrating with a warning rattle.

"For the love of St. Peter!" Heart pounding, Nola jumped back, pulling the dog with one hand, grabbing her phone with the other and dialing 911.

With one eye on the clock, Nikki made several calls, setting up appointments; then, before she left for what would be several hours, she walked Mikado down the exterior stairs. At the landing to the second floor, just as the clouds parted and allowed in a little sunshine, she saw the glint again, a bit of light catching on a piece of metal down by the trash cans. The dog sniffed at the shrubbery, then spied a squirrel in a low-hanging branch of the magnolia tree and began barking uproariously. "Forget him and get at it. Do your business," Nikki said. Meanwhile she let herself through the back gate and walked to the far side of the alley.

Glancing up at the third-floor window, she tried to determine where the offending glint had originated, based on the angle necessary to refract light into her eyes. A fence on the far side of the narrow alley separated the neighbor's yard from the back of Nikki's place, and a tall utility pole rose above the garages and roofs.

"Mikado! Enough!" she said as the squirrel found its way onto a wire running across her yard and deftly skittered over the fence and across the alley to the pole, where posters and signs had collected. The rodent scurried down the pole and past one of the rungs. As she watched it land on the fence and scramble down the far side, she saw a tiny black object wedged between the boards of the "good-neighbor" fence. It was just above her reach, so she stretched, her fingers brushing the cool metal.

It's just a piece of junk, and here you are making a fool of yourself. If anyone looks out the window, Nikki, they'll think you've gone around the bend.

Still, with one hand she balanced herself against the side of a board and extended her other arm upward. She couldn't reach it, but she could bat it down if she was careful and didn't push it through to the other side and onto Mrs. Milliford's garden, which was overrun with bamboo.

One more slap and the object fell onto a clump of weeds near the trash bins. She picked it up and stared at it, her heartbeat accelerating. This wasn't a piece of junk or leftover trash some hot-shot teenager had tucked into the boards of the fence; this little object, she was certain, was a tiny surveillance camera. Holding it in her palm, she let her gaze climb up the walls of her house to stop on the third floor, where her kitchen, bed-room, and living-area windows overlooked her back garden.

Someone was spying on her?

"No way," she whispered, but she could feel the cold prickle of fear as it climbed up her neck. Who would care what she did? Who would try to get a picture of her doing what? Working? Cleaning house? Dancing to an exercise tape? Undressing?

Weirded out, she thought of her enemies.

Norm Metzger didn't like her much at all and had made no bones about it, but she couldn't really see the crime writer at the *Sentinel* caring what she did in her off hours. He wasn't a perv, as least as far as she knew.

Someone else from the *Sentinel*?

Kevin Deeter, the computer tech, the editor's nephew, and the newspaper's resident odd duck? Kevin was a loner whose social skills were just about nil, and who had creeped her out on occasion, but really?

Then there was Effie, who seemed to show up everywhere Nikki did and who'd followed her from the coffee shop. But, again, really? Effie was overzealous, for sure, but this was . . . something else.

But maybe it wasn't someone connected to her work at all. For reasons she didn't want to explore too closely, her mind jumped to Sean, her ex-boyfriend. He was back in town and had called a couple of times but had, she thought, gotten the hint.

Or maybe the camera's aim was off and the target was really the Arbuckles. Her gaze drifted to the second-story unit.

Or . . .

She looked at the first-floor unit where Leon Donnigan resided. Talk about a loner. When he wasn't inside the apartment he shared with his mother, he was outside, walking in the back yard, smoking and talking on his phone.

Nikki had always gotten a weird vibe from him.

But was he a Peeping Tom?

The idea seemed far-fetched, yet someone was definitely watching the building.

Not knowing who was behind all this, she slid the camera into the pocket of her coat. "Sorry, bastard," she said, as if whoever had planted the camera could hear her. "Show's over." Hurriedly, she crossed the alley and walked back through her gate. Whistling to Mikado, she scurried quickly up the exterior stairs.

Inside her apartment, she bolted the door and tried to keep a panic attack at bay. Maybe it was an old camera, left years before, someone having ditched it quickly—if so, what was on it? She gave thought to the idea that it might be aimed at someone else, another apartment, but deep in her heart, she knew better.

Hadn't she sensed that someone had been following her? What about the guy in the park when she'd gone running? And then there was that time when someone had tried to run her down with a sports car—or at the very least scare her. She'd thought it just a lack of judgment, a near miss by a speeding driver, almost an accident.

Now she wasn't so sure.

"Don't let it get to you," she said aloud, wondering if whoever was on the other end of the camera could hear her—a possibility she didn't like. She considered destroying it but immediately reconsidered. She needed to find out who the voyeur was first. But she didn't want the damn thing still functioning, so she located the battery pack, opened it, and removed the power to the little device. "Take that," she said, then glanced around her unit. Surely there were no other bugs or microphones.

Shivering inwardly, she recalled another time

and place, when she had been locked in a tight space, unable to breathe, a tiny microphone recording her terror. Sweat suddenly beaded along her hairline, and she felt her pulse elevate as it always did with her panic attacks. *Don't go there. Everything is fine. Just go about your business.*

Slowly, eyeing her connecting rooms, she took several deep breaths. She couldn't lose it now. She had calls in to Niall O'Henry and Holt Beauregard, along with a few other people Amity had gone to school with or who had known Blondell before she'd been incarcerated.

She just didn't have time to fall apart. At least not yet.

Nobody knew it, but Morrisette had a deep, innate fear. She hated prisons or jails or any kind of lockup, and the thought of spending time behind any kind of bars nearly paralyzed her insides.

As a teenager, she'd been caught with her boyfriend in a house they'd broken into. She'd lived in Bad Luck, Texas, at the time and had been hauled in by the city police. A big bear of a woman whose name she couldn't remember had locked her in a holding cell and warned, "You'd better straighten up, little missy, or you'll find yourself in jail for the rest of your life." She'd left Morrisette alone for seven hours, and the isolation and lack of freedom had done the trick.

From that moment on, Morrisette had taken the big cop's snarled advice and determined she never wanted to hear the sound of a lock turning behind her again; in fact, she planned to be on the other side of the barred door, and so she'd become a cop.

Not that it wasn't a great feeling to lock up some scumbag and throw away the key, but she preferred to fill out the paperwork and send the jerk up the river rather than step inside a penitentiary.

Today the old tightness in her chest was with her as she walked inside Fairfield Women's Prison. She and Reed had waited in the reception area, been escorted to the warden's surprisingly homey office, then, after a quick briefing, had been escorted to a private interrogation room that was a little too much like a prison cell, in Morrisette's opinion. Though it was insulated from the general population and the cages where they were held, it still made Morrisette need to tamp down her case of the willies and wonder why the hell she'd ever given up smoking. Right now, she could use a Camel straight.

The area had cinder-block walls painted a dull green and wasn't much larger than the bedroom in Morrisette's duplex, and it was a lot less cozy, with its jail-cell door, metal table bolted to the floor, and intense artificial light. The concrete floor had been worn smooth, paths nearly visible on it, compliments of thousands of feet that had shuffled in and out of its barred door.

They waited, as they'd planned, with Reed taking a chair at the narrow table so that he could face the prisoner and her attorney, while Morrisette hung back, leaning against the wall, observing the conversation.

She heard footsteps in the outer hallway and looked up just as Blondell appeared, shackled and escorted by an armed guard whose expression suggested she didn't know how to smile. Blondell was the older and by far the prettier of the two. Her auburn hair, strands of silver visible, was long and pulled away from her face; her cheekbones were still high, and above them large, gray eyes still held a child-like innocence, despite the charges that had been brought against her, despite twenty years of lockup.

Along with the prisoner and the guard came, of course, Blondell's new attorney, Jada Hill, who looked like some Hollywood producer's idea of a smart, black woman who had clawed her way to the top. Dressed in a suit that probably cost half a month of Morrisette's take-home pay, Jada Hill was thin and athletic-looking, with a defined jaw, mocha-colored skin, and a badass attitude that radiated from her.

"For the record," Jada said, before the interview even got started, "my client maintains her innocence, as she has for the past twenty years.

Her story hasn't changed." She smiled then, a grin that didn't touch her dark eyes as she introduced herself, snapped open her briefcase, and slid a crisp business card across the table.

"We just want to hear her side of it," Reed said affably, as if hoping to diffuse what promised to be a tense situation. "I wasn't around during the original trial, so I'd like to ask a few questions of my own."

Attorney Hill wasn't about to be smooth-talked. "You've read her testimony and gone over her deposition?"

"Yes." Reed nodded.

"So this is just a formality?" Blondell's attorney clarified.

"I just want to hear it from her own lips, in her own words, as much as she can remember. As I said, I wasn't a detective on the case at the time; in fact, I wasn't even in the state of Georgia."

"You have the records," Hill pointed out again, but Blondell lifted a hand and in her soft-spoken Southern drawl said, "Of course, I'll answer your questions, Detective. What is it you want to know?" She smiled easily, in a manner that was part innocence and part seduction, and Morrisette suddenly realized both were part of her personality. If she'd used her brain, she would have toned down the flirtatious glint in her dove-gray eyes, but she probably didn't even know she was being coy.

"Just so we're clear here," Hill broke in. "I'm filing all the papers necessary to get my client released. I've already put a call in to the governor, and I'm sure that with Niall O'Henry recanting his testimony, and the egregious amount of time Ms. O'Henry has served, she will not only be released but compensated for losing twenty of the best years of her life, as well as her eldest daughter and grandchild, while being stripped of her right to raise her two remaining children."

Reed held up a hand. "Save it for the governor or attorney general or district judge or whoever it is that needs to listen. All I want from your client at this time is to hear her side of the story firsthand." Jada opened her mouth, thought better of it, then closed it tightly.

Turning his gaze directly to the prisoner, he said, "Okay, now that we all know where we stand, let's start with your side of that night, in your own words."

Blondell glanced at her lawyer, who gave a tight nod, then finally spoke. "It's just as I said before. I took the kids out to the cabin for a break, so I could get my mind around what I thought would be the rest of my life. They were all inside, Niall and Blythe in the loft. Amity"— she blinked, cleared her throat, then went on— "was on a sofa bed downstairs in front of the fire. I was on the screened porch, listening to the rain, and I must've dozed off . . . ."

And so the story went, nearly word-for-word what she'd testified to two decades earlier. She woke up, saw the stranger, and struggled with him, noting his tattoo in the semi-dark and so on and so forth.

Reed didn't interrupt—nor, thankfully, did Jada Hill.

Morrisette realized that Blondell, whether speaking the truth or having rehearsed the story so often that now it rolled off her tongue like memorized lyrics, actually believed the tale she spun. In her early fifties, Blondell was still a striking woman. Despite her time in prison, her complexion was clear, her eyes bright, her smile, though fleeting, a little on the naughty side. Her small stature was trim and fit, and if anyone could pull off the unflattering prison garb, it was Blondell O'Henry, who looked fifteen years younger than she was.

Watching her partner's reaction to arguably Savannah's most notorious femme fatale, Morrisette finally understood the woman's allure. To his credit, Reed was professional and respectful, but he listened with an intent, patient ear, a side of him Morrisette had seen very infrequently.

". . . I really don't remember much about the drive to the hospital or, once I got there, what was going on. I had a bullet in my arm, but I didn't feel pain. I was pretty much a zombie.

Traumatized, I guess," Blondell said. "I did talk to the police and the nurses and doctors on staff, but it was almost as if I was in a dream. I mean, I really didn't come out of it for a couple of days and then"—her face crumpled and she swallowed hard—"and then I realized that Amity was gone. She and her baby. And the other kids, Niall and poor little Blythe, had been shot." Squaring her shoulders, she sat a little taller in the chair in the interrogation room. "That's about it," she said.

Reed asked calmly, "Did you fire the gun that killed Amity O'Henry?"

Jada Hill was close to going ballistic, her dark eyes flashing, every muscle near her mouth twisting down. "She just said that she didn't."

Reed didn't back down. "I know what she said. Just clarifying."

Blondell had the audacity to smile, that same knowing, enigmatic smile that had turned so many heads in the past. Was she innocent or a psychopath of the worst order? Morrisette would have bet on the latter as Blondell, her voice cool and clear, her Georgia accent audible, said, "No, Detective Reed. I most certainly did not."

Chapter 17

The O'Henry farm had seen better days, Nikki thought as she turned near a rusted mailbox with no name, only numbers painted on its side. Two signs—NO TRESPASSING and NO HUNTING—had been peppered with buckshot and hung rusting on a fence post at the corner of the property. Winter-bleached wet weeds scraped the undercarriage of her car as she drove down the twin, graveled ruts of a long, straight lane leading to a two-storied farmhouse painted on one side in lemon yellow, while the rest of the structure was a gray hue that had once been white. Peeling paint exposed layers beneath, as well as rough wood; the gutters had sagged and in one place come loose altogether.

Outbuildings were scattered around a large parking area at the end of the lane, and the sheds, barns, and coops looked in worse shape than the farmhouse that dominated the area. A pickup, circa 1969, was rusting near a pile of fence posts that were rotting in the weather; a newer-model truck was parked in an open garage, not far from a faded, red Dodge Dart, car seats visible through the grimy windows. *Darla's car.*

The yard was patchy, and as Nikki pulled into the parking area, a huge black and white dog came bounding off the drooping back porch. He seemed friendly enough, his tongue lolling out of one side of his mouth, his tail wagging wildly as he barked a warning that there was a stranger on the premises.

A screen door banged open, and a tall woman with wild brown bangs and a graying braid that fell to her waist leaned over the porch rail. June Hatchett O'Henry, latest wife of Calvin. She'd aged since the photograph Nikki had seen, but then it had been nearly two decades. "Gunner!" she yelled, sending Nikki a pissy look. To the dog, she said, "You git back here! Right now! Hear me? Right now! Gunner! Come!"

The dog, some kind of border collie mix, was unabashed that he'd somehow disobeyed and eagerly loped back to the porch as if he expected a treat rather than a scolding. Only when he returned to his spot on the porch and June leaned down did he finally let his ears fall and look up as if ashamed.

By this time Nikki was out of her car, bag slung over her shoulder and picking her way up the stones that had been buried in the grass every foot or so in an attempt to create a walk-way.

"Hi," she said brightly as the sky darkened and a flock of Canada geese flew in an undulating

V pattern just above the tops of trees that rimmed the surrounding fields. "Nikki Gillette with the *Savannah Sentinel.*"

"I know who you are." Now that she was finished chastising the overgrown puppy, June—all sharp angles and planes, her face deeply lined, her brown eyes buried in the folds of her eyelids—was irritable. She wore no makeup; the only jewelry visible was a plain gold wedding band on her left hand and a simple gold cross swinging from a chain around her neck. Her clothes were straight out of an earlier era: blue slacks, a cotton print blouse, and a sweater knit from purple yarn that had faded to an uncertain pink. "Niall said you called. Said you wanted to talk about his mother and his change of heart."

Niall hadn't been all that welcoming on the phone, but at least he hadn't hung up on her. "I would. I'd like to speak to all of you."

"About that night. When that bitch killed her daughter and shot her other two kids?" June was bitter. "For the record? I ain't interested. As for Niall, he's out workin' with his father." She nodded toward the outbuildings. "Don't rightly know where."

"Does Niall have his phone on him?" Nikki asked. She'd crossed the lawn and was standing on the lowest step leading to the back porch, from which a retractable clothesline stretched across the yard, though nothing hung from it.

Plastic pots and a few glass terrariums were stacked against the house near a covered porch swing, its cushions covered in plastic. A row of paint cans, one splashed with the yellow of the house, were stacked on the porch floor.

"Now, how would I know that?" June's hands were on her hips, and she looked like one of those women who had spent all of her weary adult life mad at the world. "Well, look at that. You're in luck, now, aren't you?" Her gaze had traveled over Nikki's head to the barn lot; two men were opening a gate from a field where a herd of Black Angus beef cattle was grazing, picking at the winter grass. Blondell's ex was carrying a shovel in one hand, his son Niall hauling a toolbox.

Catching sight of the men, Gunner whined and bounded off the porch to run across the yard, his tail wagging furiously, his white front paws coming off the ground.

"Down!" Calvin ordered sharply. His jaw was set, his fingers clenched over the shovel's dirty handle.

The dog heeded Calvin's sharp voice and was rewarded with a quick pat on the head from the strapping man with a craggy, timeworn face and leathery skin; he wore jeans held up by suspenders and an unbuttoned flannel shirt over a black T-shirt. He squinted at the house and said something to Niall, who, no longer in his suit for the cameras, was wearing camouflage pants and a jacket.

At the quick word from his father, Niall seemed to flinch, then closed the gate behind them while Calvin crossed the wet yard in long, athletic strides. His deep-set eyes were focused on Nikki, and she didn't doubt for a second that he remembered her.

"What the hell are you doin' here?" Calvin demanded, his face set and hard, the fingers gripping his shovel showing white at the knuckles.

She forced a smile she didn't feel. "I called Niall and asked to interview him."

"For that damned paper." Calvin swung his head around, to watch his son struggle with the gate latch.

"That's right. For the *Savannah Sentinel*. I'm doing a series of stories about the attack on him and his sister, as well as Amity's murder, and I hope to write a true-crime book about it."

June gasped, flattening a hand over her chest. "Not on your life!"

"No way," her husband agreed, his scowl deepening. "I already told my story to the press. Years ago. I see no reason to rehash it all again, even if he does." Calvin hooked a thumb at his son as Niall, having finally finished securing the gate, was striding toward them across the uneven grass.

"I told her to come out here," Niall said as he

reached the house. "She already talked to Blythe anyway."

"Your sister talked to her?" Calvin demanded of his son as he hitched his chin in Nikki's direction.

Niall said, "Blythe said that Ms. Gillette offered her an exclusive deal. Promised to keep other journalists off her back."

Nikki cut in, "I couldn't promise *exactly* that," she tried to explain, "but I'll do what I can. If you give me an exclusive—"

"For free?" Calvin's eyes narrowed suspiciously.

"We don't pay for stories at the *Sentinel*."

"So what about this book you're writing?"

"Again, this would just be an interview."

"Well, hellfire, I could find me a ghostwriter and do it myself. Make myself a million or two, what with all the interest Blondell's story's kicked up." June visibly paled and touched the porch pillar for support, though her husband didn't seem to notice as he barreled on. "What the hell would we need you for?"

"Dad," Niall whispered.

"I was Amity's friend," Nikki said once again, hoping her connection to his family might help.

"Then you know she was trouble."

"Troubled," Nikki clarified.

"That what you wanna call it? That girl was a bitch in heat when boys were sniffin' around. Just like her damned mother."

"I don't think—"

"She encouraged it, y'know." He glanced up at the sky and shook his head. "I thought we were over this. Damn it all to hell!" He turned his angry glare on his son. "Why the hell couldn't you leave well enough alone?"

"Dad," Niall said softly.

"That's the end of it. Y'hear me? The end of it!" The muscles of his jaw working as raindrops began to fall, Calvin stared hard at his son. "This is all double-talk and trouble."

"The kind of trouble we don't need," June agreed.

The back door opened, and Nikki spied a short woman holding a two-year-old child peering through the screen door.

"Go back inside, Darla," Calvin ordered, turning on her. "And take them kids with you."

Niall stood up to his father. "Darla, you come on out if you want to." He waved at the porch, and the screen door creaked open. The woman timidly stepped onto the porch. "This is my wife, Darla," he introduced. "Darla, Ms. Gillette from the paper."

As Calvin seethed, Nikki said to Niall's wife, "Call me Nikki."

"How'd'ya do?" Apple-cheeked and round-faced, Darla offered a nervous smile, while the boy in her arms sucked his thumb as if he were afraid it might disappear. With tousled, blond hair and eyes with visible bags beneath them, he stared suspiciously at the group gathered on the lawn. A second child, a boy of about five with a crew cut and freckles, was hiding behind one of Darla's legs until he spied his father on the lawn below.

"Daddy!" he cried and ran down the steps to fling himself into his father's arms.

"Hey, Rock," Niall said.

"This ain't no conversation for the boys," Calvin said, glaring at his son and grandson. "They don't need to be hearin' about what happened to their aunt." He blinked at that moment, and for a second his face softened. "Helluva thing."

"Cal!" June reprimanded. "Your language. The children."

"I don't think they'll be able to avoid the subject of my sister," Niall said, but he glanced worriedly at his wife, and she, taking a cue from her mother-in-law's harsh demeanor, responded, "I'll take them inside." To Nikki, she said, "Nice meetin' you." Motioning to her eldest, Darla opened the screen door again. "Come on, Rocky, you and your little brother need to come inside and read a story."

"Noooo!" Rocky began to wail, then caught his grandfather's harsh glare.

"Don't be arguin', boy. Y'heard yer mama. Now go on. Git!" Calvin was firm.

Niall looked about to say something, then set

his oldest son onto the ground. "Better go inside, Rock. Run along. I'll be right there."

Dragging his feet all the way, Rocky climbed the steps and disappeared into the house. The second the door shut behind them, Calvin turned on his son. "I don't know what you're thinkin'." He was so angry his lips moved over clenched teeth. "It's bad enough that because of you your mama will get out of prison. Is that what you want?" He was nearly spitting. "She killed Amity, you know. Put a bullet in her and then fired at you and your sister. Blythe's still in a wheelchair, and look at you, you can barely speak, your throat all messed up."

"I can't lie anymore, Dad, I don't remember what happened, and Jesus said—"

"Do not be quotin' the Bible to me, son. Do not!" Calvin slammed his shovel into the grass near the steps and said, "I've heard enough." Then as he walked up the stairs, he pointed a gnarled finger at his wife. "This is all yer doin', y'know. The whole God thing and takin' it to extremes."

"Calvin, you believe! You have faith!" June was aghast at her husband's display.

"Sometimes it's sorely tested!"

"Then you need to speak to the reverend."

"I don't need to talk to yer brother. I know what's right and what's wrong, and that murderin' whore out of prison, that's just wrong." He spat a stream of tobacco juice off the porch that arched to the ground near his shovel. "Ain't two ways about it!"

He disappeared into the house, and June was right on his heels. "Calvin! Your boots!" she was yelling as the door slammed behind her.

Pushing his hair out of his eyes, Niall stared at the empty porch. It seemed as if he might be having second thoughts, so Nikki said quickly, "This won't take long, I promise. We can talk in my car, if you like. Just tell me what you remember about that night."

He hesitated. "I don't know if I should."

"We all want the same thing, Niall. And that's the truth."

"I already talked to the police."

"I know."

"My attorney won't like it."

"That's his job."

Frowning, obviously wrestling with his decision, he let out a long sigh. "It's pretty simple. I just don't remember much about that night other than it was dark, and there were gunshots and a lot of screaming."

"Did you see anyone else in the cabin, other than your mother?"

He stared at her long and hard as the sky darkened with a coming storm. "That's just it, the reason I'm doing this. I don't know what I remember, but I do know that I felt pushed into saying my mother shot us."

"Pushed?"

"By the cops. Flint Beauregard. It was like he was on a mission. I had the feeling he would have done anything to see that my mother was convicted, and my testimony was the surest way that would happen."

"What about Leah Hatchett?" Nikki asked, remembering what Blythe had said.

"My stepsister? What about her?"

"She was your nurse."

He lifted a shoulder. "Kinda."

"But later, when you were older, you two were . . . more than friends."

"What! God, no!" His face showed pure disgust, and yet his eyes shadowed a bit. "Who told you that lie? Oh, it was Blythe, of course. That little—!" He cut off the rest of what he was going to say as his right fist curled in anger.

"It wasn't true?"

"Hell, no!" His face had turned red with ire. "That's all I've got to say!"

"But there's got to be more," she said as he started walking toward the house.

"Probably. Sure. Lots more. But not from me." With that he headed up the stairs, his boots thudding on each step.

"Your impression?" Morrisette asked Reed as they drove away from the prison. She was at the wheel again. She liked to be in charge, though not

~cessarily in the interviews. Those she and her partner shared; sometimes he took the lead, and other times she did.

"She's telling the truth, at least the truth as she sees it, but that doesn't mean she didn't do it," he said, eyeing the countryside as they drove along the interstate, through farmland and a few wooded tracts. The sun was fighting a losing battle as storm clouds gathered, the day growing gloomy.

"So a stranger comes in, around six feet, a hundred and eighty to two hundred ten pounds, Caucasian male, probably around thirty. She just described half the male population of the state of Georgia."

Reed drew a breath just as his cell phone rang. Seeing it was a Phoenix number, he said, "Looks like it's Acencio, Flint Beauregard's partner."

Morrisette sent him a pissy look. "I know," she said, but by that time he was already answering and the farmland was giving way to subdivisions and tracts, the city of Savannah rising in the distance.

Reed and Jasper Acencio went through introductions and explanations before they got down to business, while Morrisette slid her sunglasses from her nose and snapped them into a strap on the windshield visor.

"She was the doer all right," Acencio told Reed. "We couldn't find anything to substantiate that someone else besides Blondell and her kids were there. No sightings of a tattooed stranger other than from Blondell. No fingerprints, no footprints, nothing. If there had been tire prints of another vehicle, they'd been destroyed with the storm. A real gully-washer that night. The cabin had been used by others previous to the crime, so we had to sort through the evidence, but there was nothing conclusive to put another person there at the time of Amity O'Henry's homicide. Just the kid's testimony."

"He's saying now that he was coerced into testifying."

"Saw his statement on the news."

"He says Beauregard pushed him into it."

There was the slightest hesitation on Acencio's part, then he said, "I wouldn't go that far."

"But Beauregard did put the pressure on?"

"He buddied up to the kid. Saw him in the hospital and then again after Niall was released. I got the feeling Blondell's boy was a little at sea, confused, a little scared, you know. He'd been through hell, and he had a father who came from a military background. Didn't believe in 'sparing the rod,' I think. Calvin O'Henry wasn't the least bit warm and fuzzy, and that wife of his belonged to some splinter sect."

"There aren't any churches like that in Savannah. We've looked."

"You haven't looked far enough out. Get twenty or thirty miles out of town and things change, some of these weird religions get a toehold. The deal is that the O'Henry kids were raised with an iron fist and a worn family Bible. Hard on Niall, I'd say. On top of his mother going to jail for killing his sister and shooting both him and the little girl, he's got a whacked-out religious nut for a stepmom."

"Difficult."

"An understatement, for sure. And I didn't see any of his grandparents or aunts or uncles stepping up and coming to the kid's rescue, so it's no big surprise that he kinda turned to Beauregard. Flint let him."

Reed felt his jaw clench. "So with a little coaxing, the boy testified."

"Well, yeah. That's what happened. I wasn't completely comfortable with it, but I was the junior."

"He coerce the kid?" Reed asked.

"Bribed him some with candy bars and Cheetos and that kind of junk food, but I wouldn't go so far as to say 'coerce.' The boy was impressionable and yeah, Beauregard used that to his advantage."

Morrisette had turned off the freeway and was heading into the heart of the city, maneuvering around cars quickly, eliciting an angry beep from the driver of a racy little Mazda. "Oh, stuff it, a-hole," she muttered under her breath.

Acencio was saying, "Flint was kind to the kid. He wasn't getting a lot of that at home, so he was . . . malleable, for lack of a better word."

"So Niall's recanting isn't a surprise to you?"

"Frankly, I'm kind of amazed it took this long."

"You never said anything at the time." Reed was having difficulty not coming down hard on the man.

"Look, all I can tell you is that Beauregard really had a hard-on for nailing Blondell O'Henry, and he had a reason for it. The DA was all over him, the press practically rabid, the public outcry so loud it was deafening."

"Sounds like a witch hunt," Reed observed as Morrisette slowed for a traffic light turning from amber to red.

"More like a vendetta."

"Personal?"

"For Beauregard? Who knows? I don't think so. But we all wanted to solve this one. Everyone working the case tried like hell to be professional and just do our jobs, but those poor kids. Jesus. Never seen anything like it." He let out a long breath.

The light changed. They were rolling again.

"We all thought the mother was the doer, but we couldn't prove it, not and make it stick."

"So Niall had to testify that his mother shot him or you had no case," Reed said, caught in his own thoughts, not noticing the familiar sights on Bay Street as it turned from West to East.

"That's about the size of it. Amity was already

dead, and little Blythe really didn't see a whole lot that we could determine. Plus she was only five, hardly a credible witness. But that scared eight-year-old boy, who had to whisper his testimony because of what his own mother had done to him, he was a different story. Flint and the DA knew no jury on earth would let a mother get away with the cold-blooded murder of her child and unborn grandchild if her own injured son put the blame on her."

"You had nothing else?"

"If we had, we would have used it. As it was, we had the son. Niall, he was a nice kid. Shy. Scared. Not some punk. So anyone on the jury would feel for him. Helluva case, y'know. I remember Beauregard saying to me, 'The kid's testimony is gonna take out that whole damned reasonable doubt clause.' "

"Therein lies the problem," Reed pointed out.

"Just so we're clear. Flint Beauregard was a helluva cop. Sometimes a bit . . . enthusiastic, and he occasionally bent the rules, but I trusted my life with him. He was one of the good guys."

Reed wasn't convinced, but having suffered the tarnishing of his own reputation, he wasn't eager to go down that path with Beauregard, even though Flint was dead.

"Well, look, if there's anything else I can do, just call," Acencio said. "But that's about all I know."

"Thanks."

Reed hung up as Morrisette turned the corner and the red bricks of the station house came into view. "Acencio throw any light onto the situation?" she asked, tapping the wheel impatiently, waiting for jaywalkers to hurry across the street.

"Just more about Beauregard's ham-fisted technique."

She lifted a hand and spread her fingers at the pedestrians in a "what gives?" gesture. "In front of the damned police station? They're lucky I don't write them up!"

As if they heard her, the couple hurried to the sidewalk.

"That's right, move your lazy asses," she muttered and pulled into the lot. "So did Acencio know what a jackass Beauregard was?"

"He used the terms 'enthusiastic' and 'a helluva cop.' "

"There it is again, more boys' club shit." After pulling into a parking lot, she rammed the car into park. As she cut the engine, she added, "I'm telling you, Flint Beauregard was a rogue cop who did things his own way."

"The same could be said of you."

"What? I stay within the law." She skewered him with a blistering glare. "And I don't mess with scared kids' heads to make my case." Yanking the keys with one hand, she opened her door with the other. "If you ask me, Beauregard was too lazy to go at Blondell the right way. And now, you and me, bub, we get that little privilege!"

Chapter 18

Nikki parked on a side street three blocks over from her uncle's house, then checked her phone. No return call. No responding text. So far, Reed wasn't answering. She wasn't surprised. Of course, he couldn't tell her anything about his interview with Blondell, but it didn't mean she didn't want to know. Beyond that, Reed had other cases as well and was inundated with work.

She placed another call to the elusive Holt Beauregard, but once again he didn't pick up. She wanted to talk to him, but so far he'd ignored her messages. Well, too damned bad, she was getting just frustrated enough that she intended to show up at his office if he didn't get back to her soon.

Checking the time, she made one more quick call to her aunt's home. When no one had answered by the fourth ring, she hung up before their antiquated answering machine could pick up. Silently praying no one was home, she switched her cell to vibrate only for all incoming calls and texts. Ever since visiting Uncle Alex, she'd been bothered. He'd seemed lucid when he'd warned her away from Blondell and the investi-gation, but then again, he'd gone in and out of reality.

What was the danger he'd spoken of, if there was any?

The only way she knew to figure it out was to go over the defense attorney's case and notes, try to learn what he knew.

Taking only her phone and a jump drive, she locked her car, then walked the three blocks to her uncle's house, the same path she'd taken as a kid when she and Hollis had been sneaking in or out of the house. Overgrown, littered with some bits of trash, the trail wandered between the fence line of the neighboring lots and a green space designated as wetlands years before.

Shade trees canopied overhead, their branches, aside from the live oaks, bare and gnarled, rain beginning to drizzle from the gray sky.

"Lovely," she murmured as she stepped around a small campfire pit where beer cans and ciga-rette butts had been left among the ash and charred bits of wood.

Rain was starting to fall as she slipped noise-lessly through the back gate of the McBaine property. She felt a little bit like a criminal, a trespasser, but she knew that this was the only way to get the information from her uncle's case files.

She'd considered calling her aunt and asking, but knew the answer before she'd dialed the phone. "Absolutely not, Nicole. Your uncle would never allow you or anyone else to violate his client's privacy." Of course, Aunty-Pen had a point, but Nikki didn't care. If there was something in his notes that would help solve the case, all the better.

Rationalizing her way around her aunt's shrubbery, she edged along the greenery flanking the fence, hoping no one would see her. As she sneaked around the perimeter, she thought of Reed and what he was doing. Surely he was out of his interview with Blondell O'Henry by now. She was desperate to talk to him, just to see how his face-to-face had gone.

At the side of the garage, she paused. Then, mentally crossing her fingers, she looked up to the space between the gutter and the eave and spied the extra key Hollis had kept hidden just out of eyesight. She had to stand on a decorative rock to reach it, but by stretching up her hand she was able to retrieve the key.

Of course, there was always the chance her aunt and uncle had installed a security system in the years since they'd lost their children, but Nikki hadn't seen it when she'd stopped by the other day.

She unlocked the door to the garage. Her aunt's older Mercedes was missing from its spot in the garage; the concrete, stained from years of tires and oil leaks, was all that met her eyes.

She skirted past Uncle Alex's pickup and sleek Jaguar, both of which he'd driven until he'd given up his license over the last couple of years. Tucked into a deep bay behind the Jag was a draped vehicle she knew was Elton's old Porsche, a vehicle her aunt hadn't been able to part with. The Porsche wasn't alone, as Aunty-Pen had never wanted to give up anything owned by her children.

Though Nikki really didn't have a lot of time, she lifted the drape and remembered riding in Elton's car and how her own mother had said her cousin was "over-indulged," that giving a sixteen-year-old boy such an iconic and still speedy car was "just asking for trouble." How ironic that he and Hollis had died not in the Porsche but in his father's SUV.

Get on with it. You've got no time to trip down some melancholy memory lane.

She let the cover drop, and feeling as if she were tiptoeing through an automotive cemetery, one haunted by the ghosts of people she'd once known, she headed through the door leading into the utility room, closing it softly behind her. The dryer was still spinning, its digital display indicating there were still thirty-seven minutes on the cycle. So her aunt, or someone else, hadn't been gone long.

Nonetheless, she had to work fast so as not to get caught and have to explain to Aunty-Pen why she'd parked her car three long suburban blocks away and come in through the back gate that she'd used as a child.

She was uneasy walking through the quiet house where the only sounds, other than some metal fastener rhythmically clicking against the dryer's revolving drum, were the hum of the refrigerator in the kitchen and the soft rumble of the furnace as it blew air through the house, causing the drapes to wave gently. The billowing sheers reminded Nikki of ghosts dancing and she had to give herself a quick mental shake to keep her fears at bay.

Getting a grip on her over-active imagination, Nikki made her way to the den, a room near the front of the house that had an entrance from the foyer and another that Uncle Alex had jokingly claimed was his "escape route"—a long hallway, used for storage, that led back to the garage.

A large bay window looked onto the front yard, and its blinds were open, so Nikki decided against lights, but she did snap the blinds shut, just so some nosy neighbor didn't happen to see her going through her uncle's computer files. Aside from the desk, with its massive executive chair, there was a long credenza with pictures of the family spread across it, above which were displayed all his diplomas, including a law degree from the University of Mississippi's School of Law, and a few framed pictures of Uncle Alex with various local politicians.

The file cabinet was locked, but surely he'd converted all his paper documents to digital files, even old cases. His desk computer was turned off, so she sat in the executive-style chair and booted up the hard drive. When was the last time he'd sat on these leather cushions and checked his monitor? Six months earlier? A year? Three? As a teenager, she'd seen him working here often, although at the time it was evening, after-hours work, as he'd had an office downtown.

The computer monitor glowed, program icons beginning to appear on the screen, and there, in the upper-left-hand corner, was a shortcut labeled simply "legal cases."

"Okay, so let's see what we have," she said aloud, her fingers on the keyboard, her nerves strung tight. She clicked on the icon and the screen changed to "Alexander McBaine, Attorney at Law" and then requested a user name and password.

Refusing to be stymied, she tried every combination she could think of, using family dates and names, and knowing it would be impossible. A computer hacker she wasn't.

Think, Nikki, think. It has to be something simple, so he could remember it.

She looked around the desk, in the drawer, searching for any clues. Her uncle had been slowly losing his memory for years, so he would have needed some reminder in order to get into his own files.

Unless he relied on his wife to remind him.

Sweat began to bead over her forehead as she found a set of keys in the desk that opened the long, sweeping credenza situated behind his chair. The second key worked, and she flipped through files, mostly financial reports, health records, bills, receipts, and tax files.

Nothing about his cases, and no hint about his name and password.

It has to be somewhere nearby so he could remember. Somewhere close to the computer.

She closed the credenza and relocked it. All the while she was aware of time ticking by, seconds and minutes wasted; Aunty-Pen could be back at any minute. She looked in the obvious places—in the drawer below the computer, on the underside of the keyboard, on the CPU cabinet—and found nothing.

What to do. She tapped her fingers on the desktop. The code had to be close by . . .

Her gaze landed on his wireless mouse. On a whim, she turned it over and there, taped away from the roller, was a typed scrap of paper.

Bingo!

AGMAAL was written above 8JDOM3.

He'd used his initials and occupation as his user name, no big surprise there: *Alexander Gregory McBaine, Attorney at Law* and the password . . . She didn't really have time to figure it out, so she just entered the information into his computer and waited. Still, as she put in the information and was allowed into his private legal files, she wondered why those numbers and those letters. No one in the family was born in August, the eighth month, nor March, the third.

Of course not, it has something to do with his profession. An address, or some significant date . . . oh, crap. As she waited for the file folder to open, she looked at his wall of awards, to the law degree she'd just read, his Juris Doctor degree. He'd laughed about it with her, she recalled, claimed he was a JD, just like some of Elton's friends, which caused Hollis to roll her eyes and Elton to remind his father that none of the kids he hung out with were juvenile delinquents.

She looked at the degree. The eight and three were split, but he'd graduated from law school in 1983. From Ole Miss, hence the OM. "Got it, Uncle," she said under her breath, though she didn't understand why she was whispering or why her ears were straining; she was certain no one else was in the house.

The documents finally loaded, and she was in.

"Here we go," she murmured, scrolling first the years and then the names. Spying "O'Henry, B." she started to click on it.

Bleeeeeat!

An alarm sounded.

She froze. What the hell had she tripped?

Had her uncle booby-trapped his file and . . .

Bleeeeat!

Her heart nearly stopped.

No, the sound wasn't coming from the computer.

Ears straining, she barely dared breathe. Had her aunt returned and . . . ?

Bleat!

"Oh, for the love of God," she whispered in relief as she realized the alarm was just the dryer's end-of-cycle signal. She'd been inside the house exactly thirty-seven minutes.

Already too long.

Aunty-Pen could arrive home at any moment, and what then? She really could be trapped up here. "No way."

Removing the jump drive from her pocket, she wondered how many laws she was breaking. Probably half a dozen, but she kept at it, downloading all the information pertaining to Blondell O'Henry onto her portable drive. "Come on, come on," she whispered, as time seemed to stretch and . . . Oh, no! The sound of the garage door rolling upward reached her ears.

Oh, Jesus!

Panicked, Nikki stared at the screen. Her file was still loading . . . *sixty-five percent, sixty-eight percent.*

She heard a car pull into the garage.

Damn!

A car's engine purred loudly, the smooth rumble audible through the walls. *Aunty-Pen's Mercedes.*

Eighty-two percent.

"Oh, please."

The engine died.

Ninety-five percent.

Almost . . . almost . . .

A car door slammed shut with a solid thud.

Oh, God!

Ninety-eight percent.

Nikki was sweating now, her palms and fingers damp.

The back door opened and footsteps sounded.

One hundred percent.

On automatic, Nikki pulled the jump drive out of the CPU, crammed it into her pocket, and shut down the computer as footsteps clicked across the hardwood floor of the kitchen and Nikki heard a rustle of paper—grocery bags?—as she climbed out of her uncle's desk chair, slid it into place, and tiptoed to the door of Alexander McBaine's escape route. It was her only way out because the front door was visible through the foyer to the kitchen.

Her throat as dry as sand, she tried the door.

Locked.

Damn!

But she still had the keys she'd found in his desk in her pocket. Maybe . . . *Oh, please!* With fumbling fingers she extracted the ring and put the first key into the lock. *No go!* The metal clinked softly. Another key into the lock. It too wouldn't turn. Surely one of these opened the door. If not . . .

She slid in the third and then the fourth key as the computer's shutdown music played.

Oh, no!

"Hello?" her aunt called from the kitchen.

Nikki, mentally making up excuses for when she had to face her, tried the fifth key just as she heard footsteps against the marble in the foyer.

Click!

The lock sprang.

Quickly, she opened the door and slid through and, as it shut softly, heard, "What the devil? I was *sure* I opened these!"

The blinds. Nikki had forgotten to reopen them. Praying not to catch her aunt's attention, she slowly turned the lock on the inside of the door and tried to ignore the fact that she was in a tight, closed space. Yes, the hallway ran behind her, but she couldn't move yet, couldn't take a chance that her footsteps would be heard, so she had to fight the feeling that, in the darkness, the walls seemed to be closing in on her and she was having trouble getting enough air.

"What's going on here?" Penelope McBaine asked, and Nikki prayed it was a rhetorical question that wasn't aimed at her, hiding as she was, one six-panel door separating her from her aunt.

Holding her breath, Nikki could only imagine that her aunt was eyeing the computer, or feeling the CPU to find out that it was still warm, or turning it on to view the past history, to see what had been accessed and when.

All this cloak-and-dagger stuff was about to become her undoing. Her entire scalp prickled and she could scarcely breathe. She heard her aunt walk around the room, and then heard a door creak open. The closet. Next, of course, Aunty-Pen tried the door to the passageway, and it rattled in front of Nikki but didn't move.

What if Aunty-Pen has her own key?

How would she explain herself?

From the other side of the door, she heard: "For the love of Mike, I could have sworn . . . Now, where is that key?" More footsteps. The creak of a drawer being pulled open. "I *know* I put them in here the last time I used them."

Nikki closed her eyes. Her blood pounded in her brain. The drawer was shut with finality.

"What did Alex do with them?"

Another drawer was opened and slammed shut. It was only a matter of time before she either realized the key ring dangling from Nikki's fingers was missing or found another set somewhere.

At that second, her cell phone vibrated in her pocket, jangling the keys. *Crap!* She jammed her hand deep into the pocket and retrieved the vibrating phone to see that Reed had finally called her back. Too bad. She couldn't talk to him now.

Carefully, Nikki felt around the wall and found the light switch. Wondering if she was making a horrible mistake, she clicked it on and then removed her shoes.

No longer hearing any sounds from the other side of the door, she turned and walked in her stocking feet along the unheated corridor, which ran alongside an interior wall and eventually dumped into the garage. Her uncle's escape route was now, hopefully, hers.

Quickly. Quietly. Running on tiptoes along the plywood floor that ran the length of the house, she reached the far end. Paused. Heart thudding. Listening hard. She heard nothing in the garage. Snapping off the light with one hand, she cautiously opened the door and found herself one step away from Aunty-Pen's Mercedes, its engine still ticking, raindrops running down the windshield and off the hood. Wasting no time, she cut across the cement, skirting the water dripping from the luxury car, hoping she was leaving no footprints. At the main door, she slipped through. But only when she was on the far side of the property, out where she could breathe the fresh, rain-drenched air, did she pause to slip on her shoes and then hurry along the path wedged between the fence line and the foliage.

The day was dark, clouds blocking the sun, rain coming down in a torrent. Nikki glanced back once and saw, in the warm light of the kitchen window, her aunt's silhouette as Penelope peered through the gloom.

For a second Nikki felt a twinge of remorse. What she'd done wasn't right—was downright criminal, actually—as she'd committed a theft. But it was done now, and she realized she should probably feel a whole lot worse than she did.

Get the hell out of here before you get caught. She probably sees you already, so you'd better come up with a damned good story when you meet her again.

Feeling like a traitor, the keys and jump drive in her pockets suddenly weighted down like lead, Nikki let herself out the back gate to run past the campfire as she made her way to her car.

Once behind the wheel and on her way home, she could breathe again, feel a little better. Learning more information on what had led to Amity's death would be worth it. Maybe she could finally help bring justice to her friend by exposing the truth. Maybe she could even assuage her own guilt a little.

"Come to the cabin, okay?" Amity had begged, her words seeming to echo through the interior of Nikki's Honda. ". . . Please. It's a matter of life or death!"

December 12th
Fourth Interview

"If you would just tell me your story, how you remember things," Nikki Gillette begs from her side of the glass window, as if she pleads with me enough, she will finally get through. She's gripping the dirty receiver as if her life depended upon it, her fingers clenched tight, her knuckles showing white in her desperation. "Talk to me. Let me know what really happened. If not to clear your conscience or to vindicate yourself, then, at least for those who died because of you."

"Everyone dies," I say before I can stop myself.

She blinks. Surprised. Her eyes spark with anticipation, as if she thinks she's broken the dam of my silence, and when I don't elaborate, she tries to bait me again. "I know, but this is different. This is murder."

An ugly word. In an ugly place. My skin crawls whenever I let my mind wander down that forbidden path that reminds me I'm not free but locked away. If some had their way, the key to my freedom would be thrown away forever.

"I can help," Nikki is saying, and I want to

believe her—oh, how I would love to give into that soothing balm of trust, to open up and tell her everything, but it won't help. Of course it won't.

"You're accused of awful crimes," she is saying, her eyes wide, her eagerness for the truth palpable, despite the smudged glass and thick walls separating us. "Either you're innocent and should want to clear your name, or you're guilty, and if so, everyone wants to know, I mean *I* want to know the answer to a simple question: Why? Why would you do something so heinous?"

I bristle a little at that and feel my eyes narrow a fraction. Who is *she* to judge me? Who is anyone? Hopefully, I hide my irritation, and my facade must work because she's still blathering on.

"Just help me understand. I know we've had our differences, for years. You never liked me hanging out with your daughter, but . . . please, for your children's sake . . ."

My *children*. Oh, dear God, the innocents in all of this. I blink against a sudden wash of unwanted tears, and Nikki reacts.

"Tell me about them. The children."

As if she doesn't already know.

As if she hasn't lived with the knowledge as long as I have.

As if she hasn't had her own secrets.

"I want your story told," she says, for what? The dozenth time? The hundredth?

I stand, slamming the receiver back in its cradle and motioning to the guard in one quick motion.

"No!" I'm sure she says, but I can no longer hear her or see her as I've turned my back to the window. Oh, I can feel her staring at me through that little pane, but I don't look back. I thought I could do this, I thought I could say something, but I can't, not yet.

I wonder about life and death and God and heaven and hell as I'm walked back to my cell. I believe in God. I do. I have. Even when heaven and hell were used to torment me and coerce me and the fear of God's wrath was the reason I surrendered.

Once alone, I walk to my bed and fall to my knees to pray again. Squeezing my eyes shut as I invoke His name, I hope by everything that is holy that God is still listening.

Chapter 19

"Okay, I'm outta here," Morrisette said as she stopped at Reed's office.

It was after eight. They'd spent the day going over files and evidence and, of course, interviewing Blondell O'Henry and her daughter, Blythe, at her apartment and had tried to determine if talking to anyone else in the case was worthwhile. Tomorrow Reed would go over the testimony he hadn't yet perused, and hopefully the lab would come back with updated reports on the evidence that was being retested. The DNA information would take several weeks, even though they'd asked for a rush job. They also wanted blood-spatter analysis and anything else with trace evidence that could be tested with new equipment and new eyes.

"It could be that she'll be released," Kathy Okano had told them earlier in the day at a short meeting in her office after lunch. "The state could decide that twenty years is enough, one way or the other."

"But not if you have anything to do with it?" Reed had guessed from the side chair near her desk. For once, Morrisette had been seated as well.

"That's right." Okano's jaw was set, her eyes thinning a bit behind the lenses of her glasses as she'd thought. Situated on her desk, her cell phone had started playing some tune and she'd quickly snapped it off, not missing a beat. "I told you, from reading the evidence, I think Blondell is guilty, but"—she'd held up one long finger and looked from him to Morrisette—"on the off chance she is innocent, then, of course, she should be freed immediately and somehow compensated." Okano's lips had pursed thoughtfully. "If that's the case, and she really did not pull the trigger, then we need to find out who did."

"The stranger with the serpent tattoo," Morrisette had said. "Talk about a needle in a haystack!"

"I don't care if it's twenty haystacks. If we have to enlist the help of the public, through the press, then that's what we need to do. Whatever it takes. We have to find the guy and put him away. Once we find him, we've got to have an air-tight case against him, get a conviction, lock him up, and throw away the key."

"If the killer isn't Blondell O'Henry," Reed said.

Okano nodded, her blond bob bouncing. "Goes without saying."

Morrisette outwardly agreed, and only later, as they were out of the ADA's earshot, did she add,

"Sure, why not?" She'd been walking quickly down the hall, her boot heels clicking on the hard floor. "And in our free time, we'll find the Loch Ness Monster, Big Foot, and Amelia Earhart," she'd added to Reed as they'd reached his office. "Isn't it just great that some people think we can work miracles? It's not just Okano. At least not for me. My kids are the worst. The absolute worst. They seem to think I can solve all the problems in the world, or at least in their world. I tell them life's not fair, then work my ass off to try to make things right for them." As Reed opened his mouth, she held up a hand. "I know I've done it to myself. Guilty as charged, but my point is, there are only so many damned miracles I can work in any given day. Like it or not, the assistant DA might just have to stand in line."

She'd taken off again, her footsteps fading down the hallway, and Reed had decided to call it a night himself. He was tired and hungry and probably needed to work off some steam and frustration with a case that seemed to get more complicated rather than less as he tried to put together the pieces of a crime that was committed two decades earlier.

Mentally, he attempted to close up shop as he drove to Nikki's house near Forsyth Park. The rain had stopped, the streets were drying, and the streetlights cast their blue glow over the city. At least traffic was light, though it wasn't usually a problem as Nikki lived close enough to the station that often, if he'd spent the night, he walked to work the following morning.

Tonight he expected Nikki to pounce on him the minute he walked through the door. However, as he let himself into the apartment he was bombarded by a happily yipping Mikado; Nikki didn't appear.

"Nik?" he shouted as he shrugged out of his coat.

"Up here! Down in a minute."

He snagged a couple of bottles of beer from the fridge, opened them, then walked up the curved stairs to her working loft, where he found her at her desk, her fingers flying over the keyboard.

"Deadline?" he asked, then dropped one of the long-necked bottles onto the corner of her desk.

"Ummm. Yeah. Seems like there's this big story, a woman convicted of killing her children twenty years ago is about to be released from prison? You heard about it?" She glanced up, her smile impish as her gaze met his, but her fingers kept moving, the keyboard clicking.

"I might have heard a rumor or two around the station."

"Give me a sec." She turned her attention to the computer monitor again. "I'm just about finished."

"Take your time." He unbuttoned his collar, then sat on the padded cushion of her window seat. It was dark now, but the backyard was visible because of landscaping lights placed strategically in the shrubbery.

She barely looked up, her attention riveted to her computer screen. As she concentrated, her smile fell away and her eyebrows drew together. He figured she might still be pissed at him for not taking her to the women's prison today, but she seemed over that argument, at least for the moment.

As he took his first swallow of beer, he thought about their plans to live together after the wedding. They'd agreed that he'd give up his apartment and move in. It was the sensible solution. He'd put what he'd saved for his own house into their combined finances, and they'd refinance the house together. It sounded good on paper, but there was a part of him that worried, as this was really *her* house, great as it was. He'd use the second bedroom as his home office and study, and ditch everything but his flat-screen, recliner, and desk. Still, he knew it would be better if they found a place together. He'd said as much, and she'd shrugged, saying there was plenty of room in this house, that they could, as their family grew, expand to the lower levels and give up the tenants.

He hadn't fought the idea.

And it was an incredible house, close enough that he could walk to the station house.

For now, they could make it work.

"There!" She looked up from the computer and

gave him a satisfied smile. "Done and submitted. Take that, Norm Metzger." Snagging the beer from the corner of her desk, she joined him on the bench seat, sitting close enough to drape one leg over his. "So are you going to tell me about your day? How'd it go with Blondell?" She took a long swallow from her bottle, and he noticed her throat as she swallowed.

"As well as could be expected."

"She's still claiming her innocence?" she asked, shifting, her leg sliding against his.

"Not just claiming. Shouting it. At least her lawyer is."

"Jada Hill isn't known to be demure."

"Ha."

"Anything new on the case?" She feigned innocence as she lifted the bottle to her lips again, but he saw the eager spark in her green eyes.

He shook his head.

"No surprise there."

"Unfortunately, no surprises anywhere."

"Hmm, too bad." She arched a sexy little eyebrow at him, and her hand touched his shoulder. Warm. Soft. Breaking his concentration. The corners of her lips twitched, and her green eyes darkened a bit.

"Ms. Gillette, are you flirting with me?"

"Never."

He let his free hand fall to her leg. "What is it you want, Nikki?"

"Just you." She whispered the words into his ear.

"Yeah, right," he murmured, but he couldn't deny the heat that was suddenly invading his blood, the hardness that was growing between his legs. "I know you better than that, girl, but you know what?" He plucked the bottle from her hand and set it, along with his, on a small table. "You asked, so you're gonna get."

"Just what I wanted to hear." Wrapping her arms around his neck, she kissed him hard. Lips parting, tongue touching his, she pulled him down to the floor with her and made him lose all doubts about the upcoming marriage.

He knew very well she could be the most frustrating woman on earth, and yet the most fascinating. His fingers, tongue, and lips explored every inch of her, her hands warm and magical against his bare skin. She traced the length of his spine with her fingertips, stopping just short of the split of his buttocks.

"Chicken," he whispered, kissing her, feeling a tingle that spread through his body.

"Not me." Grabbing the flesh of his cheek, she licked his inner ear and he groaned, desire racing through him until his head was pounding, his heart thudding wildly, his lips finding hers before dipping lower to touch the tip of her breast. Already button-hard, her nipple tightened, and as she began to moan, he rolled her over and, holding both breasts in his hands, forced her knees apart and pushed himself into the slick heat of her. She cried out as he began to move, and his mind went blank to anything but the pure carnal feel of her. Sweat. Salt. Drumming heartbeat. Rising pulse. Blood roaring in his ears. And the hardness of his cock straining until it was nearly painful. Faster and faster. Friction and heat. Rapid breathing, crazily rocketing heart.

"Nikki," he whispered hoarsely as he tried to hold back. "I can't—"

She bucked, crying out in a rasp he didn't recognize as he let go, the dam breaking, all his energy expelled in a rush of heat and soul-rocking desire.

Collapsing upon her, he twined his fingers in her wild reddish curls and wondered why it was always this way with her, the need always so crushing, the desire bordering on catastrophic. "You're killing me."

Laughing silently through rapid gasps, she twisted her head to look up at him through a tangled lock. "I'm assuming that's a compliment, Detective." Her cheeks were flushed, her eyes bright, and he knew then why he loved her so much.

He kissed her shoulder. "Yep."

"Okay," she said on a soft sigh, "I guess I'll have to believe you."

He traced a finger along the curve of her neck.

"If you doubt me, I could try to convince you again." Her lips stretched a little wider, showing off her teeth and, between them, a bit of tongue.

"So soon? Hmm. Okay, Detective. I dare you. But you'd better try harder this time. Really hard."

"You're on," he whispered, already feeling his cock start to stiffen. "Oh, honey, you are *so* on."

Chapter 20

"I need to show you something," Nikki said as she padded into the kitchen from the bedroom where they'd taken their lovemaking. She was dressed only in her underwear and Reed's dress shirt, the sleeves rolled up, the tails hanging over her rear end.

"I think you already did."

"Very funny," she called over her shoulder. It was all she could do not to demand to know everything he'd learned from Blondell, to try and convince him to spill the tiniest of details, but she was smart enough to know that wouldn't get her very far. She had to be patient, and Lord knew that wasn't her strong suit.

She also had to be careful not to let him know she'd been snooping around her uncle's house or that she'd made copies of his computer files. Reed would be furious with her, and so, in the hours between taking the files and his return, she'd copied them onto her hard drive and read through as many of them as she could, skimming the text, her heart pounding for fear he would somehow come in and catch her, and jumping every time the phone rang, as she was certain it would be her aunt, who had either seen her or figured out what she'd done.

Thankfully, the only people who'd called were Trina, trying to set up a time they could go out for a drink—she was having boyfriend problems —and Nikki's mother, with a dozen questions about the seating arrangements for the wedding reception.

She found the camera she'd discovered earlier in the day and carried it back to the bedroom.

"What the hell is this?" Reed asked as she dropped it into his open palm.

"I think someone may have been spying on us. I saw something glinting from the window, and there this was, the lens pointed upward at this apartment."

"You're sure?" He was still on the bed, lying naked on the rumpled sheets. The duvet had slid to the floor. As he studied the little spy camera, she hauled the downy coverlet onto the foot of the bed.

She told him the story of retrieving the camera, but left out any mention that she thought she was being followed because it was all just little pieces with no substance. The guy in the park hadn't chased her down. The car that nearly hit her as she stepped from the curb was most likely just another idiot behind the wheel. She'd had no phone hang-ups, seen no one dogging her as she walked through town, detected no headlights boring down upon her as she drove.

Maybe just your paranoia working overtime.

"I don't like this," he said, turning the camera over.

"Me neither."

"I'll have the lab look it over, see what they can find," Reed said and set it on the nightstand before walking to the window and peering into the night. "Good thing you found it or someone would have gotten a show tonight."

"Maybe they've seen others."

"Maybe." He stared outside. "But the angle would be tough. From this window to the top of the fence is what? Twenty feet? You're sure our apartment was the target? From where you said it was mounted, it seems to me it would have been set to view the first or maybe even the second floor." He squinted. "Now if it was higher on that utility pole, then maybe. But I'd bet it was aimed at the Arbuckles or the Donnigans."

"Let's hope."

His glance moved upward, along the utility pole. "You didn't find any others."

"Nothing that I saw."

Raking his fingers through his hair, he said, "I'll look into it."

"Because you don't have anything better to do." She tried to lighten the mood a little as she saw the muscles tightening in his neck and back.

He glanced over his shoulder. She'd found his boxer shorts, which she now tossed to him. He caught them handily as she said, "Talking about putting on a show, better cover up. These days everyone and their dog has a cell phone or pocket camera and could be snapping us as we speak. I don't think you want a picture of yourself in your birthday suit splashed all over the media."

"And here I thought you wanted me to get dressed because the sight of me naked was driving you crazy."

"The ego of men," she said, but she did notice the dimples on his buttocks, little indentations she'd always found fascinating.

"Yeah, you're probably right," he agreed. "I don't need to be dealing with all those women who might see my picture splashed all over the news throwing themselves at me."

"Man, you've got a pretty damned high opinion of yourself, Detective Reed."

"Just tellin' it like it is. But don't worry." He stepped into his shorts and moved away from the window. "There's only one woman for me."

"Lucky me," she said.

"Glad you know it. Now throw on some clothes and I'll buy you dinner."

Glancing at the clock, she said, "It's nearly nine."

"Murphy's serves Irish stew all night."

Her mouth watered at the thought. "Come to think of it, I missed breakfast, and lunch was a cup of yogurt."

"Then we'll get you an extra-large bowl. Get a move on." He'd been picking up his T-shirt and snapped it at her butt.

"Aye, aye, sir!" she mocked. "*You* get a move on."

Twenty minutes and a brisk walk later, they were settled into a booth in their favorite Irish bar near the riverfront. Murphy's, a long-standing fixture in the historic district of Savannah, had a somewhat murky past, a dark history that the current owners exploited. There had been rumors of shanghaied patrons in days long past; a network of tunnels that ran beneath the city added to the notoriety, and some of the drinks on the menu were named after pirates of long ago.

They settled into one of the booths that had been built along the wall opposite the long bar, its tall mirror flanked in stained glass.

Paddle fans swirled from a tin ceiling, and the two-hundred-year-old planks of the floor were worn. A waiter in a long, white apron quickly navigated a gamut of tables in the dining room to take their drink orders and drop off menus and a basket of warm biscuits.

Once the waiter had wended his way through the swinging door to the kitchen on the other side of the bar, Nikki couldn't contain her curiosity any longer. "How did Blondell look?"

"Older."

"And mentally?"

"We *are* off the record here," he said.

She held up two hands in surrender. "Absolutely."

He nodded. "So I might have a deal for you."

"What kind of deal?"

He waited, allowed the waiter to deposit two frosty mugs of ale onto the table. They placed their meal orders as a shout went up from the back of the establishment, where a dart game was in progress.

Once the waiter was gone, they automatically clinked their glass mugs and each took a swallow. "I repeat, 'what kind of deal?' " Nikki asked.

"One where we join forces."

"On the O'Henry case?" She couldn't believe her ears. This was a complete one-eighty from his position earlier.

"Okano wants us to pull out all the stops, so we could use your help. Or if that doesn't work, someone else from the media, I suppose—"

"Whoa, whoa. Slow down. If you're talking to anyone, it has to be me." She'd almost come off the bench on her side of the table.

"I've worked with Lynnetta Ricci at WKAM before."

"Cute," she said. "You've also worked with me. A lot. And you said we might have a deal. Well, I'm in. You know it. This is mine, Reed. Don't even joke with me about it."

His lips twitched as another couple came in and took a table next to theirs. "Figured that's what you'd say," he said and finished his beer just as the waiter arrived with two steaming bowls. "Let's eat and discuss this once we're home again." He glanced pointedly at the two new patrons, twenty-somethings, both in business suits, she in heels, he in wingtips, close enough to overhear their conversation.

Even though Nikki wanted nothing more than to talk more about the case, she turned her attention to the meal, which, as usual, was fabulous. The stew was made with beef and root vegetables simmered in a rich broth flavored with beer and spices. Served piping hot, with a dollop of mashed potatoes spooned on top, Murphy's stew was, in Nikki's opinion, the best in town.

They ate without interruption, and all the while the gears in Nikki's mind were turning rapidly, questions about the case whirling through her brain. She knew the relationship would be symbiotic, and she would have to give as well as get information, but she knew this was a major step toward driving into the heart of the story and finding out what really happened.

"I would still like to interview Blondell," she said to Reed as they were walking home.

"We'll see."

"Is it up to you?" She glanced over at him as they crossed a street where the traffic was slow, headlights and taillights illuminating the cobblestones. All the way back, Nikki thought about the computer files she'd "borrowed" from her Uncle Alex's den. She couldn't mention them to him. She was walking a thin line between the prosecution and the defense, even though she was just a private citizen. In order for justice to prevail, she had to uncover the truth without sabotaging either side.

"Just so we're clear," she said as they reached the back door of the house. "As soon as this is over and Blondell's fate is determined, I can publish the book."

"I don't care what you do once the case is closed," he said.

"But let's just say she's innocent, for the sake of argument, and the real killer isn't located, that would still be okay?"

"Yeah. As long as you don't do anything stupid and break the law, by, let's say . . . going through my files, or using police information that you get your hands on that isn't for the public. Then, I'd say, all bets would be off." He unlocked the door to an area that had once been the foyer and that still opened up to wide, curving interior stairs. Originally there had been several hallways and doors off the main area, but they'd all been sealed with fire barriers, and now the only doors opening off the former foyer were one to a storage area to the right of the stairs and, to the left, the entrance to the Donnigans' apartment. Behind the staircase were French doors that opened to the veranda and the fenced garden area, and beneath the stairs was a locked door that led to a narrow staircase and basement that Nikki never used. It too had a separate entrance and egress windows, so there was a chance the rooms below could be renovated into two more apartments, but so far she hadn't had the time, money, or energy to tackle what promised to be a huge project.

Once inside her apartment, Nikki flipped on a few more lights and picked up a dancing Mikado, letting him lick her face. "Okay, so how are we going to do this?" she asked Reed as she placed the dog on the floor again. She was eager to start the investigation.

"It's pretty simple and one-sided for now," he admitted as he left his wallet and keys on a table near the front door. "Since I know you're going to investigate the hell out of the Blondell case, whether I tell you to or not, you're going to share what you learn with me."

She didn't like where this was going. "And you?"

"I'll give up what I can to you, and you can work with me, not just the public information officer, but you can't report on anything that isn't approved by her. Not until this is over. You're trying to find the truth, as we are, but the difference is the state thinks we've got the murderess behind bars, and we want to keep her there. If she gets out, she can't be retried. You don't really care about that."

"True, but dealing with Abbey Marlow isn't going to be that easy; she's not exactly known for being forthcoming." Nikki conjured up a mental image of the new police department spokesperson, an ex-newswoman with a keen mind, thoughtful demeanor, and flaming red hair. She'd kept all her press conferences on point and brief, a professional to the nth degree. No way would she ever give Nikki an advantage. Unless she was instructed to do just that. "So Abbey will know that I'm on the inside."

"Maybe. Eventually. I'll run it by Okano."

From the studio overhead, Jennings appeared, trotting down the spiral staircase and meowing loudly.

"Sorry," Reed said, but it didn't sound at all like he was. "Those are the rules."

"I don't do well with rules."

"I know." He walked to the window, peered out, then shut the blinds. "But take the deal or leave it."

"You know you can be infuriating, don't you?"

"Good thing you *never* are. Right now, I'm calling all the witnesses at the original trial to see if they remember anything they didn't testify to. I've spoken to Niall and Blythe, the victims, as, I gather, you have."

"And Blondell," she reminded him as she found Mikado's leash. "You know, I haven't had that privilege yet."

"I haven't forgotten. But next up for me: Roland Camp and Calvin O'Henry."

She nodded. "And I plan to check with the men in Amity's life. Someone got her pregnant."

Mikado barked impatiently near the outside door, and Reed said, "Give me that," indicating the leash. "I'll take him." As he scrounged for a plastic bag in the junk drawer tucked under the eating bar separating the kitchen from the living area, he added, "You knew her better than anyone other than her family. Who do you think was the father of her child?"

"I don't know," Nikki admitted, "but I intend to find out." What she didn't add was that the first person on her list was Holt Beauregard. There was no reason to let Reed know that she suspected the lead detective's son of being involved, not until she knew a little more, so for the first time since she'd heard the news that Blondell O'Henry might be released, Nikki changed the subject.

"Here we go, boy." Reed snapped Mikado's retractable leash onto his collar.

"We have some other really important things to talk over, too," she said.

"Such as?"

"Seating arrangements for the reception. Mom wants to know if you want your family to sit together or mix them up with some of your cop friends."

"Seriously." He rubbed his jaw, fingers scraping against his beard while shaking his head. "I really don't give a rip about this, you know, but to think of Morrisette seated next to Luke kind of makes my blood run cold."

Nikki smiled. She tried to picture Reed's younger brother at the wedding ceremony and reception and failed. "My mother thinks who sits next to whom is damned near earth-shattering."

Lifting a shoulder, he said, "Then sure, toss them together. Could be interesting."

"Interesting," she repeated.

"Not good. Not bad. Just interesting," he said as he held the door and they headed outside with Mikado together.

Chapter 21

Nikki was tired of drawing blanks when it came to the investigation. Two days after she and Reed had come to an agreement that she could be a part of it, she'd still made little progress, and she hadn't seen enough of him to even compare notes.

While working at home, she had reached Leah Hatchett on the phone, and the woman had been in the same major state of denial as her step-brother. "I liked Niall; of course I did," Leah admitted. "I guess maybe we flirted a little, but that was it. Innocent kid stuff. He was too young for me, for one thing, but the worst of it was he was part of the family. It didn't matter that we weren't blood-related; he was still part of it. All I wanted was out. I couldn't wait to turn eighteen and walk out the door." Barely pausing to take a breath, she asked, "Have you met my mother? Mommy Fearest? That's what I called her behind her back. So did Cain, but he's a wuss and always kind of sucked up to her.

"Not me, and I caught my share of hell for it. So I want nothing more to do with them. And as for getting involved with Niall, there was just no way. I wouldn't have done anything that would keep me close to June. The only reason I see her at all is out of some warped sense of family duty."

"But Cain's different?" Nikki had asked.

"My brother's a piece of work. Spent his life wanting to please Mom and Dad, then having to deal with Calvin and that whole male, 'I'm the boss' thing.' Calvin thought he could come in and take Dad's place. Fat chance."

"Your father died in a boating accident."

"Yeah." A snort of disdain. "That's the irony of it. He died trying to save June. The summer before she hooked up with Calvin and got pregnant with Emma-Kate . . . oh, God, you've got me talking about it, and I don't want to think about my whacked-out family ever again. Impossible, I know, with all the crap that's coming down right now, but I don't have anything more to say. Good-bye."

Nikki hadn't had much better luck with Mary-Beth Emmerson Galloway, the girl Elton had dated forever. On the same day that she'd connected with Leah, she'd called Mary-Beth, who had answered, then grown almost silent when she'd realized she was talking to Nikki. "I don't want to talk about Elton," she said coldly, as if Nikki were a stranger she'd never met before. "That part of my life is over and has been for a long time. I've been married to Rupert for thirteen years, and that's that."

Rupert Galloway had been one of Elton's

friends, and the way Nikki remembered it, Mary-Beth hadn't wasted any time grieving for the boy she'd once been certain she was going to marry. Nevertheless, Nikki had plunged on, "I'm trying to tell Amity O'Henry's story."

"Why?" Mary-Beth's voice had all the warmth of an arctic night. "Oh, for your writing? Fine. Go ahead," she said disdainfully, "but leave my name out of it. I didn't know Amity, and I didn't want to know her." She hung up with finality, and when Nikki tried to call back, there was no answer.

Frustrating, that's what it was. And it didn't help that so far all the information she'd found on Uncle Alex's computer hadn't given her any more insight into Blondell's guilt or innocence.

Now Nikki was seated at her desk, about to call it a day, her stomach a little sour from too much coffee. She dialed Holt Beauregard one more time and was shocked when he actually answered.

"Ms. Gillette," he said before she could introduce herself. He didn't sound happy. "I got your messages and see that you've called six times in about as many days. What is it you think I can do for you?"

"I want to talk to you about Amity O'Henry," she said without any prelude. After spending the past forty-eight hours reading testimony, watching pieces of the original trial on her laptop, and chasing down leads that proved futile, she wasn't going to waste any time on subtleties. "I know that you were seeing her before she died."

"Oh, Jesus." He hesitated, and Nikki waited, holding her breath. "How did you find out?" he demanded.

Well, at least he wasn't denying it. That was a start. "I was a good friend of hers." Nikki saw no reason to tell him that she'd learned the information from a woman who'd been five at the time.

"She told you?"

"Some of it." This is where it got tricky; she didn't want to outright lie. "I was hoping you would fill in the blanks."

"Have you told your boyfriend or fiancé or whatever the hell Detective Reed is to you?"

"Of course not. I'm doing a series of articles for the *Sentinel* on—"

"I know what you're doing," he cut in angrily. "I can't tell you anything that would be of interest."

"Let me be the judge of that."

"I don't think so."

"Does your brother know that you were seeing Amity?"

"Deacon? Hell no! I don't know what happened to Amity, and I don't see that I could be of any help whatsoever."

"Your father was the arresting officer," she reminded him.

"You can't make something out of that. Oh, for the love of—"

She knew what he was thinking. That she'd print half-truths about him or tell the police or both. Though she had no intention of doing any such thing, she let him run with the idea; perhaps his own fears would spur him into an interview.

"Look, Mr. Beauregard, I'm just looking for the truth."

"No, Ms. Gillette," he said tautly. "You're looking for a story." He let out a long sigh, and she could envision him shoving his fingers through his hair in frustration. "Fine. Let's meet."

"When and where?"

"Nowhere too public. How about Salty's, tomorrow night, around seven? You know where it is?"

"Absolutely. I'll see you there," she said and felt a sense of elation mixed with trepidation. Salty's was located in an alley, one block off the waterfront, and was a real dive. But so be it. She didn't blame Holt for wanting to keep their meeting under the radar, considering his family ties to the case. She just wondered what it was he was so afraid of.

She remembered him at the trial, where, as Judge Gillette's daughter, she'd been able to get into the courtroom and watch the proceedings. Holt and Deacon had both been there too. Deacon was intent and interested, his face chiseled even then, revealing the man he would become. Holt, blonder and more boyish, had seemed uncomfortable, as if he'd rather be anywhere else in the world than in the audience of the Blondell O'Henry trial. He was the wilder of Flint's two sons, but in the courtroom, any hint of his rebellious swagger had disappeared, and she'd thought she'd seen him more than once rubbing a worry stone between his finger and thumb during some of the testimony. She'd caught his eye, and when their gazes had locked, a dozen questions had leapt to her mind, only to disappear when he'd quickly looked away.

Of course, she hadn't known then that he'd been seeing Amity before her death, that his interest in the case, like hers, had been personal. Now she understood why he might have been so worried.

"Good news?" Trina asked as she dropped a can of diet Coke onto the corner of Nikki's desk.

"Maybe." Nikki opened the can and took a long swallow. "How could you tell?"

"Oh, I don't know. Maybe it was the 'cat who just swallowed the family's favorite canary' smile that you can't quite hide." She opened a second can for herself. "I heard you stole Norm Metzger's story while he was home sick, poor thing."

"Untrue. Fink handed it to me."

"I'm just reporting the gossip floating around the office," she said with a lift of an already-arched eyebrow. A tall and willowy black woman, Trina had been a model just out of high school, then had sent herself to college and, eventually, after a couple of years in Los Angeles, had landed back in Savannah, where she'd been born and raised. "We good for that drink you owe me?" she asked.

Nikki glanced at the clock and saw it was nearly four. "Sure," she said automatically. "At Catfish Jake's?" A cozy bar with an open mic and hot New Orleans Cajun cuisine located about midway between Nikki's place and Trina's apartment, Catfish Jake's was their favorite meeting place.

"Perfect. But I'll have to miss happy hour. Antoine's leaving town, and I want to stop by the apartment to say good-bye. How about six-thirty or seven?"

"That works." Nikki had a few errands to run as well.

"You're on for the cosmos, er, no, I think I'll have a mint julep. Or maybe a mojito?"

"Tell ya what, I won't order until you arrive," Nikki promised as Trina headed out of the building.

"Good. See you there," she said and belatedly realized that Effie Savoy, who'd been walking back from the break room, had been within earshot. Effie's gaze held Nikki's for a second, and once again she reminded Nikki of someone. Who? she asked herself, but again couldn't place it. Well, she would remember in time.

So far she'd found nothing in her uncle's files that surprised her, no hidden evidence that hadn't come out in the trial and certainly nothing that would be dangerous to her, but what she had noticed about the computer notes was that they were neat and concise, nothing abstract included, no theories or suppositions. It was almost as if these notes had been compiled after the trial, that the pertinent information was elsewhere, maybe elsewhere on the computer's hard drive, or even more likely, given her uncle's old-school ways, written down in some form and stored in a filing cabinet or box or crate, locked away somewhere.

She hated to think she'd done all that skulking around and thievery for nothing, nearly giving herself a heart attack when Aunty-Pen had returned, but so it seemed.

That was the trouble—she felt as if she were spinning her wheels. And all of Reed's talk about working together hadn't added up to much.

Somehow, she had to ram this investigation into high gear, and that would start, she was certain, with Blondell. She *had* to get an interview with her.

After putting the finishing touches on the next article in her series about the mystery surrounding Amity O'Henry's death, Nikki swallowed the last of her soda, grabbed her jacket, purse, and computer case, and headed outside, where dark clouds, their bellies swollen with rain, were scudding across the sky. The air was thick, heavy with the scent of the river and the coming rain.

Flipping up the hood of her jacket, Nikki walked to the parking lot, where a few cars remained, including Norm Metzger's Chevy Tahoe. Norm himself was in the idling SUV, talking on his cell phone.

Spying Nikki, he threw open the driver's door and said into the phone, "Call you back in a few," before clicking off. After hauling his bulk out of the car, he stalked across the parking lot to Nikki's car. "What the hell do you think you're doing?" he snarled, his cheeks reddening above the graying goatee he always kept clipped and neat.

"I don't know what you mean, Norm."

"Yes, you do!" he roared and hitched up his pants. "The O'Henry story should be mine. I'm the crime writer here!" He jerked an angry thumb at his chest.

"You were sick and—"

"And so you swooped in and took it. Just like you've been doing from the minute Fink hired you. Jesus Christ, Gillette, isn't it enough that you can work part-time at the paper and write your books? Do you have to steal my job too?"

Her back was up. "When I started with this paper, I made it very clear I wanted to concentrate on crime. Hell, I was raised on it, with my father being a judge and all."

"Big Ron has nothing to do with this," he said, grabbing at the air in frustration. "I'm talking about my job, the one that supports my family.

You know, Della and my kids? The oldest are already looking at colleges. Do you know how much that costs?"

Nikki clamped her lips closed. Better to say nothing than have his argument escalate.

"Probably not. The judge probably paid your way. Shit!" He glared across the parking lot, his eyes following traffic on the street, but she doubted he saw any of it as he tried to compose himself. A little more in control, he said, "What happened to you quitting and taking a job somewhere else? I heard that's what you planned after the Grave Robber case blew up in your face."

"I decided to stay. My family's here," she clipped out.

"Well, so is mine, but it looks like I'm gonna have to move."

"What?"

"For the love of God, don't look so shocked! You know how it is with the newspaper business. Everything's gone digital and online, papers are closing all over the country, and the *Sentinel* is hanging on by a thread. We've lost advertisers, and the paper's half the size it was ten years ago."

"Yes, but—"

"I've been put on part-time, Gillette. Kind of like you. Only I don't have a big book deal in the wings to fall back on. And I haven't been assigned to the O'Henry case, just the biggest crime story to hit this town in years."

"But there are other news stories," she protested.

"An assault on the waterfront? A break-in out on Victory? Maybe a domestic violence call somewhere in the suburbs? Sure. Those stories are out there, but come on, *the* story to rock this town, the one that will sell papers? It's yours."

"I won't lie," she admitted. "I want this one."

"So you can write a damned book about it. You know what that means? I'll tell you! It means Della and I are probably packing up the kids and moving to Atlanta or Jacksonville. Luckily, I've got a couple of leads on jobs there. It would be reporting on their Web sites, not the actual paper, though, but I can't even do that here. Effie Savoy's already tied up that job."

"I'm sorry about your position," she said. "I didn't know."

"Yeah, well. 'Them's the breaks,' eh? I've even enrolled in a couple of computer classes to get me up to speed so that I can compete with twenty-two-year-old kids who have been using computers since they were teething." His eyes narrowed as the first drops of rain began to fall. "How do you think that'll go? And I'm looking the big five-oh in the eye. But you, with your whole damned life ahead of you, planning a big wedding and writing books and picking the plum stories for the *Sentinel*—for you, life isn't quite so tough." He shook his head in disgust. "Why the hell do I bother?" he muttered, then stormed back to his SUV, threw himself behind the wheel and drove off, his tires squealing as he punched the gas.

Nikki stood for a minute, rain now peppering down as she watched him leave. He wasn't wrong. Everything he'd said, including the ugly part about her ambitions trumping his need to make a living, was true. As she walked to her car she couldn't help but feel bad. The guy was older than she was, fifty pounds overweight, and a smoker, all of which didn't mean diddly, but he was raising five kids and was caught, like so many people, in the economic changes affecting their industry. Should she hand him over the story?

No. The O'Henry story was one symptom of a larger problem: that Norm had let himself become a dinosaur. His downward spiral didn't have anything to do with her personally. He would have to fight back any other ambitious reporter who wanted to take over the crime beat, as would she. Norm had been part of the "good ole boy" network for years, and now she was making him work a little harder. That's the way it was in this cutthroat business.

Still, her already sour stomach ached a little more as she drove out of town by rote, turning on the wipers, stopping for red lights and pedestrians, making the proper turns without really thinking about it.

Metzger was on her mind, true, as was all the other information she'd gathered in the past few days on the O'Henry case. She thought about her uncle's files, wishing she knew where the rest of the information was. Typed up on hard copy or stored somewhere else, she believed.

Her mind wandered to Amity O'Henry, and she made a sudden decision: she would go to the cabin herself and take a look around. If she couldn't find any hard facts, she would at least get a feel, a mood for her book.

Acting on her new plan, Nikki drove past the city's storefronts and subdivisions into lush countryside and rolling fields. Storm clouds rolled across the thick grass where horses and cattle grazed. A frisson slid down her spine, and she glanced in her rearview mirror. Cars were following her, of course, but at a distance, and she doubted any of the drivers were tracking her. She was just being spooked by thoughts of the cabin.

With an effort, she turned back to her thoughts. She hadn't had any luck connecting with Roland Camp, and when she'd tried for another, more personal interview with Calvin O'Henry, June had said flatly, "Leave us alone."

She hadn't added a threat. No "or else" tagged to the end of the edict, but Nikki had gotten the feeling that it was implied. She'd done some research on Calvin's second family and found that all the children from their previous marriages had abandoned the couple. Just lately, Niall seemed to be reunited with his father, but Blythe was estranged from June and Calvin, and as for June's children, Leah Hatchett was married and living in Augusta, more than two hours away, and seemed to keep her distance. Cain Hatchett remained closer and resided in a small town to the east. A logger who drove monster trucks, he too had his own life, separate from June's. As for Emma-Kate, the child Calvin and June had brought into this world, she was living on her own, downtown, but Nikki hadn't bothered with her yet as she hadn't even been born when her oldest half-sister was killed.

Her phone rang, and she attached the headset for her Bluetooth device into her ear. "Hello?"

"Is this a good time to talk?" Ina's raspy voice came in clear as a bell.

"Good as any."

"I spoke with Remmie. She read your synopsis and flipped over the idea. She's taking it to the editorial meeting, and I'm sure they'll accept it, but here's the deal: Knox is going to want a fast delivery on this, and they want it unique, you know, like the first two books. The more insight into the Amity character, the better."

"She was my friend. Not a character in a novel."

"I know, but you get what I mean, right? Let's

tell the story through her eyes, if possible, and then after she's killed, it can be a little more clinical, less personal, except—and here's the kicker—Remmie would like the telling of the murder to come from Blondell's viewpoint. In the end, since this is true crime and not fiction, you can go more into the police work, and anything from your fiancé's perspective would be great."

"I'm not sure I can deliver on all that," Nikki said, a little uncomfortable.

"Well, just keep on it, and push that personal connection. I'll keep you posted on what Remmie says."

She hung up, and Nikki was left feeling as if she were treading on Amity O'Henry's grave, trying to sensationalize and make a buck out of a tragedy, rather than present a true account of her friend's life and death.

Her thoughts plaguing her, she yanked off the headset and tossed it onto the seat.

Between Norm Metzger's rant and Ina's scheme for the book, she felt a little bruised. *This is just the business. You know it. You didn't steal Metzger's job, and you surely didn't have a hand in Amity's death. And don't even think about the phone call she made to you. So what? Do you really think you could have stopped a killer's bullet?*

She closed her mind to all the arguments

waging in her head and paid attention to the road. Traffic was light, the road slick with rain, drops pouring from the sky. Turning up the speed of her windshield wipers, she achieved a clearer view of the surrounding farmland as it gave way to woods, pine and oak trees growing along either side of the road. Another two miles and the lake would come into view. Very soon she would be at the spot where Amity O'Henry had lost her life.

Chapter 22

"I haven't seen him in what? Five? Maybe six days. Let's just call it a week," the woman on the other side of the rusty screen door said. Rain was pounding on the sagging roof of the porch that fronted the small bungalow, the last known address of Roland Camp, who until a week ago had worked the night shift at a mini-mart and gas station just west of town. According to the manager, Roland had called in sick and hadn't returned. He'd given Morrisette and Reed the number of Camp's cell, but so far no message had been returned.

So they had decided to pay Camp a visit. They'd been blocked at the door by a short, skinny woman with a ragged mop of brown hair that kept falling into her eyes—Peggy Shanks, the latest in a string of Roland Camp's girlfriends—and she wasn't giving the detectives the time of day. Balancing a baby of about eighteen months on one hip, she stared through the door at Morrisette and Reed as if they were planning to rob her rather than ask questions of her boyfriend. "Roland, he does this sometimes," she explained. "Just goes and does who knows what? Hunts sometimes. Goes and finds a poker game. Whatever."

Morrisette wondered how much BS they were being peddled. A couple of tons, she'd bet. Peggy tried to act cool, as if nothing bothered her, but she had a nervous tic near the corner of one eye, and it looked as if she hadn't slept in about a month. The kid on her hip had a nose that kept running, no matter how many times Peggy swiped at his little red nostrils with a tissue. He made a face and turned away with each pass, and so the button of a nose remained wet.

"Did Roland disappear before or after Blondell O'Henry's son recanted his testimony?" Reed asked.

"Beats me, but he *didn't* disappear, okay? He'll be back. I told you, this isn't the first time, and I don't know when exactly it was he took off."

"This is his place of residence, though. He lives here. Most of the time," Morrisette said.

Peggy's gaze sharpened a bit, as if she thought Morrisette had thrown her a trick question. "Yeah, but it's not a big deal that he took off for a few days. It's not like we're married."

"Probably a good thing if he up and leaves whenever he wants."

Reed slid her a look as Peggy protested, "It's not like that."

"You just said you had kind of a no-strings-attached relationship." Morrisette looked pointedly through the ragged screen at the little boy, who was starting to fiddle with his mother's hair. "Is Roland his father?"

"What's it to you?"

"Seems like you have a pretty tight connection even if you aren't married."

"As if it's any of your damned business. Look, I'm busy. I told you Roland ain't here, and if he shows up, I'll tell him you called," Peggy said with a superior tone that irked the hell out of Morrisette. "But for the record, he ain't a real big fan of the cops."

"I'll bet." Morrisette didn't even bother with a fake smile.

"Have him call," Reed suggested, sliding his card through a tear in the screen.

Peggy snatched the card from his fingers.

Checking his watch, he said to Morrisette, "Let's roll. We're late as it is."

As they stepped off the porch and into the driving rain, Morrisette said, "Where are we going in such an all-fired hurry?"

"Nowhere. Coffee maybe. And then a circle back."

"A stakeout?" she asked, brightening.

"He probably never left town," Reed observed.

"I like the way you think." They climbed into her car, and she glanced back. "Look at that," she said as a curtain moved in the window of the ramshackle house. "She's watching us. Probably on the phone to Camp as we speak."

"Better make it drive-through coffee, then," Reed said.

A key from Uncle Alex's ring fit the padlock on the gate, and Nikki sent up a quick prayer of thanks. While other reporters were locked out of the property marked clearly with NO TRESPASSING signs, she had access.

As ever, it paid to be the granddaughter of Eleanor Ryback. Even if someone saw her and found out her key had been "borrowed" from her uncle's desk, Nikki had a reason and a right to be on the property owned by her grandmother's trust.

She drove through and quickly shut the gate behind her, then, soaked to the skin, returned to her car and bumped down the overgrown lane leading to the cabin. As dark as it was, she had to turn on her headlights, and even then it was hard to see, an effort to keep the Honda's tires in the overgrown dual ruts. Where there had once been a passable road cut through a stand of pine, oak, and ash, now potholes and weeds prevailed. With her wipers slapping away the rain, she edged carefully forward, bouncing and jarring through the woods before the trees gave way to a clearing where the hundred-year-old cabin was settling into the ground.

The cottage had aged in the past twenty years, the gutters broken and filled with leaves and debris, the one visible downspout broken but gurgling. The wood siding had never been painted and was dark with age, shingles on the roof patched in some places, missing in others.

Sitting in the car, staring at the decrepit old building, Nikki listened to the rain pound on the Honda's roof and watched as it dappled the steely waters of the lake. With the gathering darkness, she thought today was much like the night Blondell had sworn she'd awakened to find a murderous stranger in the cabin.

You shouldn't be here. Not alone. If this place isn't dangerous physically, it is emotionally. Tread lightly.

Exhaling, she grabbed her camera and cell phone and stepped out of the car. Her boots sank deep into the mud. "Great. Just great." After closing the door shut with her hip, she walked around the front of her car and stopped to take a few outside pictures of the cabin before the light faded completely. She doubted any of the shots she took would be used in the book, and they certainly would not appear in the paper, but she'd print them and tack them to the bulletin boards above her writing space to keep her focused as she put the chapters together.

She also took a picture of the lake, whitecaps brewing on the inky water, before heading up two rotting steps to the porch, where a screen door listed from one hinge.

Once again, a key from her uncle's ring worked its magic, and with a click the old door creaked open and she stepped inside.

Morrisette pulled out of the drive-through window at the same moment Reed's cell phone rang. He cleared the cup holder of trash and set his coffee in it before answering. "Reed."

"Hey. Monty Hemler." Hemler worked in the lab on the technical side, his specialty being electronic equipment. Tall and broad-shouldered, with oversized horn-rimmed glasses, Hemler, at around twenty-six, looked like Clark Kent in a lab coat. "I just checked out the little camera you brought in, and you're right, it's the type that's used for surveillance; it can be bought online, and it isn't cheap. I went out to the place you told me it was found, on the fence, there behind your house, and from what I can figure, the lens could have been tilted to view into your window, or more probably the French doors, but unless the lights were on, the view wouldn't have been that great."

"How about looking into the apartment below us?"

"Possible, but I took the liberty of climbing the utility pole near the fence. It was clean, but about thirty feet up, a branch from one of your neighbor's trees hangs over the fence. On that limb, taped down where the branches split, was a remote lens."

"Meaning what?" Reed asked, the muscles in his jaw tightening.

"That whoever was spying could look right into *your* apartment."

"Damn!" he spat out the word so hard that Morrisette, taking a swallow from her paper cup, peered over the rim at him. Her eyebrows raised in question as he said, "Any way you can find out who bought the camera? Or what's on it?"

"Probably not what's on it. The way it works is that the pictures or video are sent to a receiver. Whoever has the receiver sees the pictures, probably on his computer."

"And can download them, or upload them, or whatever."

"I'd say so. Yeah, probably."

"Were there any prints on the lens or camera?"

"None on the lens, but some smudged ones on the camera, which I'm guessing are yours and your fiancée's."

"I'll get you my prints and Nikki's, in case you can get a clear print."

"Okay," he said dubiously.

"Can you track down the manufacturer, maybe a local outlet, so we find who bought it by its serial number?"

"Already on it."

"Good. Let me know." He remembered making love to Nikki on the floor of the apartment just the other night, their playful banter and hard sex. That sex-charged incident probably hadn't been recorded—she'd already found the camera, and the remote lens would have needed it to record the images—but there had been other times as well. Many and just as carnal. Heat climbed up his neck. He was a deeply private man. His passions were no one's business, especially not some sick voyeur who got off looking through keyholes.

Morrisette was driving slowly, for once staying within the speed limit, as she drank coffee and wended her way back to Roland Camp's house.

"Can you spare a tech to sweep the apartment?" Reed asked Hemler as it suddenly hit him that if there was a camera outside the house there could be more spy equipment inside Nikki's home. He conjured up an image of some pervert jacking off while drooling and watching Nikki and Reed in bed. They might have unwittingly created their own not-so-private sex tape. Or there might be film of Nikki undressing, or stepping into the shower . . . "Sweep the entire apartment," he told Hemler as his mind spun out other private scenarios. Maybe the voyeur had gotten bolder, come inside and turned himself on while lying on Nikki's bed, or fingered Nikki's bras and teddies, maybe caressed her underwear and masturbated.

He'd been a cop long enough to have seen some sick things, so it wasn't too hard to visualize what someone with a fascination for Nikki might do.

"I'll let you know when I can get a couple of techs together," Hemler was saying. "I'll give you a call so that you can let us in."

"Good. Thanks." He hung up and saw the questions in his partner's eyes. "Looks like someone's been spying on Nikki. Maybe me too." He quickly filled Morrisette in.

She whistled softly. "You don't think this has anything to do with the fact that she's writing a story on Blondell O'Henry."

"Don't see how. The equipment was probably put up there before the news came out about Niall O'Henry recanting his testimony."

"You sure?"

"Hell, no, I'm not sure," he said angrily, then stared out the window. "Sorry. Let's do this thing."

"You got it." Morrisette could be bossy at times, nosy at others, but she read her partner well enough to leave him alone when he needed to cool off.

Reed picked up his coffee and told himself to

get his head on straight. No matter what else was happening to him personally, he had to put it aside.

"You okay?"

"Just . . . fine." He shot her a look he knew said otherwise, but she got the message and stepped on the gas.

By the time she turned the corner onto Roland Camp's street, Reed was finished with his coffee and focused on the case again. As Camp's house came into view, Morrisette slowed down, and there, big as life, parked in the driveway, was a Dodge pickup that hadn't been there earlier, with plates Reed recognized as being registered to Roland Camp.

"Looks like the prodigal boyfriend has returned," Morrisette observed as she nosed her car into the spot behind the huge truck's bed and the street. The only way out was through a dilapidated garage or the fences lining the drive or, Reed supposed, over the top of Morrisette's Chevy, and if Camp tried that, Morrisette might shoot first and ask questions later.

Before they reached the porch, the front door banged open. "What the fuck do you want?" Roland Camp, all six-feet-five of him, demanded. His head was shaved, his jaw was set, and he looked as if he worked out seven days a week.

"Detective Pierce Reed, Savannah-Chatham Police Department. This is my partner, Detective

344

Sylvie Morrisette, and we just want to ask you a few questions."

"About that fuckin' Blondell! Shit! I ain't got anything further to tell you, man, I swear. Whatever I said before. It's golden."

"Just checking some facts."

"Then haul me the fuck in. I got a good job now and a good woman and a kid. All that other shit, it's ancient history, man, so leave me, leave us the hell alone!"

"You know Ms. O'Henry might be let out of prison," Reed said.

"Who cares? She did her time, let her be. Why the hell are you all nosing around, anyway? Don't you have other cases? You know, people who were killed this week or last week or sometime in the last twenty years? Let this one go, for Chrissakes!" Some of his belligerence had begun to fade, and he seemed a little calmer as they reached his porch. Behind him, barely visible, Peggy, her boy still attached to her hip, peeked around Roland.

"Hey, look, I didn't mean to fly off the handle," Camp said. "I just don't need any more head-aches now, any more problems. I wasn't kidding. I've got me a kid to raise."

"And that's important?" Morrisette asked.

"Damned straight."

"So you changed your mind. With Blondell, you had no use for children," she reminded.

345

His face darkened into a scowl. "I won't deny it. I wasn't interested in raising another man's kids. Still not. But your own kid is different."

"And Blondell was pregnant at the time you were with her."

"I wasn't that kid's father. Me and Blondell, we'd broke up, and she had other boyfriends, if that's what you'd call 'em. I wasn't the only one. That was the trouble with that woman, she could reel in the men. And we'd go! Find ourselves doin' stuff for her we didn't even want to."

"Like maybe kill her kids?" Morrisette said.

"No way! No fuckin' way! Is that what this is all about?"

"No one's here to accuse you of anything," Reed said.

"I was just pointing out that you changed your mind," Morrisette clarified, though Reed knew she was trying to get a rise out of the guy. It was just her way.

"We have a couple of questions," Morrisette said calmly, and Camp, folding his massive arms over his chest, muscles bulging, bald head shining under the porch light, unintentionally did his best impression of Mr. Clean. His demeanor had changed, and he was suspicious once more, but as they asked about the night in question, he decided to give in and talk to them.

"I'm not changin' my story," he began, "and if you want to check it, go see my stepbrother,

Donny Ray Wilson. I was with him and he'll tell you the same . . ."

He went on to say that Donny Ray now lived closer to Riceboro, off Highway 25, but that they'd been together the night Blondell's kids were shot. Roland's take on the situation was that Blondell had tried to kill her kids because, though she was "cattin' around," she had kind of settled on him. He was up front with her about how he felt about another man's offspring. He would never even be with her when Amity, Niall, and Blythe were around, and that frustrated her. He repeated what he'd said on the witness stand— that he thought she was the kind of woman who was good for one thing only and that was a hell-fire hot time in the sack. He figured because she'd been married and had kids already she wouldn't be foolish enough to get "knocked up" again, but when it turned out she was, he swore up and down it wasn't his. "I was suspicious, y'see. Didn't trust her claimin' she was on the pill, so I took care of things myself."

"But you are able to father children," Morrisette pointed out.

" 'Course I can, but it's when I want to. My terms. Back then, it wasn't the right time and it wasn't the right woman." His eyes glittered for a second before he pulled in on the reins of his temper and said, "Look, man, if I knew anything more, I'd tell ya. I ain't got nothin' to hide." He rubbed his arms and sighed through his nose. "To tell you the truth, I wish I'd never laid eyes on Blondell O'Henry, and I'd lay odds that I ain't the only son of a bitch who feels that way."

Chapter 23

Nikki felt as if she'd stepped back in time.

An eerie feeling crawled over her skin, causing goose pimples to rise, as she eyed the interior of the cabin where her friend had been shot. Involuntarily, though she'd not been raised a Catholic, she crossed herself, as she'd seen her friends do so often. The cabin was as she remembered it, but it appeared smaller and darker than it had when she was a child.

Using the flashlight app on her cell phone, she scanned the interior and even took a few photos, though they too were dark. She flipped a light switch, but though it clicked loudly, no illumination was forthcoming.

She studied the area where Amity had been sleeping—on the pull-out sofa, where it had been tucked under the loft.

What really had happened here that night? The prosecution and defense had laid out differing stories, but the truth was still a mystery.

Nikki's gaze drifted upward to the floor above, where Blythe and Niall had been tucked in for the night. Blondell had either opened fire on her own daughter as she slept or found an attacker looming over her . . . no, wait. That wasn't right. If Blythe had been correct, Amity had already awakened in a panic as she'd discovered a live snake in her bed. The puncture wounds and venom found in her bloodstream confirmed the reptilian attack.

Carefully, making no sound, her muscles taut, Nikki peered into the adjacent rooms, although out of respect for her claustrophobia, she wouldn't step into the tiny bathroom. She did walk through the old kitchen, with its sloping, rotting counter-tops and leaking windows, and outside to the once-screened porch where Blondell said she'd dozed. Rain was pouring in now, and there was no furniture on the wraparound porch. The view of the lake was partially obscured by brush.

Nikki wondered about Blondell's story yet again as she returned to the house and started hesitantly up the stairs. Her great-great-grandfather had built this place, if family history was correct, and had raised his family here before the newer, modern home was constructed on the site across the water, the farm where her family had kept their horses.

And yet Amity O'Henry had died here.

She felt a strange little frisson slide down her

spine, a niggle that told her she was more than connected to what had happened here, that she was the catalyst, that Amity's blood was somehow on her hands.

As she stepped through the old rooms, she imagined the terror of that night, heard the blood-curdling screams and the crack of gunfire ricocheting through the rooms, felt the frantic, confused horror as the kids tumbled out of their beds and made their way to the stairs. Niall was first, racing down, only to be hit, then little Blythe, shot and sent reeling through the rails. Nikki shivered when she saw the stains still on the wall near the stairs. Though the tragedy had happened twenty years earlier and the dead were long buried and the survivors now adults, she felt her eyes well with tears and her soul darken a bit.

Norm Metzger had accused her of being a daughter of privilege, and he wasn't far from the truth. The fact that she'd come so close to witnessing the horror unfold, had nearly been a part of the terror, reminded her how lucky she'd been all her life.

Hadn't Amity accused her of such on the days they'd been riding with Hollis? "You two are so lucky," she'd said as the horses had stopped to graze. Nikki had been astride Vixen, the pinto mare she'd come to love. Hollis had been riding her sorrel mare, while Amity had chosen Rebel, a bay gelding who was Uncle Alex's favorite.

They'd been riding by the lake, just across from this cabin, Nikki recalled now, and as they'd returned to the stable, she'd spied Uncle Alex, who had stopped by to talk to the foreman. He'd smiled at the teenagers, his eyes hidden behind dark glasses, his smile wide. He'd waved and walked into a barn with the foreman, but Nikki had experienced the sensation that he'd been watching the three of them together.

As rain peppered the roof, she made her way to the loft, and from that position high over the living area, she took another picture, of the blackened fireplace below, with its rock face and thick mantel. How had Blondell and her kids ended up here? Nikki asked herself again. *Before* the attack. *Before* she'd been accused of murder. *Before* she'd needed to hire Alexander McBaine as her attorney.

Had she read the answer to that question in Blondell's testimony? Surely someone had asked it. Just as she had when Amity had called that night. Nikki asked herself, and not for the first time, whether somehow, inadvertently, by showing her friend the cabin, she'd set the wheels in motion for Amity's death.

Don't go there. It's not your fault. You know that.

She'd seen all she needed to have seen, and what little light was left, filtering through the windows, was swiftly fading. The place felt haunted, as if whatever evil had gone down that night had seeped into the walls and floorboards of the old building, as if a residue of the depravity still lingered.

She had loved this cabin as a child, but it now seemed to have a blackened soul.

Don't be ridiculous.

From the loft, she took a step onto the stairs.

Thud!

She nearly tripped at the sound, then caught herself by grabbing the rail.

She was alone.

Right?

No one else was here, and no one had followed her. She'd checked.

Something blowing over outside and hitting the house? The thud had been muted, more like the sound of a car door closing than something falling onto the floor.

Her instincts were on alert, her nerves strung tight as she started downward again. Her ears were straining as she reached the first floor, and her heart was thudding wildly.

Letting out her breath, she started across the room when she heard a low, warning growl.

What?

Something was *inside?*

Oh, God.

The saliva dried in her throat as she strained to see.

Where was it?

What was it?

Heart in her throat, she swept the beam of her phone screen across the floor, making certain she had a way out.

Again the rumbling growl, and she froze, the hairs on the back of her neck raising one by one.

Was it an animal? A deranged person?

Passing the beam of her flashlight over the floor, she saw nothing. No glittering eyes and bared fangs. She eased across the room and tried to ignore the fact that she felt as if she were being observed, her every move noted.

Don't be such a—

The growl rumbled again.

Heart thudding, she twisted her flashlight in the direction of the noise, near the archway to the kitchen.

Reflecting the light, bright eyes glared at her from the shadows. "Oh, God," she whispered, frantic for a second. Another growl, and she realized she was looking at a gray cat crouching near the cabinets.

"It's okay," she whispered, as much to calm herself as anything else. "We're fine here."

The feral cat gave out that soul-numbing growl again, then hissed, showing its teeth.

"No worries, kitty," she said and realized it wasn't looking directly at her, but at something near her, something on the floor near her feet, something . . .

Oh Jesus!

From the corner of her eye she caught movement, a rapid slither. She whirled, the beam of the cell phone landing on a snake as it eeled toward the fireplace, its smooth scales glistening in the light.

Her heart turned to ice as she noticed the hourglass pattern of its scales and recognized the sibilant creature as a copperhead, the same kind of snake that had struck Amity O'Henry in this very room.

The cat let out a piercing cry, and the pit viper coiled, its reptilian eyes tracking the animal.

Nikki backed toward the door, but even as her mind screamed at her to run, she had the presence of mind to hit the button on her phone and take pictures of the copperhead coiled and ready to strike near the old stone grate.

The cat finally got smart and scrambled away, through the kitchen.

Nikki too couldn't get out of the cabin fast enough. Her fingers fumbled as she relocked the door behind her, ran down the porch steps, and squished her way through the mud to her car. Rain was still falling and darkness had descended, the lake barely visible. Climbing into her car, she tossed her phone into her cup holder and her uncle's set of keys onto the passenger seat near her purse, then jabbed her key into the ignition, threw the gear shift into reverse, and hit the gas.

The Honda's tires spun, the engine whining.

The car didn't budge.

"No way!" Panic was taking over. Being in the dark cabin and stumbling on first the cat and then the snake had stretched her nerves to the breaking point. She jammed the car into drive and this time slowly touched a toe to the accelerator. Again her tires spun, spraying out mud. "Come on, come on," she said as the rain poured from the heavens. A little movement. Then more spinning. The car had all-wheel-drive, thank God.

Despite the cool air, she began to sweat. *Calm down. You're safe, just freaked. Pull yourself together!*

Reverse again.

"Not today. *Not* today!" Her nerves were already shot, a headache building behind her eyes. The car rocked a little. "Go, go, go!" Desperately, she wanted to get out on her own and fast, putting distance between herself and the dilapidated cabin. She could call Reed, but would prefer to tell him she'd visited the old crime scene on her own terms.

She threw the car back into drive and the tires began to spin again. This time it moved enough to find traction away from the ruts she was creating.

"That's it," she whispered as the tires gripped the sodden ground. "You can do it," she said to either the car, or herself, or both, as she eased on the gas and the car slowly inched forward, finding a little traction in the weeds.

Now drive and get the hell out of here!

Finally, the tires caught solidly, wheels no longer spinning. On solid ground, she drove in a tight circle to be facing out the way she'd come in.

She let out her breath and felt her heartbeat slow a bit. She was free, and if she stepped on it, she still had time to race home, shower, and meet Trina at Catfish Jake's.

Headlights on, windshield wipers swishing the rain from the glass, she pulled away from the cottage and was about to reach for the radio, to find some music to calm her shattered nerves when she glanced in the rearview mirror and saw a figure in the gathering darkness.

What?!

In a blink, the image was gone. Glancing over her shoulder, she saw no one, just a huge cypress tree that she must've mistaken for a person. Was it her imagination? Was it? The atmosphere of the cabin had certainly gotten to her. Fighting the urge to call Reed, she set her sights on the rutted lane. There was no way out of the property but by the lane, so if she had the inclination, she could drive to the end, hide the car by the side of the main road, and follow the next car out that came along.

If there was a car.

But even so, it could be parked miles away and drive off in the other direction and—

There is no car. No one was in the mirror. Don't let your damned paranoia get to you.

Letting out her breath, she reached to turn on the radio again, but stopped short.

Venomous eyes glared up at her from the floor in front of the passenger seat.

"Oh . . . God . . ."

Curled into a tight circle on the floor, blending into the darkened interior, the pit viper locked its reptilian gaze with hers, its arrow-tip-shaped head raised high above its coiled body.

Her heart nearly stopped.

Fear strangled her.

She stood on the brakes.

Too late.

The snake's head twisted, its eyes, with slitted pupils, still fixed upon her.

No!

The Honda jerked around. She flung open the door and threw herself outside. The SUV skidded sideways, slewing and throwing up mud, and crashed against a fence post.

Bam! Metal crumpled. Barely breathing, Nikki ran forward and slammed the door shut, then realized her phone was in the car, which was still in gear, engine grinding.

"Damn! Hell!" She stared through the window, where the reptile was still glaring at her, unblinking eyes fixed. "Bother and blood," she said under her breath as her heart hammered and the car's engine still ran, inching the car forward. *Now what?* She'd heard snakes would rather slither away than attack, but she felt she had to keep the viper trapped. Someone had put the damned thing in her car. Hadn't she heard the quiet thud of the door closing? The trapped snake was evidence!

Of what?

Someone trying to kill you? With a copperhead? Not likely, but . . .

She needed to reopen the door, push the car into park, cut the engine, and snag her cell phone—all with the car moving and the snake lifting its head, poised to strike.

Gritting her teeth, she inched the door open.

Noiselessly, the pit viper watched.

Carefully she reached toward the center console and rammed the car into park. The snake reared higher. *God help me.* Whether the wound would be fatal or not, she didn't want to get bit. Slowly, she let her hand slide down to the cup holder, her fingers wet with sweat, as she plucked the phone from its resting place.

Muscles in the copperhead's coiled body seemed to flex.

Oh, sweet Mother Mary.

The keys were dangling so close to the snake . . .

Reptilian eyes held hers. Seeming to dare her.

For what? It wasn't worth it. She backed out

slowly and closed the car door. Her keys would have to stay put, as would the second set, her uncle's, which were lying on the seat, and she hoped she wouldn't have to explain them to anyone. She just didn't have the nerve to risk the snake striking.

Heart thudding as the rain poured over her, she hit the speed-dial button for Reed's cell phone. As the call connected, she searched the darkening forest for answers.

Who the hell was trying to scare her off the case?

And why?

Chapter 24

"I don't know why you're freaking out," Nikki said as they headed back to her house in Reed's boat of a Cadillac. Too old to be cool and too new to be "classic," the car was a beast that Reed loved, and today, after her experience at the cabin, she was thankful he was at the wheel as they drove into the city.

"If whoever it was who planted the damned snake had wanted me dead, I would be. Anyone could have followed me out there and killed me, but they didn't. They used a couple of snakes to scare me."

Cold to the bone, she rode in the passenger seat of the Caddy. Reed's jacket was slung over her shoulders as she sipped the coffee they'd picked up at a diner on the way into the city.

"Why would they go to all this trouble?"

"I don't know, but I think someone's trying to scare me off investigating what happened twenty years ago. It's no secret that I'm digging around on the Blondell O'Henry case. Two articles have already come out in the paper, and another one is due the day after tomorrow. Maybe I'm making someone nervous, and they're afraid I'll uncover something they don't want to see the light of day. A secret. A crime. I'm not sure, but it obviously has something to do with Blondell's release and Amity's death."

"How did they know you were out here?"

"I don't know." God, she was tired of admitting that. "I didn't tell anyone, not even you."

"No one at the office?"

"No." She frowned and looked out the window.

"So they must've followed you."

She thought of her run-in with Metzger in the parking lot. Could he have watched her leave and what . . . followed her, parked somewhere nearby, grabbed a couple of snakes he just happened to have with him, and stick one in her car? She almost laughed at how ludicrous that was. Or how about Effie? Did she follow Nikki, and instead of surprising her at the coffee stand, just

360

happen to show up at the cabin with, again, a couple of pit vipers?

"Someone planned this," Nikki said, cradling her cup in her hands for warmth. The Cadillac's heat was blasting, but she couldn't seem to get rid of the chill that had seeped into her blood after being eye to eye with the copperhead.

Reed's eyebrows were drawn together as he drove, the beams of headlights from cars and trucks moving in the opposite direction washing the interior of his car and illuminating his worried face. "How did whoever it was know you were going to be at the cabin?"

"Maybe they were already there, going to let the snakes loose or expecting someone else."

"Who?" he asked.

No one. You were the target, Nikki. You and Reed both know it.

He answered his own question. "No one. This message was for you, Nikki."

She couldn't deny the obvious. She was making someone very nervous, and in a sense that was a good thing. It meant she was getting close to something, she just didn't know what.

Yet.

Fortunately, Reed had arrived at the cabin in record time, beating the animal control folks, who had captured the snake, and two other officers, who had helped him do a quick search of the house and grounds. She'd told him about the other copperhead she'd seen inside, one she was almost certain was smaller, and the feral cat, along with what she saw as a "dark figure" in her rearview mirror, but on first sweep, in the darkness, the officers had found nothing. No second snake. No cat. No human lurking in the shadows.

However, Reed had taken the warning seriously, not even allowing her to drive back to Savannah. Her SUV was being taken to the police garage, where it would be dusted for fingerprints and examined for any other evidence, including the set of keys she'd taken from Uncle Alex's den. Those, she thought, could be hard to explain.

Then, of course, she would have to have the damage to the car assessed, and she hoped it was still functional, as she planned to drive north to meet with Lawrence Thompson as soon as possible.

She'd already texted Trina and begged out of their meeting tonight.

"Really sorry," she'd texted after sending a quick message about what had happened. Of course, the text had prompted a call in which she'd explained in further detail about the snake, cabin, car, and rescue.

"This is getting dangerous," Trina had said.

"Yeah."

"You've put new meaning into 'stirring up a viper's nest.' Well, just be careful, and I'll take a rain check on the drink. You're not getting out of it."

Now, as they reached the outskirts of Savannah, the rain had stopped, the sky clearing, a slice of moon visible over the city skyline.

"Maybe this time was just a warning, but who knows if this yahoo won't escalate? This is personal, Nikki," Reed said. "Morrisette and I are investigating too. That's no secret, but whoever this is came after you."

Cradling her cup, she took a long sip and felt the coffee warm her from the inside out. "I know."

They drove in silence for a few minutes. Then Reed said, "I took the camera you found on the fence into the lab."

"And?" she prompted, not liking the tone of his voice.

"And you were right. Looks like someone's been spying on your apartment." He explained about the second lens in the tree and how they were trying to find out who had purchased it. He'd spent the day on the case. After interviewing Roland Camp and his most recent girlfriend, he and Morrisette had returned to the station. He'd been on his way to her house with a couple of electronic specialists from the department when he'd gotten her panicked call about the snake.

"That is so sick." Nikki's blood ran cold all over again at the thought of someone watching her in her private life. She saw herself doing the most mundane of chores, sitting cross-legged on her bed watching television, working at her desk, playing with her animals, and cooking. What about when she used the bathroom, took a shower, or was trying on sexy lingerie in front of the mirror? And all her phone calls, or just her stupid mutterings to her animals. Could he hear her, listen in? The skin on the back of her arms actually pimpled at the thought. She was beginning to feel completely and utterly violated. "What pervert is doing this?" she wondered aloud.

And if they had been taped, how long before images might be leaked to the Internet? Lost in thought, she chewed the rim of her coffee cup. She pictured herself singing off-key in the shower, flashing her breasts as she warbled into a bar of soap, and mentally groaned. "This could be bad," she whispered, her stomach clenching.

"Trust me," he said, sliding her a quietly determined glance, "we're going to find this freak and shut him down."

"Do that."

Slowing, Reed guided his car through the city streets, and as they passed Forsyth Park, she looked at the tiered fountain, now lit strategically, sprays of water illuminated in the night. The oak trees stood guard, Spanish moss dancing ghostlike in the breeze.

No one was loitering in the park right now, but she couldn't help but think of the man she'd seen observing her on her run, the dark figure. *Not necessarily a man, Nikki. You didn't get a good enough look at the figure, did you? You just took off running.*

"You know," she admitted now, "I've had this strange feeling that I'm being followed."

"What? When?" He cranked the Caddy's wheel as he turned into the alley that ran past the side of her house.

"That's just the thing. It happened *before* I even knew Niall was going to change his testimony." As he parked the car, she explained about the stranger in the park, then mentioned the black BMW that had nearly run her over in the crosswalk.

"Why didn't you tell me any of this?" He snapped his keys from the ignition.

"Because I didn't want to worry you."

"You were afraid that I wouldn't let you in on the O'Henry case," he accused. "That I might think it's too dangerous and should be just the department's investigation, without any help from my fiancée the reporter."

"Well, yes . . . I did consider all that."

"Nik." His eyes were dark with worry. "This is just a case to me and a story to you. It's not worth putting your life in any danger!"

"I told you, it started *before* I was assigned to report on Blondell O'Henry's release, *before* I sent in an idea for a new book. It could have nothing to do with the case."

"Fine. Great. But you have to admit that you

going to the cabin where Amity was killed and finding a snake in your damned car is the direct result of your work on the O'Henry case."

"Apparently I'm getting close, Reed. Worrying someone. Making them nervous. Flushing them out!"

"I think we should reconsider this whole deal we had. It's too dangerous. I don't know what I was thinking!" He slammed his door shut, then started toward the house.

"Reed—" She scrambled out of her side of the car. "Damn it all to hell!" Hurrying around the Caddy's wide trunk, she caught up with him at the gate. "You can't renege now."

"I can damn well do anything I want."

"Calm down. I'm okay."

"No. You're not. And it's because of this case, so all bets are off."

He was through the gate and cutting through the garden, letting himself in the back of the building's large foyer. Nikki took off after him again, her boots tracking mud over the polished hardwood and up the main staircase, but she didn't care. He couldn't stop her now. "I never thought you'd back out of a deal," she accused, chasing after him, leaving more prints left on the carpet that covered all three flights of the old wooden stairs.

"Then you thought wrong."

"Reed. Wait. Just listen!" But he was already at

the third floor, where the door was open and a lanky man in a brown jumpsuit and owlish glasses was crouched just inside. A few cobwebs clung to his shoulders and hair as he snapped a toolbox closed and greeted Reed familiarly.

"Hey, just finishing up."

"Nikki, this is Monty Hemler. Monty, this is my fiancée, Nicole Gillette." As they nodded to each other, Reed continued, "Hemler here is the department's technical expert. He and his assistant have been searching the place."

"Barry's already gone," Hemler said, explaining why he was alone.

He pulled off a pair of tight-fitting gloves, then stuffed them into his pocket.

From the bathroom, there was a series of frantic barks. "Oh, had to lock up your pets," Helmer said. "Sorry."

"I think they'll survive," Reed said.

Hemler nodded. "Anyway, I was just on my way out. The place is clean. No unwanted bugs of any kind. No video, no audio. I checked the attic and even the basement, but I didn't bother with the first- or second-floor units, just the hallways, as you said they were occupied."

Nikki felt a wave of relief. "Good. Thank you."

"No problem." He flashed a smile, then picked up his toolbox and said to Reed, "As for the equipment you located outside, it was pretty low-end. I'm thinking amateur. Could be just some nerdy kid like I was who's into electronics, only this one gets his jollies spying on people."

"That innocent?" Reed was skeptical.

Hemler lifted a dusty shoulder. "Maybe."

"Thanks," Reed said, and shook Hemler's hand.

"Anytime."

He let himself out, and they heard his footsteps retreating down the stairs.

"See," she said, some of her anxiety eased. "No reason to worry."

He scanned the inside of the apartment. "Lots of reasons to worry," he disagreed. "And I'm thinking that with you as my wife, it's only going to get worse."

"There's still time to back out on the wedding, y'know," she said, hitching up her chin. "But you can't weasel out of the deal we had about the case. That's set in stone." She stalked to the bathroom and let a frantic Mikado out. Jennings, true to his lazy personality, strolled into the living area and, disdainful of the jumping dog, wound himself through her legs. She petted both animals, and Mikado calmed a bit, while Jennings, as if bored with the whole scene, wandered off toward the dining area. As she stroked the dog, something nagged at her, something she couldn't quite call up. What the hell was it? Something she'd heard when she was dealing with the dog? That was it. When she was picking up Mikado from Ruby's

Ruff and Ready. Something about Ruby's brothers being hot for Blondell . . .

"You're okay with me backing out of the wedding but not the investigation?" His tone was light, but his jaw was steel. Her answer was important.

"I'm not okay with you backing out of either one," Nikki said tautly as he tossed his wallet and keys onto the side table.

"We're getting married, Nik. That's a fact. But I almost lost you once to the Grave Robber, and that can't happen again, not on my watch." Looking at her, his expression softened. "Look, honey," he said, closing the gap between them and grabbing her shoulders. "I'm mad at myself for agreeing to our partnership in the investigation. It's not professional, and it's not smart, and I let my need to please you cloud my judgment."

Her heart cracked a little. "Okay, I get it. But let's not let one snake throw this whole thing out the window."

"It's not the snake that worries me—or the two snakes, if there really was another one in the cabin. It's the guy who put the damned thing into your car that's the problem. You know, there's a chance he's the same nutcase who took one to the cabin years before, and look what happened then."

"What you're saying suggests that Blondell might not have been lying," she pointed out.

"Suggests, yeah. Not proves."

"But who?" she asked.

"Someone nearby who can handle reptiles. That's got to narrow the field."

"You'd think." She slid out of his coat and handed it to him. "Thanks. For the coat and everything." She placed a kiss on his cheek and added, "I'm in dire need of a hot shower."

"Is that an offer?"

Leaning over, she unzipped her boots and kicked them off. "Take it any way you want it."

"As long as you understand that our deal is off."

She started working on the zipper of the lightweight jacket she'd been wearing under Reed's larger coat. "I'm not talking about this now. I figure we can do it later." She let her sweater fall open.

"You think if you get me interested in you that I'll forget that I'm changing the rules. Or that you can convince me to agree to let you work on the case."

"I'm just going to take a shower, Reed," she said. "You can join me if you want. If you don't, fine."

"I think I'd better deal with the dog."

"Your choice." She was already peeling off her clothes.

Once inside the bathroom, she turned on the taps of the shower, which was rigged over an old, claw-foot tub. The pipes groaned as the water turned hot, steaming the room as she dropped her clothes into a pile on the floor. She'd barely stepped inside the curtained enclosure when the door opened and Reed, stark naked, appeared.

"What about the dog?"

"He's quick."

"I guess. So did you have a change of heart?" she asked lightly, reaching for the soap.

"More like I saw an opportunity to spend some quality time with my fiancée."

"Quality time," she mocked. "Is that what this is?"

"What it isn't, is you seducing me to get what you want."

She watched as he deftly plucked the soap from her hand and stood between her and the spray, turning her to face the wall as he ran the slippery bar over her wet skin, causing the goose bumps rising on her flesh to disappear in the heat. Warm water sprayed over them, and she nestled against him, feeling the flat of his hand against her abdomen, drawing her near while her buttocks were pressed into his groin, his thick shaft already at attention and rubbing against her.

She closed her eyes and let the eroticism of the moment overtake her. Hot water, warm flesh, sudsy lather running down her legs and body. He kissed the back of her neck, where it joined with her shoulders, his lips tender, his tongue slick. His hands moved, one caressing a breast and toying with a wet nipple, the other, reaching lower, down her abdomen, to the juncture of her legs, where his fingers probed and her need began to pulse. She moaned over the rush of water, and she felt him lift her up as he thrust hard against her, driving deep, causing her to gasp.

Blood pounded in her ears, and her heart couldn't keep up with her shallow, rapid breathing. Water splashed, she gulped in air and he moved inside her. Harder. Faster. Hotter.

"Oh, God," she whispered as he held her fast to him. "Oh, God, Oh, God . . . oh . . ."

In a burst of heat she convulsed, gasping, panting, hearing his primal groan as his muscles tightened, then released, and his breath came out in a rush against her ear.

She went limp against him, but still he held her close, breathing hard, his slick body pressed intimately to hers.

"What got into you?" he asked on a gasp, and she laughed, realizing they were still joined.

"I think the answer to that is pretty obvious."

Chuckling, the water still flowing, he kissed the top of her wet head and finally took a step backward, their bodies disconnecting. "Wanna hear the good news?"

"Mmm. Tell me."

"At least we know we aren't making a sex tape."

"What a relief." She turned and wound her arms

around his neck, warm water spraying her face. "You know, Reed, while you were washing me? I think you missed a spot," she whispered and kissed him hard on the lips.

"Did I?"

"Uh huh."

"And I think you're trying to mess with me."

"See, you are good at your job," she said and dragged him downward into the tub, where they were crunched in a tangle of arms and legs. "From now on, I'll just call you Ace."

His laugh was a deep rumble. "And you'll be Bambi."

"Bambi? Why?"

"Because you, darlin', are trying to bamboozle me, and it's just not going to work."

"We'll just see about that," she said, because she knew, deep in her heart, she wasn't going to quit her investigation. She had a job to do and she'd do it, with or without his help. For now, though, she'd close her mind to everything that had to do with the Blondell O'Henry case and pay attention to the man she was going to marry.

Chapter 25

Any way you cut it, the drive to Charleston was going to take more than two hours, probably closer to three. One way. And it would have to be in a rental car, as Nikki's Honda was still being repaired. Well, so be it. As soon as Reed left for work in the morning, she found her way to the nearest agency, rented a subcompact, and was on her way. She'd mentioned to Reed that she planned to drive north to locate Lawrence Thompson, and he hadn't been happy about it. He'd sternly told her to keep in contact. Their argument of the night before had diffused a little, and he was being more rational, accepting the fact that her job did come with a few built-in dangers, though he didn't like it and made that point very clear as he'd dressed for work.

"Just be smart," he'd cautioned as he found his keys near the front door. "And be careful."

"I will."

"And for God's sake, keep me posted."

"Don't worry," she'd said, bussing his freshly shaven cheek, the scent of aftershave tickling her nostrils. "I will. Promise."

With that, he'd rolled his eyes and left, his own

job calling. "I'm holding you to it," he'd yelled over his shoulder.

As soon as the back door slammed shut, she'd gotten to work. Her calls to Jada Hill had gone unreturned, and she wasn't having much luck with anyone else, including Steve Manning, the stoner whom Amity had dated in high school and who was now a security guard for On the River, a hotel not six blocks from where she worked. She'd learned when he would be on duty and planned to visit him when she returned from Charleston. Brad Holbrook, after college, had taken a job in Japan with an import-export business; as far as she could tell, he was married, with three stair-step children, and though he'd been in and out of the country, his work kept him mainly on the West Coast. According to his widowed mother, he "never came and visited, not like Peter," who obviously, at least for the time being, was the "good" and favored son.

She would still love to talk to Brad, whose dreams of a career in major league baseball had fizzled out at Georgia Tech. Since Brad had been in school in Atlanta when Amity had been killed, he might have some insight into what had happened to her. She figured it was a shot in the dark, but worth the try.

The one person she did connect with was Ruby, Mikado's dog groomer. "Does that little one need an appointment already?" Ruby had asked.

"Not yet," Nikki said. "I was actually calling about something you said about your brothers and Blondell O'Henry."

"Oh. All I can say is that they thought she was the hottest thing to ever hit Savannah. Woowee!"

"Did they ever say who was dating her? I mean, before Calvin?"

"That was a long time ago. I don't think it was just one boy, and I didn't pay much attention anyway, y'know. Oh, but there was something. The one of them that had been with her in high school? That would be Flint Beauregard."

"Beauregard. Are you sure?"

"Oh, yes, ma'am. The boys were all goin' on about it. And then he ends up bein' the detective on the case."

A cold feeling stole through Nikki. "Anyone else besides Beauregard?"

"Well, they were all braggin' about her. That's the way they were. Flint, though . . . they all knew about him."

"Do you have their numbers? Your brothers?"

"Oh, no. The boys are gone now. Passed on a few years back, within six months of each other. Frank had a heart attack while he was workin', and cancer got Jeb."

"I'm sorry," Nikki said.

"That's just the way of it sometimes."

A few minutes later, Nikki had hung up, lost in thought. She felt hollow inside. It couldn't be, could it? That Flint Beauregard had fathered Amity O'Henry? Had he known? Why, then, would he pursue Blondell so vigorously, and why hadn't Blondell cried foul, whatever the case?

No, she was missing something. An important piece. She thought of the girl she'd befriended. Amity had taken after her mother in so many ways, physically as well as in her attitude toward men. But Flint Beauregard? Maybe . . .

Amity, the girl everyone knew of, but no one really knew. "What happened to you?" Nikki wondered aloud.

"Tell me more about the lake," Amity had pleaded once when they'd been hanging out that summer, just listening to CDs in Nikki's room on one of the rare times Amity had come over. "Do you swim in it?" She was sitting on the bench at the vanity Nikki's mother had insisted she needed, while Nikki was stretched out on her bed. The sun had been streaming through the windows, some Michael Jackson song playing, Amity picking up bottles of nail polish and reading the labels as they talked.

"We used to go there a lot when I was a kid, and yeah, I swam in it," Nikki had admitted.

"It must've been fun." She'd seemed sad for a second, as if reflecting on her own home life and making comparisons. For the first time, Nikki had actually been embarrassed about her bedroom, with its designer quilt and coordinating curtains.

"It was."

"With your cousins. Hollis and Elton?"

"Sometimes. Mom and Hollis's mom don't really get along."

"Why not?"

Nikki had shrugged. "They just don't like each other. Hollis seems to think it has to do with some big secret, but then Hollis is always thinking there's a major scandal somewhere."

"Is there?" Amity had asked quietly, as she stared into the mirror, her gaze finding Nikki's in its reflection. "A scandal."

"I don't know, but Hollis sure thinks so. She thinks her mother is a big fake or something."

"Maybe she is."

"I guess." Hollis had always been making up stories, creating drama, believing the worst about anyone, including Amity, though Nikki hadn't mentioned *that*. Instead, she'd picked up her old stuffed elephant, which at the time had been fifteen years old and missing an eye.

"Can we go there sometime?" Amity had asked, her eyes shining with anticipation. "To the cabin?"

Nikki had shrugged. "It's pretty rustic. I never really liked it, and most of the time we went, my sister and brothers and me, it was with Hollis and Elton and their parents. But that was a long time ago. No one goes up there much anymore."

"We should go!" Amity had said. She pulled her hair away from her face in both hands and turned her head, looking this way and that, eyeing her reflection in the mirrors. "I mean it. Let's go there."

"Sure, I guess."

Letting her hair down, Amity had twisted on the bench. "It could be fun," she said, never mentioning the two bottles of nail polish she'd hidden in her hand and, when she'd thought Nikki wouldn't notice, had tucked into the pocket of her jeans, folding her T-shirt over the bulge.

Nikki had never mentioned the theft to anyone.

Now, as the miles rolled under her rental's wheels, she thought about Amity and her desire for things she couldn't have. It had been hard for her to be Nikki's friend, hard to want so many things that were out of reach. Was Flint Beauregard Amity's father? If so, what difference would that have made in Amity's life if it were known?

With an effort, Nikki dragged her thoughts back to the case itself. She'd already decided that she was going to attend the next service of the Pentecostal sect run by Ezekiel Byrd, June Hatchett's brother. She didn't really see why anyone who was religious enough to handle snakes would use one as a weapon or a threat, but it was the only lead she had. Earlier this morning, she'd called all the legitimate reptile dealers in the area and, as it was early, left messages asking about recent sales of copperheads. She'd looked online, at craigslist and other Web sites, even searched through the previous week's free advertisements in the *Sentinel*, but so far she'd found no copperheads for sale, nor any that had gone missing from a lab that collected snake venom; she'd even called the local zoos.

Nothing.

Not that she couldn't have missed something, and there were dealers who worked under the radar, as well as hunters who trapped their own. So far, the whole snake lead was a bust. But it was still early. She could get lucky with one of the dealers. Well, maybe.

Reed was still working on the DNA of the old cigarette butt found at the scene. Nikki hadn't spoken with Roland Camp, but any conversations she'd tried to have with Calvin O'Henry had been useless.

She felt as if she were getting nowhere, trudging in quicksand, and the more she struggled, the less footing she found.

But someone who had a fondness for snakes apparently thought differently.

"I've got good news and bad news," Morrisette said when Reed arrived at the office and caught up with her at the coffeepot in the break room.

"I'm not in the mood for jokes," he warned her as she filled her cup from a fresh pot that had the room smelling of some kind of fresh roast.

"There's a surprise," she said with more than a

smidgeon of mockery as she returned the glass carafe to its warming plate.

A couple of uniformed officers sat at a table near the windows, perusing the headlines of the paper and sipping from their cups before starting their shift. A huge bowl of popcorn, half eaten and left by someone from the night shift, sat on the table, and one of the officers was picking at it as he read the news.

"So what is it?" He poured himself a cup as they left the room, passing Agnes, one of the clerical workers, as she headed in the opposite direction. Phones were jangling; a printer somewhere spewed out pages, as laughter and conversation eased through the hallways.

Morrisette and Reed made their way through the rabbit warren of offices to the room where they'd been working on the O'Henry case. Boxes were stacked on the ends of tables that also held labeled evidence, and two standing corkboards displayed pinned-up photographs of the crime scene, suspects, and notes about everything. Front and center was a glossy eight-by-ten of Blondell O'Henry, the photo Morrisette bitingly called her "professional head shot," though it wasn't all that flattering.

"So, okay," he said. "What's going on?"

"Actually, I have good news and bad news and worse news," Morrisette said.

Irritated, he said, "Whatever."

"The lab ran down the serial number of that camera you gave them and tracked it to a store right here in Savannah. They've called the owner of the shop and we can swing by there today. It's a place called Max's Spy World, on the south side, not far from the mall. If they keep decent records, you should know by the end of the day who bought the equipment and who's been surreptitiously observing Ms. Gillette."

"Good." He couldn't wait to come face-to-face with the bastard who was playing Peeping Tom. "So what's the bad news?"

"DNA came back on the cigarette found at the cabin twenty years ago. It was pretty degraded, but it looks like it doesn't match up with any of the known players back then. All they can determine is that it is a Winston and was smoked by a male."

"The Winston part we knew," Reed said; the name of the brand had been visible on the butt. "And the rest of the information eliminates half the population but won't exactly break the case wide open."

She nodded. "You ready for the worst?"

"Hit me."

"Blondell O'Henry's going to be released," Morrisette said.

"It's decided?" Reed asked, surprised.

"Jada Hill pled her case, and the powers that be decided not to pursue keeping her locked up.

Twenty years is enough if she did it, and way too much if she didn't. The statement's going to be announced later today, and she actually gets out tomorrow, after all the red tape is cut. So all of this," Morrisette said, motioning to the boxes of evidence stacked onto the tables, "is moot."

Reed stared at the piles of evidence sorted and stacked on tables. "So it's over. Just like that."

"It's over as far as prosecuting Blondell O'Henry is concerned, but now the case is open because we can't prove that she did it. Looks like she'll be suing the state for her pain and suffering or whatever, and let me tell you, Deacon Beauregard is fit to be tied, claiming his father is 'rolling over in his grave' and that a 'grievous injustice' has been done to Amity O'Henry, her siblings, the constituents of the great state of Georgia, and all people everywhere, or some such shit." She drained her cup and set it onto the table with a bang.

"But you agree with him?"

Her lips pursed and she looked away. "I thought I'd never say this, but unfortunately this time, yeah, I do."

Leaning a hip against the table, he said, "You know, Morrisette, it's barely eight. How do you know all this?"

"Got here early this morning. Bart had the kids, and I thought I could get something done here when it was a little quieter, y'know, just before the shift change, but that didn't work out. The department's gearing up for a press conference sometime tomorrow. Abbey Marlow's already all over it, talking with everyone, getting her ducks in a row. I talked to her already, but she might want to double-check with you."

"Fine."

"She won't be the only one talking to the press. I'm pretty sure Jada Hill will hold her own chat with the media, with or without Blondell. That woman loves the cameras."

"Comes with the territory," he said, glancing around the room. Most of the musty, twenty-year-old evidence had been sorted through and organized, important pieces clipped together or added to the corkboards outlining the crime. Though Reed wasn't a hundred percent convinced that Blondell O'Henry was the shooter, he'd been working on that assumption.

"Someone tried to warn Nikki off yesterday with snakes up at the cabin," he said.

"I heard." Morrisette glanced at the suspect board and stared at the woman in its center. "But not Blondell. She's still locked up for another day." Running a hand through her short, choppy locks, she walked toward the board. "Who the hell left the snake in the car? If she hadn't just seen a copperhead in the cabin itself, I'd have maybe thought it was a coincidence."

"No coincidence," Reed said grimly. And if

there was a chance Blondell was innocent, the perpetrator could very well be Amity O'Henry's killer.

"She's getting out?" Nikki said, dumbfounded. Her wireless connection was weak for some reason, and she was having trouble hearing Reed over the road noise.

"That's what it looks like. Probably . . . tomor . . ." Reed's voice was cutting out. "There will be . . . pr . . . ference . . . I'll know more . . . afternoon."

"Look, if you can hear me, I'm on the road," she yelled in frustration into her Bluetooth as she passed a gasoline truck. "I'll call you when I've stopped and you can fill me in." Hanging up, she mentally kicked herself from one end of the state to the other. If she'd had any idea that Blondell was going to be released, she would have postponed this trip. As it was, though, she had plenty of time to talk to Thompson and return to Savannah to both meet with Holt Beauregard and attend the press conference tomorrow.

If she stepped on it.

Which she did.

With the aid of the GPS on her phone and a heavy foot on the accelerator, she made it to the garage outside of Charleston in record time. Located in an industrial area far from the heart of the city, Ace Auto Repair had seen better days.

The garage of six bays was built of metal and concrete, all six doors wide open, four mechanics working on vehicles, two hoisted off the floor, rolling boards with mechanics lying on them protruding from their sides, three more with their hoods up. Some kind of rock music played over the din of the noise of the shop.

Larry Thompson was standing at a tall metal cabinet near a side wall where tools and parts were kept. She probably wouldn't have recognized him except that she knew he worked this shift and the badge on his gray jumpsuit read: THOMPSON.

"Lawrence Thompson," she said, and he visibly stiffened before warily turning to face her.

"I'm Nikki—"

"I know who you are." He sounded angry and his features were set. Hard. Almost defiant. "I knew someone would show up with all that's going on with Blondell. I guess I should have expected you."

"I just want to ask you some questions."

He glanced around to the other stations where the mechanics, after watching Nikki approach him, had turned back to their work. "I could use a break." With a hitch of his chin toward an exterior side door, he said, "This way," and led her through the door as if to avoid questions from any of the others who'd looked up as she'd zeroed in on him. She had walked straight into an open bay without bothering to stop at the front counter and deal with whatever roadblocks might have been set in her path.

"I can't tell you anything that hasn't already been printed a dozen times over," he said, wiping his hands on a faded red rag as they walked out of the garage.

"Just humor me."

"I don't see why."

"Because Blondell O'Henry is news again, Larry, and come on, you were in the biz, you know how these things go. Talk to me, and then you can tell the next reporter to take a hike, that you've already talked to me. Or answer their questions too, but you may as well get it over with."

He made a disparaging sound but nodded, seeming to accept the inevitable.

He'd aged since the last photograph Nikki had seen of him, taken more than fifteen years earlier. His face had grown jowly, his eyes guarded by lightly shaded glasses, a short, graying beard covering his once-strong jaw. His sandy hair had been thick and long, brushing his collar, but now it was only a silvery stubble, at least what she could see of it from beneath a Braves baseball cap.

They walked down a worn path to a concrete slab that had been fitted with two folding chairs that looked to be at least fifty years old and a picnic table from the same era. The sky was blue, with only a few clouds skimming across the vast expanse. On the chain-link fence that separated the back of the shop from a parking lot filled with shells of cars, a couple of crows flapped noisily away, their black wings shining, their cries piercing.

This industrial area outside of Charleston was in stark contrast to the beautiful city of elegant Southern mansions—clapboard siding, tall windows, and white pillars, bordered by palm trees—on the harbor.

"I just want to forget all that," Thompson said in a low tone, as if anyone inside the shop could hear over the hiss of air hoses, the whir of electric lug nut removal, and the general clang of metal parts being refitted.

"Is that why you changed professions?"

"Partially. And the fact that no one would hire me." He lifted a shoulder. "Times were changing anyway, newspapers and magazines folding. This was steadier." He thought for a second, his gaze, from behind his tinted lenses, taking in the Dumpster and broken-down cars beyond the fence. "And yeah, I miss it, but not that much."

"She's going to be released soon. Probably tomorrow."

He visibly started, his eyes refocusing on Nikki. "Good," he said, obviously digesting this new turn of events. Nodding, he added, "Yeah, that's . . . good. I don't believe she did what she was accused of, so justice will finally be served."

"She never told you differently?"

"No. Not in the correspondence before . . . you know . . ."

"Before you helped her escape."

"Yeah, and not after, either." He adjusted the bill of his hat, and Nikki noted there was a line of sweat on what was left of his hair. The cuff of his sleeve pulled upward, and she saw the slightest discoloration on his wrist, evidence of the tattoo he'd had removed, the picture of a chameleon that had been the identifying mark that had led to his arrest.

"Look, I don't want to be quoted in the articles you're doing nor in the book. I've carved myself out a new life and it's working, so I don't want to mess it up."

"I understand, but your name is a matter of record."

He said bitterly, "I should never have gotten involved with her. Now that I look back on it a lot more clearly, I think she wanted me so she could get pregnant again. It was her thing, y'know. She had Amity in high school, then two more with her ex, then was pregnant with that fourth one. I mean there is such a thing as birth control. I figured I was just the latest sperm donor who got close enough to her to stick his neck out and help her find a way out of prison." He closed his eyes for a second as if he couldn't believe he'd been so stupid.

"She wanted to have another baby?"

"Oh, yeah. She was all about it. No, I never saw her cry a tear for the daughter who was killed or the ones who were hurt in the attack, but she was hot to trot to have another one. The damnedest thing. So, no, I don't believe she tried to wipe out all her kids."

"You were in love with her." It wasn't a question.

He lifted a shoulder, then the fingers of his right hand scrabbled in the breast pocket of his jumpsuit as if searching for a pack of cigarettes that didn't exist. "At least lust. Whatever you want to call it. I was nuts about her." He looked at the concrete, where an ant was crawling toward a crack. "But the trouble was, my feelings weren't reciprocated."

"No?"

Shoving his hands into his front pockets, he shook his head. "Nope. I think she was still in love with the last guy she'd hooked up with on the outside, before she was locked up."

"Roland Camp?" Nikki said automatically, but Larry's head continued to wag.

"Maybe, but I don't think so. She had nothing but bad things to say about him, put him in the same category with her ex-husband. She never mentioned his name, but I got the idea he might be an older dude. She'd use words like 'mature' and 'sophisticated' and 'smart,' or was it 'well-educated'? Yeah. That sounds more like it. Didn't exactly remind me of Roland Camp."

"No," Nikki agreed. "She didn't mention his name?"

"No."

Another man appeared in the doorway. "Hey!" he called, giving Nikki the eye. He too was wearing a gray jumpsuit. "I could use a little help, Tom!"

"In a sec, Chet," Larry responded.

"You don't go by your first name?"

"Nope. Just easier. Most people don't know about my past, and that's the way I'd like to keep it, but now that she's going to be released, I think it's probably going to be a problem. You found me. You won't be the last."

"Probably not," Nikki said, and then, though she was starting to dread the answer, she asked, "What about her attorney? What did she think about him?"

He snorted. "That snob? Alexander Whatever? Yeah, she thought he walked on water, even after she got put away for life. Somehow she didn't blame him. I told her to find someone new to represent her, to file an appeal with some big gun from New York or Chicago or Atlanta, but she wasn't interested. If I hadn't known better I would have sworn she was in love with him."

"But you did? Know better?"

"I know about the rumors, but I didn't want to think about them. Legally, it was a nightmare, right? Anyway, what happened between them, she never said, but I do believe she was half in love with him, as much as she could be. Look, I gotta go," he said, catching a harsh glare from Chet, who once again appeared in the doorway. "This job is important to me."

"Just one more thing," she said quickly, thinking of the viper in her car. "Amity was bitten by a snake before she died. Did Blondell ever talk about that?"

"Only that she's deathly afraid of all kinds of snakes. Hates 'em," he said, "Would turn the TV to another channel if a snake came into view, and visibly cringed when one was mentioned. Now, look, I really have to go." He didn't wait, but slipped back into the interior of the cavernous garage, and Nikki, hearing the crows cawing as they returned, made her way back to the car. All the while, she tried to tell herself that her uncle had *not* been involved with his client, that he wouldn't have betrayed his marriage or his professional reputation, that his rumored romance with Blondell O'Henry was just that—pure, spiteful gossip.

But now she wasn't as convinced.

Too many people, including Larry Thompson, believed differently.

She thought of her uncle as he had been twenty years earlier. Tall. Strapping. Successful. With a winning demeanor and a killer smile.

As she climbed into her rental car, she realized that everything she'd believed for most of her life had been a lie.

December 15th
Fifth Interview

This is difficult.

Harder than I imagined.

I've come here and tried to reach out to this woman, only to be thwarted at every turn. The prison walls are getting to me, the smell of pine cleaner not able to cover the smell of body odors and despair. I cannot imagine how she can stand to be locked away, but there she sits, her face impassive through the glass, her pain, if there is any, well hidden.

Why?

It doesn't matter any longer. I'm done. I'll write my story the way I want to, and she can sit in silence behind these thick, concrete-and-steel walls.

Trying to communicate with a woman whose heart has turned to stone is just too much for me. I'm tired of arguing and certainly tired of pleading, but most of all, I'm tired of the lies. So many lies.

My attempts to be fair and to tell her side of the story, to let her explain what she did, to try and exonerate herself, have gone unheeded. As if it's all a game. As if playing along will ensure that I return.

The woman behind the glass can rot in hell for the rest of her life, if she wants to.

"This is the last time," I tell her from my side of the glass, the old receiver resting against my ear, the muted conversations of others reaching me. "I've tried my best to give you every chance to tell your side of things, to explain about your children, to come clean, but you aren't interested." Sighing, I lay it out to her in the only terms I think she'll understand. "I can only surmise that you just don't care what the world thinks."

For the first time, a blaze of indignation flares in her eyes, and her lips tighten almost imperceptibly. "So I'm writing the book the way I see it," I continue. "I hope you can live with that."

The face cracks just slightly, a bit of sadness showing. "I've lived with far worse," she says to me, her voice as hollow as her eyes. "This is nothing."

"So be it." I start to hang up, but she taps on the glass and her eyes, for a second, soften.

"I loved my children! That's all anyone has to know, all you have to know. I loved them!"

Chapter 26

"Here's the receipt." Max slid a copy of an itemized sales slip across a glass display case to Reed. Barely twenty-five if he was a day, Max Huber was the owner and manager of Max's Spy World, a shop dedicated to surveillance equipment and decorated with posters from James Bond movies. The display cases held all kinds of cameras, listening gear, mini-computers, phones, tiny microphones, night-vision goggles, and even some drones marketed as toys. Max's red hair was cropped short, his soul patch thin, his skin fighting a losing battle with acne.

"I can give you a copy of the surveillance tape for that day," he said, pointing to the date on the receipt. "Since I'm in the biz, I run surveillance twenty-four/seven on the shop. Got lots of equipment that people might like to steal." He lifted his shoulders. "Want a copy? It'll just take a second. All filed digitally, and since the guy came in less than two weeks ago, right at my fingertips. Just give me a sec . . ."

Before Reed could answer, Max hit a few buttons on a computer at the desk and seconds later handed Reed a small jump drive. "I remember this dude. He was like, really nervous. Asked a butt-load of questions, but was kind of a cheap-ass. I could see he wanted the better camera, but he wasn't going to part with the bucks, but hey, y'know, ya get what ya pay for. He asked about a GPS tracking device too, to hide in the undercarriage of a car or something, but opted out, said he could use the phone." His mouth twisted. "I couldn't talk him into the GPS, but hey, what're ya gonna do?"

"Thanks," Reed said.

"Hey, any time. And if the department ever needs state of the art equipment, I've got it. I can make a deal for Savannah's finest."

"I'll bet," Morrisette said under her breath, a comment that was no doubt caught and amplified by the microphones and video equipment in the store. A little louder, as they walked through the glass door, she added, "We'll keep that in mind."

Outside, the sun was peeking through the clouds, and a few errant rays were reflecting on puddles drying in the parking lot. " 'Never stop selling' must be his motto," Morrisette said. "The kid's got moxie, I'll give him that."

Once inside the car, she started the engine. "You're not saying much. You know the guy who bought the stuff?"

"Oh, yeah," Reed said, still thinking it over.

"You gonna tell me?"

He pocketed the disk and receipt. "On the way to the place where he works."

"You know where that is?"

"That I do," he said, and looked as if he could eat steel and spit nails. "Let's go."

Nikki flew down the highway, pushing the rental car and the speed limit as her thoughts burned through her brain, thoughts she hadn't wanted to consider. Had her uncle really been involved with Blondell O'Henry? Is that why she chose him as her attorney rather than some high-profile criminal lawyer who would have loved to have made his name representing a beautiful woman accused of the most atrocious of crimes, a monster who was nearly movie-star gorgeous?

If so, Nikki wondered, had her parents known? Her father, the judge who presided over the trial? The prosecution? Garland Brownell, the district attorney?

She saw a patrol car on the highway ahead, checked her speedometer, and saw she was fifteen miles above the speed limit. "Damn," she muttered, but lucked out as the patrolman had already pulled someone else over. *Slow down. You'll get there; five or ten minutes one way or another won't make any difference. You're not Danica Frickin' Patrick, for crying out loud!*

Her phone rang, and she popped in her ear device, then answered. "Gillette."

"I guess I'll forgive you for standing me up," Trina said, a smile in her voice. "A snake in the car trumps a friend at the bar any day. So how're you doing today?"

"Busy and lucky. Almost got a ticket. Just passed a state cop doing a few miles over the limit."

"Yikes. Slow down, lead foot."

"Believe me, I am. So how about we have that drink tomorrow?" Nikki asked, with one eye on the speedometer. "Tonight I'm booked."

"With that hunk of a cop, I hope."

"Not quite. The hunk part is probably right, though, of course I wouldn't really know as I'm an engaged woman these days, but the cop part is off. I think he tried to be one once and it didn't work out for some reason." *Damn but the speedometer kept inching up.* "I'm talking about Holt Beauregard."

"Ahh . . . The black sheep of the Beauregards?"

"Could be a whole flock in that family."

Trina laughed. "You're right. But there is a reason I called, you know, and it's because of the whole snake thing."

"Yeah?" Nikki forced herself to stay in the slow lane even though the guy in front of her in an aging Pontiac was taking the speed limit literally.

"This is probably nothing," Trina was saying, "but a guy by the name of Alfred Necarney died today, at a hospital in north Georgia."

"Never heard of him."

"I know. No one has. His home is an old family spread located in the hills outside of Dahlonga. First report is that he's an Army veteran who lived alone, kind of a hermit. His sister hadn't heard from him for a few days, got worried, and found him near dead from a blow to the head; he died at the hospital."

Where was this going? *"And?"*

"So far, the news is sketchy, but he ran an interesting side business. He sold snakes for a living, completely black market, under the radar."

Nikki's hands tightened over the wheel. *"And?"* she said again.

"And a lot of the snakes were let loose, running, er, slithering around free. They hadn't bitten him, the theory being that he was just lying on the floor, unconscious, not threatening, so they left him alone, just sidled up to him for warmth. Anyway, either he lifted the lids from their cages or someone else did and let them out."

"What?" Nikki's pulse elevated a bit.

"From what I can piece together, they're trying to figure out how he slipped and hit his head and knocked off not one, but several lids of the terrariums he kept them in."

"Not likely," Nikki said.

"Uh-huh, and when the animal handlers came to recapture the snakes, six seemed to be missing from their marked cages."

Nikki felt both dread and exhilaration steal through her. Maybe they were on the verge of some answers.

"Three coral snakes and the same number of copperheads," Trina went on. "Two of which, I'm thinking, maybe you met last night. Could be a coincidence, I suppose."

"No. Someone stole the snakes from Necarney, murdered him, then came back to Savannah and slipped one into the cabin and another in my car." Nikki was certain.

"That's what I think," Trina agreed. "Your buddies from last night had to come from somewhere. Even if you argued that the copperhead in the cabin could have been there for a while, had a nest or whatever, it is November, and don't they like hibernate or something in the cold weather?"

"Or something," she agreed. Geez, could the guy in front of her go any slower?

"And there's just no way one got into your car without a little help."

"You got that right," she agreed grimly.

"So far the police upstate are investigating, and there's no official word, but the sister, her name is Nola-Mae Pitman, has been spouting off. I found her number—she's in the book—so I'll text it to you just in case you want to give her a call."

"Thanks. I do."

"And by the way, Effie's been hanging around.

Of course, she asked all about you and what happened last night."

"I guess that was to be expected," Nikki said, her mind on other topics.

"Yeah, I know, but some of the questions were kind of personal. She was all about who owned the cabin and how you were related and why you were there."

The driver ahead of Nikki slowed yet again. She couldn't stand it, checked her mirror, and blew around the guy, who obviously didn't know his old GTO had been considered a muscle car in its day and should be driven faster than fifty friggin' miles an hour.

"I don't know what Effie's deal is," Nikki admitted, tucking back into the lane and slowing a bit.

"I told her to take it all up with you."

"Okay."

"She's also all over the Blondell O'Henry release tomorrow. I guess the blogosphere is blowing up about it."

"Major news."

"Yes, ma'am."

"Okay. I'll deal with it when I get there. I'm on my way back—oh, crap!" In her rearview mirror she saw flashing lights and, glancing down at her dash, realized she was once again speeding ten miles over the limit. "Talk to you later." She slowed, hearing the siren screaming as she pulled over, and wondered how in the world she'd talk herself out of the ticket. It crossed her mind to use Reed's name and title at the department, but she decided that was too low; it would put everyone on the spot. Heart sinking, nerves stretched, she waited . . . but the cop car shot by at a speed that far exceeded her max. Letting out her breath, she noticed that the other cars on the road ahead of her, which had also slowed onto the shoulder, were ignored as well.

Pulling into traffic again, she forced herself to drive at the speed limit as she headed back to Savannah and wondered who had put a snake from the hills around Dahlonga in her car.

"What is this?" Charles Arbuckle demanded, shooting up from the leather chair behind his desk as Morrisette and Reed strode into his expansive corner office with a wide view of the river.

"I tried to stop them!" a petite receptionist said in her high-pitched voice. She was wearing five-inch heels, a short dress, and a telephone headset that barely disturbed her shaggy, streaked hair. "I'm so sorry, Mr. Arbuckle, they just barged right in after I told them you were busy." Indignation poured off of one hundred pounds of her. "I can call the police."

"We're already here," Morrisette said, showing her badge.

"Oh." The receptionist, flustered, her gaze glued

to the badge, actually gulped back anything else she'd planned to say.

"It's all right, Daisy," Arbuckle said, holding up a staying hand. "Really. Just close the door and postpone my next appointment."

"With the Quinns? Really?" She looked positively stricken and glared at Reed and Morrisette as if they were emissaries from Satan himself.

"Yes, Daisy, please," Arbuckle said firmly, though obviously it pained him to waylay clients of the Quinns' stature, whatever that might be.

Reed didn't give a damn.

The starch having seeped out of her, Daisy left, pulling the door shut behind her. Once it closed, Arbuckle said stiffly, "What can I do for you?" Then before they could respond, he read the serious expression on their faces and said, "Do I need a lawyer?" He looked from Morrisette to Reed. "Because it sure feels like I should call my attorney."

Morrisette said, "Only if you have something to hide."

"Of course not!" He was emphatic, even offended, but as if he realized how sharply he was reacting, he dialed his attitude down a bit. "I mean, I don't even understand why you're here."

"Well, let's clear that much up." Reed retrieved the receipt from Max's Spy World from his pocket. "It seems that you purchased camera equipment used to spy on Nicole Gillette, your landlord. You probably recognize me, as I'm sure you filmed me too when I was there."

Arbuckle turned white as a proverbial ghost, and he nearly collapsed into his chair. "Just my luck, a cop," he said, and waved them into the plush visitors' chairs positioned across the expanse of polished rosewood that was his desk. "Oh, dear God. Look, I understand, but it was a mistake," he said to begin with, not denying anything.

"Care to elaborate?"

He closed his eyes, and his hands on the arms of his chair clenched into fists. "I was just trying to spy on *my* apartment, not *hers,* not Nikki's."

"You were photographing your own place?" Reed asked skeptically. He was holding down his escalating temper with an effort.

Arbuckle exhaled and looked out the window for a second, his eyes following a fishing vessel as it headed downstream, though Reed bet he wasn't seeing the boat. "It's my wife. She . . . Oh, God, this is so damned . . . she's been . . . unhappy and the word 'divorce' has come up a few times. I think she might be seeing someone, so I thought I'd find out for myself."

Reed said, "By taking pictures of Nikki Gillette's apartment?"

"I told you it was a mistake. The angle was all off!" Arbuckle said. "I told that idiot Donnigan I wanted to look into *our* unit. *Our* bedroom, but what can I say, he's a moron. I don't know why I trusted that pothead in the first place!"

"You asked Leon Donnigan to help you?"

"Not just asked him: I paid him!" Arbuckle admitted, folding his arms over his chest. "So I guess I'm the idiot." He let out a long sigh. "Look, I'm no computer geek, okay? I do investments and I'm very good at it. But I can't program computers or hook up cameras or locate wireless signals or do whatever it is I needed to do to spy on my own apartment, and Donnigan, he's a real nerd; holes up in his bedroom and plays war games or whatever online, spends his time fixing computers and he's always strapped for cash, so, I thought, 'He's right downstairs. Let him do the work.' But he fuck—fouled up. I figured it out when the first images came in, but by then someone had already taken down the cameras." He actually seemed a bit contrite. "If it's any consolation, I didn't see much, just Nikki at her computer." He actually had the decency to blush a little.

"Still, an invasion of privacy."

"Look, I'm sorry. When I saw the first pictures, I flipped out, couldn't believe it, and I told Donnigan to take the cameras down, but by then, it was too late. You and your officers had already done that. I didn't know who had removed them, but I figured it wasn't good." He looked defeated. "If you talk to Donnigan he'll confirm all this."

"Oh, we will," Morrisette assured him.

Either this guy was a really good actor or he was telling the truth. For the time being, Reed decided to believe him. "You know, you might just try talking to your wife."

A muscle worked in the corner of Arbuckle's jaw. "I think it might be too late for that," he said wearily. He drew a breath and then asked, "So are we done here? There's really nothing more to say, and I'm really busy."

"We know. The Quinns are waiting," Morrisette said as she glanced at Reed.

"Am I going to be charged with anything?" he asked.

Reed, disgusted, headed to the door. "That'll be up to Ms. Gillette, but I think you'd better start looking for somewhere else to live."

"So Blondell's release is all set?" Nikki said to Trina upon returning to the office.

"As long as everything goes as planned, that's the latest." Trina pushed out her desk chair and stood in her favorite spot, on her side of the partition, where their desks merged, as Nikki switched on her desktop computer. Around them other reporters were on their phones, and keyboard keys were clicking, monitors glowing, a printer pumping out hard copy across the room.

"You look remarkably okay after your ordeal last night."

"The wonders of Cover Girl."

"Yeah, right."

Nikki was known for her lack of beauty routine. She just didn't care enough, unless she was going out. Then she would hit the mascara, lip gloss, and fingernail polish a little harder.

"I would have freaked out if it had happened to me, I mean *freaked.* Antoine would have had to put me in a mental ward."

"I'm really okay," Nikki said, lying a little. She didn't want to think too hard about the snake. "My car took a beating."

"Is it bad?"

"Not good. I should find out today."

Trina glanced across the spacious room, cut up by cubicles, to the wall where several computers were stretched along an expansive counter. "Everyone's been asking about you, of course, once the word got out, but with her"—she glanced over toward Effie's empty work station and Nikki's eyes followed; Trina didn't say Effie's name aloud—"it's different."

"What specifically did she ask?"

"Oh, you know. 'Where did it happen?' 'What was she doing at the cabin?' 'Does this have anything to do with the Blondell O'Henry story she's writing?' 'Was she alone?' 'Was she hurt?' 'Did the snake strike?' 'Was she meeting anyone there?' 'Did Detective Reed know what she was doing?' Maybe it's nothing, but she seemed a little too eager for details and then she asked about your family, not just your father, but about your siblings and even your cousins, y'know, what were their names?"

"Hollis and Elton McBaine?"

"Lots about them and about their mother."

"You mean their father. He was Blondell's attorney."

"Nope. She asked me if I'd met Penelope McBaine, and I had to tell her I'd never had the pleasure."

Nikki's gaze met Trina's. "What?"

"I caught her a couple of times here, at your desk. Never really sitting in your chair, but just kind of hanging, y'know. A little too interested in what you're doing."

"She wants us to work together on the Blondell O'Henry stories, even worked it out with Fink," Nikki said slowly.

"Hmmm. Good luck with that. Did you get the text I sent you with the snake guy's sister's name and number?" she asked; then, as her phone rang, she glanced down at her desk. "Oops. Gotta take this. Big benefit auction tonight, and somehow all the questions are routed to *my* desk. Guess it comes with the territory."

Nikki wasted no time. She couldn't worry about Effie and her seeming fascination with her, at least not today. Daylight was fading, and she had a lot to do before Blondell O'Henry was released.

She listened to her messages and learned none of the legitimate reptile dealers she'd contacted earlier had sold any copperheads, but they all were very interested in selling her another kind of snake or turtle or even alligator. "No thanks," she said to herself. Her close encounter with the pit viper was enough.

She then tried the number Trina had texted her for Alfred Necarney's sister and was shot right to voice mail. Drumming her fingers on her desk, she tried to remember something that was nagging at the back of her brain, a bit of conversation she'd had recently that she thought she should remember, but couldn't. She shook her head and jotted down notes from her meeting with Lawrence Thompson, then added a few more questions to ask Holt Beauregard. Still online, she attempted to check out the Reverend Ezekiel Byrd and his congregation, but that group was pretty much under the radar, which wasn't a surprise. No Web site or social media presence.

She was reviewing footage of Blondell's trial, clips that had been posted on the Internet, when she was struck again by how much Amity looked like her mother. And Flint Beauregard, when he took the stand, was a handsome man, and steady in his testimony. He didn't appear angry or rattled, just gave out the facts as he'd recorded them.

During the entire time, Blondell O'Henry sat unruffled, staring at the cop who was trying to send her to prison for life as if she didn't care, her expression nearly blank.

"Odd," Nikki thought as the phone rang and she saw Reed's number.

"Hey, handsome," she said. "I was just about to call you, to see if there was any update on Blondell's release. Our connection earlier was almost nonexistent."

"Nothing yet. As I understand it, there are some details to be worked out, but it still looks like a go for tomorrow."

"I want to be there."

"I think Jada Hill will probably discourage the press."

"I could call her a nasty word, but I have too much respect for her, grudging though it may be," Nikki said, rolling her chair away from her desk.

"I thought you'd like to know we caught our personal stalker."

"What?" She sat up straighter in her chair. "Who?"

"Turns out it was kind of a mistake. Sorry to disappoint, but you, darlin', weren't the target, after all. Our man was none other than Charles Arbuckle, who thinks his wife might be cheating on him."

He explained about Arbuckle's fears and how

he was trying to spy on his wife but had left the details of the electronic hookup to Leon Donnigan, who, apparently, had messed up big-time and ended up focusing on Nikki's apartment. He finished with, "I called Donnigan and he confirmed, so I think another big mystery is solved, except that it doesn't explain the feeling that you've had of being followed."

"No . . ."

"And it's not tied nicely in to the case we're investigating."

"Just a coincidence," she said aloud, troubled.

"I don't like coincidences," Reed said.

"And I don't like tenants who run around like they think they're CIA operatives and spy on me. Once we get married, maybe we should kick them all out, remodel the whole damned house, and forget about renters."

"I know," he agreed. "Though Mrs. Donnigan is an innocent in all this."

"Yeah, and so is Gloria Arbuckle, but they have lousy taste in family members. Even if this was a mistake, I wouldn't put it past Leon to post some of the pictures on the Internet." Her stomach soured at the thought.

"I'll make sure he doesn't by reminding him about all the laws he's broken."

"If I don't get to him first. I think I could get some good shots of him smoking a—controlled substance—if I really tried."

Reed actually laughed and said, "We'll talk later. I gotta run now."

"Much later. I've got a hot date with a private detective."

"Holt Beauregard?" He let out a low whistle. "Good luck with that. I don't know what his feelings on the matter are, but let's just say Deacon isn't taking Blondell O'Henry's release all that well. Thinks it's a travesty of justice and is taking it as a personal black eye for not only the department, but especially his old man."

"He'd better get over it." She thought about telling him her suspicions about Flint Beauregard but decided against it. So far it was just a theory, with nothing much to back it up.

"Not happening," Reed said. "At least not today. Oh, and the garage called. The lab's finished going over your car. I can pick it up anytime."

"Don't bother. I'll do it. I can get a ride from the rental car agency." She was thinking of her uncle's set of keys that she'd had to abandon in the car. If she could avoid it, she didn't want to explain to Reed how she'd ended up with them. Until the key ring was returned, she'd basically stolen Uncle Alex's personal property, no matter how much she sugar-coated it to herself.

"You're sure?"

"Positive," she said and decided she'd better return the keys at the first chance she got. "I'll take care of it. You keep on chasing the bad guys." Her uncle's warning flitted through her mind.

She's dangerous . . . Leave this alone!

Had his words been just the delusions of an older man battling with reality? Or had the warning been a ploy to keep her from finding out the truth—that he was romantically involved with his client? There was also, of course, potentially another more dire implication in his words: that Blondell O'Henry, the woman about to be released from prison, truly was a cold-blooded killer and that digging up her past was only asking for trouble.

Chapter 27

Sometimes things just seemed to work better without a man involved, Morrisette thought as she eased the nose of her Chevy off Victory Drive and into the neighborhood where Deacon and Holt Beauregard had grown up. She'd done some digging about their father, Flint Beauregard, and learned that he'd gone to school here, in Savannah, the very same high school Blondell O'Henry—well, actually Blondell Rochette, at that time—had attended, though, of course, years before.

Still, it was a little detail that had nagged at

Morrisette for days. Today she was going to do a little poking and see what she could find. Sliding a pair of sunglasses onto her nose, she headed her car to Stevenson Street.

With aging post–World War II bungalows lining the streets, this part of Savannah could have been Anywhere, USA. Basketball hoops had been bolted to garage roofs, and cars were parked against the curbs. The sidewalks were lined with shade trees planted so long ago that their branches were tangled in the electrical wires overhead and their roots had buckled the cement.

The Beauregards' house was in the middle of the block, painted khaki green, the decorative shutters the same brown as the trim; a walkway split the scraggly lawn, its mortar chipped and cracked, and weeds sprouted between the faded bricks. Morrisette walked up to the front door, rang the bell, and waited on the outside of an aluminum screen door.

As she dropped her sunglasses into her pocket, footsteps heralded the arrival of someone on the other side, and seconds later Flora Beauregard, in a sweater and jeans a size too tight, opened the sticking front door with an effort.

Morrisette flashed her badge and introduced herself. "I'd like to come in and ask you a few questions," she said.

Flora's hand reached for the latch to the screen door but paused. "I don't know . . ."

"It won't take long. I promise." Morrisette managed a "we're just girls here talking" smile.

"Well . . . I suppose," Flora said in her soft Southern drawl as she unlatched the screen. She was thick in the middle, her hair a carefully styled blond bouffant, stylish glasses bridging her nose. "I've been expecting someone like you would be coming by ever since the talk started about *that woman*." She held the door open for Morrisette. "I can't believe she's being released. I just can't believe it. After what she did!" Latching the screen behind Morrisette with one hand, she motioned her into the living room with her other.

The room, dominated by a big picture window, looked as if it had been redecorated around 1975 and not touched since. The heat was blasting—the temperature had to have been pushing eighty degrees—and an underlying odor of cigarette smoke and bacon grease lingered in the air.

"Is there anything I can get you?" Flora offered. "Sweet tea? Coffee?"

"I'm fine."

"Well, then." Waving Morrisette into a striped side chair, Flora took a seat in what seemed to be her favorite rocker, positioned to face television, a knitting bag overflowing with balls of yarn at its side. Several tabloid magazines were strewn across the worn carpet, though she gathered them up and tucked them into a rack

416

that also served as an end table. On the muted television set, a cooking program was in progress, a stout woman frying some kind of sizzling meat while furiously chopping bell peppers and onions, from the looks of it.

"Deacon said someone would probably show up," she admitted.

"Yeah." Morrisette couldn't help but stare at the thick wooden mantel upon which rested framed photos. In the place of honor, just under an antique rifle and a picture of Jesus mounted on the chimney face, was a framed, oversize portrait of Flint and Flora, their two sons flanking the happy couple. The boys, appearing uncomfortable in creased shirts and narrow ties, had probably been in high school at the time. Flint hadn't yet begun to flesh out; his jaw was still strong, his eyes intense, his mustache thick and dark. Flora too had been twenty or thirty pounds slimmer as she smiled, hands folded, into the camera.

"What is it you want to know?" she asked. As in the photo, she sat with her hands folded in her lap.

"I wondered if you had any of Detective Beauregard's personal records, his notebook, tapes, that sort of thing, that he might have kept while investigating the Amity O'Henry homicide," Morrisette told her.

Behind her glasses, Flora's eyes narrowed a bit. "Why?"

"Because the department could use anything you have that might be helpful in keeping Ms. O'Henry in prison."

"I wish I could help you. I really do." Her lips tightened, and almost as if she didn't realize what she was doing, she picked up her knitting needles, which were entangled in a pink yarn. "I can't imagine that she'll be set free. Flint worked very hard to see that she would spend the rest of her life in prison for what she did to those poor children." Though she attempted to appear calm, Flora was obviously agitated, a little twitch visible just above the bow of her glasses, her needles moving fluidly as she unconsciously added row after row of stitching to what appeared to be the beginning of an infant's sweater.

Click. Click. Click.

"My husband worked tirelessly on the case against Blondell O'Henry."

"I understand. But the primary witness has recanted."

"Ridiculous!"

Click. Click. Click.

"You met your husband in high school?" Morrisette tried, hoping she would open up some.

The needles stopped for a second. "Actually sixth grade, but I don't see what that has to do with anything."

"Did he know Blondell Rochette?"

"No!" she said vehemently. "She was much younger, so he didn't know her when we were in school. He met her during that investigation, of course."

Again the needles began moving rhythmically.

"She had older brothers, I think. It's not impossible to think he'd met her."

Her lips pulled into a knot, and she dropped her knitting into her lap. "Detective Morrisette, what are you getting at?"

"Nothing specific. I'd just like to know how personal this case was to him."

"Very personal." She was angry now, her needles silent, her knuckles bent and showing white. "He was a father, and he found it incomprehensible and cruel and evil that a mother would do such a brutal act. Garland Brownell, the DA at the time, didn't press for the death penalty. They used Old Sparky, back then, y'know, and Blondell, she would have fried, but no one wanted that. Personally, I think it would have been the best thing, saved the state a ton of money keeping her locked away." She looked up, her eyebrows vaulting over the rims of her glasses as she kept right on knitting. "Considering all this business now, this testimony changing, having the switch thrown would have saved everyone a whole lot of trouble!"

Man, Flora was really worked up, her color high. "Did you know her?" Morrisette asked.

"No, and I didn't have to." She kept on furiously knitting. "That woman is evil. Pure evil." Taking a deep breath, she stopped and sketched a hasty sign of the cross over her ample bosom. "Since you're here, I'll tell you what I think. Blondell O'Henry should never be allowed out of prison. Never! Find a way to keep her in there, Detective. Make sure what my husband worked so hard for remains as it is. Lock her up and throw away the damned key!"

Nikki picked up her car without incident and was relieved to find both sets of keys inside. She signed for everything, swore what was listed was, indeed hers. If Reed saw the inventory, he might wonder about a second key ring listed along with her gloves, keys, half-used box of Tic Tacs, registration, insurance forms, and umbrella, and, she supposed, she would have to come clean and admit to her crime. However, she doubted he would ask and felt only a smidgen of guilt that she hadn't confided in him. Of course, she really couldn't, as it would make him an accessory to her "crime," so she figured that in this case what he didn't know wouldn't hurt him.

Her CR-V was drivable, if dented, so she figured she'd deal with the insurance later. Right now, she had too much to do to worry about the damage. All she needed was a set of wheels that would get her where she wanted to go.

First up, Steve Manning, who would start his shift within the hour, which was perfect.

Except that as she drove her Honda into the hotel's underground lot, her cell phone rang, and she saw that it was her mother. No doubt there was another wedding emergency looming, but Nikki thought she could handle it later and didn't pick up. She was already running late as it was, so she parked in the first space she saw, marked HOTEL GUESTS, then took the elevator to the main lobby. With marble floors, glass walls, and twenty-foot ceilings, the hotel was sleek and modern, in stark contrast to most of the older buildings in this part of town which oozed with the charm of the Old South. She made her way past the registration counter and concierge desk to a doorway marked SECURITY and stepped inside.

Two men were talking, both in the navy-blue uniforms of the staff. They looked up, and the taller man, a heavy-set African-American with a broad face and silvery hair, asked, "Can I help you?"

"I think she's here to see me," Steve Manning said. Time hadn't changed much for Steve; he was still slim, tanned, his hair longer than the fashion, though he'd traded in his jeans and T-shirts for the company uniform.

"Hi, Steve."

To the black man, Steve said, "Raleigh, this is Nikki Gillette."

"Big Daddy's daughter?"

She tensed a little. "One and the same."

"Nice to meet you," he said. "Your father gave my Camille a break and it changed her life, for the better." He smiled then, showing off one gold tooth. "You two go talk all ya want. It's been slow this afternoon." And with a shooing motion of hands, which were large enough to belong to a pro ball player, he swept them out of the small space.

"Never thought I'd see you in uniform," Nikki said as they stepped into the grand lobby, her shoes clicking against the marble floor, a few travelers pulling roller bags to an interior elevator with glassed-in cars.

"Stranger things have happened." He still had a boyish smile; though a few lines fanned from the corners of his eyes, Steve could have passed for a man ten years younger. "You know I had such a crush on you in high school."

"Really?"

He nodded as they walked past an escalator leading to the second floor and a few potted ficus trees, to a tufted bench by the windows, where the softest notes of piped-in music could be heard and the view of the river was nearly panoramic. "You didn't know?"

She shook her head. "You were out of school when I got there."

"Yeah, but I knew you because of Elton McBaine. He was your cousin, right?" When she nodded, he added, "We had the same extra-curricular interests back then."

"Drugs?"

Rather than answer directly, he said, "The same connection."

"Your dealer?" she asked, remembering that Elton had "dabbled," according to her parents, which could have meant anything from having an experimental joint to being an out-and-out druggie who used any and every illicit substance known to man. From what Hollis had told her, she thought he was somewhere in between.

"I don't smoke and tell," he said with that charming grin, "but those days are behind me now. So what is it you want?"

"You dated Amity O'Henry when she was in high school."

His smile slid off his face. "Well . . . we went out a couple of times. Maybe three times. But we weren't going together or anything like that." He looked decidedly uncomfortable.

"No?"

"It wasn't for me not trying. Hell, I thought she was incredible. Hot. But," he lifted his shoulders, "I didn't like her old man, the one who'd come back from the war. He gave me the evil eye, and I had the feeling that it was 'hands off,' if you get my drift. But the deal was, Amity wasn't all that interested anyway. I'm pretty sure she had her eye on someone else."

"Who?"

"I don't know," he was shaking his head as if digging up ancient high school history was nearly impossible.

"Brad Holbrook?"

"Nah. She thought he was stuck on himself, and she was right. Dumb-ass baseball jock."

"What about Holt Beauregard?"

He looked out the window, where dusk was settling. Nikki turned to follow his gaze and saw both their pale reflections, ghostly images that reminded her of how they had looked at Robert E. Lee High School, which seemed, now, a lifetime ago.

"Beauregard. I don't know. As I said, Amity and I really didn't spend much time together. Too bad you couldn't ask Elton; she was always calling him. Bugging him, but he loved it."

Again the connection. And hadn't Hollis said once that her brother and his friends had basically used Amity? At the time Nikki had thought it was all just teenage boys with their inflated egos and largely exaggerated sexual tales. "Did they date? Amity and Elton?"

"Not officially, but I got the idea she had the hots for him. I figured because he had a hot car and money, and could get drugs pretty easily, but that was maybe wrong. The way I remember it, Amity really wasn't into smoking weed or anything. At least she never did it around me, and you know, at that time, I was into being stoned." He thought for a second. "Does it really matter? She's dead. Her weird mom spent most of her life in prison, and her siblings are all messed up. So it's ancient history."

"Except that someone fired a gun at point-blank range and killed her."

"You don't think it was her mom?" he asked, astounded, as if he'd never considered another person could have pulled the trigger. "They sent her to prison."

"And now it looks like she's getting out early, that her son might have lied on the stand. She may very well be innocent."

"That would be something." He shoved his hair from his eyes and looked faintly disturbed.

"Did you ever meet Blondell?"

"Like I said, I didn't like Amity's old man. I tended to avoid parents back then. I did see Amity's mom from a distance once, though. She was getting into her car as I was walking up the street."

"And?"

"Amity definitely got her looks from her mother." He stopped for a second. "So you're writing about Amity's murder and Blondell's release, for the paper. I saw your name on a story in the *Sentinel*."

"I'm doing a series on Blondell."

"Sells papers. And you're writing a book too? You did that before."

Nikki nodded.

"You sure you want to do that?" he asked, rubbing his chin.

"Why?"

"Sometimes it seems that it's best to leave well enough alone. You know, let sleeping dogs lie."

"You think I won't like what I find."

"I think there's just no point to it. Amity's dead. Yeah, someone killed her, most likely her old lady, but no matter what kind of digging around you do, whatever truth you're trying to uncover, nothing will ever bring her back."

"But maybe justice will be served."

"Maybe it already has been."

She thought about that a minute, then decided it wouldn't hurt to tell him about what had happened to her at the cabin.

"Someone tried to scare me off just last night by leaving a snake in my car. A copperhead."

"Oh, shit! Really?" He took a step back. "That's serious crap. Why would anyone do that?"

"I don't know. Yet. But maybe it's because of my investigation. Maybe it was a warning."

"That's what I'm tellin' you. People have died. I'd stay as far away from Amity O'Henry's murder as I could. I still think Blondell did it, but just in case she didn't, you'd better watch your back."

• • •

"Let's get something to eat," Morrisette suggested as she poked her head into Reed's office. "I think we missed lunch."

"And breakfast," Reed said.

"I'll just be a sec. Meet you in the hall."

Reed's stomach was starting to burn a little from a day of too much coffee and too little food. Since Nikki was going to be late again, he planned to stop by his apartment, grab some clean clothes, and head over to her place to spend the night. Little by little, her old manor was beginning to feel like home, even if it was split into three apartments.

He was giving up his lease come the first of the year, so he figured the more used to her place he could get, the better. But all that was just a cover-up for what he was really feeling today. And the truth of the matter was, since this whole Blondell O'Henry case had been reopened, he didn't like Nikki to be too far out of his sight.

His mind was on the conversation, but his brain kept turning back to the snake that had been left in Nikki's car. She was shaken up last night but had pulled herself together. She'd woken up more determined than ever to write the damned book about the O'Henry case, as well as the continuing series of articles for the newspaper, and that, it seemed, was worrying someone. Who the hell was it, and why were they so concerned? He thought of all the players in the O'Henry case and couldn't come up with anyone who would be deadly.

But there was someone.

Amity O'Henry's murder was proof enough of that.

Reed had hoped that when he located the person who'd been spying on her apartment the mystery of her stalker would be solved and she would be safe again. Not so, it seemed, and trying to talk her out of going after a story when it was in her blood was like trying to stop a rushing freight train by holding up one hand.

Reed feared some nutcase had Nikki in his crosshairs again, and he was pretty damned sure it wasn't Charles Arbuckle or Leon Donnigan. No, whoever was targeting her was far more dangerous, and it was all he could do not to order a bodyguard for her. She'd be upset, but it didn't matter. Let her be mad. As long as she was safe.

He grabbed his jacket and sidearm and patted his jacket pocket to make certain he had his badge and wallet. His keys jangled in his pants pocket as he stepped into the hallway and nearly ran into his partner.

"You know," Morrisette said as they headed downstairs, "Reverend Ezekiel Byrd's congregation does use copperheads in its snake-handling rites. But they're not just into coppers. They are an equal-opportunity user of poisonous snakes, so they've got rattlers and cottonmouths, and even an occasional cobra, but they're rare since, you know, they're not indigenous to the area—or the continent, for that matter." She seemed proud of herself as they headed down the steps together, her boots ringing loudly on the stairs.

"You visited the reverend?" He'd learned the church was forty-five miles outside of the city and, of course, outside their jurisdiction, but the various departments across the state worked together more often than not.

"Of course not. I called, but I just got a voice recording. I'm hoping he'll call me back."

Reed almost laughed. "You think the reverend would tell you?"

"He will if he's an honest, God-fearing man, I think," she countered. "And even if he isn't, I have a cousin whose friend belongs, and Corinne, that's my cousin, double-checked about the snakes."

"I would have liked to have heard that conversation. Was it casual, maybe over an iced tea? 'Hey, by the way, what kind of serpents do you all handle at church?' " He stepped closer to Morrisette at the landing, to allow room for a couple of uniformed cops climbing up the staircase.

"Make fun all you want, but that's what she said. I don't know how she found out, but according to her, lately it's only been rattlers. I guess there's been a run on copperheads."

"The kind someone used to scare Nikki." At that thought, he lost his sense of humor.

"According to Corinne, the congregation is small, maybe sixty people, and was started by Byrd, who originally hails from Kentucky. Appalachia. His daddy was a coal miner and started the group. Byrd apparently brought Daddy's beliefs with him. The members stand out a little. Don't smoke. Don't drink. The women don't cut their hair, the men wear long-sleeved shirts, and they speak in tongues, though Byrd's sect has drawn the line at drinking poison."

"There's a line?"

"Every religion is different."

"I still think we'd better talk to the good reverend himself. Your cousin's anonymous friend's tip has to be checked out."

"Amen, brother!" They reached the bottom of the steps and started for the main doors.

They had just stepped outside when Reed's cell phone went off. He glanced at the screen. "Deacon Beauregard," he said. "Wants a meeting." He frowned. "In his office. And he wants it now."

"Of course he does." Morrisette rolled her eyes. "He's no better than his old man."

Elton has to be a part of this, Nikki told herself. *You know it. Whether you like it or not, you have to face the fact that your whole family is involved in this mess. It's sicker and more twisted than you thought.*

She parked her car in the *Sentinel*'s parking lot and cinched the belt of her sweater a little more tightly around her as she hurried along the cobblestones near the waterfront. She walked quickly, but was wary, half-expecting some stranger to leap out at her. She hadn't told Reed that the night before she had barely slept, with thoughts of snakes crawling through her mind and dreams of scaly bodies, open mouths, and sharp fangs dripping with venom. Amity O'Henry had been bitten by a copperhead in her bed; now Nikki had been warned with the same slinky reptile, so tonight she was careful, on edge.

Within minutes and without intervention from a tall stranger or a slithering viper, she found the alley and Salty's bar, an establishment that had been in existence, under different names and a variety of owners, for a hundred and fifty years.

Inside, the bar was dark but warm, a long, narrow room with black wainscoting, gray walls, and decorative tin ceiling tiles, all illuminated by a dozen sconces. It was early for the evening crowd, only a few tables occupied, so she spotted Holt Beauregard easily, a lone man nursing a drink in one of the booths near a back corner. He had been gazing at the door, so he noticed her as well, and lifted a hand as she wended her way through the tightly packed tables. Physically he resembled his older brother, aside from his coloring, but that's where the likeness ended.

While Deacon was always clean-shaven, his black hair neatly trimmed, his suits expensive and pressed, Holt exuded a total disrespect for fashion. Tonight he hadn't bothered to shave; his hair was on the shaggy side, the sleeves of his work shirt were shoved up, his jeans faded and probably in need of a wash.

He rose as she approached.

"Nikki Gillette," she said, extending her hand.

Dark blue eyes assessed her as he took her hand in a firm, brief shake before they sat down on opposite sides of the table. "Buy you a drink?"

She nearly declined as she wanted to keep her wits about her, but she needed their conversation to be easy, almost friendly, so that he felt he could confide in her. She guessed his drink, a short glass filled with ice and some kind of whiskey, from the looks of it, wasn't his first. "Sure," she said brightly. "But I can buy my own. Yours too."

With a shake of his head, he said, "My mother would kill me if she thought I let a woman pay, no matter what the circumstances." With a glance and a crooked smile in Nikki's direction, he added, "Flora is *very* old school. There are rules, you know, and they *must* be followed."

"What your mother doesn't know won't kill her."

"S'pose not." He flagged a waitress at the bar. "But just the same, this one's on me." As the unenthusiastic waitress shuffled over, he said, "Whatever the lady wants."

"*The lady* will have a . . . cosmo," Nikki decided aloud. "I haven't had one in years."

Holt said, "Then it's time."

"'Kay. Got it. You?" the waitress, a frizzy-haired girl with dangling earrings and an oh-so-bored attitude asked.

"I'm good."

As the waitress disappeared, Holt leaned against the tall wooden back of the booth. "You said you wanted to talk about Amity O'Henry."

"That's right."

"I already told you: there's not much to tell."

"Humor me."

"Fine." He expelled a rush of air. "I dated her. Yeah. Three, maybe four times before my old man found out and totally freaked out, and I mean freaked with a capital F." He picked up his glass and took a swallow. "Nothing had happened between me and Amity. Really. Nothing. We went to a dance and then out for burgers and to a party once. Lots of underage drinking, and somehow the word got out, and Flint came unglued. When I got home, he was waiting for me, and he blew his stack. Came at me, hauled me off my feet, and slammed me up against the outside wall of the house. I'd never seen him like that. He told me in

433

no uncertain terms that Amity O'Henry was off-limits."

Nikki thought she understood the older Beauregard's reaction, and she'd always heard Flint had a temper, even though the man she'd seen in the video clip of Blondell O'Henry's trial was calm, even reserved. "Did he say why?"

"Nothing except that her mother was trash and bad news, and that I was to stay as far away as possible."

The waitress returned with her drink and set it on the table. "Anything else? A menu?"

"We're good," Holt said and she moved off.

As Nikki picked up her cosmo, she asked, "So did you? Let it go with Amity."

A slow grin crawled across his scruffy jaw as she took her first sip. "What do you think?"

"That you ignored your father's edict," she said. Holt had always been the rebellious one, the son of a cop, who pushed the boundaries, a cocky athlete in high school who never lived up to his potential and had bombed out of the police academy. She might never have known that detail except her older brother, Andrew, had known both Deacon and Holt and she'd heard the gossip.

"Yeah, we snuck out together, but it wasn't a big deal. No spark, I guess you'd say. It was like she got the same advice and took it."

"Did she say so?"

"Didn't have to." Lost in thought, he rotated his drink on the table.

"Was she interested in someone else?"

"Probably." He nodded, as if to himself.

"Any idea who?" she asked, sipping the cosmo but barely tasting it.

He looked up at her. "No."

"Steve Manning? Brad Holbrook?"

"They were before me, I think. But I really didn't keep track."

"Maybe an older guy?"

He zeroed in on her as he tossed back his drink. "Anyone ever tell you that you're pushy?"

"I may have heard it a time or two," she admitted.

"I bet. Well, as I said, don't know. Could've been someone older, I s'pose."

"Maybe Elton McBaine?"

He shook his head. "I think she kinda liked him, but he wasn't the one. Didn't he go with, oh, what's her name?" He thought for a second. "Mary-Beth Emmerson. That was it. I remember she was really broken up after the accident, but as 'in love' with Elton as she was, she found a new boyfriend pretty quick. Ended up marrying him, didn't she?"

"Yeah, that she did," Nikki said, then turned the conversation back to Amity. "So what about the guy Amity was interested in?"

"I don't know, but I saw her once with her

mom's boyfriend, and she was like, all giggly and girlie. Not like her."

"You think she had a crush on Roland Camp?" Nikki asked, surprised.

"I don't know what you'd call it, but there was something going on there, something I didn't really want to think too long and hard about." With that he twirled his drink, ice cubes clinking.

"One more thing," Nikki said, now that she'd gotten all the information she could from him about Amity. "What about your dad and Blondell? They knew each other, you know, growing up."

"Don't think so." He shook his head, his blond hair catching in the soft light.

"I heard he had the hots for her. That a lot of guys from that neighborhood did."

"What're you getting at?"

"That Amity wasn't Calvin O'Henry's biological child," she said boldly.

"So?" He glowered at her. "Oh, you think my old man was? Come on. Amity was younger than I was and Mom and Dad have been married for . . ." He squeezed his eyes shut for a second. "Just because Dad blew a gasket that I was seeing Amity . . ." He stopped short and set his drink on the table and said through his teeth, "You know what, this interview is over." A vein was throbbing near his temple as he glared at her. She knew she'd pushed him as far as she could.

"I'm just trying to find out the truth."

No answer. Just stony silence.

"Fine, but if you change your mind . . ."

His eyes were cold as a glacier.

"Okay, then," she said. "Thanks for the drink."

Then she left, and as she pushed open the door to the outside, she heard him order another whiskey on the rocks.

Chapter 28

Deacon Beauregard was furious, his face a color Morrisette had never associated with the human complexion as he leaned over his desk. His office was small, crammed floor to ceiling with books, with barely space for his law degrees to be displayed.

"I find it impossible in these days of DNA analysis and photographic enhancement and all the other effing forensic advances, that you couldn't find enough evidence to keep Blondell O'Henry behind bars!" He was leaning forward over his desk, looking for all the world as if he truly were going to have a heart attack or stroke or some kind of major health trauma, all of which was just fine with Morrisette. She'd always figured him for a prick, and he was doing his best this afternoon to prove it.

"All the evidence hasn't been gone over yet," Reed said, "even though the lab is working overtime. We hoped that there would be something found, like epithelial tissue collected under Blondell O'Henry's nails or DNA that matched from the cigarette butt, or that the weapon could be located or something, but in this case time was our enemy. The DNA is inconclusive or too corrupted. It's been too many years since the crime occurred and too little time since Niall O'Henry decided to recant his testimony. We even had the lab check those love letters that were located in Blondell O'Henry's house. Her fingerprints were all over them; they were all written in her hand and are assumed to have been meant for Roland Camp. She'd testified to the same in the original trial."

"You just didn't look hard enough," Deacon accused. "This is my dad's case. His reputation!"

Morrisette had heard enough. "Maybe if he would've worked harder on building his case on evidence rather than the testimony of one little kid, we wouldn't be where we are today. The fact is your dad had a hard-on for nailing Blondell from the get-go," she said, then, hearing herself, stopped short.

Deacon charged, "And maybe if you'd been following legitimate leads instead of visiting my mother and asking for *her* help with *your* case, we would have wrapped this up by now and

Blondell O'Henry would be staying where she belongs: in Fairfield Prison."

"That's enough!" Kathy Okano must've heard the last part of the conversation as she walked into the room, because she too was agitated. She and Beauregard were both ADAs, but she'd been with the department longer and was therefore his senior. "Let it go, Deacon. It's over."

"The case was solid!" Deacon insisted.

"Not solid enough." Morrisette wasn't backing down. The guy was no better than his old man.

"Enough said." Through her glasses, Okano looked from one to the other. "We have other cases. Was justice served for Amity O'Henry? Who knows? Was Blondell O'Henry put away for a crime she didn't commit? Again, who knows?"

"The problem is," Beauregard pointed out, "if we do find evidence now that proves undeniably that she's guilty, then she can't be tried again. Double jeopardy applies."

Okano inclined her head. "She's served twenty years."

"And her daughter is dead, along with the child that daughter was carrying. And two other people—"

Okano cut him off, "It is what it is. Tomorrow she goes free."

"Unless we come up with something in the next twelve hours." Deacon looked from

439

Morrisette to Reed. "Come on. Let's not let her walk. She can't win."

"I don't think anyone could accuse Blondell O'Henry of winning anything," Reed said.

"She's a murderer, Detective. You know it and I know it, now just find a way to prove it!" He glowered at Okano. "And it's not over. Not until tomorrow."

She looked about to argue, then simply turned away. "Fine," she said, "Twelve hours."

"Working late. Beauregard's on the warpath. Will explain soon."

Reed's text came in just as Nikki walked into her apartment and dropped her computer bag onto the couch. "Looks like it's just us again," she told the animals, at which point Jennings accepted a few pets and Mikado did his happy dance at her feet. Surprised at how disappointed she felt that Reed was delayed, she decided it was a good sign. After all, they were getting married soon. Thanks-giving was next week, and then the countdown really began.

"Wonder if we'll make it?" she joked to the dog, who was having none of her small talk. He yipped loudly and kept up his frantic twirls, toenails clicking on the hardwood. "I know, I know. Dinnertime. But first, let's go out, shall we?" The dog was already racing to the door, and as soon as she pulled it open, he shot through, little legs jetting him down the steps. She followed after him and noticed Leon Donnigan on the patio, cell phone to his ear, cigarette burning in his free hand.

"Hey!" she yelled at the big lug. "Hey!"

He looked up and pointed at the phone with his cigarette.

"I don't care, I want to talk to you!" She was already at the bottom of the stairs.

". . . have ta call ya back, dude," he said and clicked off, the expression on his face one of exasperation and disbelief. "I was on the phone."

"I saw."

"Well, that was rude!"

"So is setting up spy equipment. Not only rude, but illegal. What the hell did you think you were doing?"

"I messed up. Okay?" he muttered.

"No. Definitely *not* 'okay.' "

"Don't get mad at *me*. Charles needed to look in on his old lady and he hired me to do it. But I got the angle off. I was gonna fix it, but you found it first. It was an honest mistake."

"Dishonest mistake."

He lifted his shoulders. "So sue me."

"Maybe I will," Nikki ground out.

"And are you gonna tell my mommy on me too?"

"You bet I am." Some of her anger was starting

to fizzle out, but staring up at the big galoot, she wanted to shake him. "Get it together, Leon. For your mother's sake, grow up."

"I don't know why you're so pissed at me," he said with a smile that suggested he knew something she didn't. "I made a mistake. It wasn't like I was tryin' to get a picture of you or anything. Not like that stalker you picked up."

"What stalker?"

"I've seen her, taking pictures of the house. Even saw her on your deck, clicking shots through the door." He pointed toward the back door of her unit. "Climbed all the way up there."

"You're lying," she said, but the gleam of satisfaction in his eyes told her he enjoyed thinking he had one on her.

"You don't know?"

"Leon . . ." Her patience was about to snap.

"That woman who writes the blog for the damned paper. I recognized her from her picture on the *Sentinel*'s Web site."

"Effie Savoy?" she asked, stunned.

He shrugged. "Yeah, that's her, I think."

"She was here? At my *house?*"

"That's what I just said," he pointed out, as if she were thick as a brick.

"I'll check on that," Nikki assured him.

Smoke filtered out of his nostrils, and as he tossed the remainder of his cigarette onto the patio, crushing it beneath the heel of his boot, he asked, "Has anyone ever told you you're a bitch?"

"I'll take that as a compliment," she snapped. "Pick up your trash. This is my patio, not a garbage dump, and I'm tired of cleaning up after you."

"It's just a butt, for crissakes!"

"Just do it." She whistled to Mikado and made her way up the stairs as the dog bolted up in front of her. When she reached the third floor, she heard Leon's voice rising upward from the patio as he reconnected with his call.

"Yeah, sorry about that . . . just my bitch of a landlady . . . who knows? Probably on the fuckin' rag or somethin'. 'Cept she's always like that." He chuckled deep in his throat, and his skin-crawling snigger filtered up through the branches of the magnolia tree. Then she heard his lighter click as he lit up again.

Nice, she thought. If she didn't have so much to do, she'd take up his attitude and actions with Dorothy. If not for his mother, Nikki would evict him on the spot. But not tonight.

Tonight, it seemed, she was going to deal with Effie Savoy.

"What the hell was all that about Flint Beauregard?" Reed demanded as they walked to an all-night diner a few blocks away. Night had fallen, the streetlights were glowing, and only a few other pedestrians were walking along Oglethorpe, the traffic remarkably thin.

"Something went on with Beauregard," Morrisette said. "I found out he knew Blondell before she was married. They went to the same high school, though he was a few years older."

"This isn't exactly a newsflash. He's lived in Savannah all his life."

"And Flora didn't like it much when I brought it up. Practically came unglued when I mentioned Blondell and her husband in the same breath." She glanced up at him as they walked past Colonial Park Cemetery, where gray headstones stood out starkly against the night.

"So what're you getting at?" Reed asked.

"I was just wondering who Amity O'Henry's biological father was. Blondell has never said, not once, even when asked. It didn't come out in the trial, probably wasn't considered relevant, and no name was listed on her birth certificate. I double-checked. So I figure most likely it wasn't Calvin, as he adopted her and wasn't around when Amity was conceived."

"And you think Flint Beauregard knew," Reed said, though he was beginning to understand where Morrisette was heading with all of this. "Or that he was Amity's father?"

"I'm saying it's a possibility. He sure was pissed at Blondell. Did everything he could to convict her," Morrisette said.

"Why would he do that?" Reed asked, trying to understand her logic. "If Amity was his kid?"

"Who knows? He probably thought Blondell was behind Amity's homicide, or at the very least should have protected her."

"Kind of a big leap, isn't it?" he asked as they crossed the street. Rain was just beginning to fall.

"Maybe. But I'm checking. I even have a call in to Jada Hill, because the easiest thing would be for Blondell to tell the truth, especially now that Flint's dead."

"Why hasn't she?" Reed asked as they reached the diner and he held the door for her.

"She must have her reasons. Enough people have asked—at least they did during the trial—and she wouldn't say. It's funny, you know."

"What?"

"For the past twenty years, I've thought Blondell O'Henry pulled the trigger and that justice was served. I went into this investigation hell-bent to prove just that, but now I'm not so sure. That twelve-hour ultimatum Deacon just delivered? I think it might just blow up in his face."

"We have DNA from Amity."

"Which wasn't available twenty years ago."

"We've got nothing from Beauregard."

"But we have both his sons, now, don't we?" she said, "Should be enough of a match to prove if Amity was their half-sister."

"Okay."

"Deacon Beauregard gave us twelve hours to figure out this case," she said. "I just want to make sure he gets what he deserves."

"You do that," he said. "Meanwhile, I'm going to talk to a guy about a snake."

"And who would that be?"

"The good reverend Ezekiel Byrd."

"You think he put a copperhead in your fiancée's car?"

"I think he might know who would be a likely candidate. Either Byrd catches his own pit vipers or he buys them. One way or another, he's as close as anyone to the reptile trade."

Fired up from her confrontation with Leon, Nikki was laser-focused on having it out with Effie. By rote she fed the animals and ate a slice of cold, leftover pizza that she washed down with the remains of a half-drunk bottle of diet soda she'd found in the fridge, then headed for the *Sentinel*'s records and Effie's address. It turned out to be less than half a mile away from Nikki's house, on the far side of Forsyth Park.

Close enough that Effie could have walked the distance. So near, in fact, that Effie could easily have been the person Nikki had felt was watching and following her.

But *why?*

She was afraid she might not like the answer to

that question, but was determined to learn what it was anyway. Grabbing her purse, her uncle's set of keys, and her cell phone, she was nearly out the door when her phone jangled.

She didn't recognize the number and almost didn't answer, but thought better of it. "Hello?" Holding the phone to her ear, she shouldered her bag, walking outside and locking the door behind her.

"Is this Nikki Gillette?" a woman's voice asked tenuously. "I got a call from her. I'm Nola-Mae Pitman."

"Ah, yes, Ms. Pitman." Finally Alfred Necarney's sister had returned her phone call. "Thank you for getting back to me," she said as she hurried down the stairs, where the scent of Leon's latest smoke still lingered. "I'm glad you called. I'm a reporter with the *Savannah Sentinel.*"

"I know. I googled you. I figured this was probably about my brother, Alfred."

"Yes. And I'm so sorry for your loss."

"Oh, my." Her voice cracked a little. "Losing Alfred was a blow," she admitted, sniffing loudly. "Thank you. But you didn't call me to offer your condolences."

Nikki unlocked the gate and shut it behind her as she made her way to her car. "No, that's true." After unlocking her Honda with her remote, she quickly slid into the car's interior; she opened the console, found her notepad and a pen, and was ready to take some notes. "I'm doing a series of articles about Blondell O'Henry's release and double-checking some facts."

"Well, I don't know anything about that, except what I read in the papers. As for Alfred, I'm certain he never met her. He was a solitary man. Lived alone. Liked it that way. He rarely went into town, and I'd be surprised if he'd ever been to Savannah."

"But he did sell snakes. For quite a while."

"We never discussed it, but yes . . . he did."

"How long was that?"

"I'm not sure. A while, I suppose."

"Years? Ten? Twenty? Maybe more?"

"Probably started soon after he got out of the service, I suppose. He'd always liked those kind of things, but after the war, he well, he was different, and snakes held a new fascination for him, but as I said, we never discussed it."

"At least twenty years, then." Nikki was scribbling on her notepad.

"I'd say so. I don't really know, but . . . Oh. Are you trying to connect Alfred with the O'Henry murder?" She sucked in her breath. "There was a snake . . ."

"I'm not accusing your brother of anything."

"Well, I should hope not! Alfred was a good man! A veteran! It wasn't his fault that horrid little Mandy-Sue dumped him! He never got over her, y'know. Even though she was a tramp. I know she was messing around with Bobby Fullman while Alfred was in Vietnam and still writing my brother love letters," she said, her voice trembling with outrage.

"I'm interested in Alfred's customers," Nikki cut in. "Who would buy his snakes—specifically, his pit vipers."

"His . . . what?"

"The copperheads. Last night someone left one in my car."

"Oh! That was you? I read about that in the *Sentinel*'s blog!"

Effie again. Nikki couldn't wait to confront the woman. "I understand your brother was missing some of his . . . merchandise."

"Well, I think so. The police seem to think he'd sold some snakes that night because there was some cash on him and several of the cages were empty, but their heaters were going and there was water in them . . . you know, Alfred wasn't one to waste electricity! He was a bit of an environmentalist, y'know."

An eco-friendly snake dealer. Perfect.

"Do you know who his customers were?"

"No."

"He didn't mention anyone who collected snakes? Dealers or zoos or someone from one of those tourist spots that display wild animals and reptiles?"

"I said, 'no.' " She was getting huffy.

Nikki couldn't let it go. "What about a church group?"

"*What?*"

"There are sects that use serpents in their religious rites."

"That's crazy!" she said, aghast.

"Did he ever mention Reverend Ezekiel Byrd?"

"I'm sorry, but I really don't know anything more. If anything, I think Alfred might have been the victim of foul play. The police aren't saying anything, of course, but I told them what I thought. There's no way Alfred would have fallen and hit his head, even with his bad leg. He was careful. Meticulously so." She sounded as if all she wanted was to get off the phone. "I don't think I should be talking to you. I don't want anything negative published about Alfred. He was a good man, you know. A veteran."

"So you said. I just want to know—"

"Oh, dear," she said anxiously. "I—I've got another call coming in!" Before Nikki could say a word, she'd hung up.

Well, fine.

Nola wasn't much help, Nikki thought, backing her CR-V out of the parking area, but maybe Effie Savoy would be.

It was time to find out.

Chapter 29

"I wish I could help you," the reverend said in a soft voice that Reed was certain could be raised to a thunderous boom if called upon. Byrd was a short, stocky man who was going bald, but he made up for the lack of hair atop his head with a thick chin curtain of beard that allowed for no mustache. He wore glasses that seemed to enlarge his already owlish eyes, and he was wearing a suit with a bolo tie as he stood just inside the door of his modest rural home. Whitewashed and tidy, the porch held two chairs and an old-fashioned porch swing. He'd opened his door quickly when Reed had knocked and hadn't seemed the least bit nervous when the detective had shown his badge. "I don't know anything about missing snakes. All of mine are accounted for." He smiled then, showing off tiny teeth.

"Did you ever purchase any snakes from Mr. Alfred Necarney?"

He was shaking his head, the top of his pate shining under the single bulb of the porch light. He opened the door and stepped onto the porch. "I trap my own. It's just less complicated. I know that people think I'm practicing some quack religion out here, but my congregation is just exercising our religious freedoms as stipulated by the Constitution of our great nation." His smile was beatific, his demeanor calm, his accent smooth as wild honey. "We believe in the scripture of Mark. 'They shall take up serpents.' "

"I'm not here to argue theology or even discuss the legality of your owning venomous snakes. I'd just like to see the ones you have."

"Why certainly," he said congenially. "They are not to be feared. Respected yes, but not feared."

Reed waited somewhat impatiently. He wasn't going to talk the pros and cons of this religion, which he considered whacked out. For now, he was just trying to find the person who had wanted to use a snake to scare and potentially harm Nikki.

The pastor led him through his small house, where several lamps burned and a woman, presumably his wife, was washing dishes in the kitchen.

He stopped to call to her. "Annie," he said loudly, and when she didn't turn around, a little louder, "Annie!"

"Oh, what?" She started, her hands in plastic gloves shooting out of the water, suds flying against a garden window where African violets were blooming. "Ezekiel, you scared me to death!" She snapped off the faucet, and the sound of rushing water disappeared. Turning around, she said, blinking in surprise, "Oh my. I didn't know we had company."

"Detective Reed, my wife, Annabella."

She pulled off her gloves and shook his hand. Her hair was long, streaked with silver, and she wore neither lipstick nor mascara. "Welcome. Nice to meet you. Uh . . . Detective?"

"Nothing to worry about, Annie. He just wants to check the serpents," Byrd said.

"Why?" she asked quickly.

Ezekiel sent her a warning look. "Nothing to worry about. We'll discuss it later. Now, Detective, this way." He showed Reed into the hallway again, and from the corner of his eye he saw the reverend's wife stare after them before she turned back to the sink and stuffed her hands into her gloves again.

"Here we go," the reverend said, unlocking the door to a back room that might have once been a porch; the screens had been replaced by windows, now with their shades drawn. The room was small, but warmer than the rest of the house. At waist level, stretched along long tables, were individual terrariums, each complete with its own soft light, mulch or sand, a chunk of some kind of wood, and a very live rattlesnake.

Seven sets of tiny eyes with slits for pupils were trained on Reed.

A soft rustle started as the first rattler vibrated

his tail, and then another sounded a warning that caused the hairs on the back of Reed's neck to lift. "Just rattlesnakes?"

"Currently yes," the reverend said, "but, of course, we've had others. Cottonmouths. Copperheads. Once a cobra, but that didn't last long. I prefer domestic."

"You're June O'Henry's brother," Reed said as he watched one of the rattlers slowly uncoil to slide across the bottom of his Plexiglas cage.

"Yes."

"And she attends with her family? Calvin and Niall?"

"Some members of the family attend," the preacher agreed. "Others do not. Leah gave up the faith, but listen to me, I shouldn't be discussing members of the congregation even if I am related to them. So . . ." He motioned toward the trapped reptiles. "Did you want a closer look? I can certainly take the snakes from their cages. They're used to it."

"I'm good," Reed said and searched for a glint of anger, even superiority in Ezekiel Byrd's gaze to see if the minister were testing him. It appeared not. The man seemed to be a true believer in his unusual faith.

"Do you have anyone in your congregation who keeps snakes?" Reed asked.

"Oh, yes. A few."

"Calvin O'Henry?"

"He and June did at one time. No longer, I think, though."

"Can you name anyone else?"

"I suppose it wouldn't hurt," he said, a little more anxious than he had been. "I think Herb Curtis, he had a couple of rattlers, and Willie Carter had a cottonmouth a few years back." He was thinking hard, actually scratching his chin. "Oh, yes, and Donny Ray Wilson, he and his stepbrother, they used to trap them."

"Roland Camp?"

He nodded. "But I think Roland gave it up because he was having a child and the mother insisted. She's a fearful one. Doesn't understand God's will."

"Imagine that," Reed said. He felt a little twinge of excitement as he drove away from Byrd's home.

Roland Camp and Donny Wilson.

Stepbrothers with an affinity for snakes.

How convenient that twenty years ago Wilson had been Roland Camp's alibi.

Nikki parked in the first spot she found near Effie's apartment, located in a tall, older building. Effie's unit had its own entrance through a wrought-iron gate and a small garden area that was three stairs below street level. The gate creaked as she opened it, and the path was covered in leaves wet enough from the recent rain to be slick beneath her boots.

She rang the bell, hearing it peal inside, and waited. Impatiently. Ready to tell the woman exactly what she thought.

If Leon's telling the truth.

But something felt right about this.

"Come on. Come on."

Nothing.

But there were lights on. She could see the glow of a television. Standing at the door, Nikki realized how little she knew of the woman who lived so near to her, worked with her. Effie was single, she'd said as much, and wore no wedding ring and, Nikki thought, lived alone. She'd been in Savannah only a month or six weeks, had lived in Texas before moving to Georgia, though she had mentioned she had family living in the area and that she was originally from around here. It seemed that recently she'd been with a newspaper in Dallas, but Nikki wasn't sure. She'd never paid much attention.

Again, Nikki pressed the bell, and this time she beat on the door. "Effie!" she yelled, and when there was no response she tried the door. Locked.

She should just leave. She had things to do. But the thought of Effie Savoy cowering in her apartment after spending weeks following Nikki, scaring her, taking pictures of her, was too much. Had Effie been the dark figure she'd seen at the fountain? Or had that been Nikki's overactive imagination conjuring up a stalker?

And what about the time she'd been nearly run over? Right after Effie had come up to her in the coffee shop. Had that been Effie, or just some negligent driver?

Why in the world would she target Nikki?

She rang the bell one final time and was turning back to her car when she saw the path leading around the building. Without hesitation she followed the brick walkway, lit by small outdoor lights. It led to another gate, which she reached over, tripping the latch to let herself into a back courtyard. The upper units had decks, but Effie's place had a small patio surrounded by shrubbery and a sliding door.

The curtains were partially open, as if someone stepped out here regularly, and the ashtray on a small table seemed to confirm that Effie spent time out here.

Nikki peered inside. She could see into the living area, where a love seat and two chairs faced a television set. There was no dining table in the space allotted for it. Instead a computer sat atop a scarred desk pressed against one wall.

"Effie?" Nikki called, listening for a response. So far she hadn't heard a dog; that was a good sign, but Effie could be in the bedroom, earbuds in place as she listened to music, or in the damned shower.

She tested the slider and found it unlocked. An invitation if there ever was one. Despite her elevated heart rate and the arguments pounding through her brain, she stepped inside.

You're getting good at this, aren't you? Breaking into places? First Aunty-Pen's and now here . . . a regular cat burglar.

But if Effie had been spying on her, she figured turnabout was fair play. But what if Leon, the insufferable idiot, had been lying? Baiting her? What if Nikki was about to walk into a bedroom where Effie was sleeping or a bathroom where she was taking a shower, water rushing . . . Nikki would be hard pressed to explain herself.

So far, though, the place seemed empty, and the slider *had* been left open. Softly, every muscle tense, she walked through the apartment.

She heard no signs of life.

A galley kitchen was near the front door, countertops littered with dishes, a slight odor suggesting the garbage should be taken out to the Dumpster.

The bedroom was empty, the bed unmade, an older television propped onto a chest of drawers at the foot of an unmade double bed, laundry tossed in or near a basket by the closet. The bathroom was also empty, towels scattered on the floor, half-full bottles of shampoo and a razor in the shower. Several bottles of prescription medications were lined on the counter, all issued to Effie Maria Savoy.

At least she hadn't broken into the wrong apartment, Nikki thought, frustrated that she couldn't have it out with the woman.

She walked back to the dining room, where the computer sat, a tiny light visible on the keyboard indicating the system was turned on, the monitor dark. Of course, she shouldn't snoop in Effie's digital files—that would be a real invasion of privacy—but as she thought about Effie taking pictures of her home, of peering inside at her, she didn't really give a damn.

Who knew if she'd ever get this opportunity again?

Yeah, and who knows that Effie won't walk in the door at any second? She might have run to the convenience store for cigarettes or milk or whatever.

Nerves strung tight, every little noise making her jump, Nikki touched a finger to the keyboard. The monitor began to glow with a screen saver that was a picture of the cabin by the lake, but it wasn't a recent photograph, or even one of the old crime-scene photos of the night Amity was killed.

Nikki's lips parted in shock.

This was a much older picture, in which the sun was shining, the cabin still tended, a canoe pulled up to the porch. Seated on the step, staring into the camera, was Nikki's much younger self. All of seven years old, her teeth too large for her face, her freckles in full bloom, Nikki Gillette grinned happily into the camera's lens.

"He's not here." Peggy Shanks stood at the door, blocking any view into Roland Camp's house; from beneath her shaggy bangs, she glared at Reed as if he were trying to break in to do her bodily harm. Her thin arms were folded across her chest, her small jaw jutting in anger, her attitude as bristly as ever.

"When do you expect him back?"

"Don't know. He's been gone a while." She slid her gaze away from Reed's.

"How long is 'a while'?"

"Since last night some time."

"Can you call him?"

"You don't think I've tried that? Sheeeiitt. I've called and texted, but he's not picking up." She lifted a scrawny shoulder. "It's no big deal," she said, as if to convince herself.

"Tell him I'm looking for him."

"Oh good. He'll like that." Again she glared at him with pure, undisguised hatred, the kind of loathing, he suspected, she felt for any officer of the law.

From inside the house a baby began to wind up, his cries becoming louder and louder.

"I'm serious, Ms. Shanks," Reed insisted, his gut warning him that Camp's disappearance was trouble. He had no serious evidence of it, but he'd been in law enforcement long enough to sense when something was coming down. "It's important that I speak with him."

"Yeah, me too. I'm pretty sick of him just takin' off!"

"Could he be with Donny Ray Wilson?"

"I just said, 'I don't know.' Look, I gotta deal with the baby. If Roland . . . I mean *when* Roland gets home, I'll tell him to call you, but, really, I wouldn't hold my breath."

"Maybe he's planning to meet up with Blondell O'Henry tomorrow," he said, just to rattle her cage a bit.

"He is *so* over her," she snapped. "She cheated on him, and Roland, he can't abide that."

"It was twenty years ago."

"Exactly."

"Does he still hold a grudge?"

"No." But she looked away, avoiding eye contact.

"Does he still care about her?"

"No way!" she nearly yelled, her lower lip trembling just slightly. "She did a number on him. Throwing him over for her stupid attorney, but Roland, he's got me now. Even if she does get out of prison, he's got me. And his son. And that's enough!"

Donny Ray Wilson was nervous. Lately Roland had been going a little crazy, more than slightly off the rails, and Donny knew why. It was because that bitch Blondell O'Henry was getting out of jail. She was the one woman who'd turned his stepbrother into a head case, and once again, Roland was talking all crazy-like.

"Look, just leave it alone, man," Roland was saying, pacing in front of the couch, destroying Donny Ray's view of the basketball game in progress on the big screen, a monster of a television set Donny had bought just before flat screens had become the thing. It filled up a third of his single-wide, but he really didn't care, the picture was just so damned big. "Chill out," he advised his stepbrother. "Who cares if she gets out?"

"I do. And you should too."

"She didn't rat us out before. Why would she now?" He and Roland had had this conversation a hundred times in the last twenty years—no, more like a thousand times. Roland just didn't know how to calm down.

"Not only the police, but that bitch Nikki Gillette is poking around. She's called a couple of times."

"You talk to her?"

"Not yet, but she's not the kind to give up."

"We're free, man," Donny Ray insisted. He'd been Roland's alibi for the night those kids were shot up, and it had worked out just fine for him as well, as he'd been cheating on his wife at the time. Sayin' he'd been with Roland, rather than admitting to banging Wanda Colbert, had saved his marriage. For a little while anyway. Eventually Sharon had found out and served him with papers—the bitch!—but for *that* night, he'd been safe. Not that he'd ever felt good about it. After all, a girl had *died,* a *pregnant* girl. But Donny Ray had been true to his word, and luckily for everyone involved, Blondell hadn't named Roland as being in the room with her; she'd come up with the stranger story instead.

Weird, that.

It was something he didn't really get. Hell, he didn't want to think about any of it, but here Roland was so nervous he was just twitching around, almost tweaking, though Donny Ray had never seen Roland touch meth or anything stronger than an occasional joint.

"Just be cool," Donny Ray advised. "Everything will work out."

"Not if that bitch gets out, man. No way. And not if that stupid Nikki Gillette keeps at it."

"You gonna try and stop her?" Donny waved Roland off and caught the end of a three-point play. Beautiful shot. Nothing but net!

"I'll have to. I'm gonna be counting on you again, man."

"For an alibi?" Donny Ray didn't like the sound of that. He'd stuck his neck out for Roland more times than he wanted to count and kept his mouth shut about the big one because it had served his purpose as well.

"What're you plannin'?" Donny Ray asked cautiously.

"Don't worry about it. I'm here, remember. If anyone calls, you just say I'm in the bathroom and I'll call them back, then you phone my cell, tell me who called and what the score of the game is. Who made the last big play, so pay attention."

"Jesus, Ro, what's in it for me?" he asked, half-joking, then saw the glimmer of rage in his stepbrother's eyes. He knew what that meant and backpedaled fast. "Just kiddin', man—you know it. I've got your back. If anybody comes askin', you and me, we were watchin' this here game." He pointed at the TV. "That's it, tossin' back a few cold ones and rooting on the Jaguars."

"That would be good, bro," Roland said as he opened the door of Donny's mobile home. "That would be real good."

As he left, Donny Ray didn't know if his stepbrother's final words were an observation or a warning.

Nikki stared at the images on Effie's computer, and as she did, her shock gave way to anger, a sharp, pulse-pounding rage.

The picture of her on the porch of the cabin was just the first of dozens of photographs of Nikki and her family. Snapshots at the lake when she was a child, photos from school albums, Hollis riding her horse or in the dance studio, Elton in his football uniform or behind the wheel of his car, Aunty-Pen as a girl riding dressage or in college.

"What is this?" she said aloud.

There were newer shots as well. The house where she lived currently was featured, along with the one where she'd grown up. There was a photo of Uncle Alex's home and the farm by the lake. Some of the pictures were older, some more recent. The cabin was featured prominently. Older shots, some with members of Nikki's family, but newer ones as well.

What the hell was this and where the hell was Effie? Nikki had been sitting at the computer for more than half an hour and half-expected Effie to walk into her apartment and discover her, which, Nikki decided, would be just fine. She was itching for a fight, and she sure as hell needed to know what was going on.

She sorted through Effie's pictures and realized she was in a folder marked "Family." Yes, it was Nikki's family, but . . . holy crap. Not Nikki's family. But Effie's. Somehow Effie had adopted Nikki's family . . . *adopted.* Her mind began spinning with all the innuendos and quiet whisperings she'd heard, the skeletons that had kept rattling in the family closets, one of which was about her aunt. Hadn't Nikki's own mother intimated that Aunty-Pen wasn't as lily-white as she'd pretended to be? And Hollis had made a few similar remarks.

All of a sudden the reason Effie reminded her of someone became increasingly clear. She was large for a woman, like Aunty-Pen, her eyes as blue as Penelope's and Hollis's.

No longer worried about breaching Effie's privacy, Nikki kept searching the documents in her computer, looking for clues to the woman. She had little trouble as Effie kept her password taped to the desk on which the computer rested, allowing Nikki access to ever-more-personal files: a copy of Effie's birth certificate, with Aunt Penelope's name listed as the mother, the father blank; adoption papers signed within two months of Effie's birth; and finally the obituaries and death certificates of Nelson and Vivian Savoy, who, according to the obits, had no living relatives other than their daughter. Newspaper articles about the automobile accident that had taken their lives were in the file.

"Dear God," Nikki said under her breath, as if the very walls could hear her. She found that Effie had joined a couple of Web sites dedicated to connecting adoptive children with their birth parents.

All of it was starting to make some kind of sense until she opened an album marked "Blondell

O'Henry." Just as there had been pictures of Nikki's family, there were photos of Blondell and her children, her ex-husband, even some of June Hatchett, Leah, and Cain, a virtual family album of people connected to Blondell O'Henry. What now? Nikki wondered. Pictures and links to footage from the trial were included, and Nikki saw her own father in his judicial robes, as well as Alexander McBaine on the courthouse steps, smoking a cigarette, and Garland Brownell standing at a microphone.

It didn't stop there, either. Not only did Effie have pictures of the players at the trial and shots of the crime scene, but there were photos of Blondell's home before she was incarcerated and ones of the exterior of the prison. "What the hell are you doing, Effie?" Nikki said. Then she saw why Effie had been seen hanging around her station at work: she'd obviously lifted some of these pictures from Nikki's database.

"Tit for tat," she whispered, angry all over again, and when she opened Effie's Word document file, she saw, big as life, the start of a long document with the working title "Mother or Monster: The True Story of Blondell O'Henry," by Effie Savoy.

"You bitch," Nikki whispered in wonder, realizing that Effie planned her own true-crime book about Blondell O'Henry's case.

She went back to the photo library again and found an album marked "Research with RC."

With a click of the mouse, Nikki was exposed to Effie Savoy's private sex diary, photographs primarily shot in the bedroom of this apartment. The man who was tending to Effie's sexual needs was obviously tall and muscular, with a few tattoos emblazoned across his broad back, but his face was generally turned away from the camera's eye.

Only one photograph showed his features clearly.

Nikki's heart nearly stopped.

There, on the computer screen, big as life, was a naked and sweating Roland Camp.

"I knew you'd show up again," Flora Beauregard said quietly. As before, her jeans were too tight, her hair a perfect cap of soft waves. "I just didn't know it would be so soon." Through the screen, with only the porch lamp for illumination, she looked defeated, as if she'd done some serious soul-searching since Morrisette's last visit.

"There's not a lot of time. Blondell O'Henry is about to be released. If you won't tell me the truth, I'm pretty sure she will, and I thought you might want to unburden yourself first." It was a ploy, but Morrisette pushed it a little. "I know there's more to the story, and I'm willing to bet you know it."

As if she held the weight of the world on her shoulders, Flora unlatched the door. "I don't know if it matters anyway," she said wearily. "From what Deacon tells me, it's a done deal, but come in. I suppose it's time to tell the truth. Flint is long gone, the boys are men now, able to fight their own battles, and I don't really care any longer anyway." She looked at Morrisette with sad, defeated eyes, then led her back to her living room, with its pictures of her family proudly displayed on the mantel, attended by Jesus and the antique rifle.

Flora dropped into her chair. "All right," she admitted, "It's true. Amity O'Henry was Flint's daughter. He and *that woman* had an affair. It was short-lived; she was little more than a girl and ended up pregnant." Flora's lips tightened at the memory. "We were going through a rough patch in our marriage, the boys young, not enough money, me dealing with my father's failing health, and we just drifted apart for a while, though, of course, I didn't know that he'd . . ." She squeezed her eyes so tight that her whole face crinkled, and she looked suddenly ten years older. "It was a nightmare. Lord knows he was at fault, being as she was so young, but that woman was sly and calculating, demanded money."

"Child support?"

Absently Flora picked up her knitting needles. "Oh, no, Detective, this was blood money."

"She *blackmailed* him, that's what you're saying?"

"Her boyfriend came back from the army, and he was in on it too. Though O'Henry formally and legally adopted Amity, Flint was always expected to pay. If he didn't, she swore she'd cry rape." The needles began clicking furiously. "And then, where would we have been? It all came to a head when Amity was killed. Flint was beside himself and blamed her . . . oh, well, he blamed himself too. So he pushed hard to have her put away, and she didn't dare tell the truth, not with her life in the balance. He promised to push for life rather than the death penalty."

"There was no deal," Morrisette said.

"Of course not. That entire trial was a sham." Her mouth twisted at the irony of it all. "And then *she* ends up getting involved with her lawyer."

Click, click, click.

"I'm pretty sure nothing about the State of Georgia vs. Blondell Henry was legal, but everyone just played their part," Flora continued.

"So Blondell did shoot her kids?" Morrisette asked.

"Of course she did, Detective. But the prosecution just couldn't prove it, not without that little boy's testimony."

Click. Click. Click.

"But it doesn't really matter anymore now, does it? Amity's gone. Her baby, Flint's grandchild, gone too." Flora's lips quivered.

"Amity's baby," Morrisette said. "Do you know who the father was?"

She shook her head. "But it wasn't Holt's. Flint made sure of that. When he found out Holt was dating her, I thought he'd wring Holt's neck."

"You're positive?"

Her needles stopped for a second, and her lips twisted in distaste. "Yes, ma'am. And now that woman is going to be set free, her crimes suddenly erased."

Click. Click. Click.

"What a banner day for all of Georgia," Flora Beauregard declared, holding back a flood tide of emotion Morrisette guessed was just about to burst through.

Chapter 30

Now that Nikki knew what Effie was up to, it was time to leave. She'd love to confront her right then and there, but obviously Effie was out for the evening.

Convenient, Nikki thought, as she scooted the desk chair back. She was about to exit out of Effie's desktop when she spied the online calendar on Effie's monitor.

Could she get so lucky?

With a click, she was on a page for November, and, sure enough, work info and appointments from doctors to hairdressers were listed on the virtual page. On today's date, she had a note: meet at cabin.

Cabin? Meet who?

No note.

It had to be the only cabin pictured in the laptop's memory, the very spot Amity O'Henry had been killed.

Why would anyone want to meet there?

Nikki's first thought was that Effie had set up a meeting with her birth mother, but no way would Penelope Hilton McBaine go to that dilapidated cabin at night. Besides, according to Nikki's mother, she and Penelope were scheduled to attend the Benefit for the Arts.

So that left Roland, right?

Or someone else?

Another player in all of this?

Someone who could give her a little more insight into the book she was writing.

Nikki thought about it hard. She should crash that meeting, find out what was going on.

Are you crazy? You haven't forgotten staring nose to nose with a copperhead, have you?

Her doubts kept pounding through her brain, but her determination to learn the truth won as she made her way out of the apartment the way she'd come in, walked around the building again, and slid behind the wheel of her dented Honda.

She could just drive home. It was only a few blocks. That would be the smart thing to do.

Or if she needed to feel as if she were doing something useful, she could even stop by Aunty-Pen's while she was out and return the keys.

But she didn't heed any of her saner options. From the second she'd seen the note on Effie's calendar, she'd known, deep in her heart, what her next plan of action would be.

She took the time to text Reed, saying she was still doing research, but she didn't have the heart to admit that she was going back to the cabin. Still, she couldn't go out there and not tell anyone, so she left another text with Trina and asked her to call her in an hour.

Just in case there was trouble.

Then she headed out of town.

"That's right," Reed said to the dispatcher, "I want a BOLO alert on Roland Camp's Dodge pickup." Driving back to the station, he rattled off the license-plate number and hung up. Maybe he was jumping the gun on Camp. The guy hadn't done anything illegal that Reed knew of, but there were those missing snakes in Dahlonga and a dead man to go along with them.

Roland Camp could have had nothing to do with Alfred Necarney's death, but Reed wanted to be sure. Truth to tell, he didn't like the guy.

His cell phone blasted, startling him out of his thoughts of Camp and Blondell O'Henry and religious ceremonies with snakes.

Adjusting the ear device on his Bluetooth, he said, "Reed."

"I'm on my way back to the station." Morrisette's voice was weak, background noise distorting it a little, as she was also driving. "But I thought I'd give you the rundown. Looks like Flint *was* the father of Amity O'Henry. The missus finally spilled the beans." As he maneuvered his Caddy through the streets of the city, she told him a story of statutory rape, unwanted pregnancy, and blackmail. When she was finished, she sounded pleased with herself. "You know, Deacon might just regret forcing another twelve hours on us."

"Who're you kidding?" Reed asked, slowing for a traffic light and watching a jogger overtake an older man with a cane who was crossing more slowly. "You would be doing this, deadline or no. You love this."

"Yeah, you're right. Hate to admit it, though." He knew she couldn't deny what was so patently true. As opposite as she and Reed were, when it came to working doggedly on a case until it was solved, they were totally in sync. Neither could stand a case going cold. "So what about you?"

"I'm looking hard at Roland Camp again."

"For Amity's murder?"

"I don't know. I just found out he has an affinity for poisonous snakes." He launched into his meeting with the Reverend Byrd and his association with Camp. "Since Roland's MIA again, I put a BOLO out on him. Just to talk to him."

"And maybe scare him a little. I like it. You're kinda pushing the limits," she said.

"Guess you've rubbed off on me."

"About damned time. I'll meet you back at the station. I should be there in five."

"You got it. I'm here already."

He pulled into the lot and was getting out of his car when the text from Nikki came in.

"Working late. Looks like we may have picked up another stalker. Seriously. Effie Savoy. Will fill you in later. Meet at home and maybe eat Chinese?"

He read the text twice and didn't get it. He knew that Effie was a woman Nikki worked with and that there was some friction between them, but a stalker?

As he climbed out of the car, he had his phone in hand to call her when he nearly ran into a wild-eyed June Hatchett.

"What do you think you're doing?" she demanded.

"I'm sorry."

"Going to my church! Bothering my brother! Asking all kinds of ridiculous questions!"

"Mrs. O'Henry, slow down," he suggested.

"I am sick and tired of all the harassment my family has endured. Reporters. Police. Curious people driving past our house and up our lane! It has got to stop!" Eyes rolling until the whites showed, she said, "I want to talk to your supervisor."

"She's gone for the day."

"Well, there has to be someone on duty!" She was raving, her face drained of color, her body shivering with her outrage. "Why don't you come into the station and we'll talk this out," Reed suggested as, from the corner of his eye, he saw Morrisette pull into the lot.

"Fine," June agreed. "But don't try to placate me, Detective. I know my rights, and religious freedom is guaranteed by the Constitution of these United States."

"That it is, Mrs. O'Henry," he agreed as Morrisette parked and started toward the door. "That it is."

Nikki had never used the stun gun that Reed had insisted she carry. In fact, she always left it at home, near the bed, but tonight she took the time to find it and make certain it was working.

Just in case.

Then she drove as fast as she dared to the dilapidated home her great-great-grandfather had constructed more than a century earlier. The night was clear, a moon rising, the breath of winter chilling her bones as the beams of her headlights splashed against the trees and underbrush surrounding the cabin. The lake was much as it had been the last time she'd driven here, white caps swelling on the dark, restless water, reeds and marsh grass bending in the wind.

This is nuts, her inner governor told her, but she blocked her mind to that glimmer of sanity.

The gate to the property was open, and that gave her pause. How had Effie figured that one out? Was it left unlocked the other night after she'd had her car towed?

Setting her jaw, she drove forward, through the open gate.

Are you sure you can do this? Tread on Amity's grave all over again?

Her jaw was so tight it ached, and fear crept up her spine, but she was determined to ignore it.

The coward who'd placed a snake in her car wasn't going to stop her. And besides, Effie would be here. As irritating and deceitful as she was, Nikki didn't think she was physically dangerous.

So where was her car?

Bracing herself, fighting her inner demons, she told herself the ramshackle cabin was not evil, that just because an unthinkable horror had occurred within its crumbling walls, there was no reason to be afraid.

Get on with it, then, if this is what you're bound and determined to do.

Armed with a large flashlight, her cell phone, and the stun gun, she climbed out of the car and this time had the presence of mind to lock the door before making her way through the mud and patchy grass to the front door, which also was open.

Before heading inside, she ducked her head against the wind and walked to the back of the cabin. Parked close to the building was a BMW, the same make and model that had tried to run Nikki over. It was Effie's, she realized as she tried the handle. It was locked tight, and she turned from it to look at the cabin. No one around, no flashlight glowing from inside.

So Effie was more dangerous than Nikki had thought.

Still, she wasn't a murderer.

Right?

Nonetheless, it didn't hurt her to let Reed know where she was. Deciding that safe was better than sorry, she texted Reed simply:

"Am at the cabin."

Then she pocketed her phone and, with her uncle's key, let herself in.

The door creaked on its rusted hinges, and once again Nikki was hit with the dead, musty smell of the place. Outside, the wind buffeted the walls, screaming and howling, rattling the few windows that remained.

Nikki swept her flashlight over the interior. "Effie?" she called, though once again she felt as if the place was empty.

Her stomach roiled a bit as she stood where she imagined Blondell had stood. Fighting with a stranger? She swept the beam of her flashlight over the area under the loft and thought again of her friend who had died here so long ago.

"Effie?" she yelled again. Where was she?

Slowly she moved the beam from the area where the sofa bed had been positioned to the wall where the kerosene lamp had shattered, still a bit of charring visible. She imagined the screams and the broken glass, the bits of fire dripping down the wall and onto the floor as the kerosene spread, miraculously not catching anything on fire.

There were so many unanswered questions. It seemed that the more Nikki learned, the less she knew.

She stared at the spot where Blondell had sworn she struggled with an intruder—in front of the fire—and claimed she'd struck her head on the mantel. The police had found bits of hair and scalp that confirmed that part of her story.

Nikki crossed in front of the cold hearth and climbed the staircase along the far wall. She saw where bullets had been pulled from the wall, where the spindles of the railing had been broken;

once again, she saw the spattered bloodstains that were still visible on the wood. Her skin pimpled at the thought of that night, but she kept moving upward, one hand trailing the smooth banister.

On the second level, she had a view of the first floor, and she tried to imagine what the kids had seen.

The empty loft hadn't changed since the last time she'd been here, of course.

No Effie.

Just her car.

What the hell was going on?

Nothing good.

She felt another chill and thought she heard a soft click, as if a lock were being turned.

She started to call out but held her tongue. What if whoever was opening the door wasn't Effie, but the person who had left a snake in her car the last time out? Suddenly the stun gun in her pocket seemed like a small weapon.

As if a spider had climbed up the back of her arms, her skin crawled. Turning off the flashlight, all the while telling herself she was a ninny, she strained to hear over the rush of the wind and the scrape of a branch against the siding.

It's nothing. Just a case of nerves.

Her finger hesitated on the button of the flashlight.

Creeeeaaak.

A floorboard groaned.

Her mouth turned to dust, her throat suddenly dry.

Squinting into the lower level, she thought she saw a shadow move, then realized it was that same skeletal branch near the window, casting an eerie shadow, dark on dark, through the living area.

Time to get the hell out, Effie or no Effie. Something just wasn't right.

Walking as softly as she could, she reached the top of the stairs, still not turning on the flashlight, when she heard the noise again. Definitely footsteps. She stopped, ready to take another step, but held herself still. Frozen.

"I know you're here," a man's voice called out, and she nearly fell through the floor. Definitely *not* Effie. "Come out, come out, wherever you are."

The voice was familiar, and now she knew who it was: Roland Camp. Effie's lover.

"You just couldn't stay away, now, could you?" he said as she tried to melt into the shadows. Here, in the loft, she was trapped, couldn't sneak down the stairs, and there was no window, just a sloping roof.

Darkness was her friend as well as her enemy.

"Oh, well, Nikki, there's no need for you to expose yourself, I suppose." He struck a match, scraping his thumb over its tiny head. With a hiss a little flame appeared.

If only she had a gun—her father's tiny pistol he'd kept strapped to his ankle, which had come in so handy the last time she was in trouble, or even her uncle's gun. But no. The stun gun required close contact, and she was going to avoid that at all costs.

She did have her phone, though, and if she could switch off the ringer and other sounds, she could call Reed and—oh, God, was that a knife, glinting in his other hand? The match's flame was reflected on a long, shiny blade.

She swallowed hard.

"Let me guess. You're upstairs," he said, and her heart fluttered in fear. "Thinking you would find Effie."

He knew her plan.

Panic threatened her, and her fingers fumbled, but she reached into her pocket and speed-dialed Reed without exposing the cell to the light, not taking a chance that its glow would expose her position.

He waved out the match, the smell of burning phosphorus floating on the air.

She heard him cross the floor to the stairs.

Backing up slowly, she tried to keep a clear head. The only way down was over the rail or down the rickety steps that he was steadily climbing, his footsteps slow and deliberate.

No. That wouldn't work. He'd block the path to the staircase. Throat tight, she considered her chances of going over the rail once he was on the upper level. She could vault over the railing cap, then grab the balusters, lower herself, and drop to the floor below, which, considering the length of her body, would be less than four feet. She was athletic, always had been. If she didn't land wrong and twist her ankle or, worse yet, break her leg, she might make it to her car. It was worth a try.

"Nikki," he called, sending terror through her.

Don't let him get to you.

"You couldn't let it go, could you?" he taunted. "You had to dig up the past, bring it all out into the open again and fuck up my life. Just like that stupid bitch, Effie."

She wanted to argue that she wasn't the one who had started the avalanche of truth from becoming known, nor had it been Effie—it was Niall's recanted testimony that had begun the events that had brought them here. But there was no reasoning with him, she knew that. She hadn't believed it, but now she knew he was on a path, a deadly path, that led straight to her.

Edging closer to the railing, she heard him land on the top step, and when he did, he didn't bother with a match for effect. This time he used a small, bright flashlight and swept the beam across the loft's interior.

She didn't think twice but dropped her own flashlight, grabbed the top rail, and, with a leap, vaulted the railing, grabbing two balusters with her hands on the way down, sliding her weight until she had gone as far as her straining arms allowed.

"Son of a bitch!" he hollered. Footsteps pounded above her, as she stretched as long as she could to minimize the drop. With a silent prayer, hoping the worst of her injuries would be bruises, she let go.

Thud!

She landed in a heap.

Hard.

Pain screamed through her right ankle.

"God *damn* it!" He thundered toward the stairs.

She kept moving.

Clambered to her feet.

The spotlight of Camp's flashlight washed over her. "You little bitch, stop right there!"

She kept reeling forward, ignoring the dull ache pounding up her calf. Staggering, she threw herself forward, toward the door. Only a few more steps!

"Oh, no, you don't!" he yelled, on the stairs, running down, his flashlight trained on her as she staggered toward the door. She grabbed the knob as he dropped his flashlight. It hit the floor and rolled, its beam wobbling crazily. Oh, Lord, he was close. So damned close! Yanking on the knob, she forced the door open, only to have it slammed back with the flat of his massive hand. "Gotcha!" He sounded so pleased, his breath hot against the back of her neck.

He grabbed hold of her hair, but she twisted, turning, and before he could use his damned knife, rammed her knee into his groin.

With a roar, he let go and doubled over.

She yanked the door open and ran outside, all the while fumbling for the stun gun and her keys.

Where the hell were they?

Wind was rushing over the lake, her hair blowing in front of her eyes as she half-ran, half-hobbled across the porch, all the while searching her pockets. The keys in her jacket pocket were her uncle's; the other key was in her jeans.

Her ankle nearly gave way on the step, and she heard the door open behind her.

"No you don't!" he yelled.

Across the yard she flew, her ankle throbbing, yanking the car key from her pocket, but he was behind her again, propelling himself across the porch and onto the yard.

He caught her at the hood of her CR-V, and this time when he grabbed her, he wrapped a meaty arm around her abdomen, and her keys slithered to the ground.

Oh, Jesus!

Before he could use the knife, she jabbed the stun gun against his arm and hit the button.

Electricity jolted through him, and he screamed,

withering and flopping onto the ground. The stun gun slipped from her grasp.

She found her phone and hit the dial button, all the while skirting the big man, who flailed as he tried to grab at her ankles. His reflexes were off, and he was jerking uselessly in the moonlight, but she knew the effects wouldn't last for long.

"Where's Effie?" she demanded as he trembled at her feet. She grabbed his knife and stood over him. "Damn it, Camp, where is she?"

Reed's phone went to voice mail. "Reed, it's me," she said, never taking her eye off Camp. "I'm at the cabin with Roland Camp and Effie, I think. It's not good. Send a unit. ASAP!"

Camp was still muttering and shaking.

Slowly, with her eyes still trained on him, the knife in her hand, she crouched and felt on the ground for her keys or the damned stun gun. It was too dark to see much—even Camp was just a big, dark figure on the ground—but she knew they had to be here.

She felt blindly for the keys or the gun. Where the hell were they? Through the wet grass and the mud, her fingers scrabbled, nails breaking.

Camp had stopped flopping, but still he was groaning.

"Don't move," she warned, waggling the knife with her free hand, still searching the wet ground with the other. She felt the edge of sharp metal in the grass. Finally! Just as she grabbed the keys, he sprang. His huge body slammed into hers. Awkward but heavy, still twitching, he pinned her flat to the ground, her face driven into the wet grass, her nose squished with his weight.

"Y—yoou f-f-f-uckin' bittttch," he said, ripping the knife from her fingers. For a moment he lay breathing on top of her, gathering his strength. He was still feeling the effects of the stun gun; through his jacket she felt him move, his muscles seeming to writhe.

Desperately she tried to wriggle free. "I'll cut you," he warned, his voice low and deadly against her ear. "You fight me and I swear, I'll cut you to ribbons." She froze as she felt the blade of his knife against the soft tissue of her throat. He was still a little jumpy from the volts that had swept through his body; the knife in his hand felt unstable.

"You . . . you couldn't leave well enough alone. You and Effie," he said in disgust as he took in a long breath and, with what seemed to be supreme effort, hauled both himself and Nikki to their feet.

Chapter 31

Reed's cell phone went off again. He'd ignored it for the first few minutes of June O'Henry's ravings, but now he checked his messages as June was on her third rant about the violation of her civil rights or religious rights or whatever rights crossed her mind at the moment.

"I swear to God, I will take this all the way to the Supreme Court, if I have to! I'm going to sue the city of Savannah and the police department and both of you!" she declared, pointing a long finger at first Reed and then Morrisette.

"You do that," he said as he stepped into the hallway, leaving Morrisette to deal with the indignant woman in the interview room.

As he closed the door behind him, Nikki's message came through loud and clear.

His heart nearly stopped.

She was at the cabin? With *Roland Camp?*

He dialed 911 from his cell phone and took off at a dead run.

Nikki knew she had to fight Camp now, while he was still not at full strength, but the blade against her throat kept her from struggling.

He was unsteady, his steps halting, but he was determined as he marched her ever forward. Over the howl of the wind, she thought she heard a car's engine.

Reed! Her knees went weak to think that he was close by and could help her escape the madman.

Was it her imagination, or had she seen the flash of headlights in the distance? Maybe Reed had received her earlier message. Oh, please! *Hurry, hurry, hurry! There isn't much time!*

Slowly Camp turned her back to the house, and all the while the blade was pressed to the underside of her chin, its sharp edge beginning to dig into her flesh. Desperately, she tried to think of a quick way to escape.

If Reed didn't reach her in time . . .

But he was close. She was certain that a car's engine was roaring ever nearer.

Don't react. Let him take you inside. Do not let Camp think that help is on the way.

With the knife digging into her flesh and his hulking body pressed hard against her backside, the smell of his sweat heavy in her nostrils, he drove her slowly forward, toward the cabin.

Come on, Reed, hurry!

She was thinking of another way to escape, any way, but she could scarcely do more than breathe shallowly. She could feel his rage and decided her best ploy was to appear to comply, to act as if he'd scared all the spit right out of her, that her injuries were worse than they actually were.

"You know," he said, urging her forward, his body pushing hers over the wet grass, his knee at the bend of hers, his shin pressed into the back of her leg. Obviously he wasn't quite in control of his body; nonetheless, they inched ever closer to what she knew to be her doom.

"You spent all this time tryin' to figure out what happened that night, the night your friend was killed?" he pointed out, breathing hard. "You never got it, though, did ya? So maybe it's time you had all the facts, huh, sweetheart?" His voice was becoming steadier again, the effects of the stun gun wearing off.

Nikki didn't have to ask why he would finally tell her; it was obvious. Not only did he want to brag, but he already knew she wouldn't be able to spread the story because he intended to kill her.

Hurry, Reed!

"What are they? Those facts?" she asked, trying to stall him, staggering on her weak ankle. Whatever his plans were, she had to keep him talking, delay him, give Reed time to get here.

"Stand up, bitch! I'll tell you, since you won't be able to share the story after this place goes up in flames."

What? No!

Fear curdled through her blood, but she didn't admit it, wouldn't show that she was scared as hell, her body beginning to perspire in the cold night, her mind threatening to run away with all kinds of horrid scenarios of what he would do to her.

Hurry, Reed! Hurry. If there was just a way to get the jump on him, to turn the tables, but the wicked knife shoved hard against her throat kept her from doing anything rash.

"It was all because of Blondell," he said. Now they were close to the cabin, to that gaping door where the tunnel of light from his dropped flashlight cut through the night. She couldn't die like this, not at some maniac's hand.

"It was her fault. She's the one who cheated. I found out that she was fucking that high-priced lawyer, McBaine. Your uncle." He jabbed the blade harder against her flesh for effect. "That's why she insisted they come here. Because he owned it. This is where they got together to fuck. But that night she had the kids, and after they were asleep, she and McBaine were having it out in her car. A big fight. I heard 'em screaming at each other. About her losing the baby."

They were close to the porch now. Too close, but Roland kept talking, and all the while, as he spilled his guts, Nikki sought for a way to escape, to save herself.

"It pissed me off, let me tell you," he said. "When I found out, I saw red. I could've killed her with my bare hands. I thought we were good together, but it turns out she had 'something special' with McBaine and played me for a damned fool." He was breathing harder now, his anger evident in the muscles tensing around her. "But no one gets one over on Roland Camp, especially not some crazy nympho whore!" His anger radiated from him in waves. "I decided to teach her a lesson, you know, scare the living shit out of her. That's why I brought the snake. She hates 'em. So while she and McBaine are yelling at each other in the car, so mad the windows are fogging up, I wait and wait, until he's gone and she's on the porch, and then I sneak into the cabin, plan to leave the snake in her bed. Would serve her right, y'know.

"That's when I saw Amity, there, on the pull-out. She was a looker too. Like her mama."

Nikki thought she might be sick as she thought of Amity. Camp, however, seemed to revel in his sexual prowess as he propelled her up the steps. She tripped a little, but Camp's arm around her middle kept her upright, his blade slicing into the skin, blood beginning to run.

"Watch it," he growled angrily.

And then they were across the porch and inside the cabin, with its weird half-light from the flashlight on the floor.

This was no good! No good! All too vividly she remembered the last time she'd been under a psycho's control and how the bastard had locked her in the casket. She'd hardly been able to move, barely able to draw a breath, the coffin close, so airless, so unbearable. In a blink, she was there again, in that awful space.

She was starting to hyperventilate, though Camp didn't notice as he held her tight, his jacket bunching between them, the fabric moving as he propelled her forward.

Don't freak out. Don't go there, Nikki. You have to stay clearheaded, you have to find a way out of this mess. Think, for God's sake, and listen to him. He enjoys reliving his victory over Blondell. He might forget about you for a moment . . . just a moment . . . Keep him talking. Whatever you do, keep him talking!

Reed took a corner a little too fast, the tires of his Cadillac screaming in protest.

His phone rang and he connected. "Reed."

"What the hell happened to you?" Morrisette demanded. "You go out to take a call, and the next thing I know I get a message saying you're going to that damned cabin."

"Nikki's there. With Camp."

"What? Holy Christ."

"I called for backup. I'll be there in five."

"I'm on my way!"

Reed hung up and only hoped he wasn't too late.

"I . . . thought Blondell loved you," Nikki said.

"So the fuck did I! That's why I wanted to have

it out with her, clear the goddamned air." He was furious now, reliving that night in his mind. "But things changed when I saw her with that bastard McBaine. Then the goddamn snake got loose. Everything was going to hell in a fuckin' handbasket, but then McBaine finally leaves and Blondell goes to the porch. I wanted to kill her. I really did. But then I saw Amity lying there on the couch, dead to the world. And God, she was beautiful. More beautiful than her own mother. So I think to myself, what better way to get back at Blondell than to fuck her daughter. Jesus, I got hard just thinking about how she would react. It was, like, almost too good to be true, just there for the taking, like God wanted me to do it or somethin'."

He said it as if he believed it, as if divine intervention were the reason he planned to rape a teenager. Dear God . . .

"But I never got the chance. The damned snake must've crawled into the sleeper, under the covers somehow, and bit her. All of a sudden she's screamin' bloody murder, and Blondell runs in! It was as if she'd been waitin' for me to show up! But we never struggled for no gun. I didn't have one. I just ran."

"But no. . . . the gun, the kids," Nikki said weakly, trying to keep her wits about her, to process his confession even while she searched for an escape.

"I figured, like everyone else, that she shot 'em to shut 'em up. Probably thought they'd all die on the way to the hospital, and she even shot herself too, to make it look like someone else did it. I always wondered why she didn't recognize me, but figured it was too dark or she was just too damned freaked." The knife twitched in his hand, and Nikki sucked in her breath. Already she was bleeding, could feel the warm drizzle of blood sliding down her neck and under her collar. Any second he could slit her throat.

Camp seemed unaware that he'd already cut her as he continued, caught up in his memory, "Maybe she just didn't see me or was afraid that I'd let on about McBaine being her lover, the father of her new bastard, so she made up the story about some guy with a serpent tattoo—probably thought of that because of the snake. Jesus H. Christ, that woman was a cat in heat and always lookin' to get pregnant," he snarled in disgust. "And then she shoots her kids? She's a freak, let me tell you, a goddamned freak of nature, and should be locked up for life or worse."

"You could do it. With your testimony," Nikki ventured. They were halfway across the room, their legs illuminated by the flashlight, the upper area of the cabin dark.

"Who'd believe me? Nah!"

"You could get immunity from perjuring yourself in the first trial, work a deal."

"Shut up. With the cops? No way. No fuckin' way. And I'm in too deep. And she's goin' to be out anyway. Can't be tried for the same fuckin' crime twice, so what good would it do?"

The stairs were directly in front of them, running up the back wall. Did he think he could get her to climb up there again? If he did, he'd have to take the knife away from her throat. Maybe he thought he'd throw her over the railing, make it look as if she'd had an accident.

That would be good. She could risk jumping over again.

But he knew that too. Wouldn't give her a second opportunity.

Where the hell was Reed?

They were at the base of the stairs now, and all of a sudden she realized his intention. It was not to force her up the narrow, open staircase, but to thrust her into the closet of the bathroom, a tiny space filled with spiders and mold without a window or any air.

Oh, God, no!

Images of being locked in the coffin shrieked through her brain.

"She got what she deserved. Twenty years locked up and that fuckin' attorney, your uncle, him too. Had to live with what he'd done and lost his damned case."

Her heart twisted as she considered Uncle Alex, a weak man who couldn't resist the seduction of Blondell O'Henry, like so many others. He'd given up his integrity for her, but then maybe he didn't have much to begin with.

"It was his gun, y'know."

"What?"

"Blondell didn't own a gun, but she'd been with him, so I figured he brought it."

She wouldn't believe it. "No way."

"Then she took it from him, 'cause it was his. I figured she intended to kill the kids anyway. They were just added baggage that kept her tied to her ex, and by the way, he's a real bastard."

"But to shoot her children . . ." Even to plan it was too gruesome and horrible to consider.

Camp walked her to the closet of the bathroom, an awful, tight place that was so small she could barely turn around, the air inside thick. *No, no, no!*

"That's why the gun was never found. I figure she ditched it, called him, and blackmailed him, and he came and got it before the cops got here."

"That's all just conjecture, and if he were here," she said, suddenly desperate to vindicate her uncle, a man who had considered her his favorite niece, "why were there no tire tracks, apart from Blondell's?"

"For a big deal reporter, you're pretty damned stupid. He used a canoe, at least that's the way I figured it. Didn't he have him a house across the lake?"

"No, he lived in town, but . . ." She thought of

the farm with the horses. Oh, God, Uncle Alex had known the truth all along! Had been a part of it! Her knees felt weak at his complicity. She'd discovered his affair with Blondell and half understood it, as his marriage to his wife had withered over time, culminating with the loss of their children, but she hadn't been able to believe that he'd been here, at the cabin, on the night Amity was killed and the other children wounded. He would've heard the shots, even over the rain. And he didn't turn around, try to come back and save them. But then, neither had the monster who held her in his grip.

"You had to have had a car," she said, panicking as the door of the bathroom was suddenly in front of her face. She couldn't go into that bathroom. Couldn't! Still he propelled her onward.

"Truck," he said. "An old beater I borrowed from a neighbor who was out of town and barely used it anyway. I parked a mile away near an old huntin' blind." He laughed a little. "I know how to make myself disappear, y'know. How to cover my tracks. Been a hunter all my life. That's where my truck's parked tonight, and Donny Ray, he's got another alibi for me. Just like before. Now let's get this over with."

Without another a word, he kicked in the door. Claustrophobia closed in on her, but rather than scream or cry out, she bit her tongue. She couldn't show him that he'd somehow blundered into her worst fear; she was certain that if she did he would only make it worse.

He gave her a shove, and she stumbled over the remains of the sink, landed on the toilet. "You can just stay in here," he said, and even in the partial darkness, with only the dim glow from the fallen flashlight seeping around Camp, she saw Effie Savoy, stuffed in the old shower, duct tape over her mouth, her body bound, her eyes open and fixed.

Screaming, Nikki tried to back away to the door, but Camp blocked her exit, his knife in his hand.

No, no, no! It was just like before. Stuffed into a small, tight space with a dead body.

"Surprise," Roland said with a laugh. "You and Effie, you never should have started messing into things," he said. "Because now I'm going to have to kill you too and get rid of the evidence." He reached into his pocket again and this time came up with a lighter rather than a match. "Time to burn the place down. Too bad you have to go with it."

He clicked the lighter, and in the illumination from its tiny flame she saw the evil on his face, the lines of pure hatred. And then he smiled. "But first, maybe some friends to keep you company."

Reaching into the large pocket of his jacket, he withdrew a leather bag, and with his knife, slit open the string holding the sack together. Immediately three small snakes slithered out, their distinctive bands of red, black, and yellow visible.

Her insides curdled in fear.

The coral snakes belonging to Alfred Necarney.

"These little fellas, they're shy," he said as the snakes shrank from him, curling upon themselves, their tiny eyes reflecting the light as they wriggled away. And then another copperhead poked its head from his bag and dropped to the ground.

Oh, God.

"You'll probably be all right if you don't move, and if you do, don't worry. You won't suffer long. The fire will take care of you."

Chapter 32

Nikki freaked!

No way was she going to be locked up in this tiny room with coral snakes and another copperhead and a dead body. No damned way! It didn't matter that their venom might not kill her. She was not going to take that chance. As he chuckled at how clever he was, she reached into what was left of the sink, her fingers scraping around the rim until she touched the old pipe she'd seen the last time she was here.

Without thinking, she pulled it from the sink and, using all her strength, hurled the heavy elbow joint at his head.

Thud!

With a groan, he went down to his knees, the knife clattering out of his hand. Moaning, about to pass out, he reached for the knife.

She stomped his hand with the heel of her boot and grabbed the knife.

"Oooowwwweeee!" Camp let out a howl of pain guaranteed to wake the dead in five counties. Then she tried to climb over him, to get away, but his free hand grabbed hold of her injured ankle and he squeezed. Hard.

Pain splintered up her leg and she screamed.

"You little bitch!" He grabbed her other foot just as she felt something slither down her leg. "Aaawwwwe!" he cried, and she knew one of the snakes had bitten him.

Good!

For good measure, she kicked his head, then scrambled forward.

Where the hell was Reed?

"C'mere!" Camp growled, rising to his feet again, ready to lunge.

Blam!

In a deafening flash of light, a gun fired, and Roland Camp, six-feet-five inches of muscle, bone, and hatred, jerked backward. He hit the bathroom wall. The entire cabin shook as he sank to the floor, a huge man caught in the light of his own flashlight as a growing red stain seeped through his jacket.

Nikki felt the urge to fall apart and sob in relief when she heard the footsteps approaching. "I thought you'd never get here," she admitted, climbing to her feet and wanting nothing more than to fall into Reed's arms.

"What took you so long?" She was hobbling forward and was surprised that he stopped to pick up the flashlight on the floor.

The muscles in her back tensed. Where were the other cops? The sirens? The team running through the house to secure the building?

"Nicole," a female voice said, and it was tinged in disgust.

"Aunty-Pen?" Nikki was confused. What the hell was her aunt doing here and why did she . . . ?

The big man on the floor groaned.

"I heard his story," Penelope said, the flashlight blinding, as it was now trained on Nikki's face. "And he got it all wrong anyway. But then what can you expect from a cretin?"

"I don't understand."

"Of course you don't," Aunty-Pen said wearily, but with her trademark supercilious sneer.

"The gun? You have a . . . ," Nikki stopped. "Why are you here? To meet Effie?" And then it hit her. This was all a setup. "You knew what would happen," she whispered in disbelief. "You knew that Roland would kill her . . . and me."

"Did you really think I didn't know what you were doing, Nicole? That I didn't see you skulking around my house, that I didn't figure out that you were going to tell that little slut's story? Like mother, like daughter, don't you see?" She shifted slightly, and Nikki's eyes, adjusting to the darkness, caught a glimpse of her in her suit and open-toed heels, the diamonds around her wrist catching in the flashlight's beam. She'd been to the auction, of course, establishing her alibi.

"What are you getting at?" Nikki asked, hearing another groan behind her.

"And here you were supposed to be so smart. Blondell and your uncle? They weren't fighting over her baby. The bastard was Alex's, of course, and she was devastated that she'd lost it, but she was even more upset to learn that her own daughter was carrying his child."

"What . . . no! Amity and . . ."

"Your dear, sweet Uncle Alex."

Nikki's stomach threatened to heave. All the conversations came back to her, about the older man, about a secret that would be life and death. Another wave of nausea hit her hard.

"He had this problem, you see. An eye for pretty women. Always. I should have known but I was *in love*. I gave up everything to be with him, to have his children, and then the bastard let our son drive that damned car when he knew

Elton had been drinking! It was Alex's fault that they died that night, you know. If he hadn't given Elton the keys, both of them, Elton and Hollis, would be alive today!" Her voice cracked with heartbreak.

"But there was Effie—"

"Effie?" Aunty-Pen sneered. "She was never my daughter. Never. I could never have acknowledged her, the shame of it all."

"She's dead, Aunty-Pen. Roland killed her! She's in the shower in the bathroom. Your own daughter."

"Didn't you hear me! She was *not* my daughter. She was fathered by my stepfather. The bastard who raped me every chance he got. Don't you see? She should never have been born!" Aunty-Pen was shaking now, the gun wobbling, and over the sound of the wind rushing through the open doorway, Nikki thought she heard the sound of another car's engine. Reed's Cadillac! Aunty-Pen didn't seem to notice. "Alex. He was my savior. He was supposed to take care of me. Of us. But he fell for that horrid tramp and her daughter while my precious babies died. He didn't even care enough to protect them!"

The rumble of the engine was no more.

Nikki's heart was pounding, her eyes trained on the pistol being waved in her face, the weapon that had ended Amity O'Henry's life.

"You killed Amity," Nikki said, finally understanding. "It was you. You wounded the others and shot Blondell."

"Roland ran out like a scared rat and I stepped in."

"But why didn't Blondell say anything . . . ?"

"Because she didn't know. I wore a disguise, you see. Bushy hair. Fake tattoo . . . your uncle's gun. I thought that was a nice touch. I even left the cigarette butt that he smoked here, but no one figured that out. Not even you. You know he was interested in you too, don't you? His favorite niece."

"No . . . Aunty-Pen, don't even—"

"Shut up! I'm not 'Aunty-Pen'! Do you know how I abhor that?"

"Penelope—" she tried, but the older woman swept on in a righteous fury.

"The irony of it all is that he asked me to be his alibi for that night. Isn't that rich? Not only was I his, but he was mine."

"You were both here."

"He paddled over in his stupid little canoe, but I rode my horse around the perimeter of the lake. He never saw my car as I parked it in the garage at the farmhouse, but his was right in front. I knew where he was, where he was going. I *always* knew," she said sadly, then as if realizing she was getting caught in her memories, she cleared her throat. "Now, you get back into the bathroom!" She waggled the gun toward the open door. "As

505

much as I hate to admit it, I think the moron had a decent idea."

"No," Nikki said, not budging. She wasn't going to be locked in that tiny room with the corpse of Effie Savoy.

"You want me to kill you right here?" Penelope asked.

Out of the corner of her eye Nikki saw one of the coral snakes moving silently across the floor, closer and closer to the open toe of Aunty-Pen's shoe.

"I think you should turn yourself in," Nikki said. The snake had chosen a path between her aunt's legs. And better yet, another one was joining it. Penelope didn't seem to notice. The copperhead moved silently too, so close to Nikki's feet that it was all she could do to stay still as it brushed her boot and continued on its slithering path.

"And I think you're a foolish, foolish woman!" She leveled the gun at Nikki just as one of the smaller snakes started an inquisitive path up Aunty-Pen's leg.

"Whhaa . . . ?" she cried, then let out a little screech of horror. With a scream she started running, shaking, trying to get rid of the snake that had crawled up her leg. "Get it off me! Oh, God, get it off me!"

"Police!" Reed's voice boomed as he stood in the doorway. "Drop your weapon!"

Penelope spun, falling onto the floor, screaming as she dropped Uncle Alex's gun, and the sounds of sirens could be heard cutting through the night. The flashlight twirled in an arc as, squealing, she writhed, crying and screeching, the copperhead wrapped tightly around her ankle, its mouth open wide, its fangs visible.

Nikki made her way to Reed, who held a gun on the stricken woman with one hand, while with the other he called for backup, barking out orders for an ambulance and animal control.

Gingerly, he picked up her gun as the first of the backup units arrived, sirens screaming, lights flashing. By this time Penelope Hilton McBaine was nearly catatonic and Roland Camp was unconscious.

Nikki threw herself into Reed's arms, thankful for his strength and wondering how she ever thought for a second that she couldn't marry him.

Finally, after twenty long years, the scandalous truth of Amity O'Henry's murder could finally be told.

December 17th
Last Interview

Now I know the truth as I stare through the smudged glass at the broken woman, a maniac whom I once thought I loved. It's hard to imagine that hatred could rot a person's soul to the point that now, this woman I cared for, is nearly unrecognizable to me.

"Good bye, Aunt Penelope," I say.

"Go to hell!" is the sharp, concise response. She's recovered from her snake bites but never again will find peace, if she ever had it in the first place.

"Sorry. I've already been there, thanks to you." I give her a hard smile and get off of my stool. "But now I'm back and have my life again. I'm getting married tomorrow."

"That's a mistake," she snarls.

"I don't think so."

"You'll find out," Penelope says with a bitter, hard-edged cackle, as if she knows better, just as the guard reaches for her. "Men," she advises with a pinched face. "They're all the same."

She seems so sure of herself. So convinced. And yet she is on the other side of the bars;

she is the one who is caged. Who is she to give out any kind of advice?

"Blondell's finally spoken," I say. "She was dumbfounded to learn you were the stranger who attacked her. She really did have car trouble on the way to the hospital. Turns out she loved her children, as best she knew how. She loved Uncle Alex and kept silent rather than implicate him in any way, even with his betrayal with Amity."

Penelope's face devolves into a mask of hatred.

I leave then, get up from the uncomfortable chair and walk down the long hall, hearing the gates clang shut with finality as I pass. I won't miss the smells or the sounds or the sights or the feel of this place, and I know I won't be coming back.

As I gather the things I left at the admittance area, I close my mind to my childhood and the hours I spent with my cousins and aunt and uncle, the halcyon days that now I realize are just a nostalgic figment of my imagination, a fragmented and unreal part of my family history.

I'm escorted out of the prison area to freedom, and as the final gates close behind me, I draw in deep, cool breaths. Bars and cages, tight places and locked doors—not my thing.

Roland Camp died on the way to the hospital, but Penelope survived. Is that justice? Maybe there is no such thing. I don't know. Donny Ray Wilson is talking, and he's agreed to be interviewed for the book, so that's a good thing. As for Calvin O'Henry, he and June refuse to acknowledge me, and they resent the fact that Blythe is willing to be a part of the story. Niall feels vindicated, of course. He didn't see his mother shoot him as she was struggling with a stranger for the gun that Aunt Penelope hid for twenty years and Uncle Alex never admitted was missing. Uncle Alex was as guilty as she in many ways, though I don't believe he ever knew his wife was a murderess. I won't let myself think that horrid thought. My mother never liked Aunty-Pen and wasn't all that surprised, though my sister, Lily, found the scandal "delicious." Yeah, well, she didn't have to live through exposing it.

Uncle Alex lives in an ever-deepening twilight world. Is it payback? Karma? Maybe.

In the end, the snakes were captured, and it was determined that Roland Camp had killed Alfred Necarney, though why Roland was so upset with my digging up the past will remain a mystery.

I wonder about Effie Savoy, but I'll never really know her. Not now.

It's mind-boggling.

I leave the prison behind me. Forever.

Reed is waiting for me. Wearing jeans and a

ght jacket over a long-sleeved T-shirt, his hips leaning against the dirty fender of his ridiculous Cadillac, his hair teased by the winter wind, he smiles as I approach—that slow, sexy smile that always gets to me. "Hey, Hot Stuff," he says as I draw near.

Damn—I can't help but grin.

"What do you say we elope?"

"Tonight?" He's got to be joking, right?

But the spark in his eye says differently. "I'm talking about right now. You hop in and I drive."

"Seriously?" I can't believe it. "But . . . the wedding and . . . the guests . . . and the church and the country club . . . My mother will be mortified. She'll kill me. And she'll kill you too. Both of us."

"So what? I want to just get married, the two of us. You and me. No muss. No fuss."

"Romantic."

"It could be." Again, that irreverent grin stretching across his beard-shadowed jaw. I really can't tell if he's kidding or not.

"Well?" he asks.

"Well." I stare at him long and hard, and suddenly I feel free. Light. Even giddy. Those ponderous ropes of convention, the ones that have been weighing me down, the seating charts, and menu options, and limits on the bar tab, the need to please my mother . . . they finally snap. "Okay, Detective," I hear myself say as I slide into the warmth of the Caddy's passenger side, "Let's run away together. Right now. Take me to the nearest preacher and make me your wife!"

Reed switches on the ignition and we stare at each other a moment, then both of us start grinning as the Caddy rolls forward.

A
WHISTLING
WOMAN

Louise Shivers

LONGSTREET PRESS
Atlanta, Georgia

The author would like to acknowledge
and thank the National Endowment For
the Arts for the Grant provided for the
writing of this novel.

Published by LONGSTREET PRESS, INC.,
a subsidiary of Cox Newspapers,
a division of Cox Enterprises, Inc.
2140 Newmarket Parkway
Suite 118
Marietta, Georgia 30067

Printed in the United States of America

2nd printing, 1993

Library of Congress Catalog Number 93-79654

ISBN: 1-56352-085-0

This book was printed by R.R. Donnelley & Sons,
Harrisonburg, Virginia.

Jacket design by Honi Werner
Book design and typesetting by Laura McDonald

To Julia Cooke Shingleton

A WHISTLING WOMAN

*A whistling woman and a crowing hen
never come to any good end*
                        — old folk saying

*Whoever tells the truth is chased out of
nine villages*
                        — Turkish Proverb

One

ALL MY LIFE I'VE BEEN able to watch myself do things. See myself . . . stand off and look over at a chair or table and see myself there where I'd walked before . . . see the muslin sheets flap on the clothesline and see him stretched out on them beside me, or see the big oak tree by Contentnea Creek and see the other one push me against it and himself against me.

Right now I can see my whole life like that, some of the parts clearer than others, some real dim and shadowy.

The first thing I remember was when I was a baby. I had a bad dream: frogs were crawling in my bed, slithering right in it.

And then a few years later I remember us moving. It must have been 1867. I was about eight years old then. It was in the fall; I remember the cut hay in the fields. Mama piled our things in a big flat wagon and a man drove us to a different house to live. It wasn't my papa that helped us 'cause I didn't have a papa. Never did that I knew anything about. I didn't even know him from pictures. The only thing I ever could get Mama to say about him was that he was a hardluck fella from Fool's Bridge who didn't come back from the war.

I remember sitting high up on the seat of that wagon. Mama sighed and said, "Ever stitch we own in the world," as she looked at the feather bed, the iron bedstead, the trunk and the old ballyhacked dresser. The bed shook from side to side as the horse clip-clopped along, making a kind of rhythm.

The places in the town looked so funny to me as we passed them with me perched up there. We rode and rode out into the country. Before we got too far out we passed the Sandpit where Laffton used to take me swimming sometimes. Laffton was my brother who had just up and left a few months earlier when he had turned sixteen. Mama was still mad as a wet hen about it.

There was a sorry-looking house near the Sandpit. "Looka yonder at the limber-necked chickens," I called out, pointing to the yard, but Mama shushed me and sat up real stiff. I expect she knew the people that lived there, but she looked straight ahead as we passed.

"Sick chickens," she said after we were down the road. "That's Bad Alley down there." I peered down the lane trying to see what was bad about it. The colored man that was driving the wagon broke my thoughts.

"Mr. Fleeting's hoping you'll get there in time

to give him a haircut befo' dinner."

"Well, I've got right smart to do to get settled in," Mama spoke up.

"I can hep with that," the man named Slender said. "Me and Maebelle are mighty glad to see y'all come. Mr. Fleeting hadn't had too much attention since his Missus died. We've got just about all we can handle with the harvesting and all."

"Is Maebelle your wife?" I piped up.

"Yes, and my woman, too," he chuckled.

When we went around the hill, I sucked in my breath. There in front of me was the plantation called Fairfield and I'd never seen anything like it.

I stood up in the wagon and crowed like a rooster, "Pinniney Yeargin went to Phil-a-ma-york." Mama said, "Georgie, sit down and be quiet. What is the matter with you?" I didn't know myself but it was all so new and exciting that I felt like I had to say something!

When we rode up to that great big house and I saw it in front of me, I let out another whoop.

The house had long porches on both sides, and there were a lot of little buildings around it, and a big round waterhole near the long grape arbor. We went on past the house and down a lane. "Yonder where me and Maebelle live," Slender gestured with a sweep of his hand towards the woods.

We went on around for a ways and came to a little house with a big umbrella tree beside it. The

way Mama got down off the wagon kind of nim-
ble I could tell she liked it. The porch had a rail
around it and a wooden shelf for the water bucket. In one direction there was the lane to the big
house, in the other a path to the creek.

We unloaded our things from the wagon and
placed them around in the two rooms. Then we
walked away from our house with its unpainted
silver-gray boards and went to meet Mr. Worth
Fleeting. Mama never had seen him, she'd just
been sent for. Mrs. Fleeting had been dead three
months when we got there.

When we went into the door to the side porch,
a big rawboned woman smiled at us from the
kitchen. She called out welcome and nodded at us
as she kept right on sifting cornmeal from the
round sifter with one hand and turning the chick-
en frying in the black pan on the biggest wood
stove I've ever seen with the other.

Mama nodded back at her and said, "Smells
mighty good." I can still remember the whiffs of
baking sweet potatoes and the wood smoke all
mingled together.

"Maebelle, aren't they here yet?" It was a fine
sounding voice that called out from the front of
the house—what I later learned to call an aristo-
cratic voice.

Slender hurried us on into the room where Mr.
Fleeting sat. While we were being introduced to

the man, my eyes swept around that big sitting room. It was a grand room with sunshine coming in the long windows. Big-headed pictures hung on the wall, their eyes following me around.

When I set my mind to it, I can see Mr. Fleeting just like he looked that day. He was a medium-sized man and when he'd been young he must have had that kind of hair they call strawberry blonde. He still had a lot of sandy gray-streaked hair and a moustache the same color. His skin was kind of pink and he had real light blue eyes. I remember noticing right away that when he'd try to talk, a little trickle of slobber would run out of the side of his mouth. You see, he'd had a little stroke before we came and he was shaky and addled. Mama said it sure could have been a whole lot worse. "He can walk and talk, and that's a blessing," she said.

I liked him right from the first. You don't know why you like some people the first time you see them but you just do. And some people you don't even want to like.

Of course, all of this was long before I even knew what the Ten Commandments were, let alone what they meant, and long before I pointed to the big framed copy of them in the hall and asked, "What does commit adultery mean?" and he had cleared his throat and said, "Mess around with bad women."

Two

WELL, I CAN TELL YOU it was a different life for us as soon as we moved in and Mama went to work. I don't mean that things were grand; there wasn't much of that around in those days so soon after the war and all. Why, they always told me that when the surrender came General Sherman wasn't more than twenty miles from here. He'd have burnt Fairfield for sure if the war hadn't ended right when it did.

But before Mama got the work, we'd been living on peas and cornbread as long as I could remember. You see, it wasn't just that Mama didn't have a man to take care of us (a whole lot of women were left in that fix) but she didn't have any other family either. It was hard for her to find any way to make any money. So I could see right away that Mama was pleased by us being at the plantation. I heard her talking to Maebelle and saying so.

"This is a real blessing. I've got another one I'm trying to raise . . . Laffton's his name. He just turned sixteen and as soon as he did he lit out somewhere, bound to find some kind of half decent job . . . and I guess he was tired of being around women."

"He just fixed himself a lard bucket full of peas and went, didn't he Mama?"

They both looked at me and didn't say anything. I knew what they were thinking . . . that I talked too much for a girl. But remember, I was eight years old and there weren't any children anywhere; Mama and Maebelle were the youngest people around and of course I thought they were ancient. Maebelle and Slender had some children but they were grown and had moved off the place long before we came.

So you can see the situation. That frail old aristocrat and two tenant farmers who did everything from plant the crops, keep the big house in some kind of repair and cook the meals. We were out there in the country in a run-down place that the world seemed to have forgotten about.

Like Maebelle said, "Everybody is in the same fix these days."

Soon Mama and Mae were thick as thieves, sewing and cleaning and thinking of things to tickle Mr. Fleeting's fancy. Part of the time Mae had to work in the fields. Slender had all he could do. I'd help Mama in the big house then. I kept wanting to go to school, but Mama said, "Maybe one of these days." Children came and went in school. Mr. Fleeting had good and bad days. On the days he felt good he started teaching me how to read. I'd already figured a lot out by looking at his books. After that I'd read to Mama and Mr. Fleeting. I made me a little book and I'd record some of the things I'd read to Mr. Fleeting on the days that he'd be feeling weak and Mama would be busy in the kitchen. He had a room full of books that he'd let me read out of.

During that time we didn't meet any of his kin. A week before Christmas a package was brought out from his son, Mr. John Fleeting who lived in the old Albemarle area up near the Virginia line, where his mother had come from. That was the first time I'd heard of him.

It was at Christmas that I got to love old Mr. Fleeting. Santa Claus brought me a little birth-stone ring. Looking back I don't know how Mama managed that, as poor as everybody was back then. But she did, somehow. We all had a good time that day, Mae and Slender and their children visiting, all dressed up and happy. We all laughed and talked together and I showed off my ring with the emerald-colored stone.

But after sundown when they all went off and Mama had made Mr. Fleeting his toddy and got him ready for bed, I noticed that my finger was starting to swell. The more I pulled at the ring to get it off, the more my finger swelled. It started to ache and get red. That's when I started to get scared. I could tell that Mama did too. No matter how much soap we put on the finger trying to ease the ring off, my finger got redder and redder and throbbed more. Finally Mama set me down in a straight chair in the big kitchen and told me we were going to have to file it off. That's when I started to feel panicky and started to cry. Mama filed and filed. It felt like she was hacking as she ground back and forth with the big metal file.

I was so miserable that I slumped over and felt like I was going to die. Terror went through me as I thought of the things I'd heard of, like blood poisoning. Suddenly I felt a cool hand on my forehead and then a cool washrag, clean and sun-smelling, laid across my eyes. When I opened them I saw that Mr. Fleeting had come in and was sitting in front of me on the round piano stool that Mama must have brought in. The light from the lamp shone behind him and when he smiled at me, it was like I was seeing him in a kind of dream. He reached over and took my hand and wrapped it in a big cool white rag and we sat a minute. He kept dabbing it with icy water from the bucket outside. He said, "Now be real quiet and think of the best thing you know of." In a minute he said, "Now tell me what you're thinking about."

"Bananas," I said, and he smiled. We'd had some since we'd moved to Fairfield and it was the first time I'd ever seen any.

After we'd sat for a while, he took a thin black file he'd brought from his room and slowly, very slowly but with a hand so firm I couldn't believe it was his, filed until the ring broke in two and fell away from the sides of my finger. After a kind of hiccup sigh, I closed my eyes and lay my head against his warm arm and rested.

A sound from the porch woke me up, and when I looked up I thought I was dreaming because I saw a strange dark man standing in the doorway not making a sound.

"John!" Mr. Fleeting exclaimed, making an effort to get up.

"Chaney, Chaney," he called to my mother. "Come here! Call Mae to get out the supper. Doll's home!"

That was the first time I ever saw him.

Three

WE SETTLED DOWN AT Fairfield. Before I knew it I was thirteen and then everything started to change.

Like I said, I've always been able to step back and watch myself. Well, I can tell you exactly what I looked like then. I was tall and straight, taller than Mama even when I was just thirteen. When she'd go to tie a sash around my waist she'd laugh because it was so little. My legs were long and thin like bird legs. When I'd pull the black stockings on to go to school they'd look even skinnier, and I know I was a funny sight. My bosoms were high and little. Mama said she didn't even see any need for me to wear a waist except to keep the cold air out. My face was long too, and my eyes were black, like muscadines, Mae used to say. My hair was dark and straight.

I came in one day about that time, whistling and skipping, whistling up on the porch. Mama came out of the house, drying her hands on her apron, wringing her hands, looking anguished. "*George*, stop that whistling. Have you never heard that girls shouldn't whistle?"

"Ma'am?" I said.

"A whistling woman and a crowing hen never come to any good end," she said.

I looked at her. I could tell she was serious.

She went on in a lowered voice. "I don't want you getting on Mr. Fleeting's nerves. I need this job mighty bad, and men don't like to hear a big ole growin' girl."

A school had started up between Fairfield and town and I'd been going since I was ten. I would walk about an hour to that little building in the grove of oak trees. If it was too cold or icy, Slender would give me a ride in the wagon on his way into town. He was always going back and forth taking care of business for Mr. Fleeting. But most of the time I walked. It gave me a chance to get off by myself and think things out. And I liked to investigate things. I'd collect different kinds of leaves and rocks. I had things I'd check on every day, ant beds and bird nests. In the fall I had a favorite thing, a big garden spider who'd spin a wide web every day, take it in at night after he'd caught his dinner and then spin another one early the next morning before I'd even come by. I'd heard them called writing spiders, and people said that if they wrote your initial in the web you'd die. I didn't ever see a G. Sometimes I thought there was a W, but then it would turn into something else. Some days I'd be so excited when I left the house for school that I'd wave my hands in the air. Mama would say, "Whatcha flittering for?" and chuckle at me.

On the trail that I walked in the winter, I'd watch the trees lose their leaves. When they were bare and black, they laced against the sky like fans. I thought that was the prettiest sight I'd ever seen in my life. I still do.

Once or twice over those years when the leaves were all off the trees and I could see the road, I saw the man in a black and brown buggy hurrying by.

There were two main kinds of churches in Tar County. Methodist and Baptist. First you'd see one, then the other. There was a Free Will Baptist one between Fairfield and town. The Fleetings had gone to the Methodist church in town before the war. Mr. Worth didn't go anywhere when we lived there. Mae and Slender went to their own African Methodist one, on the other side of the creek. Before we'd moved to Fairfield, we hadn't gone to church, but out there Mama got a hankering to go.

It all started when Mr. Fleeting offered an announcement at supper one spring night. We generally all ate supper together. "There's a big

Baptist camp meeting going on next week," he said.

"A camp meeting?" Mama's voice sounded flat, but my ears perked up. Something to do. Somewhere to go. But she didn't sound like it was going to have anything to do with us.

Finally, after a long quiet, she said, "I've heard tell of camp meetings all my life, but I never have thought to go to one. Do you feel like going?" she asked Mr. Fleeting.

"No, no, my churching's finished, but you and Georgeanna ought to go. If it's farther than you want to walk, Slender can carry you in the wagon, or he could get out the buggy."

It was settled then, and we did go. The meetings were outside, under a shelter they'd made. They called it a brush arbor because it was made out of little trees and branches put over a wooden frame, like a grape arbor, to make a tent.

It was the first preaching I'd ever been to. It was funny seeing folks from school and their families out there like that. That part was nice, being out of doors and all, but I didn't like the preacher from the minute I laid eyes on him. He was a real long-legged fellow with a sort of whinny laugh. "The ladies, God blessem, hey hey." He patted me on the top of the head when he walked by. I took my hand and brushed my hair all around to get the touch off. But the crowd got caught right up in the ranting and swelling and carrying on. When we got home I heard Mama talking to Mr. Fleeting. "Georgeanna didn't seem to care much for the preacher." He chuckled. "That girl never did suffer fools gladly."

But Mama was caught up in it, and it wasn't long after that before we started going to the regular church by the creek.

Contentnea Free Will Baptist Church was a pretty little white building, and the preacher that was there was as different from the evangelist as dark night is from bright morning. When I think back I realize that the preacher, Luke Swann was his name, must have been a young man, about thirty-five. But of course he seemed as old as the hills to me then. Still I enjoyed seeing the people and just the *going*. Afterwards I'd sit outside on a tree stump and eye everybody as they headed to their wagons, while the mules whinnied and grazed in the corners of the churchyard.

Folks at that church dearly loved Mr. Swann's sermons. Mama and the other ladies would sit on the edge of the wooden pews just eating up every word he said. That's where I learned what it means when somebody says something is "*gospel*." What Reverend Luke said was gospel. He was a fine-looking dark-haired man, medium height and straight in his black suit, but when he walked he kinda drug one of his legs. From the way the women looked at him, that made them like him even more. "It was infantile paralysis," I heard a woman say to Mama.

He had a farm over near Eureka and came to our church on the second Sunday of every month. "He farms during the week," we heard, but we never saw him in his everyday clothes. We knew he preached at other churches too sometimes. In fact, before it was over, Mama got to wantin' to go other places to hear him. She talked about it, but she never did. No way she could have.

Mama wasn't all that pretty, but her skin and hair were soft and smooth. Compared to me she was almost short, but I always thought she was just the right size for a woman to be. She was rounded and shapely and the few times she ever hugged me it felt as good as a feather bed. Something about her shape and coloring reminded me of a dove. But there wasn't anything soft about the way she talked. Straight to the point, with a bite to it.

Mama changed after we started going to church. Her face kinda opened out. I'd hear her and Mae singing hymns about loving Jesus while they worked. Mr. Fleeting spoke out about it one day while she had him out on the porch sunning in the rocking chair. "Well, I don't see a thing wrong with it. It makes ladies feel good to go to church," he said.

I believe going out to that church gradually made Mama feel like somebody. There at Contentnea Church she could speak up and be a person. She'd fix her hair, and we'd be right there along with everybody else. It didn't even matter all that much that she couldn't read; a lot of the others couldn't either. I remember seeing one man holding a hymn book upside down and singing away. She could listen to the Bible readings and learn the songs. There was always someone leading the singing. Since there were so few hymn books, the leader would line out the words. You know, In the sweet *In the sweet* Bye 'n bye *Bye 'n bye*. The preacher wasn't one of the kind that looked down his nose at women. He would listen to what they had to say, each one of them, and seem to care. The women ran the church mostly. There were three times as many women as men. I s'pect for a lot of them it was the only time they ever got to have any say-so about much of anything. I even got Mama to let me teach her some reading and writing, something she'd always been too ashamed to do before.

One day, after we'd been going there for awhile, I stood outside after the service and watched the women close in around the Reverend Swann. One of them nudged against his black sleeve like it was an accident. I remember shutting my eyes and feeling and tasting moist wool in my mouth. I stood far back from the circle and heard, just slightly above the sound of the women's voices, a man behind me mutter, "Timothy I, Verse 2, 'Converse sparingly and conduct yourself prudently with women.'" I could see out of the corner of my eye one of the impatient husbands standing tapping his foot. But Reverend Swann talked earnestly on. Every time he ever stood in the pulpit he said, "All souls are precious in the sight of God." And it seemed to me that he meant those words with all his heart.

About the time the churchgoing started, I woke up one day with a strained feeling between my legs. Waves of uneasiness moved through me from one bone to the other. My sharp hipbones stuck up when I lay down flat, and between them it seemed like a new ocean lapped with thin water. Something like an eggshell and eggwhite started happening. After I had stood up for a while, I pulled down my drawers and saw weak pink stains in the eggwhite. I stood there for a long time. It didn't go away. I put my finger in and took it out. It came out sticky and red.

The air around my ears felt heavy. As I stared at the wall, little black specks like gnats flew between my eyes and the wall. Standing there, I could see a thick veil of myself leave and float out the window like a butterfly. The stains from the ripe mulberries that lay crushed on the ground turned the path that led to the creek red.

I'd told Mama when I went into the house. "I started," I said, and Mama had looked at me real strange and had given me a pile of clean white rags. She'd shown me how to fold them and pin them inside my drawers: "You'll need them every month, so keep them clean," she'd snapped. Then she'd slammed the door as she left to go to Mr. Fleeting's room. When I'd done what I had to do and gone up to the Big House, I could tell Mama had told Mae, because Mae put her big arm across my shoulder and leaned close so no one could hear.

"And one more thing, George, stay away from menfolks when the curse is on you. They don't like to have that around."

After that there were still a lot of long slow days. Days when we didn't see a soul but each other. Days when we made lye soap, or boiled the washing and didn't hear a sound but the birds. Months would pass by like that, dusty days, moldy days, but Mama had different things to think on now, and she'd have me read from the Bible every night before we'd turn down the lamp.

But when spring came I'd go for long walks in the woods and across meadows. I'd watch the sweep of the fields just plowed. The curve would follow the line of the woods. The rows would make designs as pretty as ribbons, low and smooth, then ridging, washboarding. I'd want to go lie down in that sweet plowed dirt and wallow like a pig. At nights sometimes that feeling would come over me when I was in my bed and I'd think of those sights and I'd feel like I was about to bust. I'd get so full of it that I'd bite the sheets and shake. I couldn't wait for the next morning — hated to take my clothes off at night because it just took time to put them on again the next day — only went to bed so that night would be over so that I could see what the next morning would bring.

One day while we were sitting outside in the back yard, Maebelle told my fortune by looking at the lines inside my hands. The main thing I remember her saying was, "Old, you're going to live till you're real old, and you're going to have two men, one light and one dark." Then she dropped my hand and looked at me hard. "And a secret, you're going to have a secret."

"A good one?" I asked.

"Good and bad, bad and good — now don't ask me no more," she said.

Later on she taught me how to read palms myself. "The main thing," she said, "is to be real quiet and you can feel something come out of the person to you, like a little whisper — it's more *that* than the lines." She also told me to be careful whose palm I read.

"Be careful reading men's palms. It's something you have to be careful about, it catches their soul — and it's a right smart *burden* havin' somebody's soul."

Four

IT WAS MY FOURTEENTH birthday and hot for May. I remember the tub sitting out on the sunny side of the back porch at the big house. It had been there all morning, warming in the sun. Shadows of the leaves from the maple trees lay in the water, and as I stuck my toe in, they skittered like minnows and tadpoles.

My big toe was long, but the one beside it wasn't longer like Mr. Fleeting's and Maebelle's were. Maebelle had told me a long second toe meant that you were boss in the family. "See," she'd pulled her bare foot out of her slipper.

There wasn't anybody around the place, so I took off everything but my drawers. The tops of my legs were white as starch with little goose bumps on them.

Maebelle wandered by and saw me wondering about them. "It's cause you're so skinny. After you fatten up some, you'll have some butter inside you to smooth out the places." She laughed and slapped her behind. "Now, I've got plenty of butter. Slender says I'm rich as cream." I blushed because I knew what she was referring to, but I couldn't imagine such a strange thing. I was realizing there was something that went on between women and men and it made babies happen. All that talk about hollow tree stumps didn't fool me anymore, but I still couldn't really imagine such a thing.

Mae left me alone as I got into the tub. Slender was in town and Mr. Fleeting was staying in bed feeling poorly, so I soaked and dreamed in the water with only the birds watching, the trees wiggling their leaves at me. I felt so happy. Everything in the world seemed possible. I just knew I'd grow up to be fine looking . . . maybe I'd even go off to school to get an education like Mr. Fleeting. The sunlight danced through my eyelids like millions of diamonds.

Mama let me go into Snow Hill by myself for the first time that day. I think it was her way of accepting that I was getting older. Slender had come back and rigged me up a little pony cart.

I was high with a free feeling all the way into town. When I got there I tied the pony in front of the store, then stopped to look into the window. I saw myself reflected in the glass in my pinafore with eyelet embroidery on the edge. I thought I looked right good. But my mood changed quickly as I gazed.

A man was standing across the street, about to step out of the doorway of the bank. I could see him reflected behind me in the store window. That image of him, standing there in his prime, froze in my mind forever. I recognized him immediately even though I hadn't seen him for a long time. It was Mr. Fleeting's son, John. I'd heard Maebelle refer to him many times by his nickname, Mr. "Doll." When I'd first heard it I'd snickered — a great big grown man called Doll. I figured she'd known him when he was little and maybe his mother had called him that and it had stuck. His father called him John most of the time. But over the years everybody else referred to him or called him Doll.

After I'd first seen him standing in the doorway that night when my finger was swollen, I remember seeing him from time to time. He'd moved back from Albemarle and was building a big house in Tar County between his daddy's place and town, not too far from where my school was. "He inherited that parcel of land from his mother," I heard Mr. Fleeting say.

He never lived at Fairfield in those days but had lodging in town while the building was going on. He'd left his family back in Albemarle while the house was being built. That's all I knew about him when I saw him that day in Snow Hill.

There was no doubt that he was watching me. He slowly crossed the street. I felt so self-conscious that I wanted to run.

"Georgie?"

I wanted to say, "Don't speak to me, I'm just a little girl. I shouldn't even be in town without my mother."

"Is that you? Do you know me?"

"Yes, Sir," I stuttered.

He stood looking at me. He was such a tall, slender man. His coloring was completely different from Mr. Fleeting's. His hair was almost coal black, and thick. I'd seen pictures of his mother; he was the image of her.

"I thought it was. But you've changed — you were just a little girl . . . what brings you to town?"

I started to talk but it seemed like words just babbled out of my mouth.

"A birthday present . . . your daddy . . . the pony . . . ." I realized that I wasn't making much sense.

He stood smiling down at me and it seemed like there wasn't anybody else on the street, although there were people bustling all around.

He was as old as my mother — thirty-five or more — but for some reason he was making me feel strange.

"So, Papa gave you some money to buy yourself a present and let you bring the pony into town," he said.

He kept looking at me, somehow making me look up into his eyes. It was his cold blue eyes looking over his sharp nose that made me nervous. They were as fierce as some kind of bird.

"The Hat Shop," he pointed to Bonnie's by the bank, "has pretty things." I noticed how thin his lips were. I could hear words in my head. Maebelle saying, "I never have trusted anybody with thin lips — that's a sign of meanness!"

Then he smiled a charming smile reminding me that he was Mr. Fleeting's son, mumbled "Nice to see you," and turned and went off down the street.

I went into Bonnie's and picked out a card of lace but I hardly saw it. I was so addled the rest of the time I was in town that not a thing I did made a bit of sense. When I headed for home that day, right after I'd passed the Sandpit, I saw his horse and buggy up ahead, waiting for me.

"Georgeanna," he said as he tipped his hat, "I thought since you were passing right by my new house you'd like to see how the building is coming along. It is going to be a real show place." The idea scared me a little, but I reminded myself again that he was, after all, Mr. Fleeting's son. What harm could there be? So I let him lead me off the road towards Contentnea Creek.

When I got to the house there weren't any workers there, but I stopped the pony and got down anyway. There wasn't any sign of anybody; Mr. Doll Fleeting had disappeared. I walked around looking at the foundation of the house and the supplies that were stacked up.

It sure was a pretty spot — I remember thinking that, up on a rise with big oaks all around shielding it from the road, and Contentnea Creek flowing behind it. I walked down towards the creek letting my hand brush the tops of the ferns growing along the bank, forgetting for a minute why I'd stopped off at the spot.

"I could hug your neck," I heard Doll Fleeting's voice saying. He stepped from behind a tree, appearing out of nowhere again, like he could do.

Five

THAT WAS ALL THAT happened that day. He showed me around the place like he'd said he was going to and then sent me on my way to Fairfield.

But I couldn't go to sleep that night for thinking of that thin-lipped mouth and the strange way the man made me feel.

When Mama and Maebelle asked me about my trip into town, for some reason I didn't mention anything about Mr. Doll Fleeting.

I know now that there are some men in the world who seem to know by instinct that if they just wait and watch, they'll end up getting exactly what they want.

It was about the middle of June when he came out. I was by myself on our little porch, trying to get the rust out of the bottom of a blue speckled basin. I kept turning it round and round. Mama had told me that if I rubbed it good with sand, most of the rust would probably come out. The day was warm and humid, and my hands were getting splotchy like the basin. I was just starting to take it inside but for some reason it aggravated me and I fell into a frenzy scrubbing at it. A sound in the distance made me glance up. A man riding a horse was coming. Before I could collect myself, he was in front of the porch. He just sat up there looking at me. The horse pawed the ground and when he finally spoke he asked, "Where is your mother?"

"At the big house."

The man sat there a minute more, still looking right at me.

"When are you planning to take another trip to town?"

"I . . . I don't know." I felt miserable, but he kept staring at me in that way until I had to look up at him.

Then he sort of jerked his hand and clicked his mouth for the horse to go. He reached over and slid his hand over the cane handle of his long keen whip.

I shivered. He'd come around a different way, not past the house, and I saw him leave that way.

I thought about telling Mama about him coming by, but I didn't and I didn't know why I didn't. I guess I thought that I must be mistaken.

After that he showed up about once a week. He wouldn't stay long, just pass a few words. He'd ask me if I had any messages for him, in a kind of teasing way. I'd feel real bashful and blush. Sometimes I'd hide when I saw him coming. I'd watch from behind the curtain until I saw him leave. Then he started appearing on the path. He didn't ask me to

get in the buggy, just got down and walked alongside me a little ways and then left.

Sometimes he'd come up to the big house.
Sometimes he'd just stride up and down the long
porch shaking the boards with his walk, his boots.
I felt so strange when he did that. I was afraid
he'd look at me in that way, or tease me. Sometimes he'd stay for dinner. Mae would get something from the smokehouse and cook a special
meal for him. The way he'd talk and move and
eat was so different from his Papa's. I'd keep quiet
and out of the way, but I always watched him.

On those days they would talk about the house
that he was having built. I'd sit out in the yard
and listen to the talk. After he'd leave I'd go to my
secret place at the creek. I'd sit down there with
my back up against the big chestnut oak tree and
reflect on all different kinds of things. Even
though I'd try not to, I'd think about how he
looked, and I'd carry on little conversations with
him in my head. Sometimes I'd laugh out loud at
myself, at how silly I was, making out like I was
talking to that grown man and he was talking to
me. Some days I'd play dressup, throwing Mama's
shawl around my shoulders, and walk around.
After I'd glimpsed him, I'd make a whole week off
of a nod. I'd wear it clean out thinking about it
from every angle. Measure it, touch the color, the
texture. It was so strange. At first I'd been scared

to death of him and despised the sight of him, handsome as he was. But gradually I was starting to watch for him. I'd sit under my tree or up in the branches. There was one that grew across, and if I climbed in just right, it was like sitting at a piano. So I'd sit and pretend I could play.

I was sitting up there the day in July he came in from the creek. I was trilling my fingers across the branches and singing the old songs.

The tree sat right at the edge of the wide field that spreads out down near the creek. He came that day on a barge. I was sitting with my back to the field. I heard a sound, thought it might be quail, and when I turned it was him coming, striding across the field toward me. I got a flash as he walked, a flash of the sight of him. It made me jump, roughing my hands on the bark of the tree.

But he called up to me, "Come down from there before you break your neck."

I scrambled down . . . and all of a sudden I felt so tense that I laughed. When I got almost to the bottom, he reached up and caught me around the waist and swung me down to the ground. He was holding me, and for the first time I had the feeling. The feeling of wanting to push, to push myself into another person. *So this is what it is*, I thought. *This is why people do the things they do.* The feeling made me sick, scared me, and I pulled away saying, "Quit!"

But he knew how to wait, and just how to work me, and unbutton me.

By harvest time in the fall I'd be there waiting for him. He'd walk up and put his hand behind my neck and slowly pull me to him.

I remember thinking, *I am a rider on an ancient horse.*

Six

LATE IN NOVEMBER MAMA and I went to a special service at the church. One different thing about it was that it was at night. There was a whole lot I didn't understand. I couldn't really say whether that was the service itself or the confusion going on in myself. On one hand I was feeling scared and guilty, and on the other I was living in a secret world that didn't seem real or connected to anything or anybody else.

There was no question about us going. Mama was bound for us to go even though it was a long trek, and for some reason she wanted us to walk. We wrapped up and set out with Mama swinging the old lantern. As we walked I saw little slivers of ice flaking and forming on the road and in the trees. And I don't know why but that only made us laugh.

When we got there we saw a right good crowd sitting on the benches and socializing. A table was set up in the front with a cloth on it, like communion, except this time sitting on the cloth were two big white washbasins and pitchers. On the front there were little towels, a whole bunch of them. Mr. Swann was there, had ridden from

Eureka, and he came in from behind the pulpit where the wood stove was. He stepped over to the pulpit and started reading from the Bible, and I realized that it must be what was called a foot-washing service. First he read about Jesus washing folk's feet. It was from John:

"He riseth from supper, and laid aside his garments; and took a towel and girded himself. After that He poureth water into a basin, and began to wash the disciples' feet, and to wipe them with the towel wherewith He was girded . . . ."

As he read, I watched the brethren moving around getting things ready. He'd read the part about Simon Peter saying that he didn't want his Lord washing *his* feet, but Jesus said if he didn't let Him wash his feet he couldn't have any part with *Him*.

"Know ye what I have done to you? Ye call me Master and Lord, and ye say well, so I am. If I then, Your Lord and Master, have washed your feet, ye also ought to wash one another's feet. For I have given you an example, that you shall do as I have done to you."

Mr. Swann's firm lips shaped the words as he read in a strong, sincere-sounding voice:

"Verily, verily I say unto you. The servant is not greater than his Lord."

I got the idea that the service was all about everybody in the church being humble and the same, nobody highfalutin, but everybody loving everybody else. But my Mama is a servant in Mr. Fleeting's house, I thought, and she can't read or write. Reverend Swann kept on reading different verses as he stood in the pulpit with the men on the left and the women on the right.

I sat lulled by the lamplight and candles, watching the shadows loom up on the ceiling when the men got up and down. The women's shadows looked like hooded ghosts on the walls. Two of the men came from the big stove carrying a tub of hot water. They dipped it up with gourd dippers, filling the pitchers.

One by one. Sometimes it was the preacher that washed a man's feet, the man sitting on the bench with his trouser legs rolled. Sometimes it was one of the sisters washing another woman's, the woman's bare toes peeping from out under her long dress for just a minute.

Mama had told me earlier to take off my stockings and shoes in the back part of the church behind the curtains. We'd both done that and sat waiting our turn. The preacher was reading:

"I sleep, but my heart awaketh: it is the voice of my beloved that knocketh, open to me my sister."

I realized then that he must be reading from a list he had prepared of verses in the Bible that mentioned feet, but I heard his voice hesitate as he got into this one, like he didn't know whether to keep on reading or not. Mrs. Person, the little puffed-up woman who always looked like her eyes were going to pop out, was kneeling in front of Mama. She had her washrag and the basin of water. Mr. Swann kept on:

"My love, my dove, my undefiled: for my head is filled with dew."

I couldn't figure out what that verse had to do with feet, but I figured he must be leading up to something. Mrs. Person grabbed Mama's ankle, her fingers pressing right into flesh. As she took the white rag and slowly slid it up and then down the graceful foot, I saw Mr. Swann try to look away, but he seemed to be hypnotized like somebody watching a snake. He stumbled on in his reading.

"I have put off my coat; how shall I put it on? I have washed my feet. How shall I defile them?"

He looked for just a stroke or two as Mrs. Person washed and then cupped and dried Mama's foot briskly. I didn't know what to think about it then, but I saw that for just one split second Mama quit looking down at her feet and turned her eyes up to meet Mr. Swann's. I felt something in the air but jerked myself from the trance of watching and hurried to the back and put my shoes on. It was all too strange, along with everything else that was going on in my life. I just couldn't let that priss of a woman touch my feet!

The service ended quickly; everyone was anxious to get home before the ice really started forming. But Mama walked like a sleepwalker all the way, hugging herself. I wondered if that's what religion did to people. As we walked along, with me carrying the lantern, we heard a stir in the bushes and jumped — it was only a cow. When we got near Fairfield, I thought I heard a horse and buggy behind us. My throat tightened. Was it John Fleeting? I knew he'd gone to get the family, but could it be his somehow? Did I imagine someone following us in the cold? Did I imagine someone outside the little cabin after we'd hurried in? I got in my nightgown and hopped into the bed, pulling the quilts over my head, wrapping them around my icy feet.

A wild thought came into my head. I was thinking it might be John Fleeting. Why, that very morning before he'd left he'd taken me to the finished house, and there on the heart pine floor of the parlor had pulled up my skirts.

"Quick," he'd said, "they'll be here with the rest of the furniture anytime now. *Quick*, let me . . . and don't you ever ever think about telling anybody about this!"

The wild thought was this: maybe it didn't have a thing to do with me. It could be someone else. Could it be Reverend Swann? Was Mama waiting until I got off to sleep to slip out to his buggy?

Seven

BUT THERE WASN'T ANY more speculating about any Reverend Swann or much else for a long time after that. Those next few months everything in my life turned sideways.

When John Fleeting came back bringing his family to the new house, there was no more of him hanging around me. Just like that. No telling me goodbye, no nothing. When I haunted the old secret place by the creek, it was like I had imagined it all. There was no evidence that he'd ever laid me down on the mossy ground. I went there time and time again, but he never came. The stopping confused me as much as the beginning. I thought I was going to die. He had caught me in his web, his sweet sticky web. Slowly he had taught me all those longings and then with a jolt he'd just left me. I didn't know what to do with all the feelings. I'd sit in my tree and remember all the soft words he'd said to me, but then I'd look out over the creek and realize that I was completely alone except for the woodpeckers across in the deadening. I felt like they were looking at me, cocking their feisty little heads saying, "What, where is he?"

He'd always called me his little woodpecker — had said from the first that I reminded him of that bird.

Day after day I'd drag myself back to the house feeling like I was walking underwater. My arms and legs were so heavy with the sluggish pain of his leaving that I could hardly make myself go through the ritual paces of days and nights. And I couldn't share any of the way I felt with anyone. I didn't have anyone to blame but my own self. I was a strumpet and a sinner.

Just when I thought it couldn't get any worse, he showed up at the big house one evening. I was bringing water in from the back yard to the kitchen for Maebelle. I looked up and saw him standing in the doorway of the front room talking to his papa. He wasn't facing me so I tried to turn and go back, but just then he looked my way. I was glad I had the two buckets of water in my hands because my knees almost buckled, and the balancing helped me not to fall.

He looked right through me as if I was a whiff of smoke.

"Gail," he called to the woman behind him, "come out to the yard and I'll show you where I played when I was a boy."

I stood at the water shelf in the back by the kitchen while he and his wife and two little girls went out into the yard.

I'll never know how I got through the pain of that night and the next few days. If I could have died, I would have. The heartache was worse than any pain I could have ever dreamed of. And the embarrassment was nearly as bad.

He never even spoke to me — the man that I thought had loved me, cherished me. The man who had called me his little darling over and over.

I was so sick with grief and shame that for several weeks I didn't even notice the other sickness.

Eight

BUT NOT NOTICING didn't make it go away.

I didn't know what was happening to me. I felt sick, felt like I was going to die, but I thought it was all because he was gone. I knew he was really gone for good, that he'd turned himself in another direction. But one night Mama and I were taking turns at our Saturday night baths, both of us using the same water in the tub on the floor, when she said, "What are you aiming to wear to church in the morning?"

Seeing my blank look she was satisfied to say, "Go look in the chifforobe."

I walked over, and there hung the prettiest dress. The cloth was thin with all sorts of little flowers, pink and blue and yellow just like in the garden in the spring.

The next morning I put it on and smiled. It was sunshiny and Mama and I were going to start out early and walk to church and stay for dinner on the ground. While Mama came over and pulled on the hem of the dress, tugging at it to make the skirt hang straight, I thought, *I'm going to think about good things today. I'm going to make myself feel better somehow*. But right while I stood there with her smoothing my skirt I started feeling funny around the mouth, and then the flowers on the dress started turning in on me and I started feeling whirly. I was hot and pulled away from Mama's hands and bolted for the door.

Later, as I lay on the bed with a cold washrag on my face, Mama said, "We'll wait a while to see if you do feel like going. When we get home, I'm going to give you a big dose of calomel."

But the being sick in the morning kept on, and one morning when I came to the house looking peaked, I saw Mae give Mama a look. "Lordy Mercy, Lordy Mercy," she said. "What in the *world* are we going do?"

Mae called me out into the back yard, and we stood out there near the chicken pen.

"Georgeanna, there's something the matter with you, I know there is. You might as well to go on and tell it."

"I've been feeling bad," I told her, and she asked me what was the matter.

"I can't tell you," I said.

She told me, "Come here, girl." She'd seen the tears coming. "You're not scared of me, now what's troubling you?"

I told her I couldn't tell anybody. I was crying by then. I couldn't help it although I knew Mama was on the porch listening and waiting.

Mae said, "If it's what I think it is, you're not going to have to tell it. It's going to be plain as day soon."

I asked her what she meant.

"I believe you've got yourself mixed up with some boy," she said. "Is that right?" I didn't know what to say. "I believe you've let some boy fiddle with you," Mae said, "and now you gonna have to pay for it. . . . You goin' to have a *baby* sure as I'm born. I know every sign as well as I know my name's Maebelle."

I broke loose from her hand and started moving away. But I knew Mama was out there standing near the house, listening. And then I heard Mama talking to herself in a terrible sounding voice.

"I just can't stand it. I just do not believe I can stand it." Then she started talking to Mae, "I should have *known* she'd play the fool. She's never had a bit of sense; I *knew* better than to have her start going off in that pony cart, but Mr. Fleeting was bound to let her do it. I knew it! There is no telling *what* she's taken up with."

I could hear her ranting as I ran. When I looked back I saw her going round and round in the yard like a chicken with its head cut off. By then I was sobbing so hard I was nearly blind. I ran down the path to my place by the creek. I lay there curled up under the tree all night. Scared and cold and miserable. But as scared as I was, a light kept flickering inside me. A baby! Me and Mr. John Fleeting made a *baby* out of ourselves.

Mama and Maebelle came down there late the next morning and made me go home. I was ashamed to look at them, but Lordy was I glad to see them.

We talked about it for a week. At least they did. Mama got it in her head it was one of the red-headed Gardner boys, the ones that lived in the tenant house down the road. "So that's what you've been up to, gallivanting off to town."

I didn't want to be in the same house with her she made me feel so ashamed, but there wasn't anywhere else I could go.

"No use me even going over there to talk to those *common* folks. *Sorry*. That woman just lays up in the bed all day, I hear. Hear they keep a packa dogs in the house!"

"But Mama!" I kept trying to tell her I never had a thing to do with any of that family. I tried to tell her the truth, although I sure didn't know how, but she didn't want to listen. She would not *let* me tell her. When I said John Fleeting's name once, she looked right through me. Like I wasn't there. Like I was invisible, and like my voice was air.

"Don't you dare, don't you ever let me hear you say such a thing . . . drag the name of that fine family into this common mess."

She took me by the arm, her hand was trembling with rage, and bent close to me, whispering hoarsely. "You listen to me now, girl. Don't you *ever* mention that name in this house again! We're going to figure out *something* to do . . . me and Mae . . . and you're going to do exactly what we tell you to do."

That is how it was decided. Mama was going to pretend to have a baby. I was to stay out of sight while she stuffed her dress with a pillow and appeared in public. They decided that the best place would be the church where people would be sure to see her. It would cause a scandal, but the scandal would be about her, a widow, not me, a girl. It would save my reputation. "Maybe she can still find a husband later on," Mama said to Mae.

Once she got that idea in her head, nothing I said would change her mind. She made it very clear that the Fleetings must not be bothered. I was too scared to do anything but agree.

"Well, we just won't let anybody know it," she said. "You'll just have to stay out of sight. As long as Mr. Worth Fleeting isn't told, the old fellow'll never even know the difference." She laughed a bitter laugh. "I've seen men that didn't even notice their own *wives* were expecting until right up till the youngun was born. A *baby* they'd say. You mean we're going to have a *baby*?"

Much later she said, "Well, you can just forget all that *school* foolishness! But while you're doing all that reading, you might read in the Bible and see what Ezekiel has to say about things like this. I may not be much of a reader myself, but I've *heard* it read."

That night I huddled down under my sheets trying to bring the lamp close enough to see, but not let on to her what I was reading.

The Bible said, "There were two women . . . and they committed whoredoms in their youth, there were their breasts pressed, and there they bruised the teats of their virginity."

Tears came into my eyes. Was this like me, like women like me?

I read on: ". . . and she doted on her lovers . . . which were clothed with blue, captains and rulers, all of them desirable young men, horsemen riding upon horses."

And I thought of John Fleeting. I thought of one of the early days when I'd seen him there at his daddy's porch. I'd heard a horse galloping up the driveway. And as I stood dusting in the parlor, I saw him, a man like I'd never seen before. His legs were slim and the muscles tight as he swung off. I'd heard Mama draw in her breath and say to Mae, "That's the best looking man I've ever laid eyes on!"

"He's always been that way. Ever since he was

born," Mae said proudly. "A prince!" As he'd strode up the steps and onto the porch, the light hit the steel gray of his coat, and for a minute, I remember, it had looked as blue as a robin's egg.

Nine

ON EASTER SUNDAY Mama took aholt of my elbow and we set out down the road to church. My throat was dry and achy. We didn't talk any all the way there. Mama's jaw was set. The only thing she said as we walked was, "I wonder what kind of thing Mr. Fleeting is harboring up for us to do next."

Now, you may think by her saying that that he had something to do with what she was fixin' to do, but it wasn't like that at all. She just said that because she was still mad as a hornet about all that had happened. We had no more than walked up into the churchyard before the women started staring and getting off in little bunches and whispering behind their hands.

Mrs. Person came up to us and looked right straight at Mama and said, "Well, Chaney, there must be something we don't know." Then she gave a little coy laugh. "Something you've been keeping a big secret?" Mama just nodded to her and held her head up real high and kept her back stiff as she walked into the church and took her regular seat in the middle.

The people already in the church rustled around and sucked in their breath and then it got so quiet you could hear a pin drop. The only sound at all was a hee-haw from one of the mules waiting outside. The preacher didn't notice a thing though and stood in the pulpit and went on and preached his sweet sermon.

Later, out in front of the church when he came to shake hands, he turned to Mama and the look on his face was like he'd been struck by lightning. His jaw dropped and he started stammering and blushing. Mama stood facing him, looking as bold as brass, her puffed-out belly there in front of her for the world to see. She just looked straight at him, her face set in such a way that the skin was pulled tight in the hollows under her cheekbones. Reverend Swann looked like he was about to spew. He turned abruptly and went back into the church, leaving the crowd in a circle around us. Mrs. Person spoke up again.

"Tell us your news, Chaney. Speak up so that we can rejoice with you."

Mama looked her right in the eye and said, "We've not got any news to tell."

Well, you can just imagine the dither they were all in. The men started leading their wives to the buggies, getting on away. You could see that they were about to bust to start talking. There was no sign of the preacher; I guess he left the back way.

We went home and waited. We knew they would be coming pretty soon. Only the year before, a brother had been excluded from the church for the sin of intoxication and attending a circus. Adultery and fornication wouldn't take long; it was right there in the Ten Commandments. It wasn't like the time Brother Aycock had been brought to trial for drinking French brandy. He had pleaded illness as an excuse and had confessed and begged forgiveness. There would be no forgiveness for this sin.

It took them three days to come out. It was a drizzly day, and I saw the covered buggy coming down the road. Mrs. Person sat up front beside the preacher, her little round bottom perched on the seat, her face saintly looking. Mr. Swann looked like a mule had kicked him. In the back the three other members of the committee of honorable brethren appointed to investigate sat ready.

I don't know why at a time like that, when I'd been told to stay in the dark kitchen and hide behind the flour barrel and let Mama face them alone, I would think of such a thing, but a story Mama had told me when I was little came to my mind.

It was when she'd told me that my daddy was from Fool's Bridge and I had asked her how it got such a funny name. She'd said, "When the bridge was built across a stream there, with one end in a cemetery, the superstitious folks that lived nearby despised going through the cemetery at night to reach the bridge, and said only a fool would locate a bridge in such a hanty place."

I could hear some of the things they said, and some of the words would drift off. There were two women and two men besides the preacher. I guess they thought that was fair. I'd wondered before about how fair the people at the church were. Some of the things they did seemed mighty stern to me. But in this case I could see that they were trying to give Mama a chance there on the porch, a chance to say that she was married to Mr. Fleeting or somebody. But she just kept her lips tight together and snapped back at every question.

"No, 'tain't so."

I've never seen anybody more miserable than the Reverend Swann. He didn't ask any of the questions. Mostly it was Mrs. Person. "Well, what do you aim to do?"

"Take care of myself," Mama snapped.

It was dim out in the gray circle of the yard. Our dog got up and moved around and lay back down under the house. Even though it was spring, it was like winter had come back. The trees around the house looked bare and lifeless like in a deadening. There wasn't a sign of color or life anywhere, in our raked dirt yard, the unpainted house, the mud holes.

After about an hour of questions with nothing but bitter tight answers, with all of them standing on the porch in a little bunch, Mrs. Person said in a loud voice, "Well, at least you must come before the church and admit your sin and beg forgiveness." Then she whispered, "Is your husband come back? You can tell me."

"No, I'm not coming, and no, ma'am, I'm not begging anything. This is no one's doings but my own."

Mrs. Person sucked in her breath. "The Lord our Savior has something to say about it!" She sounded put out but gave it one more try and whispered, "But, Chaney, you have to confess if there is to be any hope of forgiveness, and name the man that sinned with you."

"No, ma'am," Mama said again and rared back so that her belly stretched the cloth of her dress. "I'm not doing any confessing."

"Then," Brother Sorrow, who had been quiet until now, boomed out, "the preacher will have to denounce you from the pulpit at the next meeting."

And he did. We weren't there, of course, but word got back to us quickly and with every detail . . . Reverend Swann stood there and said what was expected of him, "Caught in fornication and excluded from the church, the member Chaney Weeks . . ." and then went on with a sermon about hellfire and damnation to all sinners while all the members sat wild with excitement, but holding themselves as still as corpses.

Ten

WELL, OUR LIVES DIDN'T stop. The world didn't come to an end. It hardly ever does at the times you wish it would.

There's no way I could have known back then how much church going had meant to Mama. I really was just a youngun. It would be many, many years before I had any idea what kind of sacrifice Mama had made at that church.

But there was one thing for sure — that baby kept right on growing inside of me.

It was born in August. There would never be any use trying to tell somebody what giving birth to a baby is like. There aren't any words that could ever describe the pain of being split wide open — like having one foot tied to one taut tree limb and the other to another and then having someone cut the rope in between.

Mama and Maebelle were doing everything they could there in our little cabin that night, but I was hurting so bad and I knew I was like an animal.

"No! No!" I'd scream in terror.

Mae would bathe my face with a soft rag and beg. "Please, Georgie, try to calm yourself," she'd croon.

But not only was it the first time, but all that shame and sin was corked up in me holding the baby inside me like a stopper.

That was the longest night of my life. Three of us, two women and a girl, in the black night.

When I woke up the next morning, there was a little baby boy lying in a basket making noises like a kitten.

I named him Wilkes. I don't know why. I just liked the sound of it, I guess. Mae looked at me kind of funny when I said the name, but then she said, "It's a handsome name cause he's a pretty, dark-eyed boy. Look at him looking over at you with those bright eyes."

And he was, too, looking right at me. I had found me a friend, that was for sure.

Mae said while she watched us eye one another, "Menfolk may have the best of it most of the time, but there's never been one or never will be that'll have *that* feeling." I sighed. The baby sighed.

Everything got real quiet in that little cabin for a while after that, and then every once in a while there'd be that new sound.

Two years later we were all down at the shed for the hog killing. It was the first bright day and everybody in Tar County had been waiting for one like it, hoping to get the meat in the smoke-house by Thanksgiving.

I liked to be down there helping and watching the men. I was scared of the month of March and scared of storms, but I wasn't afraid of hog killings. I knew hogs had to be killed, and I knew better than to ever make a pet of one of them. If you even got to playing with one when they're sweet and little you never could have stood it, but hog killing was something you just knew you had to learn to accept.

We'd been out there since daylight, cold as it was, and a thin coat of ice was still on the mud-holes. Tubs of water that were drawn from the well and poured into a vat the night before had been heated real hot to scald the hogs. Right soon after sunrise the men went to the pen where the hogs had been fattened and used their axes, rifles and butcher knives. Then they dragged the hogs up to the vat and scalded two or three at a time to loosen the hair. Later, after they worked on them some more, they hung the hogs on the gallows.

Mama and Mae had to do their part by ridding the chitlins and washing them over and over and keeping the small intestines separate to make our sausage with. They'd taught me what to do to help them. It sure was a job before we got all the sausage and lard and everything done. We never would have got all the meat salted down if we hadn't had Slender's kin folks to help us.

"I want brains and eggs for supper," Mr. Fleeting said. My favorite part would come later when the little Tom Thumb sausage was dried good.

Mama'd said, when we got up that morning, "It's probably going to be the last one for Mr. Fleeting. He's gotten mighty feeble." But later that morning he'd wanted to be out there with us. So Mama had put him in his rolling chair, his gray head just a-bobbin', and brought him down to where everybody was.

Sitting there watching the ritual, he got to musing. "I used to think I'd like to be a steamboat captain," he said. "I like the names of the boats — even the ferry The Morning Star and the one on the river, The Yellow Hammer." When he said river he meant the Great Contentnea Creek; everybody used to call it the river.

He was in a talking mood as he watched the men working with the butcher knives. "Stay back, Wilkie boy," he said to the baby who was toddling around with a straw, sticking it in a doodle bug hole. He said, "This is a different kind of place than it used to be. I'm not talking about just lately — in this war either. I mean since this Carolina land was settled. Why, back in the old days up there in the Albermarle where my wife was raised, the forests were thick with longleaf pines. Right from the first the English wanted those naval stores for their fleet of wooden ships. They couldn't get enough of tar and pitch and turpentine. Millions of those trees were cut and burned for the tar that oozed out, and to get the resin for turpentine you chopped a deep hole into the base of the living tree. You don't see those great forests like you used to, I can tell you that."

He saw that I was listening to him. I always listened to him, never did get tired of hearing anything he had to talk about. He'd always taught me so much. Wilkes looked over at us. I reached over and hugged him to me. "You little doodle bug," I said into his ear. He laughed. My precious baby. Mr. Fleeting put his hand on his head. If any words had passed between Mama and Mr. Fleeting, I never knew about them. We had a baby there with us and he was ours.

At that minute I wanted to tell Mr. Fleeting all about everything, I wanted to say, "This little fellow is kin to you," but of course I had to push those words right out of my mind. So instead I asked, "How about hogs? Have there always been hogs in North Carolina?"

He laughed. "Young woman, I never know what's going to come out of your mouth . . . well, you've sure hit on it. You've always been able to hit right on it. Two of the first things anybody would ever hear about the old North State is that for one it used to be called the Rip Van Winkle

State because it was so slow to get going, and the other was that everybody always had hogs and everybody fussed over who could make the best barbecue. Well, Tar County barbecue is the best anywhere, I can tell you that."

"What makes it the best?" I asked him.

"Well, there are several things. First, the best pigs, then that slow cooking over the hickory wood. Then the chopping real fine, skin and all, and not messing it up with a lot of sweet sauce, but just putting that vinegar and red pepper. Why in the world would you want anything else when you can have it pure and simple? I tell you, I have had me some good barbecue in my day."

Slender came over and handed us a plate of cracklings that Maebelle had just fried up in the kitchen. As we all nibbled on the crusty saltiness he said, "*Everybody* thinks their barbecue is the best. But ours *is* the best."

We all laughed and I'll always remember that happy time.

Then Mr. Fleeting seemed to start feeling bad again. He sighed, "But everything has changed so. Why, after I'm gone I'll vow they'll let this place rot down."

I saw the look in Mama's eyes. She knew he spoke the truth. Slender and Maebelle had already worked something out. But where would we be? A fallen woman, a whistling girl, and a baby?

Eleven

I NEVER SAW JOHN Fleeting again until Mr. Fleeting's funeral. Wilkes was nearly three by then, what they called a "knee baby." John didn't know he existed. The day of the funeral everything was ready. The parlor was spotless and aired out. The table in the dining room was loaded down with food. Different women had come out from town with platters, and Mama and Mae had cooked a plenty.

When I saw the buggy coming I was standing in the side room with Wilkes at my knee. I saw him step down, take her arm and help her. Then I saw the girls. They looked like him, especially the little one that had been left deaf from the measles. Her hair looked soft like his. As I watched, my baby pulled at my skirt. Knowing something strange and scary was going on, he wanted me to hold him. When he asked for "Ninny," I pulled him to me and let him nurse. Mama woulda had a fit if she'd seen me, but she was busy in another room. She didn't like for me to do that. Sometimes, even way back then, she acted like Wilkes was really her baby instead of mine. But I let him suck at my breast while I watched them.

John had been there the night before, after Mama had found Mr. Fleeting dead. Dear old man, he'd been taking a nap and had just rocked back in his chair and gone to sleep forever. But I had taken Wilkes to the cabin and stayed out of sight while all the arrangements were being made.

There was a porch full of people that cold January day. I could see their frosty breath as they greeted each other. Many were from Raleigh, families of his old friends. I'd never seen so many fine clothes in my life. I could hear the tinkle of voices as people talked after they passed the coffin in the parlor and went to the dining room. There the smells of coffee and ham drifted back to the kitchen where I stayed with Wilkes. I watched from the window while the preacher from town and the pallbearers led the procession out to the graveyard on the other side of the house under the old cedar tree.

At the last, Mama and myself, with the baby between us, and Mae and Slender went out and stood in the back while the coffin was being lowered into the ground. We all stood in a little lonesome knot.

I only raised my eyes once and looked over at John. He was standing across the grave from us. Just for that one quick second his eyes held mine. He didn't look at the baby, and if he had I guess he would have thought he belonged to Mama.

I like to have cried myself to death that night. Mr. Fleeting gone, down in the ground, and then seeing John there, a stranger to me. I lay there never wanting to get up. Then a little face appeared right in front of mine and a little hand touched my wet face. It upset my little boy so much to see me cry. I knew I had to make myself stop. I knew I had to get up.

Twelve

I DIDN'T SIT AROUND AND think about this kind of thing much back then. Mama kept me busy but most of all I was busy being seventeen years old. But from the things I'd heard Mr. Fleeting say and just from the things I noticed all around me, I could see how much everything was changing.

Mr. Fleeting had said over and over, "North Carolina's got a lot to get over. So many killed, lost in their prime during that hateful war. Forty thousand men, Georgie . . . you can't even imagine . . . more than any other southern state! — and right there at the end there was the big battle, the biggest one ever fought in North Carolina went on no ways from here, right down there at Bentonville.

"It was a time, I tell you. It was a time. Slender and Maebelle stayed on here with us all during the war and stayed on after. My wife Martha helped in Snow Hill at the hospital that was set up there. I did what I could to help run it.

"John was already away at the Military Academy when the war started. He and his first cousin, Martha's brother's boy, went into the cavalry together. They took Slender's boy with them for the first two years to look after their horses . . . . Then rations got so scarce he was sent back home. I know some of the infantry boys called the Calvary the Buttermilk Brigade . . . and at first, some of them may have acted the dandy . . . but before it was all over with . . . well, there wasn't too much to joke about."

I'd try to imagine, look out across the fields and try to see it in my mind. The flash of the sight of that Confederate uniform, the steel color of berries from a cedar tree got in the corner of my eye and I couldn't make it go away. Part of me wished I'd been there, breathing the horses' dust, hearing those wild battle cries. I wondered what all the blue jays, the catbirds, the owls had thought when all that was going on.

But the war was over and Tar County had come through the worst and was starting to thrive again. It had been reconstructed.

I learned from listening that the places that were big farms and plantations before the war were now small farms. The landowners would do their best to come up with enough tools and mules and seed. Since they didn't have money to pay anybody to work the farms, they got whoever they could to work on shares. Sharecroppers didn't have much choice. They did whatever they could for a shack to live in and something to eat.

Some in Tar County had managed to hold onto a little money and they started making more by building tobacco factories. Before the war, tobacco had been raised, but the factories had just been log sheds on the farms. I heard that John Fleeting had taken what was left of his and his family's money and was doing real well in the business of tobacco manufacturing over near Raleigh.

Now that Mr. Fleeting was dead, Fairfield was to be closed up.

Thirteen

SOMETIMES WHILE YOU'RE searching for an answer, something comes along and you realize that *is* the answer. One night after Mr. Fleeting had been dead about two months, I was lying on the bed dozing while Wilkes was asleep. You never knew when he'd wake up. "You're scared you're going to miss something, aren't you! Well, everybody needs some sleep," I'd say to him, but he was just too busy to be interested in sleeping. Mama was sitting up sewing in the lamplight in the other room. I knew she was studying on what in the world we were going to do now that there wasn't any job left at Fairfield.

I woke up and looked at the door between the rooms and I thought I saw John Fleeting standing there. He was just standing there as tall and good-looking as ever, and before I could think I jumped up and ran over to him. When I put my arms out to him they went right through air. I'd just dreamed him up, but it had seemed so real. I was so shaken that I sat down on the end of the bed and put my face in my hands. Oh, it still hurt, I tell you, it still hurt. Right at that minute I heard a

noise outside and then a knock on the door.
Mama was startled but she managed to open the
door. I stood behind her looking at two strange
men standing in the doorway. Their lantern hung
flickering between them and they were just two
dark shadows at first. As the lamplight slowly
came up, I could see their faces, and I heard
Mama say "Laffton." Didn't that beat all. There
standing in the door was my brother — after all
these years without a word. He was older like I
was, his clear, open face filled out and handsome
— a good-sized man with flashing black eyes. It
was the first time I'd seen him since I was a little
girl. The fellow with him stood there, plain and
dressed in work clothes. I don't know what made
me speak out like I did, nerves I guess, but I said,
"You look like somebody; who is it?"

"I look like me," the stranger said. Thinking
about that makes me smile to this day.

After an awkward while, Mama decided to
cook some flour bread on the griddle and fry some
molasses. Laffton started talking. "This is so good
I wish I'd come home sooner. Anyhow, I'm home
to stay. Willy Stanton here is my partner. We're
aiming to set up a sawmill at Little Contentnea."

There's no telling what all he'd been up to all
those years, I thought, but then he didn't know
what all we'd been up to either. Wilkes pulled on
my sleeve, and I picked him up and twirled one of

his curls around my finger. Laffton stared at him. "Whose little boy?"

Mama snapped out, "He's mine! Did you think he was one we found in a hollow tree stump?"

"Well, he sorta favors me," he said, and seeing Mama wasn't going to give him any more conversation, he turned to me and said, "You sure growed up fast."

I shook my head, and Mama gave him a look that said, "Don't take that too far."

He had other things on his mind anyway. I've noticed over the years that plenty of times men are so caught up in some idea or the other of their own that they don't even notice things right under their noses — especially if it's something to do with women.

Laffton had made his way east after he'd left Snow Hill. "I got on a barge with some fellas there on the creek and wound up on the river and then down there on that Pamlico Sound. It's just like the ocean there on the sound and of course a little ways out there *is* the Atlantic Ocean."

"What kind of work did you do?" Mama asked warily.

"First one thing and then another there for awhile. There was always plenty of work, what with all the ships coming in and out, and all the fishing, every kind of fish you can imagine. You ought to see it down there. It's a wild swampy

place. You never saw such birds. Those bald
eagles and whistling swans seem to love those
peat bogs. It's full of red wolves, too."

Willy said, "Those wolves won't bother you.
They don't care a thing for people — and will do
near bout anything to stay outa your way. There's
plenty for them to eat: rabbits, raccoons, turtles."

I looked over at him as he spoke, watching the
way his firm lips moved. The way he talked had a
different sound to it than what I was used to. The
muscles in his neck moved as he talked and for
some reason they fascinated me.

Laffton said, "Willy knows all those woods and
bogs like the back of his hand. He comes from a
little place at the edge of the sound called Swan
Quarter. He's been a pilot of a ferry boat between
there and Ocracoke Island since he's been grown.
Ocracoke is one of the outer banks . . . ships and
boats have been going through the inlet there to
the West Indies and England and all since the state
started," Laffton said earnestly. He obviously
admired Willy. That kind of talk stirred me up. It
sounded like a different world.

We sat up half the night, with Laffton and
Willy talking about the plans. Willy said, "We
been planning it and saving up for it for right
smart two years!" Willy had an easy slow way of
talking, and he said things the funniest way. I
found out later that the way he talked was called

banker talk. The outer banks were on the very edge of North Carolina, out in the ocean by themselves, and people there had their own way of doing most everything.

The next morning we had a long breakfast after the men got up from their pallets and got hot water out of the reservoir and bathed by the wood stove in the kitchen where it was warm. Everybody sat around the table and ate hot biscuits, fried eggs, slab bacon and more fried molasses. Laffton kept swinging his foot and tapping on the table. Willy looked nice with his face shiny and his brown hair clean and slicked down. His face was wide and he had high cheekbones and a firm, smooth mouth. He was just an average height for a man, I guess, but his arms and neck and chest were strong looking, making him seem bigger than he was. His gray brown eyes looked at me and he laughed. I was intrigued.

"What are you laughing at?" I asked.

"You. You remind me of a bird."

"Well, I'm not even going to ask you what kind." I remember thinking, what am I doing laughing and joking with this fella who's just walked in here? Ever since the baby had been born I'd never get within ten miles of a man. Never even when I had to go to town would I let a man as much as look sideways at me. I never forgot for a minute that whether anybody else knew it or not — I knew it and Mama knew it. I was damaged, damaged forever. I never aimed to let a man near me again. And here I stood in our kitchen letting a young man tease me and look into my eyes, and I was laughing about it!

Willy didn't seem to be impressed with my looks a bit, like some had been in those days.

It wasn't long before I knew, though. He was looking at me, all right.

And Mama was looking at him. I could tell that she was thinking and figuring.

One night when we were all together after supper, I didn't quite know why then but I felt so lively all of a sudden that without thinking about it, I started to whistle. Mama came over and clapped her hand over my mouth. Seeing her do it, Laffton spoke up and said, "You musta heard that old saying 'A whistling woman and a crowing hen is no good either to gods or men.'"

I took Mama's hand off and said, "Well, I don't see what whistling has to do with anything."

"I used to hear tell from the seamen that you must never whistle on shipboard. It'll bring on the devil's power, or what they call 'the old woman,' and a big wind will come. I was stopped from whistling when I was a cabin boy."

Willy said, "I've always heard that, too. Another thing you don't do on a ship is mention the word *pig*. It's unlucky to see one on land just before you sail, and most ships won't carry pork on board. I think it's all foolishness myself, but many don't. That's why so many taverns are named The Pig and Whistle. Once a sailor returns safe, he's ready for some taboo."

Willy and Laffton made their arrangements in Snow Hill and then built themselves a lean-to at the creek where they were starting the sawmill. It wasn't long before they were making money. They had figured it right and had come to Tar County at just the right time.

Fourteen

WELL, IT ALWAYS SEEMED to me like life goes in cycles . . . one thing ends, another begins, and you just have to go along with it.

We got married right out there at Fairfield Plantation. The preacher was somebody Willy and Laffton knew of. We had a little ceremony. Man and wife, the preacher said, just like that.

Wilkes had a big time because we had cake and all. Maebelle had made a special nut cake from one of Mrs. Fleeting's old recipes. She'd been cracking black walnuts for a week. "I wouldn't do this for anybody but you, Georgie," she'd said. It was while we were cracking the nuts and picking out the meat that we really said our good-byes. Maebelle and Slender were leaving Fairfield too. Their oldest daughter, who worked up in Maryland, had convinced them that they should come to live with her. Fairfield was to be left just as empty as Mr. Fleeting said it would be. It was hard for me to leave Mae. She'd nearly raised me and I didn't know what I was going to do without her to talk to. But she knew the time had come.

"You be a brave girl now, Georgie. Your Mama

and Wilkes are counting on you. Let's don't have
any foolishness when you leave. There are things
between us that are best left buried right out
here."

When I walked out to the edge of the field to
throw the walnut shells away, I turned back to see
that she and Mama were holding onto each other,
both with their eyes closed, fighting back tears.

Willy and Laffton had built us a new house in a
place about twenty miles from Fairfield called Tar
Depot.

"I've always heard tell that three movings are
equal to one burning," Mama said the day before
the wedding when we were trying to decide what
to take from our cabin at Fairfield and what to
throw away.

"This is my third moving and I don't think I'm
going to take a stick of this ole furniture with me
. . . there's nothing worth even hauling to the new
house." We had a real burning. Our old things
and a lot of Maebelle and Slender's too made a
real good bonfire. We'd all scurried around
throwing things in and raking around the edges
to contain the fire. Wilkes was fascinated by the
sparks when they'd shoot into the air and then
fall gray to the ground.

I'd caught Mama just before she got too carried away with the fire.

"Mama, you know you want your feather bed! Don't burn that!" I'd said.

"Well, it's getting mighty old and needs airing out good, but yes, my Mama did make that herself, way back yonda. Pile it on in here, Laffton. Might as well."

"Nobody but pure trash goes off and leaves a house without cleaning it up good when they move," Mama muttered as she threw the last scrap on the pile.

After the burning, Laffton put our trunks in a wagon. With so much going on, Wilkes was happy. He'd draw a line in the dirt with a stick and then hop over it.

I could tell that Mama was still stunned by what was going on. It did seem nearly too good to be true for me as well. Just like that we had somebody to take care of us.

"And the last one in the *world* I would of expected it from would of been Laffton," she whispered to me. "He sure did a good day's work when he met up with that Stanton fella. You can thank your lucky stars."

Mama and Laffton and Wilkes stayed in the

back of the new house. Willy and I had a big room with a high ceiling in the front. He'd bought us some furniture.

I felt as odd that night as I reckon anybody in their life ever felt. There we were away from the country and the plantation. There I was getting into the bed with that strange fellow.

It took more than a night. It took a long long time for me to get over my stiffness with Willy. Long after I trusted him in my mind, my body just wouldn't relax. But he seemed to understand so much without me even telling him. He'd hold me and stroke me and make me laugh and slowly, slowly I started to feel more and more like a young girl and less like a hunted fox.

Mama had warned me about telling him about Wilkes. She was afraid he'd be scared off. "Men don't like to hear too much truth, Georgie. You don't want to mess up a chance like this." But I'd told him anyway. "Anybody with one eye and half sense could see that. Now be my girl and see if you can give me a back rub," Willy said softly as I cried into my pillow.

Fifteen

TAR DEPOT WAS ON THE edge of Tarborough, a little settlement that had been built on upper Contentnea Creek. The town of Tarborough had grown in the other direction, leaving Tar Depot to be like a little village of its own. I heard tell that in some ways Tar Depot wasn't too different from the way it was when it was a stagecoach stop before the Revolutionary War. That's part of what Willy said he liked about it. It was like living in the country in some ways, but having people around, businesses and neighbors. He liked people.

He and Laffton built another house beside ours. The smaller one was for Mama and Wilkes and Laffton. The town easily accepted Wilkes as Mama's child. She accepted it so totally herself that sometimes the way she acted gave me goose bumps.

It was a whole different kind of life. Willy made me laugh all the time. He was so natural and warm.

Mama seemed relieved to have a place. Wilkes was growing so fast that it was hard to believe. Soon it was as if Fairfield and the old days hadn't ever even happened. We missed Maebelle and Slender, of course, but we stayed busy all the time.

Laffton and Willy were still big friends, but more and more Laffton stayed out at the mill and Willy stayed in town. After awhile Laffton moved back out to the sawmill; he liked to be by himself. Willy liked town, and one night I overheard him talking to Laffton after the rest of us had gone to bed.

"If you think that'll work out, I believe I'll go on and do it," Willy said.

"It suits me, it suits me fine. I've been wantin' to just build me a cabin out there," Laffton had said.

I gathered that Willy was selling his share of the sawmill business to Laffton.

"Yessir, I think it's the thing to do. I've been studying over it, and I believe this would be a good time to start one of those big general stores right here in town down by the railroad track."

I thought it sounded like a good idea, but of course my life would be pretty much the same, except now he'd be coming home at dinner time. My days were laid out: wash on Monday, iron on Tuesday, sew, cook, preserve, rake, tend garden, clean house the rest of the week. I was grateful for it, for him. He took good care of us.

But life just isn't that simple. I loved Willy and loved to hear his stories about the coast, the ships, the hurricanes and the wild birds. When our little girl was born, I loved to hold and rock her. I was a respectable wife with a good home. You would have thought that I could have been happy, but something inside wouldn't let me. I'd still have the dream about frogs; every once in a while I'd wake up in a cold sweat, shaking. My head full of the slime of the dream.

And on the mornings after that I'd surprise myself when I'd look into the mirror. The girl who would get out of bed would be so dark and old inside, but when I'd look into Willy's shaving mirror I'd see another girl there — a fine-looking black-eyed one with strong cheekbones and a healthy, happy-looking face.

I'd look and I'd think — Who is that young woman? She looks fine, but she doesn't match the one inside, the strange one, the one that isn't like these other women in Tar Depot. The one in the mirror is the one everyone saw.

"Your wife is so sweet, Willy."

"Your wife is mighty pretty, Willy."

If they only knew, I'd think. You should see the real one, the one that knows. The one inside.

I'd try to keep that secret girl, that watching, sly girl, quiet. But she was hard to keep hidden sometimes. My memory was like some old hag that poked around with a stick and gathered up red rags and belt buckles from old days — you never knew what she'd come up with. Usually it was something about Wilkes . . . or about Mama. But one day she went way up under the house of childhood and dragged up, like an old bone, a day with my brother Laffton. A twilight time when we played hide as little children.

"You wanna try this?"

"What?"

"See." He held out a smoking cigar.

"Laff . . . you know . . . ."

"Oh, she's nowhere around."

I puckered my mouth in just such a way as to puff on the end of it, touching the stickiness, taking one big draw.

"Not too much! It'll make you spew."

"Augg!" I said, disgusted. "It turns my mouth inside out like 'simmons!"

"Then let's try something else. Let's try kissing. That's what folks do."

"No, I don't want to." I pushed him hard.

So strange the things memory draws up, like the way a dream unearths a thing you don't even know is inside you. And that same hant sneaked things into the days of routine and the girl inside would follow. Memories of John Fleeting and what he'd done to me, the way he'd put his mouth on me. I wondered, "Are all people like this? Do the people I see on the street of Tar Depot all have secret lives?"

After those dreams it seemed like I was split in two, like there were two of me, the one who was married to Willy and was the daughter of Chaney, and the other one, the one who stood back and watched it all. She watched the Tar Depot wife who carried the water buckets in from the pump in the yard, raised the chickens, killed the hen and boiled her in the pot. Who took the eggs and put them with the milk and made egg custard. Who lay by Willy at night, skin touching skin, and who got up first and made a crackling fire. Got the coffee boiling and put his big breakfast, meat and eggs and hominy grits and biscuits, there to hold him down till dinner. Letting him eat first, grateful for him and the house. And nearly every year she watched a sweating woman, knees up under the sheets, biting a mouthful of rags until a baby was born.

The one that watched was taller, straighter. She spoke correctly, like a teacher, and her clothes hung smoothly. She had books to read and time to read them, and she often had rides with a man in a fine buggy. He helped her down and called her darling and looked at her with loving eyes that held respect. He talked to her about all kinds of things, world affairs. She answered him easily, and the clarity in her voice was admirable.

But those were the bad spells. There were plenty of good times.

Sixteen

IT WAS ALWAYS LIVELY at the store. Willy had a joke or a little something to say to everybody that traded there.

Once in a while someone would come in who'd say, "That your boy, Willy?" pointing toward Wilkes, who loved to hang around.

"No, but he's a good one. My wife's little brother."

The store was a house of treasures, not just to a little boy but to the farmers and their families all over Tar County. People didn't just jump on a train and go off to Raleigh or Richmond then. Eastern North Carolina was made up of little towns and crossroads with just the right distance between them for a horse ride and back in a day. People from the farms didn't just come to Willy's store to get flour and salt and sugar; they came to see new things and to visit. And Willy knew how to give them a show. He had goods from all over the world — Belgium lace, Italian macaroni, wedding rings, bone buttons. A farmer might come in for a washtub, but nine times out of ten he'd leave with a little something else. And after Willy, and

later Wilkes, got through showing them around,
they'd had an eyeful. It was no wonder anytime
they had a few coins to rub together they'd find
some excuse to visit Willy's store.

We had a good time ordering things for the
store. After the days on the plantation, living in
Tar Depot and having the store right down the
street seemed almost like some kind of game.

Every once in a while about that time a little
warning bell would go off in my head. I know
now that I should have listened to it, but I was
younger then and didn't pay as much attention to
my instincts as I do now. That bell went off about
the way Mama started acting about Wilkes . . .
jealous like.

It was when Wilkes got big enough to really
help Willy at the store that I started noticing how
strange Mama was becoming. Willy and I had
four little girls by then. I guess it had gradually
been happening ever since we'd left the plantation, but I'd been so caught up in everything I
hadn't realized it. She looked different for one
thing. She'd been pretty when I was a girl . . . but
in town, when it had finally gotten easier for her,
she had, somewhere along the line, gotten swollen
looking. Her skin, which used to be so smooth

and pink, was flushed. But it wasn't so much the way she looked as the way she hovered, like she was about to sting. And she did. Me. Wilkes.

More and more about that time I'd notice that she'd call Wilkes "*my* boy." It seemed like she'd go out of her way to put her hand on his arm and say, "*My* boy is the smartest one in school." She'd look right into my eyes when she'd say that. When she wasn't taunting me she was picking on him. I really couldn't stand it when she picked on Wilkes. He was so trusting and even-tempered, it took a lot to rile him, but she kept on him all the time. Whatever he did wasn't enough. He was just a youngun, but she was after him all the time. She even picked at him for spending so much time at his school books. I started to see why Laffton had run off as soon as he got old enough to light out.

Every day she'd meet Wilkes at the door with something. "While you were hanging around the store, gallivanting off, your goose died. I've already buried it."

"But Mama . . . ." he'd start.

"Never mind. Mrs. Powell's been waiting all evening for this dress. I've been finished with it. Do you think you can manage to get it to her? And collect? Sewing is the way I make our living, you know; I've got to make some laying-down money."

I didn't understand her. Wilkes was the best boy

in the world, and Willy and Laffton both gave her money, which she put in her trunk. To hear her talk she was starving to death. Of course, I knew that there's nothing in the world like having a little something of your own.

But the way she treated me was the strangest. There we were, tied together. I did everything I knew to suit her. We lived side by side. Everything I had, she had. I did everything in this world I knew to make her comfortable. I hated it that she was so sour, so bitter. I realized that she didn't have a man of her own, and of course I'd never forget what had happened at church and what it must have done to her, but still I hated to see that taint the rest of her whole life. I didn't want her to be jealous of me, I wanted us to get along. I'd think of every way I could to include her so she wouldn't feel left out. But it got harder and harder.

One day while we were sitting out in the backyard peeling pears, the dry leaves gold and red around us, I said, "Mama, I wish you'd tell me about your folks, about when you were a girl and all."

She sniffed. "You've near bout let these pears get too soft."

"I got to them as soon as I could. You know Sally and Hally both had high fevers last week." There I was, apologizing, making excuses, like I always did with her.

"The preserves aren't a bit'a good if the pears aren't solid," she went on, like I hadn't spoken.

"Tell me, Mama, about Fool's Bridge and all. Are there any kin left?"

It was like pulling eyeteeth to get her to answer. "No."

"Where was that?"

"What they call the great Dismal Swamp."

"What were your folks like?"

"Like anybody else. Folks said I favored my mama. I might of took after her. She died young. Papa was a big black-headed man. Reckon Laffton and you and Wilkes might of took after him."

"Tell me about your mama," I said again, hoping to keep her talking.

"There's not much to tell. She came from Virginia, and she might of come from somewhere else . . . might of been a bound servant. I just don't know."

Looking back I wonder why I didn't suspect more, wonder more about how little she'd say about her folks and growing up, but she had the way about her of closing up a subject by sealing her lips.

Thinking about it now, I don't know why I didn't see that something was real, real strange. I guess that sixth sense I have now of being able to see things about people hadn't come to me yet. It may be that it was still blocked off then by the trouble that I couldn't put a name to. I did get her to talk about her mother a little more, though.

"Well, she always did like to cook that salsify."

"What's that?" I asked her.

"Well, it's a kind of plant, has a long root that you cook up. It tastes like oysters."

"I never heard of it."

"No, people around here don't seem to know anything about it, but Mama cooked it a lot. There's two kinds, the white and the black. She always loved the black. Scorzonera they called that kind."

"What's that?" I couldn't take in the strange word.

"Scorzonera. I think it means serpent. It's a long black root that looks like a snake, and I heard tell it would cure snake bite."

"It sounds nasty."

"It was tasty though — you'd scrape the roots good and boil 'em in salt water then rub that skin right off. By the time you'd put butter on them you'd have you something good, I mean."

While she talked about the cooking she seemed to be in another world, and while she was I hoped she'd tell me some more about her folks, but she stopped talking as quick as she'd started. Her face closed up.

"Well, never mind now," she said. I saw I might as well let her alone.

After that I tried to picture Mama, a soft little girl there in that bleak place. A dead mother. A sour stern Papa, tall and hard as an axe . . . and later the war had come and stripped whatever little there was. When I thought of that it made me vow to be more patient, more gentle with her.

And then her sharp tongue would cut me again and I'd bust out crying. She could always catch me off guard. Get my goat.

Of course, I had a lot of other things on my mind then. And I don't mean to sound like I didn't have some good days, 'cause there were good ones.

One main pleasure I had was telling stories. I guess you might call them ghost stories.

After I'd finish washing dishes and close up the kitchen for the night, especially on summer nights, we'd sit out on the back porch. When it was nearly dark it was easy to get everybody in the mood. The girls would hug their knees and put their faces into their skirts and giggle in a nervous way. I'd just look at the color of the sky and then look way off down the street, peering as far as I could and start off.

"Once upon a time . . . in a little town sorta like this one, there lived a family who kept hearing little scratching noises at night . . . ." I'd have their attention and I'd go on, drawing it out.

"Who was it, Mama?" Hally would usually whisper.

"Well, they couldn't see anything. They'd just feel something in the air."

And then I'd make my voice witchy and strange and say, "It was Rawhead and Bloody Bones, slouching, dragging his way down the railroad track, making his way to . . . Tar Depot."

They'd pull tight together and giggle, and when they'd get the nerve to peep around the bushes to see what the sounds were coming down the street, it would usually be Willy on his way home late from the store. They'd run shrieking out to him, calling "BOOGERS!" Then they'd run back up on that safe porch and beg for more.

I was always trying to get Mama and Willy to tell me some stories that they'd heard, but I didn't get very far. But sometimes I'd go down to the store and listen to Willy and the men who came tell jokes. If I stayed in the back, they forgot I was there. I loved stories wherever I could find them. I looked for story books all the time, but they were as scarce as hen's teeth in Tar Depot. I read Wilkes' school books until I knew them by heart.

And of course I read the Bible; there were so many good stories in there. But because of it being the Bible, it made me feel uneasy. When Mama would see me reading it, she'd look at me funny.

One I remember hearing at the store went something like this; I can hear Willy laughing and telling this: A drummer selling "unbreakable lamp chimneys" comes along, opens up his case right there on the front porch and starts his pitch. "These lamp chimneys might look like the same ones you've got at home — clear glass." (He begins tossing chimneys around as he talks, one against the wall, another off the store porch floor). Well just about the time his pitch is reaching the selling point (" . . . and you can purchase two of these remarkable chimneys for only . . .") one of his unbreakable lamp chimneys hits the floor and shatters into a million pieces. The drummer shuts his mouth, gathers up the rest of his chimneys, tosses them into his case and shuts it too. "What did the drummer do then?" the men would ask. "He *left*," Willy said, slapping his knee and laughing. One like that would get them going.

"Now tell the one about . . ." someone would say.

"Well," Willy would start off, " . . . shoe companies used to send samples in the place of catalogs to small country stores who wanted to sell shoes but didn't wish to tie up a lot of money in shoe inventory. These samples were one each of every shoe the company made, and always these single shoes would be for the left foot. Well, one night a thief breaks in, sees all these new shoes and steals them." By then the men would be laughing so hard they could hardly hear the story. "Can't you just *see* his face when he tried to put those shoes on!"

This would do them in again, and usually somebody else had a companion piece: The fella is walking around with one shoe on, his other foot bare.

"Looks like you've lost a shoe, Jimbo."

"FOUND one!" he replies.

If a customer had come in at that point, he would of had a hard time being waited on. One of the other ones that I remember was about the field hand who'd come into the store on Saturday after being paid for a week's work. He spent every last cent he had. About closing time he asks if he can open a charge account.

"I just love that wallet there in the case. I want to charge that."

The fellas at the store loved that one, but the favorite, the one they never got tired of telling, was the one about the little girl who'd come into the store and said, what sounded like, "Sir, wash your ass for eggs."

"*What*!"

"Wash your ass for eggs," she said again, holding her money tight in her hand, looking so innocent that the storekeeper felt like he was hearing things.

"*Excuse* me . . . did you want to buy something?"

"Yes, Sir, but first I got to know *what you ask* for *eggs*."

Every time that one was told they would fall completely apart, tears streaming out of their eyes. Bending double with laughter, they'd take their handkerchiefs out. Willy was always their ringleader.

Seventeen

I THOUGHT ABOUT MAEBELLE so often over those years. There wasn't any passing and we didn't hear from them. I sure hoped everything had worked out for them after they left the plantation.

When Willy started taking the Raleigh paper there at the store, I felt so pleased. After the men around the store finished with it, I'd keep every issue and read every word, if I had to sit up half the night to do it. I saw John Fleeting's name in there a lot of times. Once I saw his picture. One Christmas, I saw a picture of him and his wife all dressed up at a party there in Raleigh. The words under the picture said "Mr. and Mrs. John Fleeting spent the remainder of the holidays in their lovely home, Malabar, in Tar County. Mr. Fleeting's business, the JWF Tobacco Company, is the pride of Raleigh." I studied it a long time. Every once in a while I'd take it out and stare at his face, examine every line, the corners of his eyes. He hadn't changed, not that much since I'd seen him at the funeral.

When I looked at the picture, I wasn't comparing the men. Willy was a good man and good

storekeeper, and I don't know what I thought
marriage would be like. I guess I'd thought, the
way he and Laffton came in right wild and wool-
ly looking, that he'd be hunting and fishing more.
I guess I thought that he'd brought secrets and I'd
be in on them. He went to the store and back,
kept the accounts, rocked and joked with the fel-
lows, came home and went to bed. On Sunday he
ate a big dinner and took a long nap. Not a thing
for me to complain about; that's what most of the
men, people in Tar Depot, were like.

Over and over I heard from Mama, "You sure
are lucky to have a steady fella like Willy. Doesn't
drink. Doesn't run off after other women."

Oh, I knew it, I knew it, but sometimes I wanted to say, "Couldn't we just go to Baltimore and
get the goods for the store?"

I would ask from time to time, but he'd look at
me, give me that funny little smile he had and say,
"Now, Georgie, you know the train brings everything right here to the door. What sense would
that make?"

And I knew he was right, but I wasn't talking
about sense. I was talking about that wild feeling
that would come over me sometimes when I felt
like if I cooked one more cake of cornbread I'd
throw it in his face. On those days I'd want to
slap him just to break the routine. I wouldn't do
that, but I would pick a fight somehow, over some

silly little thing.

"You sound just like your Mama!" I'd finally provoke him into saying as he'd stomp out and go to the store.

When one of those spells would be on me, I'd get up real early in the morning, long before anybody else. I'd walk out into the backyard where I could have the air to breathe by myself, just the air without anybody else breathing it. The dew would still be on the grass, undisturbed even by a bird or a snail. There just for me. And if I was lucky and if nobody heard me get up and called "Mammy" or "wife" or "daughter," I'd slip off down to Contentnea Creek. I'd stand on the bridge and snatch a few minutes with myself, hungry, starving for something I couldn't name.

If no one was in sight, I'd sing little songs to myself or go down to the sandy bank. I'd take a sharp stick and write in the sand, things like, "I am a rider on an ancient horse made of transparent bones and soft leather . . . The horse comes apart and I lie with my face in the damp, blue earth spitting bitterweed, yellow from my mouth."

I'd never know myself what the words meant, and I'd always stomp them out with my foot before I'd leave.

❧

Then there was that thing that happened to me in March every year. I never could figure that out, but I would get so low, all my strength seemed to be gone. I'd have to force myself to get out of the bed every day. Each of my arms felt as heavy as a ten-pound sack of flour. And it seemed to me bad things always happened in March. When April would come every year I'd breathe a sigh of relief. But then the spring and summer would bring the other thing, the storms. I had to plan my whole day, my whole life around watching the sky and not letting a storm slip up on me. A lot of people are scared of lightning and thunder, in fact it seemed to me that anybody with good sense would be, but mine was more than a fear. I was paralyzed, especially by the pink nights.

That's what I called the times when the whole world would take on that eerie color that comes so many times just before a storm. I'd sense the change in the air pressure and would prepare to go somewhere and be very still, like animals do. Usually I'd stop whatever I was doing, grab the girls and hurry over to Mama's. I'd sit in her dark hall, straight and stiff. I'd remember all the things Mama and Mae had said in the old days. Scissors draw lightning, mirrors draw lightning, water draws lightning. I'd sit shut up tight in the stifling room until the storm was well over. One of the things that I had to be absolutely sure of, or I was convinced I'd be struck down any second, was that my feet were always covered. For some reason being barefoot in a storm was the worst horror. The very worst.

I don't know what Willy would think when he'd see me acting like that, but I believe he knew that I was doing the best I could.

The longer I stayed with him the better I got. I thought about the time when I was a little girl and a risen came on my leg. It was red and swollen and sore. Then one day it came to a head and burst open and the pus came out of it. Down way deep in the sore there had been a piece of dried stalk. It must have been in there for a long, long time from a fall in some forgotten field. After the risen opened, I was well in no time.

I loved Willy so much by then. My heart was full of him. The bad spells and moods didn't have a thing to do with him and he knew that.

"You know, don't you? Of course, you know."

And I did. He was always showing me, with his fairness and patience.

The nights in our soft bed when I'd touch his warm moist skin I'd be sorry for anybody else in the world. I'd feel him turn to me, his hard muscles would make me mold myself to fit his body, make me long to. Our bones came to know each other.

"You're the best cure . . . you're a honey cure," I'd whisper.

"Hush, you little mockingbird," he'd say.

But something inside me always knew, knew that sooner or later something would pounce. And, of course, it did.

Eighteen

THE YEARS WENT BY. THEY went by just like a
snap of your finger. It seemed like one day I was a
sixteen-year-old girl and a few days later I was
already starting to look back on my life.

The older Mama got the stranger she got.
Looking back I can see that all during those years
there were things about her that I should have
paid more attention to, but I just didn't have that
much patience with her.

"You never will believe in a hundred years
what I found Mama doing this morning," I said
to Willy as I snuggled up against him one night in
our bed.

"Well, I never do know what you're going to
say, that's for sure," he said.

"She was watering the chinches."

"What?" he chuckled.

"I'm serious. She was out in the backyard —
had the mattress drug out there, you know, airing
it out like we've done a hundred times. Then I
saw her bending over doing something with a little pan of water. I asked her what she was doing
and she said, 'When those ole bedbugs hop off of

there they need a little water like anything else.'
She said it just as plain as you please. I tell you, I
didn't know what to think. It made my blood run
cold."

Willy looked at me with concern in his eyes.
"What did you say?"

"Well, I didn't know what *to* say. I just told her
to quit working so hard and we sat down and had
a little snuff."

But something I'd taken pleasure in was watching Wilkes grow up. I tried to keep fairly quiet
about it since he was being raised in Tar Depot as
my brother, but he was a joy . . . the joy of my
life. Right from the time he was little he seemed to
know better than to ask Mama too much about
the past. Whatever he suspected he kept to himself. Like so many others, he thought the world of
Willy. He always called him Buddy — I guess
because Willy had a joking way of saying "Hey,
buddy, hey" to nearly everybody he saw. By the
time Wilkes was fourteen, he was already running
the store as much as Willy was. He was a quick
learner and seemed to be a natural at keeping up
with the accounts. Many a night I'd lie in my bed
and imagine holding that boy in my arms. But I
couldn't confuse him like that, so I held Willy
instead. One night when for some reason we were
especially close, I asked Willy.

"Has it bothered you a lot? You know, knowing about John Fleeting, knowing about Wilkes?

He'd put his big hand over my mouth, spreading his long fingers out on my lips, and said, "I'm the one that's got you. You're right here beside me. That's all that really matters. There's not a lot of point in raking up the past unless there's something that needs to be settled. As soon as I saw you that night, I knew that if I could get you it was settled for me." He folded me right up into him. I can still feel that to this day.

That was the night we made our little boy, Will. Our last one, our baby.

Sometimes when we were close like that, I wondered about my brother Laffton.

"Willy, do you think Laffton's all right down off on the creek all the time? He never has gotten married or anything. He seems fine but . . . ."

"Oh, George," he said, "as sharp as you are I can't believe you haven't figured that out. He's got a secret life. He and Doctor Flowers' wife have been sweet on each other for years. When Flowers is off in Raleigh at his medical meetings, I expect they play doctor. It's been going on a long, long time. I think it's a kind of arrangement that suits 'em all."

"Well, I'll be doggone. I have been busy not to

have figured that out," I said.

"And then don't forget — that creek goes down to the coast, and Laffton loves it down there. It suits him to wander here and there. He's got friends from the old days down on the coast. And, have you ever noticed, anybody that ever liked Laffton once always likes him," Willy said.

"He's kindhearted, all right," I agreed. "Where do you reckon he got that sweet nature from?" Willy smiled at me.

"Everybody has a whole different way of wanting to live their life . . . what's right for one sure is wrong for another. Laffton doesn't seem to be able to trust many. I'm just proud that I'm one he feels like he can count on." I thought he was right and I thought he was wise.

After that every time I saw Dr. Flowers' wife I noticed how happy she looked and how she doted on her two dark-eyed, good-natured children.

It goes to show, I remember thinking, things go on around you whether you pay attention to them or not. Lives change, people come and go. While you're seeing to the chicken coops, places can change forever. On one morning when I least expected it a new thing came into my life. It was a perfectly ordinary morning. I was at home cutting out the material for a dress when I heard a little scratch at the screen door. I looked up and Maebelle was standing there.

I couldn't believe my eyes. I hadn't seen her since the day of my wedding. Sometimes friends who find out too much about each other drift apart. Embarrassing secrets can make people avoid one another. I didn't think that was the case with Maebelle, but after all that time, I didn't know for sure.

As soon as I heard her speak, I knew there was no question of that.

"Isn't that Miss Georgie?" I heard a deep voice with a laugh in it.

"Is it Mae? I don't believe my eyes."

As soon as I could, I got the door open and my arms around her. Holding her, I realized that she was bonier than ever. We stood there laughing and clinging to each other.

"Where have you *been*?"

When I asked about Slender and the children, she said, "Scattered all over everywhere. But look at you. You've become one fine-looking woman. How old are you now?"

"Thirty-five."

"Well, un-uh . . . marrying hasn't hurt you one bit." She turned me around.

"Sit down here and hush that foolishness," I said as I motioned toward the table. I took out potato pie from the safe and put the coffee pot back on the stove.

When she asked about the girls I said, "I taught

them early, Mae, to get out and GO." We laughed. "And I've got a little boy. Willy took Will down to the store with him this morning. Hally is going to get him and take him to her house for dinner."

"I wish I could have seen Wilkes but I hear he's gone off to business school." Mae said. We got quiet and looked each other in the eye.

"You wouldn't believe him, Mae, you just can't imagine how fine . . . ."

"Oh yes I *can*, honey." She laughed at her words. "Do you remember how old Mr. Fleeting used to call everybody 'honey,' I mean *everybody*, and near bout *everything*? One morning I even heard him call the old rooster that. 'Hush up, honey, we heard you the first time,' he was saying when I took him his coffee."

We sat holding hands across the table.

"Oh me, oh me . . . are you all right?" she asked.

"Yes," I said. "I don't have anything to complain about. Now tell me, where have you been?"

"Well, we've had a different life, living off up there in *town* — in Baltimore, Maryland, I can tell you that. You wouldn't know us. Slender has turned into a real sport."

We laughed together.

"We're still home folks though. We've missed Carolina. When Slender had a letter from Mr.

John, we were glad to have a chance to come visit."

"From Mr. John?"

"Yes . . ." She paused and touched my hand. "He's got some business he wants Slender to see to at Fairfield. Slender's gone to meet with him now. He dropped me off here and will be back to get me this evening."

After we'd talked for a good while, she cleared her throat and looked at me in a kind of strange way.

"Georgeanna," she said, "there's something we need to talk about. There's something about your Mama I've got to mention. I feel like I've got to bring it up to you. I b'lieve she's kinda addled in the head."

"What do you mean?" I asked.

"Well, I've been over there visiting with her. As soon as I got there this morning she started talking about how you were trying to take Wilkes away from her. Her baby, all she has left in the world."

"Oh, Mae, she told *you* he was her baby?"

"Oh, yes . . . and thanked me again for helping birth him."

"Helping her birth him?"

"Out of her own body."

"*Mae*, no wonder she's been peculiar lately!"

"Yes, I spec' she's got a problem . . . more of

one than you know. She told me that Wilkes had become her whole life after his daddy left."

"His daddy! Mae, what in the world am I going to do about her?"

The shift of Mae's shoulders made me know that Mama was standing in the doorway behind me.

"Come on in, Chaney; we've got just enough pie left," Mae said.

"It was my pie, you know. I made it last night. Georgie makes hers too dry. I never could stand a dry pie."

"Well, you know how we used to love to make 'em for Mr. Worth," Mae said, trying to ignore what Mama'd said.

"I figured Georgie was taking credit for it, like she does for everything else."

"MAMA!" I said.

She turned on me. "I know you've been scheming — now you've finally got Wilkes off away from me."

"MAMA! What are you talking about? You know Wilkes is just off learning business!"

We sat there at the long table, tension hanging like bats in the room, the gray light of the morning creeping like fog, and us glaring at each other. We were the three women who knew the truth about Wilkes' birth.

Finally the tension was more than I could

stand. I got up abruptly and started spouting whatever came into my mind.

I'm ashamed of it but I got so mad that I went blind. Lord knows, it wasn't like I'd never thought of doing something to get him out from under her control. I had, many a time. But that wasn't what had happened. Willy had just arranged for him to go off to school. We'd talked to her about it before he'd left.

"Mama, I just wish you'd quit talking like that to me. I haven't done a thing to you. All I've ever done is do just like you said do, all my life!"

Maybe Mae being there gave me the courage to stand up to her, I don't know. Maybe holding the resentment in all those years it was just bound to come out sooner or later. But once it started coming out that day, it all came out.

"Well, he'd a been a heap better off to have stayed right here where he belonged instead of prancing off to some highfalutin business college!"

"Don't say that to me again, Mama," I said. "Just don't say it. I know every word you're going to say by heart." My voice was getting loud.

But there was no stopping her. "Well, we all know, don't we. We all know where you'd be if it wasn't for me. Drowned in the creek. Or an old maid sitting off somewhere. But I guess you think it's you that should be going off to some college."

She broke into a laugh.

Oh, I am ashamed to think of it now, but right then it was all I could do to keep from hauling off and hitting her. I wanted to. I wanted to beat her with my fists until she stopped making fun of me.

Mae saw the dangerous look on my face and stepped between.

"After all I've done for her, sacrifices I've made for her," she said to Mae.

"What sacrifice?" I asked hotly. "Taking my baby away from me? Going down to that church and taunting Reverend Swann with your 'pregnancy'? Strutting around making those ignorant leering dunces think you'd been in the bed with him, their darling? Or making him think, punishing him because he had been able to resist you . . . you made him think . . . that poor sweet man who was in love with you . . . that you had been with someone else . . . someone like John Fleeting, and that you were having a baby by him. Didn't you, Mama? Didn't you?" I was yelling and Mae was trying to quiet me.

I went on. I knew I was wild but I seemed to have lost control of myself.

"No, I want to know. I want to say it. You scorned him. You didn't do it to save me. You did it to control me. And you have. You've held that over me. Never letting me forget my shameful place. Never letting me tell my own boy that he is mine. And John Fleeting, you never would even let me say his name! You knew he'd been with me, but in your mind it probably suited you to think that he and Reverend Swann made love with you! And that Wilkes is your baby by one of them . . . I, I, I'm a good mind to . . . " I was crying by then. I've never been able to do much talking when I'm mad because I start sobbing, but that time I managed to get most of it out before I broke down. I pulled my apron up to my face and ran out of the house and kept walking, taking my apron off and throwing it into the bushes.

I knew that this time it was going to take more to get me over my spell than a walk to Contentnea Creek.

I went down to the corner and instead of going in and asking Willy if I could take the horse and buggy, I just waved at him through the window and went around the back and got them for myself. I was in no mood to ask anybody's permission to do anything.

I took off out into the country, not really knowing where I was going, but just going somewhere away from Tar Depot. All the time I rode I kept talking to myself, saying things to Mama I'd never dared say. It was a long ride and by the time I realized where I was, I had reached the plantation. I was spent and drained, but all the rage was gone. I've never been able to stay mad for long.

But I felt sick. How could I have talked to my Mama like that?

There I was in the yard of the old Fairfield Plantation. The roof of the house was partly caved in. The back porches were piled with hay. It was plain that the house had been abandoned ever since we'd left. A cat ran out from under the porch and up a tree. I tied the horse out in the back where the stable used to be and walked around the yard. I made my way over to the cemetery, picking some flowers on the way.

I was scratching at the dirt trying to make the flowers stand up when I heard something coming on the road. I knew, I knew as sure as I was born who it was before I even turned my head. "Oh, dear God," I thought.

I turned and there he was. All those years later there he was sitting on his horse.

"What is this?" he said, not really asking, just amazed like I was.

I watched him get down and walk over to me, and he was still fine looking.

It just happened that I had on my favorite color that day, French blue like the little flowers in the woods. It was just a cotton workdress, but it was a pretty color. I was so glad I was still slender, and I sure did wish I hadn't been crying my eyes out right before I saw him for the first time in all those years. But by the way he looked at me, I could tell immediately that he still liked the way I looked.

"How have you been, Georgeanna?"

"I've been fine, thank you."

He stepped back after coming up so close at first that we almost brushed against each other. He glanced over at the house and said, "I'm ashamed to see the old place like this. I'm away so much on business. I've been meaning and meaning to do something about this. I've just made arrangements with Slender about tearing it on down and bringing some of the lumber and bricks over to my place."

I hardly heard his words, just listened to the sound of his voice. I was stunned and shaken.

"I see your picture in the paper," I said.

"Being in Raleigh is like being in another world," he said. "How is it with you? I trust you have a husband and children?"

"Yes, I do." I thought for a second about what I'd just left and almost laughed, but I said, "All right, we have a good life."

He walked away toward the porch. I followed. When I'd thought so many, many times that this could happen, I'd imagined a scene: in the scene he would be sitting on the edge of the porch, the place where I'd first seen him; he'd turn those eyes to me and say, "Oh, Georgie, you were just a little girl . . . how could I have . . . oh, my girl, my girl!" he'd say.

I'd put my head against his chest and it would be like we were back at the oak tree all those years before. He'd jerk at the front door, and the old parlor room would become ours. He'd make love to me. Later when I'd open my eyes slowly, I'd see the winter sun filtering through my eyelashes and realize that it was the room where I'd first seen Mr. Fleeting when I was eight years old. The big-headed pictures would come back from the past and hang on the walls. When I saw them, I'd see that they were his ancestors, his kin, and their eyes would look at me, through time, and I wouldn't be afraid of them anymore. After he'd tell me how ashamed of himself he was, what a selfish man he was, I'd tell him then about Wilkes.

But it wasn't that way at all. As I looked closely at his face, I saw that he had hardened, his lips were thinner and meaner than ever. He didn't know me, he scarcely remembered me at all. He probably didn't even remember that he'd ever made love to me. Aging hadn't made him like Mr. Worth, who'd been kind and interesting; it had made him removed. The small spark of interest he'd had in me when he first saw me that day was because I was a handsome woman, not because I was the girl who'd once been under his spell. How many women he must have cast his eye on over the years.

What if I told him, I thought — what if I said,

"You have a fine son that you don't even know about." Instead, I said, "How are your daughters?"

"Fine," he said. "Mary Lee's married. Sarah teaches at the school where she was helped — in Guilford County. Mary Lee married a Daniel. He's like a son to me." He was used to answering questions.

We stood looking at each other, and there was only politeness. How could I politely say, "I had your son."

All those years I'd thought that I hadn't told him because I was afraid of Mama. Then I got the idea in my head that the reason I didn't find him and tell him was because of compassion. I mean, what could he have done about it? And he'd have been so hurt and left out. That was the thing. The truth was that I was afraid that if I caused any fuss he'd reject me even more than he already had. That was really it.

So, that day while I was facing up to a lot of other things, I decided that maybe compassion is just another thing to hide behind . . . another word for fear.

And I decided that since I hadn't had much control over anything that had happened to me in my life, I would have some that day. I decided that I wouldn't tell him.

Remembering, remembering, as I stood there,

how my girl's bones had been pulled apart as the baby had pushed out — the terror, the scream, the shame.

I said to myself: I had him alone, and I'm keeping the secret — you shouldn't have it — it's mine.

I felt a power as he walked away and I stood watching him. The beginning of my powers started right then. I almost puckered my mouth to whistle.

"I have to get on back to Raleigh," he said, his voice as impersonal as a bank clerk. He never even asked what I was doing there. Never even noticed I'd been crying. "Nice seeing you. My best to your family."

I stood by the porch of the old house watching him turn his horse and go off down the road toward Malabar. The little noises the hooves made on the hard clay echoed as I remembered the day he'd led me to the house when it was being built. I stood there for awhile before I realized that the sound I was hearing was the sound of a different horse. I turned and there was Willy standing at the fence looking at me.

"Willy . . . ."

But his face wasn't the face of the comfortable husband that I knew so well. He wasn't smiling. His jaw was set and his gray eyes looked dark. He pushed the fence post aside and walked toward me.

"Just what in the hell do you think you're

doing?" he asked.

In that flash I realized that he'd seen John Fleeting and thought that he'd come up on a lovers' meeting.

"Willy, no, I . . . ."

But he was beside me at that point, grabbing my arm.

"What . . . ."

He pulled me up on the porch. When he came to the old shackly door, he quickly kicked it open.

"Willy . . . ." I'd never seen him like this, like a storm.

"Here. Get in here."

He half drug me into what had been the old parlor and now was piled up with hay. He slung me onto the hay and bent over me, bending me back, putting his hand around my throat and then down to each breast, hard and crude, like he'd never been before.

"Is this what you want?" he said as he roughly kissed me, his mouth hard and cruel.

"So this is what your gentleman gives you that you don't get at home?"

"Willy, I can explain . . . ."

"I don't want to hear you talk. I want you to raise up your skirt where I can get to you."

He was stripping me and stripping himself, throwing clothes into the hay.

"When I get through with you, you can get up

and go to your lily-livered friend if you want to, but you owe me this. Do you want me to stop?"

"No, no," I said. "Don't stop."

When he plunged into me, hot and hard and wild, I met him halfway.

It had never been like that between us before. There seemed to be a long time then when we were enclosed in a silken cocoon. Afterwards I held him in my arms.

"Are you mine?" he asked.

"Of course I am. You know I am."

I explained everything to him — told him about the whole day.

"If you ever even thought you saw me thinking about John Fleeting, you can be certain that after this day — from this day forward — I never will."

When we gathered up our things and tried to get my blue dress in some kind of shape to go back home, I said, "Come here one more minute."

I walked into the cemetery. I picked up the little bunch of flowers that lay on the ground. We stood at the grave feeling alive and young, like we'd surely live forever. As we turned to go I nuzzled up to my darling and said, "That good man lying there is the first man I ever loved. He would thoroughly approve of *everything* that's gone on here today."

Nineteen

I'D THOUGHT ABOUT THE fact that Mama was getting older and might not be around all that much longer, but I'd never thought about such a thing as that Willy wouldn't.

We rode back to Tar Depot together that day, with Willy's horse tied behind the rig I'd come out in. We just let the horses clip-clop along taking their time. Being away from the family and the store and the town was a mighty unusual thing for us. I guess that was really the first time we'd even spoken of it.

"We sure did settle down quick, didn't we?" Willy said.

"Well, when we got married I was so young and you were too. But we had Wilkes and we had Mama and somebody had to look out for things. Somebody has to take charge of a family and make things work out — or things *won't* work out. You sure have always done your part."

"You have too, Georgie — don't think I don't know it."

"Well . . . as wild as I get to feeling at times, I know that we have to keep our family. Nothing would mean a thing without that."

"We ought to remember this day, though. We ought to get off by ourselves once in a while . . . get something straight between us without everybody around." He looked at me slyly.

I put my hand on his arm. My good, straight, kind, earnest fella.

"I never have even taken you to the Pamlico Sound. Just because I don't have any folks left there doesn't mean we couldn't go sometime. We'll do it . . . we'll surely do it."

But of course as soon as we got back into town there were problems waiting for us. In every family there are one or two people that all the other members look to to solve everything. Willy and I were called on to make all the decisions for six children, Laffton and Mama, anybody who ever worked at the store, and anybody that married our daughters. There wasn't much time for riding off to the coast.

When we rode up to the store in Tar Depot that day, the boy that was minding Stanton's ran out saying, "They've took Miss Chaney to the hospital. Nobody could find y'all."

The little stucco hospital was right across the street from our house. Dr. Flowers had built it himself about the time our house was built. It was used for many different purposes.

When we got there we found Mama in a bed in the back.

"You can take her on home, Georgie, when she wakes up. She had some kind of nervous collapse. A negro woman named Maebelle brought her over here and I gave her something to calm her."

"She's been kind of strange lately . . . and we had words this morning."

Seeing my face, he said, "Don't blame yourself too much. A lot of folks get real peculiar when they get older."

I went over the next morning and walked her back home. We were both quiet and embarrassed after the things we'd said the day before. When we sat down on her back porch I said, "Mama . . . I hate that I talked like that . . . ."

"Let's just not say anymore about it."

I felt that she was right about that, and we set to work snapping beans. I never brought up what I had intended to say the day before. I had planned to tell her that I thought Wilkes was old enough to know the truth.

I turned around and it was ten years later. It was on that same porch that she finally told me her secret, but this time she was on her deathbed.

Twenty

WILLY AND I NEVER DID get down to the Pamlico Sound. We did start taking a buggy ride together out in the country though, about once a month. I'd give him a look or he'd give me a look and we'd both know that it was time to shake up the routine. We'd drop everything for just a little while and get off by ourselves. He said I seemed to know just when to give life a slap. It seems like we had found a new respect for each other and for the work each of us had to do if life was going to have real meaning. If a man works hard all day juggling and balancing a business, dealing with drummers and peculiar customers, he has a right to expect a plate of hot food when he finally gets home. A kind greeting at the door isn't too much to ask either — and a woman, well, nine times out of ten a woman just wants to be appreciated and treated with respect. In fact, it seems to me that's just about what it all boils down to in the long run — whether people respect each other or not.

Willy died in his sleep one night when he was fifty-two years old. I was lying right there beside him and didn't know a thing until I woke up and found him still beside me. There aren't any words to say how deep the hurt was and how I still miss him every day of my life, but he is always with me. It got so deep between us those last years that I couldn't have told you where he left off and I began.

One time when he first opened the store, I went down there and picked me out a good paring knife. I used that same paring knife every day, couldn't peel or chop with any other knife. If I'd pick up some other one by mistake, my hand would know it by the feel right away, and it seems like whatever I touched wouldn't come out right. That's the way I knew Willy.

To this very day, and if I live to be a hundred, every time I see that path from the store to the house in Tar Depot, whether in my mind or in real light, I'll always see Willy. He'll be walking along with that rolling walk he had, kind of swaying from side to side. It'll be the same story it always was. Every evening it would take him an hour to walk those two blocks. Some man or woman or little child at every house would need a chat.

"Hey, Willy — how'd you do today?" Mr. Daniel would call out. "I've got troubles myself," the feeble old man would say.

"You think *you've* got troubles . . . I've got *piles*!"

There'd be peals of laughter.

"Willy — what's that one about the chicken?"

"Well, there was a man that would take a chicken and throw him up in the air, and then catch him, throw him up in the air and catch him. The chicken would squawk and squawk. I said 'What's that you're doing?' He said, 'Well, if you ever want to show a chicken a good time, this is how you do it.'"

The laughter would float up and down the street. The birds would take it as their sign to start to go to roost.

I wish he could have known me later when I learned . . . I just wish he'd lived long enough to know what I found out. Then he would have seen that there was a damaged part of me that he couldn't have known about . . . too deep even for his loving to heal.

Twenty-one

WELL, IT WAS JUST ME and Mama then. Of course, Wilkes was at the store. He had married a pretty girl and they'd built a house right downtown. He'd always had such a good level head on his shoulders and I could tell that he'd be able to handle whatever life handed out for him.

My Will was a busy little fella and always had something going on — either at the house or at one of his sisters' houses out in the country, on the tobacco farms. Or at the store. He was the spitting image of Willy.

After the day at Fairfield when I'd seen John Fleeting for what he really was, a lot of places in me seemed to heal up. Just knowing for sure that he was a selfish cold man who, in spite of money and brains and position, took advantage of an innocent trusting girl like he had. He ought to have been horsewhipped, and if his daddy had known about it he would have been.

His big JW Fleeting Tobacco Company was known all over everywhere by then. But that didn't really make him a big man.

But there were still times that things would

come into my head that I couldn't understand. The frog dreams would still come back from time to time and leave me weak and sick the next day.

I was finally going to understand why when Mama told me her dreadful secret.

I was forty-five that May and Willy had been dead for three years. Mama and I had gotten on pretty well since the day of the terrible fight and neither of us had mentioned those things we'd said again. In a way it was like we'd said: let's let Wilkes alone and let him live his life.

She had gotten sick in December, and in March she'd taken a bad turn. Pneumonia had racked her and made her weak. I'd nursed her the best I could. She'd always been so feisty I hated to see her like that.

On that day in May the sun was shining so pretty that I decided to make her a little quilt-covered cot on the back porch so we could sit outside.

We were just talking about this and that, like you do when you're piddling around, when she turned to me and said, "Georgeanna . . . I'm never going to make it through the spring. There's something eating at me inside. I know it . . . and hush . . . you know it too. I've put my house in order . . . but I've got to tell you a terrible, terrible story."

"What, Mama? What are you talking about?"

"You're not going to believe what I tell you. You're just going to think I'm rambling again, but I reckon you need to know about this . . . and you'll be the only soul in the world who does."

I looked into her eyes then and I could see that she was as rational as anybody could be.

Like I said, it was so strange seeing her like that. Lying there pale, with her eyes focused on another time, she seemed like a different person. She wet her lips and started off. This is just the way she told it to me.

"Well, I might as well tell you right now. Your Papa wasn't killed in any war."

"He wasn't?" I said. I sounded lame, I know, because every instinct in my body told me that she was fixin' to tell me things that I might not really want to hear.

"There's a good reason I never have talked about him. I didn't want you to have to know about it all, but I guess you're going to have to. Sit down, for I don't know how to tell this."

As I pulled up the rocking chair and sat in it near the cot, she cleared her throat.

"Your Papa's name was Fenton Weeks. He lived not far from where I lived with my folks. It was up toward Virginia over there towards the coast. It was on the edge of that godforsaken place called the Great Dismal Swamp.

"Our families were there because the menfolk

were shingle-getters. Those shingles were cut out
of the juniper and cypress trees that swamp was
full of. They'd cut them there and load them out
to wagons pulled by mules where they'd be carried to a ditch. At the ditch — the canal, you see
— they'd put them onto lighters — that's what
they called the flat-bottomed boats they took
them up to the rivers on. The Land Company had
built shanties for the workers, but some families
lived in farm houses. We were about the only
white families there — the others were hired
slaves or free men. My own Papa and Fenton's
Papa too, like so many of the others, spent a
whole lot of time in that swamp. They'd hunt,
fish, and trap. It got where they'd do that more
than they'd work with the lumber.

"I learned mighty young that you never know
what went on in that swamp. Men were always
going in there and never coming out. You could
get stuck in the black mire or you could make the
wrong turn and not have any idea where you
were. I never went far in there.

"Our yard wasn't such a bad place and I
always stayed close to the house helping my
Mama with the garden. Snakes hardly ever came
into the yard. We never could count on when
Papa might show up with meat, so we made sure
we had potatoes and all sorts of other things
growing. And we'd go fishing nearly everyday.

"Mama tried to teach me how to take care of myself. 'Don't depend on a soul except yourself,' she'd say. But she never was strong — she had some kind of female trouble. One night when I was eleven, she got up and tried to go out to the outhouse. We found her lying out in the yard the next morning. Papa said, 'I heard some kind of noise in the night, but I thought it was owls.'

"After that it was just me and Papa whenever he came out of the swamp.

"When we buried her out there beside the garden, I could hear her say like I'd heard her say a many a time, 'I hate it, I hate it, Chaney, that you're a girl.'

"Night after night I'd curl up on her feather bed, the one she told me she'd brought from Virginia, and squall. But nobody knew or cared.

"Fenton was a curious kind of fella . . . always was. I thought that the first time I ever saw him standing on the edge of our place. He was good looking, no doubt about that — tall, lanky with dark, straight, stiff hair and that high, wide forehead — even when he was just sixteen. I learned right quick that the sulked look he had drew girls to him like flies to gingerbread. He might of been part Indian, I don't know.

"He kept hanging around all the time, not saying much but just being there when I least expected it. It seemed like he just liked to watch things.

It got where every time I'd look up he'd be there. Well, he got me one day and no matter what I said or did to try to stop him he got himself on me. And once he got me he felt like he could get me anytime he took a notion. It was just like I was his slave, a poor slave!

"And then there I was having a baby when I was fifteen years old. You see, Georgeanna, I do know something about it, and there wasn't any Maebelle or Mama to help me. Pa did get one of the black midwives from the swamp to come in for the birthing, but that was all.

"You needn't think Fenton was anywhere around by then. No, he wandered off into the swamp or up to Virginia. I never did know where. Well, that's what Laffton came into the world to. You would of thought I'd learned something by the time Fenton showed up around there again, but no, nearly seven years later he showed back up and started up again. The next thing I knew I was going to have you. Papa saw me crying one night and this time he got his shotgun out after Fenton.

"'I've got enough mouths to feed. You're not getting away this time,' he'd told Fenton when he got us into town to get married.

"Well, you know what happened two years after you were born — that war. That was the end of his shingle-getting job. He was glad to go. He was up at Corapeake before I knew it, signing up.

"I was living at his Mama's place by then. His daddy had disappeared into the swamp years before. His Mama, bless her poor ole soul, she had a goiter. Well, one day while she was hanging out clothes she was bitten by a cottonmouth snake and died. Well, it was mighty hard after that, but I kept going. When you've got little children to take care of you just do, somehow you just do.

"When we were first married Fenton seemed fairly pleasant as long as I did everything to suit him. But even then it didn't take much to make him fly off the handle. It seemed like he'd jump on me about the slightest little thing and then as soon as I'd set that right, he'd sneak up on me with another completely different thing. I reckon he just liked to keep me dangling, sorta like the kitten that wandered up from somewhere to the place. He wouldn't feed it or let me feed it, but he wouldn't run it off either. Week after week it would hang around where we threw the slops, half starved. I'd see him looking at it out the window. Just standing and looking at it.

"After he enlisted, he came home once in a while. The only way I heard anything about the war was what he'd say or what I'd hear from some passing stranger. We lived off whatever I grew or Laffton and I caught, shad mostly. Every few months we'd try to get into Corapeake and do a little trading at the store there.

"Well, that day that he came up, I'd been there on my own for nearly a year. I saw him coming a long way off, and when I saw his face from a distance a kind of hot hate came up in me.

"Laffton wasn't there. I'd sent him into Corapeake with Papa early that morning, and they weren't planning to come back until they'd helped the storekeeper build a storage shed.

"He walked up on the porch and into the house just like he'd never been away. I heard him coming onto the porch whistling through his teeth and singing a kind of song under his breath:

I caught the rheumatism,
A-sleeping in the snow;
But I killed a chance of Yankees,
And wished I had killed some more.

He flashed a kind of smirk at me when he saw the way I was looking at him.

"'Well, you needn't look at me like that. I'm not planning to stay, though I believe I could eat a little something.'

"While I warmed up the pot of butter beans and the cornbread we'd had for our dinner, I took you up to the loft and put you in the high-sided crib I used to keep you safe while I worked. I didn't want you around him. You weren't but three, but I didn't trust him around little girls — and I knew that no matter how short a time he planned to stay, he was bound to try to get me into the bed.

"But it didn't come to that. While he was setting at the kitchen table eating, he looked up at me and smiled as I stood by the stove. He was talking about the inn he'd stayed at the night before.

"'It sits right on the state line. If you're in one part, you're in Virginia, and the other you're in Carolina. You see all sorts of people there — gambling, marrying. It's a real curiosity.'

"'I *reckon*,' I said.

"'Well, you don't have to be so sour. I told you I'm not staying. I've just come to get the feather bed. It's a heap colder in Virginia than it is here.'

"Then he looked up at me and smiled that smile. I might not of done it if he hadn't looked at me like that. Everything was in that look. How I was nothing. How he was holding me, *had* held me ever since I was fourteen and he'd sweet-talked me, coaxed me into letting him. How he didn't want me but didn't want to throw me away. How he got his pleasure was in keeping me half starved, for affection, for anything — just like that kitten by the slop bucket.

"And that smile said — and I've already plucked your bloom — you're catching on to me

— you're not young enough — not dumb enough anymore. The feather bed — mentioning the feather bed was telling me of the innocent girl on the farm in Virginia near the swamp, the girl with wide blue eyes and soft yellow hair and hardly more than a baby, with skin still smooth and soft as a baby, that he was planning to put his hands on on that feather bed. Something rose up high and hot in me again where it had festered so long. A rage like a bubbling hot lava. I turned and reached for the flat iron that I kept on the stove. I threw it and hit him right between the eyes. He looked so surprised. I believe it killed him right off. But I was in such a wild frenzy that it was hours later before I stopped hacking on him with the ax I kept by the door.

"After I'd chopped him up into as many pieces as I could, I took it all, wrapping it up in tow sacks and burying it all in the black mire under the outhouse. It took all night long. While I was still in the frenzy, I cleaned up the kitchen — it took hours of boiling water and scrubbing — then I washed myself in the tin tub. I went into the room where you were and you were screaming. You thought there were frogs in your bed. Your face was swollen with crying. I took you out and put you in the bed with me and we got warm and pressed together — on that feather bed and slept til nearly that night.

"One of the things he hadn't known that I knew was that he wasn't even in the army. A month before when I'd been standing in the store, a woman who didn't know me was saying, 'Robbie was home last Friday a week ago and he said that the Weeks man from over by the bridge deserted two months ago, right after the bad train wreck between Tarborough and Rocky Mount.'

"Nobody ever came looking for him. Nobody ever knew. I reckon those bones are still right there. I watched and waited for a long time for a chance to get out of there.

"One day a tinker was going by and I told him I'd give him our horse if he'd take us to wherever he was heading. It was a place called Snow Hill. We stopped by Papa's and I woke him up and told him we'd been sent for. That we were gone for good.

"After we were on the way, I told the old tinker man that I was a widow without a way to earn my keep, and he said he had a cousin, a seamstress who might could use me. He put us and the feather bed out at her house."

Mama looked off in the distance and said real detached like, like it didn't have a thing to do with her.

"I buried it, you see. I buried it in the swamp."

Twenty-two

IT'S 1910 NOW. I'M SITTING in a hospital room in Richmond, Virginia, where I've been for three months. I've been writing this all down to make the time go while I get well. My doctor here, that round-faced boyish fella, Dr. Eugene Long is his name, thought it would be a good thing for me to do. We've talked a lot and I believe he, like a lot of other folks, secretly wants to be a writer. Well, looking back over it all, one thing I believe is that *the hardest thing in this life is knowing what to tell and what not to tell.*

After that day Mama told me her chilling story, I sure knew that I never was going to tell anybody what she'd kept inside her all those years. I don't aim to dwell on it though. It was all a very long time ago and there's nothing I can do about it. Grieving about it forever is not going to help a soul.

I hadn't said a word the whole time she'd talked. It was like a chant. I could tell that she had told the story in her mind a thousand times since it happened. Waiting, expecting to be caught. Trying to make herself understand; exploring herself. But no one had ever asked. And then she saw the old story starting all over again when I was just a little girl and John Fleeting tampered with me.

By the time she told me, it was too late for her, but it made me understand so much about myself. The terrible spells I'd always had, the frog dreams and headaches and sick spells were the times when the truth that I'd pushed back in myself was trying to get out. I'd been right there in the loft when she'd killed Fenton Weeks. I'd known what happened and part of me had remembered it even though that kind of proud flesh in my brain had healed over it and hidden it from me. Very soon after I was able to put a name to it, my self started to heal. I'm so sorry she had to go through that horrible life, but I surely wasn't going to tell on her.

My poor little Mama died. We'd had some good talks at least. I understood by then how she had gotten so confused and why she had made the sacrifice for me at the church. It had been a real sacrifice, for she had loved Reverend Swann and he'd loved her — even though they never were able to do anything about it. The church had meant a lot to her too, but when she saw me falling into the same trap she'd been in, she couldn't stand to watch it happen. She'd fixed it so I could still be a young woman in spite of John Fleeting's selfish appetite. There was nothing I could ever do to make it up to her, but I did what I could.

I remember that old saying, "A whistling woman and a crowing hen never come to any good end." Well, I don't believe that just means that men want women to be quiet, or that if a woman whistles she's acting like a man. I've thought and thought on it. I believe that some women, most women, *know* so much that they never tell, know so many secret things that sometimes they're just making a little slow, low whistling sound of warning. Don't mess with a whistling woman.

Like I've said before, I always have thought that life goes in circles. I've noticed it over and over — you get where after a while you can see one coming to an end — then you know that you might as well get used to the fact that what you've known is gone for good. Sometimes it's people who are gone, sometimes places — when you look back on some of those days, they seem like days of heaven, and you wish you'd paid more attention to every little speck as it went by. I can see them all: Mr. Worth Fleeting sitting by a sunny window at Fairfield Plantation. Willy walking down the street slapping his leg and laughing. Laffton going down the creek to stay with his friends — the watermen, the oystermen. Maebelle and Slender, wise and funny, making their life count for as much as they could. Wilkes painting and expanding the store and taking in Will for his partner. Those times give me my strength. And somehow knowing all the secrets and not telling them makes me feel like I can see things coming too. I'll have to watch out for Will and his family, for there's something going on there.

The main thing I've learned from living all these years is this: be sure to savor the good things, give them their time, because the bad will pounce and snatch its time from you.

All of that has nothing to do with why I'm here in the hospital. One day there in Tar Depot my hip just cracked and I was in bad pain. Dr. Flowers treated me with morphine and I got caught by a horror called Soldier's Disease. They called it that because many a soldier came back from the war addicted to morphine after their wounds had been treated. I went through some mighty bad days before Will brought me up here. There are many in Dix Hill and in asylums in other states that will never get over it, but by the grace of God, that doctor in the baggy pants with the kind brown eyes tells me I'm through the worst.

I want to go home to my little white house in Tar Depot. The pair of mockingbirds that live in the holly tree out front, their soft gray wings spreading and their white underfeathers fluffing up, are probably wondering where I am. I remember a story I heard about a woman from the north who tried to take a mockingbird home with her in a cage. Well, it never would sing and just curled up and died. In fact, I've heard the colored folks say that if you put a baby mockingbird in a cage the older birds will feed them poison berries so they'll die.

I have a vision of that little town that I call home. Dominecker chickens are clucking and mockingbirds are singing. Down at the store a painted colored sign on the red brick storefront spells out our name, Stanton Weeks. A black-eyed woman wearing rusty black widow's weeds sits on a green wooden bench out front watching the trains go by.

And then I see another vision in my mind before I look down below at the hospital here and see Will arriving to take me back to Tar Depot.

I see Mama and myself there in the big backyard of our house. We stand out in the open with our long aprons tied around our waists. Between us lies a big pile of dried peas that have been gathered from the long garden. We're throwing the peas onto a thin sheet of cloth. We shake and shake, and our arms grow tired and our backs feel like they'll break. In the cloth the peas and the husks separate. The husks and little dried hulls start to blow. As we stand with our hands on our hips and watch, a quick fall wind catches the hulls. They blow like ghosts of fireflies down the street of the town, up into the sky, and down again to light on Contentnea Creek.

The author wishes to give the readers of *A Whistling Woman* the recipe for Georgeanna's Black Walnut Wedding Cake:

4 & 1/4 c. flour

2 c. & 1 tbsp. sugar

1/2 lb. butter

1/4 lb. candied cherries

7 eggs

4 c. nuts, 1/2 black walnuts
        1/2 pecans

2 tsps. nutmeg

1/2 c. whiskey or brandy

1 tsp. baking powder

2 boxes white raisins
    (golden)

Sift flour several times, measure, add baking powder and nutmeg. Sift over chopped nuts combined with raisins.

Cream butter and sugar, beat well, adding one egg at a time. Add whiskey, beat well, add flour, nuts, etc. Mix a little at a time, beating thoroughly until all is added. I mix mine in a dish pan and sometimes even use my hand to mix it thoroughly or a very large spoon.

Pour into a well-greased funnel pan which has been lined with several thicknesses of waxed paper on bottom and sides.

Bake in moderate oven at 250 degrees for two hours. Have pan of water under cake. (If you have a hot or good heating oven, you had better watch it and turn it down lower as this cake cooks fast).

This makes a thick cake and is hard to cook through sometimes.